INTRODUCTION BY CANDAS JANE DORSEY

STORIES BY
MAURICE BROADDUS
ALAN DEAN FOSTER
RICH LARSON
KARIN LOWACHEE
PATRICK SWENSON
JANE YOLEN
AND MORE

seasons between us

TALES OF IDENTITIES AND MEMORIES

LAKSA ANTHOLOGY SERIES: SPECULATIVE FICTION

EDITED BY SUSAN FOREST & LUCAS K. LAW

SEASONS
BETWEEN
US

TALES OF IDENTITIES AND MEMORIES

LAKSA ANTHOLOGY SERIES: SPECULATIVE FICTION

EDITED BY SUSAN FOREST AND LUCAS K. LAW

LAKSA MEDIA GROUPS INC.
www.laksamedia.com

Seasons Between Us: Tales of Identities and Memories
Laksa Anthology Series: Speculative Fiction

Library and Archives Canada Cataloguing in Publication

Title: Seasons between us : tales of identities and memories / edited by Susan Forest & Lucas K. Law.
Names: Forest, Susan, 1953- editor. | Law, Lucas K., editor.
Series: Laksa anthology series: speculative fiction.
Description: Series statement: Laksa anthology series: speculative fiction
Identifiers: Canadiana (print) 20190218835 | Canadiana (ebook) 20190218878 | ISBN 9781988140162 (hardcover) | ISBN 9781988140179 (softcover) | ISBN 9781988140186 (EPUB) | ISBN 9781988140209 (Kindle) | ISBN 9781988140193 (PDF)
Subjects: LCSH: Science fiction, Canadian. | LCSH: Fantasy fiction, Canadian. | LCSH: Speculative fiction, Canadian. | LCSH: Memory in literature. | LCSH: Identity (Psychology) in literature. | CSH: Science fiction, Canadian (English) | CSH: Fantasy fiction, Canadian (English) | CSH: Speculative fiction, Canadian (English) | LCGFT: Science fiction. | LCGFT: Short stories. | LCGFT: Fantasy fiction.
Classification: LCC PS8323.S3 S43 2021 | DDC C813/.0876208353—dc23

LAKSA MEDIA GROUPS INC.
Calgary, Alberta, Canada
www.laksamedia.com
info@laksamedia.com

Edited by Susan Forest and Lucas K. Law
Cover Art by Samantha M. Beiko
Cover Design by Veronica Annis
Interior Design by Jared Shapiro

FIRST EDITION

SUSAN FOREST

To *Callum, Liam, Jaxon and Lucas*
Spring, full of promise.

LUCAS K. LAW

To *members of the Law and Foo families* (wherever you are)
Identities—ever-evolving, behold a sense of wonder always

To *all of us*
Seasons—ever-changing, dreams and journeys yet to be discovered

In memory of *Daniel Frank Yochim, Suzanne Lee West,*
and *our loved ones who had left us*
Memories—ever-treasured, stories never to be forgotten

CONTENTS

FOREWORD

Lucas K. Law

What is a life well lived?

That thought stirred in my mind as I watched a slideshow at my brother-in-law's Celebration of Life. And this question led to another: *How should life be lived?*

Then, to another: *What kind of stories will you leave behind?*

Each person—including myself—must write his or her own story, but it struck me that some experiences throughout a person's life may be recurrent. Ageing, universal emotions, and relationships were three commonalities that crossed my mind.

Ageing. The changing of seasons.

What comes to mind when you see the word *ageing*? "Old people"? "Ancient," "feeble," "useless," or one of the other negatives? I used to have such associations when I was younger. Now, I connect the word with "all of us." *Ageing* is a life's journey of growing older: a journey that begins in our mothers' wombs and ends with our last breaths. No reversal, just progression.

What has shocked and alarmed me in the past few years has been hearing young people's remark that they are not afraid of death (so they say), but they worry about ageing. They fear the future. There may be numerous reasons for this, but one root cause could be the rapid social change societies all over the world have experienced in the last few decades. Although what worries a 20-something might be different from what worries a 40-something or a 60-something—and we fear or worry differently at different stages in our lives—we can nevertheless empathize across generations. The underlying emotions are universal and known to us instinctively.

There is happiness in welcoming a child into this world. There is jubilation in celebrating a milestone. There is grief in facing a sudden loss or saying goodbye to a deceased loved one. In between "arriving" and "leaving," each season is a series of waves, rising and falling between joy and sorrow, touching the range of human emotions—some named, some not, some indescribable. Though each experience is individual and unique, the stories feel familiar because they are the touchstones in our collective unconscious. We know these emotions—they are fundamental and universal to us from the moment of our birth to the moment of our death. Do we accept and embrace these emotions? Or do we fear and run from them? How do we live a life of purpose?

Living with purpose is difficult when the complexities of our world go against us—some hurdles are within our control, others not. But, as the slideshow in the Celebration of Life demonstrated, moments of joy, moments of goodness, and moments of festivity are to be found in every season. We must live, and we must dream.

How often have we heard "it's not the destination, it's the journey that matters"?

Not only do the slideshows have many stories to tell, they also impart truths if we care to look for them. One fundamental truth can be expressed as: it is not the quantity of relationships but the quality of those bonds that last over time and space. The quality of our lives—emotionally, physically, mentally, spiritually—is directly linked to the quality of our relationships. No matter our age, we are not alone, and life is a shared journey of moments to discover, explore, and rediscover in every season. We have a lot to learn from each other—the young from the old, the old from the young, and everyone in between. There's no shame in asking for support—or accepting support. Being independent does not preclude needing each other: to grow, to expand, and to flourish.

In *Seasons Between Us*, Candas Jane Dorsey and twenty-three authors examine the power of self-exploration as we cope with the undiscovered country of our journeys through growing older over the seasons. In their *Tales of Identities and Memories*, the authors leave us with probing questions: *Who are we? What is the meaning of existence? Do we make a difference?* And at the end of each short fiction, the author provides a note: *What would you tell your younger self?*

This anthology is dedicated to the memory of Daniel F. Yochim, Suzanne L. West, and all our loved ones who have gone before us. We do not say *goodbye*, but only *farewell until we meet again*. Dan and

Suzanne taught me not to take time for granted. Who or what is here today may not be here tomorrow.

Somewhere in my travels, I saw this phrase: *Each morning we are born again. What we do today matters most.*

So, go. Create memories; accept new identities; engage words for social good; listen to music; read a book; be honest and humble; connect with people, places, and things that make your life richer; savour the support and generosity given to you; acknowledge your good fortune; work on healthy ageing. And also, apply the pay-it-forward principle. When it is time for your own farewell, you will then answer your own question: *What is a life well lived?*

A portion of this anthology's net revenue goes to support the Kids Help Phone and Mood Disorders Association. Please support your local charitable organizations and public libraries. Do take care of your own health, and be kind to yourself and others. And remember: *We are never too old to dream.*

—Lucas K. Law, Calgary and Qualicum Beach, Canada, 2021

INTRODUCTION

Candas Jane Dorsey

Arriving, Pausing, Enjoying, Leaving

Recently I was in the emergency room of the closest hospital (for reasons that turned out okay, don't worry!) and when she saw my patient number, the admitting clerk said, "I've never seen one so low! Were you *born* in this hospital?" and the answer was, "Yes. Yes, I was." I discovered I could go to Records and ask to see my birth record—which is apparently written in pen in a ledger, so old am I becoming. I haven't done it yet, but it gives me pause (paws?) to think that *my* paws, for all their roamings away-and-back, are now firmly planted only a few blocks, a mile maybe, from where I drew my first breath. I have been to a lot of places in the world, but I come back here, and I am growing old here, sometimes in the same rooms.

What is the journey of a life, then? Is it geographical? Certainly, for my forbears, it was. Four generations ago, they were arriving on this landscape, full of ambitions, prejudices and misconceptions about the emptiness of the land. They had a self-image of hardy pioneerism, and their very definition of self came from a line drawn between where they started their lives and the very different landscapes they traversed to end those lives on the Canadian prairie. My mother's ashes are interred beside theirs, in a little graveyard in middle-Alberta where perspectives on colonialism, settlement and reconciliation are seldom admitted.

I am so firmly *of this land* that I never want to leave it, and yet, I am of settler stock. I have been in a lot of discussions lately about reconciliation, in the wake of the Truth and Reconciliation Commission of Canada (TRC), and I accept that those settlers in my lineage did not possess the place they lived, though they thought they did. And yet, my

geography exists: this is *my* place—and I "own" this house where I sit to write this. The difference, maybe, is the limitation of time: my *place-ness*, my ability to claim a place is mine, is time-limited to my lifespan. Which makes every moment of that life precious (no matter how, from outside, I may be relegated to margins because of someone else's prejudices or misconceptions).

So, is a life a geography all its own? History has more people who stay in one place than have ever travelled: are we to say that a life lived planted in one spot has no unique and particular landscape, no hills and valleys, no *belonging-ness*? Obviously, unless we are not paying attention, we would never say that physical, outward geography was all of one's destiny, even if place and origin is some of what makes us who we are. But yet, geography anchors the most potent of the allegories, the metaphors, the similes we use to start describing our lives and purposes. We travel through life, we journey, we explore, we arrive, we depart from the events of our lives as if they were solid and created a geography. We talk of our highs and lows, our hills and valleys, and then, we "travel" atop that geography.

Like Everyman in The Pilgrim's Progress, whose journey was a naked and unsubtle allegory full of descriptively-named regions like the Slough of Despond, we can liken life to a series of destinations where we arrive, stay and leave in a relentless peripeteia. So then our life stories are a travel memoir, and the destinations—wisdom, serenity, peace, happiness—are goals to achieve as we age.

Equally potent are the comparisons to climate, season, and weather. This very volume's call for submissions was organized by seasons, with spring defined as the time of beginning, and the journey of our lives described as the passage of time (which it is) through allegories of an inevitable progression of birth, growth, prime of life (whatever that is), senescence, and death— unimpacted by any conscious wishes to linger in any one stage. But are seasons eras, or are they but moods? Is spring instead optimism, summer enjoyment, autumn melancholy, and winter despair? Do we really move through seasons only once, or do we hopscotch through them as robustly and discontinuously as any literary or TV time traveller, exchanging summers of content for winters of discontent, or wistful autumns for hopeful springs, on a daily basis? Or perhaps we think not of seasonal change but of daily passages: dawn of life progressing to sunset and night enveloping us at last—but is night infinite to some of us, and full of life and possibility in stars and galaxies, and do we scribe our stories on that infinity, while day feels limited by the blue bowl of sky that hides or limits our fate? And weather: are we defined by our weather: grey or sunny moods or personalities, sudden storms of passion or anger, icy receptions or warm welcomes, all the weather of daily existence?

My job in writing this *Introduction* is not to answer these questions, but to pose them and leave you in a state of wondering. The writers whose work follows will move you onward into the state of wonder. That is the nature of the fictional contract (and I knew this through and through, as a writer, even before I read Barthes, Foucault and Iser!)

But those who know me will not be surprised to know that I do have some ideas on the progressions of our life. In some ways, every story written anywhere, every "speculative fiction" (which is a bit of a redundancy, I sometimes think!), is making a comment on our ages and stages of life, in one way or another, and in reading them, we draw from them and take with us both the positive and negative propellants of understanding. Having survived childhood (despite some serious illnesses), endured adolescence (despite adolescence!), bounded into adulthood and romped about in its possibilities (the people! the relationships! the creativity! the community! the achievements! the love! the sex!) while also confronting its challenges (with which I will not burden you), and now being in the process (a never-completed process) of coming to terms with the entropic advancement of ageing, I have at once achieved and abandoned perspective. Achieved it by the inevitable progression of days and understanding, but abandoned it because it was a spurious achievement.

As a writer, and now also sometimes a visual artist, I have a great deal of experience in choosing what Feigenbaum, the chaos theorist, called the "irreducible amount of detail" that has to be present to make a work of art resemble reality. While doing this I have come to understand that if life were as simple as narrative, we would all be better at it.

Here is what I think that I think: we are hard-wired storytellers adrift in a capricious, arbitrary, entropic, and disorderly Universe.

I struggled with that word "disorderly": we know we can find order that makes sense of the universe, or at least parts of it. We can cut the cake in such a way that we see a pattern. But is that pattern really there, or is it a result of our neurological tendency to impose narrative on the vast sea of information that provides input for our senses? I also wonder if "capricious" ascribes too much agency. Perhaps, instead, I should say that our Universe is completely disinterested, and, as we have constructed it, friable.

And for another nice word, our narratives as we construct them are fungible, and much of our conflict as humans come from misunderstanding that very point. So we spend our lives defending chimera.

If this is true, What joy! What freedom!

And thus, what a lovely cornucopia of reason and fiction all the ages of our lives can be. So read on, for some versions.

—Candas Jane Dorsey, Edmonton, 2021,
author of *Black Wine* and *ICE and other stories*, and, forthcoming from ECW Press, the mystery series *The Adventures of Isabel, What's the Matter with Mary Jane,* and *He Wasn't There Again Today*

CLEAR WATERS

C.J. Cheung

The deluge had begun two days earlier, the same day Hiroshi's daughter, Shizue, called. She hadn't been home for three years, but despite having to drive through the downpour on winding mountainous roads, she was coming for a visit.

And she said she had a surprise.

But Hiroshi had much more to do than prepare for her visit. The torrential rain made the river near his home rise nearly twenty-five centimetres beyond its bank, almost washing out the Shinto shrine that sat near the shore. The shrine stood taller than the roadside shrines common in Japan before the Collapse, and its upswept roof provided enough cover to keep the rain off his head and shelter the hologram of his wife who appeared and bowed whenever anyone approached. She was accompanied by two electronic candles and a small copper bowl filled with raw rice and red incense sticks.

Hiroshi spent two days erecting a sandbag barrier that snaked along the river's tree-lined banks, but the water crept up and lapped against the makeshift berm. As Hiroshi dropped another sandbag on the wall, wiping rainwater from his salt-and-pepper hair, a voice came from upriver.

"I have come to assist."

Hiroshi turned and his chest tightened. It was Karl, Tom Anderson's android farmhand. An early model android, Karl would pass for human, but for the blue stripe on each cheek that crossed the silvery eyes all androids possessed.

Karl picked up a spade and began filling an empty burlap sack with sand.

"Thank you," said Hiroshi, "but I'm almost done."

Karl glanced at the makeshift barrier. "There are three more metres of wall to build, which could take you several more hours alone. You need help."

Hiroshi sighed. Talking to an android was like talking to a trained dog. They were programmed to obey, not catch the subtleties of human speech. He would have to be direct. Hiroshi reached for the spade, catching the android's clammy hand instead. Polymer and titanium. Plastic and dead. He shuddered at the touch.

Karl stopped digging and gazed at him. Was that a shocked look in his silvery eyes?

"I don't want you. Go home."

Karl released the spade, thanked him, and walked back upstream.

"Thank Tom for me, please." Hiroshi watched Karl disappear into the trees, not knowing whether Karl heard him or not. Then he leaned over the berm, dipped his hands in the silty river, and let the fast current cleanse them. Tom was just trying to be a good neighbour. Hiroshi was sure he wouldn't take offence, but he considered sending him a gift basket for his troubles.

"Abe-san."

Hiroshi flicked the cold water from his hands. On the veranda, Mrs. Galang was beckoning him to come inside. "She's here."

Excitement swelled in his chest like a wave. Shizue was early.

He glanced back at his handiwork. The river lapped against the flood wall. Rainwater poured off the gables of his small shrine just metres from the barrier. Karl was right. There were still a few more metres left to build. Would the shrine be secure from the onrushing stream on the other side of the sandy wall?

Hiroshi couldn't worry about such things at the moment. His daughter was home. He rushed inside, took off his shoes and peeled off the heavy, rain-slicked coat and put on his slippers.

Mrs. Galang sluffed a heavy cardigan over his shoulders and handed him a towel. "Do you think she will agree?"

He wiped his hair with the towel. "We'll see. I'll let her in."

Mrs. Galang nodded and hurried back to the kitchen.

Hiroshi shuffled down the hall across the dark-stained wood floor, past shelves of porcelain geisha dolls in glass boxes, until he reached the front door of his compound and swung it open.

In the middle of the compound sat Shizue's old electric Citycar, its windows fogged up.

Hiroshi strained to see into the car. What was going on? Why wasn't she coming out?

The driver's side door opened, and a young woman in shorts and a tank top stepped out. It was Shizue, all right, just standing there, gazing up at the sky, but Hiroshi almost didn't recognize her. The shoulder-length black hair she had throughout high school was gone, replaced by a pixie cut. But it was the same silly girl, still standing in the rain.

Shizue twirled about, arms stretched out as if embracing the sky. She let out a whoop and a broad smile crossed her face.

Hiroshi smiled, remembering all the times she would dance for him as a child, twirling about in a flowery kimono like the little water sprite she was.

The passenger side door opened. A hooded figure stepped out of the car, unfurled a large red umbrella, and shielded Shizue from the rain. Too late, of course. She was already soaked to the skin.

She never mentioned she was bringing a friend. Hiroshi cursed himself for not clarifying when she called. Surprises were for parties and gifts, not unexpected guests. At the very least, Mrs. Galang would have to set another setting at the table and prepare another room.

The stranger was taller and had a larger frame. Boyfriend? Was her friend the reason she came home?

Shizue sprinted toward the front door, while the stranger opened the trunk of the Citycar.

"Papa-san," she said as she slammed into Hiroshi, embracing him and almost knocking him into the entryway. He gave her a halting hug before she pulled back, torrents of rainwater dripping from her short, black hair, reminding him of that scrawny stray cat she'd brought home when she was seven years old.

Hiroshi wrapped the towel around her and gathered her into the entryway of the house. Shivering under the towel, Shizue slipped out of her wet shoes and into the pair of pink plastic slippers Mrs. Galang kept clean and dust-free, just for her.

The door closed behind the stranger, who folded up the umbrella and backed into the entryway.

"Papa-san," said Shizue, "Please excuse my rudeness."

Hiroshi stiffened. He should have expected this day. Three years away from home and she had to have made friends, perhaps other boyfriends as well. Would she ever tell him about them?

The stranger removed the hood. Blue stripes on his cheeks crossed his silvery eyes.

Shizue took the stranger's arm. "Papa-san, this is Jin. He's my boyfriend."

The air in the house became abruptly thin.

"Surprise," Shizue said.

———•———

Hiroshi led Shizue and Jin down the hall, slippers shuffling across the creaking hardwood floor. Jin spoke in whispers, commenting on how old everything seemed, while Shizue told him to be quiet.

Hiroshi opened the door to a makeshift guest room: a small office with rosewood furniture and a squeaky old cot squeezed between two overstuffed bookshelves.

Jin sluffed his backpack onto the floor with a thump.

"I'm sorry this may not be up to more modern standards of accommodation."

Shizue glanced at him. "It's fine, Papa-san."

Hiroshi beckoned for her to follow, but Shizue shook her head. He pointed further down the hall. "Your room—"

"Is here, with Jin." She glanced at Jin who was already unpacking. "Besides, he likes the floor. Says it's good for his back." She gave her boyfriend a wry smile.

An icy coldness ran down Hiroshi's spine. *Boyfriend.* He opened his mouth to insist that her place was her old room, that Mrs. Galang had prepared it for her, but he stayed silent. No need to start an argument before she'd even settled in.

Hiroshi nodded, turned, and shuffled back down the hall toward the kitchen.

Shizue and Jin chuckled in the office.

Three years. Had it been so long? Who had just walked into his home? She resembled his daughter in all but the hair. What other surprises lay in hiding behind that three-year wall of time?

He found Mrs. Galang in the kitchen stirring a pot of soup stock, adding dollops of miso paste.

"How is she?" she asked.

"Shizue is Shizue. We have a guest. His name is Jin."

Mrs. Galant perked up. "A boyfriend? I'll set another place at the table."

"Don't bother. Just plug him in."

Before she could respond, Hiroshi stepped onto the veranda, shutting the door on intrusion. He sat on a padded wicker chair and leaned back, never taking his eyes off the rainstorm, the flood wall, and the river roaring just beyond it.

His wife loved watching the river flow by and seeing skipping rocks over the surface of a slow-moving stream. As a child, he'd amassed a small collection of skipping rocks, the smoothest and flattest ones he could find, and displayed them on a small table by his bed and kept them into adulthood. His wife saw them and chided him, saying the rocks weren't meant to be kept. Their purpose was to be thrown. But Hiroshi knew, that once thrown, they were gone.

"That's where you're wrong," she said. "The stone sinks to the bottom, the ripples on the surface disappear, yes. But the stone is still there. You can't see the stone but water flows around it, affecting the stream's path."

Hiroshi sat on the veranda for a long time.

———•———

Mrs. Galang called Hiroshi. Dinner was ready, and his guests were already at the table.

He slid the door to the dining room adorned with a half dozen geisha dolls. An electric frying pan, half-filled with bubbling soup stock, sat in the middle of a low, cloth-covered table. Shizue and Jin knelt beside it on soft cushions, gazing longingly at the pan as Mrs. Galang filled it with fish cake, prawns, tofu, and cabbage; the fragrant scent of soup stock and miso wafted toward Hiroshi like a wave lapping onshore.

"I haven't had Nabe in . . ."

"Three years," Hiroshi said. "At least."

Jin nodded as Shizue explained the dish.

"I didn't know androids could eat," said Mrs. Galang as she filled four bowls with heaping mounds of white rice.

"Yes," said Jin. "We are self-lubricating."

Shizue snickered as Mrs. Galang gave him a puzzled look.

"He means," said Shizue. "He can eat."

"Isn't that what I said?"

Mrs. Galang began handing each of them a bowl of rice.

When Mrs. Galang handed Shizue her bowl, she waved it away. "Thanks, Liza, but I only want half."

"Half? But you always—"

"Perhaps," said Hiroshi, "Shizue is forgetting her manners after being away for so long."

Shizue turned her gaze to Hiroshi. "I don't mean any disrespect. I eat brown rice now. It's better for you and more sustainable."

"Oh? Some things change."

"And some things stay the same." Shizue beckoned to Mrs. Galang, and accepted the offered bowl.

Jin examined his surroundings, his eyes wide. "The dolls are beautiful. Where did you get them?"

"Japan," said Shizue. "Imported, right?"

"Yes," Hiroshi said. "Saved from the Collapse. Very valuable."

Jin raised his eyebrows and nodded. "Does the river flood every year?" he asked. "There are a lot of sandbags."

"Yeah, the stream seems pretty high this year," said Shizue, scooping rice from her bowl onto a small plate. "And the rains, much harder."

Hiroshi shook his head. Didn't she think he would notice? "No worse than usual," he said. "It's like this every year. It will hold." He gestured to the small pile of rice on Shizue's plate and shook his head. "*Mottainai*." What a waste.

Shizue's eyes narrowed, and she let out a heavy sigh. "Fine." She picked up the plate and slid the rice into the bowl with her chopsticks. A few grains tumbled onto the table.

Hiroshi clapped his hands. "*Itadakimasu*."

Shizue and Mrs. Galang echoed him, but Jin looked confused.

"It's a Japanese custom," said Hiroshi. "You say it before you eat."

Jin and Shizue exchanged glances, and ate in silence.

Finally, Hiroshi spoke. "How was school?"

Shizue shrugged. "I have one more semester before I take another four months in a work programme. If all goes well, I might be able to get a permanent job."

"Doing what?"

"Artistic renderings of architectural designs, for sales brochures and stuff." Shizue gestured toward the android. "Jin is an engineer at the company I've interned with."

"It's very good," said Jin. "They pay well."

"And how much did you make?" Hiroshi focussed on shovelling his rice.

"A good wage," said Jin. "But I lived in the—"

"Shizue, I mean."

Shizue hesitated. "It was an internship. I didn't make anything."

"You were a slave? How did you live?"

"You don't understand, Papa-san. I didn't work there for the pay. I worked for the opportunities, the doors it opened."

"She has a very good chance of a return internship," said Jin. "My boss really liked her work."

"What kind of opportunities?"

"Weren't you listening? I might be able to continue working with Jin at his firm."

"Anywhere else?"

She shook her head. "No. Not at the moment. I'd have to continue freelancing."

Hiroshi looked up from his rice bowl, squinting at her. "And how much does a freelance artist earn?"

Shizue glanced at Jin. "I make do."

"What she is trying to say," said Jin, "is that she is comfortable."

Knight in shining armour, always coming to her rescue.

"What does that mean? Make do?"

Shizue dropped her chopsticks on the table. "Jin said I'm comfortable."

"I heard."

"No, you didn't."

Mrs. Galang piped up. "Anyone want more tofu?"

Hiroshi glanced at Mrs. Galang. Thank the gods for her, acting like a break wall against the oncoming tide. Hiroshi nodded and went back to digging through the remaining remnants of chicken and shiitake mushrooms in his soup.

Mrs. Galang poured a block of udon into the electric pan.

"I wondered," said Hiroshi, "whether you would consider a change of scenery?"

"Where to?"

"Here."

Shizue and Jin glanced at each other, and Hiroshi's heart sank. He knew her answer. Not everything had changed. He could still peer through the veil she had erected these past few years and look directly into her heart, and her heart no longer belonged here. It belonged to the thing that knelt beside her.

Shizue looked down at her half-eaten bowl of rice and shovelled down another bite. "I . . . don't know. Why?"

"I'm getting old. Mrs. Galang is soon to retire."

Shizue shrugged. "Hire an android."

"I want you."

"Can Jin come with me?"

"He can visit."

"Can he stay? Live? With me?"

Hiroshi opened his mouth but words stopped in his throat. His stomach roiled at the thought of that machine living here with him.

"That's what I thought," said Shizue.

"I didn't say anything."

"You didn't have to."

"Perhaps," said Jin, "some arrangement could be made—"

"Stay out of this," said Hiroshi, not taking his eyes off his daughter. "This doesn't concern you."

Shizue slammed the chopsticks onto the table with a loud clatter and stood up. "This was a mistake." She stormed from the room, slamming the sliding door behind her.

The Nabe continued to boil.

———•———

After dinner, the rain subsided, allowing Hiroshi to finish shoring up the berm against the rising river in the light of the lanterns on the veranda.

As he piled more bags on the flood wall, he mulled over the events at dinner. Let the storm subside. She would be much better if she had some time alone to be with her thoughts. In the morning perhaps, with a good cup of green tea, they might speak.

"Abe-san."

Hiroshi turned. Jin was silhouetted against the light of the lantern.

Hiroshi picked up the spade and shovelled sand into a burlap sack.

"Abe-san?"

"I can hear you." Hiroshi tamped the sand in the sack down before tying the drawstring.

"Excuse the interruption, but I thought I should let you know. We're leaving."

Hiroshi winced as if he were just struck in the chest by an hammer. No morning conversation. No time for reconciliation. How long before Shizue's next visit? Years?

Maybe never.

Hiroshi put the next sandbag down and turned back to dig more sand. "Roads could be treacherous at night. It'll clear by morning. At least stay the night."

Jin shook his head. "The rain let up. Shizue insisted and I . . . I agreed."

Hiroshi sniggered. Of course, he would. Hiroshi strained to shovel more sand into a bag.

"But I could talk to her. Change her mind." Jin gazed at what remained to be built of the flood wall. "Let me help."

"No." Hiroshi slammed the shovel into the mound of wet sand and tied the sandbag closed. He lifted and carried the thirteen kilo sack to the burlap wall.

Jin's shoulders slumped. "Would you accept assistance from Mrs. Galang? From Shizue?"

This was intolerable, being interrogated by a toaster. Hiroshi slammed the sack onto the wall. "I just don't want your help."

"Because I'm an android?"

Dizziness began to overtake Hiroshi. He was sinking into a quagmire. Was Jin judging him? Yes, in the mathematical way only androids were capable.

"We are no longer merely mechanical constructs with silicon brains. We—I am a biohybrid, a synthesis of artificial and organic."

"Yeah. Self-lubricating. I got that."

"More. We truly are living beings. Shizue knows this and has embraced it."

You mean, embraced him. Intimately. Hiroshi could feel the heat burning on the back of his neck. He'd heard enough. This disgusting thing was trying to tell him how to think, how to feel. How could Shizue? The little girl who danced.

He—*it*—was an affront. The sooner she got rid of it, the better.

"We are completely committed to each other," said Jin.

Hiroshi thrust the spade into the sand and squared himself before the android. "She hasn't committed to you. She pities you. Right now, you're just her latest stray. In a few months, she'll realize her mistake and throw you out with the trash. It doesn't matter that you're sleeping with her. All you are to her is a—a—"

"Sex doll?"

Hiroshi turned. Shizue stood on the lawn just a few feet away from them.

"That's what you were going to say? Huh?"

Each word was a spike driven into him. It didn't matter that she was right. No amount of cleansing could strip the stain of impurity from her.

Shizue gazed up at the sky and let out an exasperated grunt. "This is bullshit."

"No, I—"

She turned and glared at Hiroshi, her cheeks shining in the light of the lantern. "And just so you know, I'm pregnant."

———·———

The world spun around Hiroshi like a whirlpool, threatening to pull him under. Pregnant? That was impossible. With a machine? That was her real surprise. That was the news she came to tell him, the news she'd avoided.

Shizue marched toward the swollen, sandbagged river, grabbed the spade and strode to the shrine. She paused, hefted the spade above her head and struck the hologram projector. Her mother's image flickered.

"Shizue."

The river crested the burlap wall and poured across the lawn.

Shizue hit the shrine, hit it, splintering wood, hit it, knocking the coppery plates and bowls to the ground.

Water gushed against the shrine.

"Shizue!" No!

She turned and yelped. Water cascaded into her, covering her feet, and almost knocking her over. She dropped the spade and grabbed the shrine wall. It creaked at the strain of the pouring water.

The makeshift berm had collapsed, and water rushed in waves, thigh deep.

"Hang on!" said Jin. He started for Shizue.

Hiroshi wasn't about to let the android help his daughter. He grabbed Jin's arm. Jin turned to face him.

"Stay here," said Hiroshi.

Jin opened his mouth as if to protest, gazed into Hiroshi's eyes, and relaxed his arm. "Go," he said.

Hiroshi turned and ran, sloshing through water. The muddy ground sank beneath him, sucking at each step. "Shizue, come here!"

She looked up at his outstretched hand and let go of the shrine. For an instant, she reached for him. Then she sank in the rising flood.

Hiroshi strained to move toward her as Shizue pushed herself up, coughing and spitting up water. He got his hands under her armpits.

"Sorry, Papa-san." Her chest heaved as she tried to speak. "Mama. It's always been—"

"Shizue." Jin stood on dry ground only a few metres away, arms outstretched.

Shizue slipped away from Hiroshi and stumbled up the slope toward Jin, collapsing into his arms. Jin's arms.

Too much time had passed, too much water had flowed down that stream. A different Shizue. A different world passed by his home, and he had failed to take notice of the difference.

Wood creaked and splintered behind him. Hiroshi turned, bracing himself against the current. The shrine buckled and fell over under the weight of the rushing water.

Hiroshi lunged forward, grasping for one of the legs of the shrine before it floated away. His fingers closed about the leg as he fell head-long into the muddy water.

He floundered to find his feet, the shrine tugging relentlessly into the darkness, dragging him down with it.

"Papa-san!"

Shizue buttressed herself, arm outstretched, reaching out toward him. Jin held her other arm, a human chain. "Grab hold. You can't save it."

Hiroshi gazed back at the shrine, a bobbing gleam yearning for the river. His arm, shoulder strained against the weight of the rushing current. The flood was going to take it. He would be pulled into the river to crash on the rocks below the surface, the ones he couldn't see.

But did that even matter anymore? Nothing of his wife survived. Just the shrine. Nothing of his old life. Nothing of who he was and where he came from. Shizue didn't remember. She wanted nothing of it. She said so herself. And now she was pregnant with an android's child. He was going to be a grandfather to what? A cyborg? A thing? An abomination? Why bother living when everything of value was dead?

"Papa-san."

Hiroshi turned toward Shizue; she was still inching toward him.

Shizue. The river had taken her too. Long ago. She followed it to the city, to a new life, to new friends. None of them were here. His home was here. Japan was here, but she was not. Yet wasn't the reason they came here . . . to give their daughter a new life?

She had that life. It just wasn't the life he imagined for her. It was her own life.

"Papa-san. Please . . ."

Hiroshi released the shrine. He reached out and grabbed Shizue's hand. With a massive effort, they scrambled to safety. The shrine crashed against the rocks and splintered.

His wife's hologram flickered out.

———•———

"Abe-san," shouted Mrs. Galang across the yard.

Hiroshi looked up toward the house. Mrs. Galang waved at him. "She's here."

Damn. She was early.

Hiroshi put down the hammer and looked at his handiwork. The shrine was almost ready. Over the years, he'd managed to recover a few ornaments from the old shrine that washed ashore a few kilometres downstream: a small inari statue, an incense bowl, a copper plate. But there were still pieces missing. He took off the heavy apron and grabbed his cane before hobbling down the levee. He beamed when he saw the young girl dressed in a flower-patterned kimono.

"Grandpa," the girl shouted. In her hands was a cardboard cylinder almost as long as she was tall, but that didn't stop her from running across the grass toward him as fast as her bare feet could take her. She barrelled into him like a wave, almost knocking him off his feet. He dropped his cane and lifted her up as she smothered him in hugs.

Hiroshi put her down, knelt beside her, and gazed into her silvery eyes.

She handed him the cylinder.

"Thank you, Kaiya. What is this?"

"It's a surprise," she said, giggling.

Hiroshi popped the lid open and tilted the cylinder. A long paper slid out. He unrolled it. It was an ofuda, a Shinto charm. The calligraphy was immaculate, and it looked as if it would fit right where he wanted it in the shrine.

"Very nice. Where did you get it?"

Kaiya gazed toward the house.

"I made it, Papa-san."

Hiroshi looked up. Shizue walked toward them. "All those calligraphy lessons you gave me as a child finally paid off."

"Is that the shrine?" asked Kaiya.

Hiroshi nodded. "Go have a look."

"It's beautiful." Kaiya ran toward the shrine.

Hiroshi grabbed his cane and pushed himself up. By the time he got to his feet, Kaiya had already finished the ritual purification.

"Amazing," he said.

"Yes, she is."

Shizue put her arm around her father, and they walked up the levee.

"Jin?"

"He's unpacking."

Hiroshi gave her an incredulous look. "Oh?"

He had only seen Jin a handful of times since they first met more than five years ago: once at Kaiya's birth, another at her christening, and still another at her first birthday. All those times, Hiroshi had to make the journey. Jin never came here.

"What made him finally decide to visit?"

Shizue gazed at the river flowing past the shrine and sighed. "Just time, Papa-san."

They walked along the levee, hand-in-hand. Hiroshi glanced at the river as it streamed by. The runoff had been lower than usual this year, and there was no danger in flooding. But the current was fast, and these eddies would never come again.

Author's Notes to My Younger Self: Follow your dreams. Don't let anyone dissuade you from them. Don't let the voices within and without tell you that you cannot make it as an artist. You will, despite the odds. Be confident that you have what it takes. Move ahead. Work hard. And don't look back.

GROVEN

Heather Osborne

1.

"What hopes, then, for a daughter reaching womanhood?"

Firya ducked under the caustic coo of her mother's voice. She sat hunched on a stool Lerene had rapped down on the frost-hardened mud in front of their small cot. The ritual was often a shared celebration, and never hidden. For her mother's pride, it would be performed practically in the street, where all Iden town would have the pleasure of gawking. Lerene must prove she honoured the dryads.

A few desultory watchers gathered in the narrow street. Dannah, the laundress, and her friend Hezal, the brewer, were the nearest. Firya glared at them. They were both smiling behind their hands to see their scrubwoman's daughter spinning fancies.

"Well?" Lerene asked. Her fingers lay sharp as magpie's talons on Firya's shoulders. She saw the laundress too, and her hands trembled. "What daughter-dreams have you wrought?"

Firya lifted the scissors in front of her and stared at the open jaws. If she finished the ceremony quickly, she could get back inside to stoke the fire. "Travel," she muttered.

"Travel, Firya?" Dannah called from across the mud-rutted street. "And where might you be going?"

The destination didn't matter. Firya wouldn't name it if she knew. Iden town loved its gossip, and Dannah's tongue was rarely idle. She was the one who said the dryads must find Lerene lacking. When Firya's father lay abed with the pox, Lerene's sacrifices hadn't brought him back—*if* she'd even wished for his health, Dannah hinted. Firya

had raged with tears at her father's burning. The pox hadn't spread, but Dannah's whispers did.

Firya scowled. "Travel," she repeated, sitting up straighter. Herrow, with its great bronze gates. A ship, skimming across the straits to another world. Escape was a daughter-dream hot enough to burn even this snow-laden air. She thrust the scissors into her mother's hands.

Lerene tugged her hair, pulling Firya's head back. The blade of the scissors pressed against the base of her skull. Firya held back shivers.

"So high?" Dannah called. "Lerene, she'll drift away when the wind blows."

Too low and Firya would be weighted like an anchor. Better to be shorn like a sheep and be stolen by dryads, than to live in Iden town.

"What young man will want to marry a flighty woman?" Dannah prodded.

Slowly, Lerene moved the back of the blade down Firya's neck. She'd been a small-holder once, when Firya's father lived. Now she bent her back to scrubbing for the laundress's few coins. "Too high and you'll fly away," she sing-songed brightly.

Firya's shoulders knotted. Lerene would trap her if she cut so low. "Mother, please—"

The scissors closed with a *shhk* Firya could hear in her bones. Hair fell loose around her ears. Firya tucked it back, but it fell forward again, tangling in her eyelashes.

Lerene circled Firya and studied the ragged fringe her scissors had left. "Low enough for Iden town," she muttered. The lilt had disappeared from her voice. She dropped the frayed braid in Firya's lap.

Her first sacrifice. Lerene claimed magic should only be called on with the strength of desperate intention. If that were so, then Firya now had the power to stop Dannah's tongue with a wish.

Lerene took her chin in a bruising grasp. "*Some* women imagine dryads in the herb pots on their windowsills," she said. "Prove yourself better."

Her mother had woken her at daybreak and led Firya across the snowy fields to the stream and broken through the rime. She'd scrubbed Firya's waist-length hair with her own cold-reddened fingers. She'd often called Firya an untimely daughter, with her temerity to be born before the thaw. But even cowed by Dannah, she'd given Firya the gift of her womanhood braid.

Firya's wishes would be her own.

———◦———

Skiffs of snow gathered between the field-furrows. Firya chopped at the ground with a hooked hoe, digging frozen swedes for the pigs and milch-goats. No young men were beating a path to the scrubwoman's cot for Firya's sake. Like as not, she'd end up a scrubwoman herself, or spend her life at a spinning wheel. Unless she could escape.

She'd endured a cold month at her first woman's work. When the small-holder's wife came out to offer hot broth, the other women laid off and stood in a huddle. Firya refused the rest. She would earn double: half to her mother for her keep, and half tucked away for her journey to Herrow.

Her heart quickened as she reached the end of her row, leaving the others behind. She'd had no excuse yet to slip away and offer her sacrifice. Some girls went no farther than the willow-hedges shading the cart paths. But true power came from seeking the dryads hidden in the wild lands.

Beyond the split-rail fence, black spruce loomed above the pitted field. The trees marked an outcropping of rock too flinty for swedes. Firya reached through a slit in her skirt into the pocket underneath. The soft mass of her womanhood braid, wrapped in a linen rag, reassured her searching fingers.

Once she was behind the rocks, the wind dropped to a low moan. The snow was deeper in the shadows. Firya pushed past the naked thorns of wild roses. Threads from her wool skirts caught on the briar. A path to guide her back.

After a time, she found there was a woman walking at her side. Firya couldn't see her face, but she wore a loose cloak of downy grey.

"Such a prize would soften all the tongues in Iden," the woman said.

Firya caught herself on a rough-barked spruce. Beneath her wool wrappings, sweat chilled to ice. The voice was her mother's, at once querulous and sarcastic. "What prize?" she asked.

"You brought an offering."

Firya's first wish would not be for spite's sake. With an effort, she formed a word and the wind wrenched it from her lungs. "No."

"Then what would you have?"

Travel, Firya thought, focussing her intent on imagined Herrow, on ships that sailed through dreams. She was strong enough to demand, not beg. "Freedom," she said.

It was not the word she'd intended to speak.

"A wide wish." The woman stopped in thought. "Will you pay my price?"

Firya lifted the fraying braid from her pocket. The coarse brown hair had once writhed around her face, always tangling. If she went back on her word, the woman might lash out at her weakness like a weasel scenting blood. And freedom could take her further than Herrow's gates. "Willingly given," she insisted.

The dryad laughed. Her breath made no mist in the air.

Firya stood alone, enclosed by drooping branches. Her braid was gone; her wish granted.

———•———

Wind whipped through Firya's heavy skirts when she escaped the forest's eaves. Fog had fallen, erasing the field's fences.

A dark form loomed out of the mist in front of her. Firya's heart stuttered—the dryad had left no footprints. But the bulky figure was only Jonnah, the small-holder's son, dressed in leathers and furs. "There you are," he said, catching her arm.

Firya tried to shrug him off, but his grip tightened when she stumbled on the broken earth.

Jonnah tilted his head at her—a sheepdog's big, gangling whelp. "The others left at payout time," he said. "They said you were— Well." He stopped himself with a frown. "They said you were grubbing more than your share, if you weren't witching."

Witching indeed. And some women left their wages in the fields and needed someone to blame.

Firya leaned closer to Jonnah. His wide shoulders walled off the wind. Why would a small-holder's son come out to find her? He could be huddling by his mother's hearth.

Jonnah lifted a broad hand, and hesitated. Firya swallowed a sharp breath as he tucked her tattered hair behind her ear with one gloved finger. "Were you?"

Her bones felt brittle with cold. "My wishes are my own," she said. Her mother had fallen into drudgery. When Firya was flying on a tall ship, salt on her lips, she would know herself the stronger.

"My pardon." Jonnah watched her with eyes warm as honey. He tucked Firya under his arm like a motherless lamb and turned her toward the barn.

His easy swagger wasn't the charm he thought it was. Firya

stretched her elbows against his clinch. "I'm going to Herrow," she said.

"What, tonight?" Jonnah's voice rang with laughter. "I go every summer for the wool fair. It's nothing to rush for."

Firya yanked free and trudged toward the barn. "No farther?" she scoffed. A boy could disappear down the road and expect to find work. A boy never noticed that a woman couldn't. But Firya's sacrifice had been accepted. The dryad's gift would appear to her and the way would open.

Jonnah lunged after her and wrapped her in the engulfing shelter of his arm. His fingers stroked again through her close crop.

Firya shivered, more with heat than with winter. Since she'd become a woman she'd seen men's eyes on her bare nape. Jonnah's touch sparked a sudden breathless impatience.

"You could sign as a sailor. They'd take you for those shoulders alone," she said. She sounded as peevish as Lerene.

"If no witch lays a wish on me first," Jonnah said with a grin.

Firya stilled under his teasing. Why was Jonnah so warm, and so happy to have found her? Lerene always told her not to take truck with mindless men who ignored the dryads on their very doorsteps. Was Jonnah needling because he didn't trust in women's magic, or was it a sign she might capture his heart with a wish? He was the first person she'd seen after leaving the hills.

Jonnah nudged Firya's scarf open, running a thumb down to her throat. "You're warm enough, aren't you?"

Churlishly, Firya let him crowd her away from the barn door. The dryad hadn't promised *travel*, precisely. Travel suggested homecoming, like a bellwether worried back into the fold. Back to her mother's skirts? Then what would she have proved? But freedom, now. Firya tipped her head forward, letting her hair fall into her eyes, and peeked at Jonnah. His family owned more fields than her father ever had. Jonnah was tall already. Firya liked the bulk of him, the strong press of his chest against hers. Slowly she let her body melt before him, a seedling turning to the sun.

Jonnah leaned close and murmured, "I like your hair."

Behind him, a line of firs made a windbreak for the barn. How many shorn field-girls had Jonnah chivied back here? But a dryad's gift shouldn't be refused, lest she disdain Firya's future sacrifices. The bride price Jonnah could bring to Lerene would put pause to her complaints. Firya would live in a well-chinked farmhouse, not a dark cot. Food in the larder, silver in a strongbox? And she had only to claim her gift.

One fir-branch nearly touched the wall, hiding them from sight. Perhaps in the shelter, the tree had imagined a touch of thaw. A single bud, brown with spring sap, capped the tip of the branch. Firya reached out to touch it, and the sticky, papery cover fell away. Bright green needles unfurled under the brush of her thumb.

Firya laughed, and her breath mingling with Jonnah's was warm.

2.

"When did you last have your woman's blood?"

Lerene's voice had lost nothing of its sharp whine in the years since Firya's marriage. She huddled under a wool wrap with a quilt across her knees, though sunlight poured through the open shutters and the wide-propped kitchen door.

Firya sifted flour over the oak counter before turning the dough out of its bowl. Once the panbread was in the oven, there were the soaking sheets to wrangle and pin up in the snapping wind. Firya leaned forward to begin the kneading. Her back twinged sharply just above her hips.

"I haven't seen you washing your rags lately." Lerene fretted over Firya's courses just as her plump hands worried the threads from the square of patchwork in her lap. "You bore six children—"

"Four," Firya muttered. The thick smell of yeast knotted her stomach. Push, turn, fold—the morning's laundry had left Firya's knuckles swollen and red.

"You've a fine farmhouse, girl, so don't let the dryads think you've forgotten them."

Push, turn, fold. The boys' ticks needed changing from down to linen, the bulky quilts to be tucked away with sachets of camphor. "I didn't wish for a farmhouse."

Lerene's scrubwoman's hunch deepened as she pushed the rocking chair into impatient motion. "Happiness can't be paid in full."

Firya's bride price had been more than Lerene might have hoped for, but hardly a dryad's silver fountain. When she came to live with them, Lerene took up the chimney corner like a land-holder's lady. She watched Firya keep house and carelessly wondered why Jonnah couldn't hire a girl to soap the leathers and sand the floors. A trip to the groves, an offering accepted . . . Firya had proved her magic, and Lerene's price had only steepened.

"You needn't look to me for help," Lerene persisted. "I have nothing left to sacrifice but these thin bones—"

"And obviously the dryads don't want them." Firya bit her words short, too late. Lerene's sour mouth crimped into wrinkles.

"I'm sorry." The words felt heavy in Firya's mouth. When had Lerene's skin thinned to dry parchment? Firya could hear a wet draw in her mother's breath, like a baby's croupy cry.

There was a shout from the stable and the creak of Jonnah's wagon, and then the boys flooded through the door. Bellen tramped in first and leaned down to kiss her cheek. He smelled of sweaty horse and sweatier boy. Before she could stop him, he'd snatched a handful of apples from the barrel.

Jan plowed into Firya's sore hip, sticky fingers snatching a bite of dough. "Da' has a lamb," he said. His mouth was a smear of currant jam.

"One of the ewes had twins," Raff said, catching an apple from Bellen and rummaging through the breadbox for crusts. "She wouldn't take the second. She was butting the poor mite. A black one."

"She's mine!" Cade shouted over Raff. "Mother, we still have the leather bottle, don't we?"

Bellen poked his head into the cupboard. "Is there cheese left?"

There was, and Firya had intended it for her own lunch. "There's an empty firebox," she said.

Bellen grinned, as tall as his father and rangier. "Da' had us out at daybreak. I'll chop a cord by dinner." He held up his find, the corner of cheese wrapped in loose linen. "Raff will draw the water."

"It's Cade's turn."

"Cade has a lamb."

"I'll pick eggs," Jan said. "May we have eggs with dinner, Mother?"

"All right." Jonnah appeared at the door, with the bleating lamb draped around his shoulders. Those shoulders, still. He was thicker at the waist and his beard held piebald patches of tawny-grey, but he was strong as a mountain. "Let your mother bake the bread before you stuff your faces."

Jan popped the dough in his mouth like a chaw of spruce gum. "Can I sail from Herrow?" He grabbed at her arm and started swinging it. "I'm big enough."

Firya stared sharply at Jonnah. "Who's sailing from Herrow?"

Jonnah hoisted the lamb down into Cade's arms. The tiny thing kicked and struggled, while Cade crooned to it. One errant hoof caught Raff on the shoulder. Bellen yanked him back before he could cuff his brother for the insult. Jonnah settled at the scarred table with the boot-jack and laughed.

Firya rapped the bread bowl down on the counter. "Jonnah."

"Ah, Jan." Jonnah ruffled Jan's hair. "My secret's out." He held out his hand to Firya. "I've the contract for wool to Herrow, and across the straits."

"There's pox in Herrow," Lerene muttered darkly. "Spring ships carry pox."

"The boys have had the cowpox, what's a few more pits?" Jonnah said. "But I don't plan to take them—or stay in any rough inn." He grinned at Firya. "I think I'll take my lady travelling."

He looked as young as Bellen, behind his beard. Eager. Yet Lerene's worry was more than fair. Firya's father and brothers had been taken in a spring pox. "And who's to run the farm?" she asked.

"I can do it!" Bellen's voice cracked sharp on the first word and he flushed red, but his eyes sparkled with eagerness.

"He'll do a fine job," Jonnah agreed. He tucked his toes into house shoes and nudged his mud-caked boots under the table. "Your mother can watch Jan."

A year ago Jan had fallen twenty feet out of a poplar and broken his arm. Lerene didn't notice his screeches until Jan came to her sniffling with his arm in plaster. Then she'd taken time to tell Firya she'd been too rough on the child in setting the break. She'd hardly grown more mindful since.

The boys started up their clamour, shouting how they'd get their chores done, and mind their grandmama, and help Bellen with the lambing. Jonnah held out his hand again—his wide, rough hand could still make her shiver—expecting her to seal a bargain she'd never bartered. Firya's arms were flour to the elbows and the bread was no closer to the oven. "Bellen—" she said.

To Bellen's credit, he must have seen his adventure on the line. "Let's find a warming box for the lamb," he said, and herded his brothers out to the barn. The shrieks and the wrestling and the boasts went with them, for a dearly bought moment.

Firya left her loaves to the flies and climbed up the loft ladder. Jonnah followed her and settled on their feather mattress with a grunt. "I suppose after twenty years of begging, I'm to hear for the first time that you never once wanted to go to Herrow?"

He'd wanted his surprise to please her. She knew. He wanted it to be his own gift, not her will worked through him by a wish. Little did he know how badly she wanted the same.

He hadn't noticed yet, but the nights were warming. Soon she and Jonnah would sleep skin to skin, sweat slipping between them. By then there'd be no hiding from him. "Why this year?"

"The boys were young. Next year Bellen will be begging me cash money for a bride price, watch if he doesn't. This is our time."

"Every year I asked, when you had wool to sell." Firya's hair needed cutting. She could feel damp tendrils clinging to her nape. There was no pretending to be a girl at her age. "Haven't you seen my mother?"

"It'd be a strange day I saw the chimney seat empty for once."

Firya hid clenched fists beneath her skirts. Burying her soiled rags in the woods had seemed little enough to curry the dryad's favour, at first. If she gave up on her wish, then little would be left of Jonnah's love. If love it ever was. "She's ill," Firya said. "Her lungs sound like a swamp."

Her drab tiredness left Jonnah little to fight. "The boys can take care of her."

Which was it—Lerene to take care of the boys, or they of her? "She's right about the pox. In spring—"

"You won't catch the pox," Jonnah said. "You act like you never had the pus under your skin like any babe."

"Nellis visited a friend with the pox and gave birth to a deaf baby."

At last, Jonnah's gaze darted to her hand, splayed across her abdomen. Firya watched his tight mouth, his set shoulders. "You haven't kindled in years."

"I know." All these years, and this once, this once he asked. Firya cupped his face. His beard was soft against her palm. She played out her refusal sweetly, to sting him. "I can't go. My mother's sick."

"It's just the change," Jonnah insisted.

He must think she was a dried up husk already, discarded by the dryads. "So my mother would have it."

"And you said nothing." Jonnah stood up, big enough to loom under the low ceiling. "Well, I have to go. The contract's signed. I'll take Bellen—*he'll* enjoy the trip."

His words were a sharper slap than she'd braced for. A small, spiteful smile curled the corner of Firya's lips. How quick he was to pull the promised treat from her grasp. "I might lose the baby."

Jonnah stopped at the top of the loft ladder, heavyset, sombre. "You've lost others," he said. "It seems you've all the luck your dryad sees fit to give."

———•———

In some surly years, new shoots crept in under winter's bristles, a slow and hidden greening. The year Jonnah took Bellen to Herrow, to the boy's delight, the budding followed the rain in a great rush, and the flax fields rippled with blue flowers.

The turn in Firya's pregnancy arrived with the season. The sluggish heaviness in her stomach disappeared. She felt like a draft horse unchained from the plough.

In due course, Jonnah's hired hands arrived to drive the sheep to the higher pastures. Firya sent Raff and Cade with them. Jan tagged behind on the old mare who'd taught his brothers to ride. Firya wrapped a sandwich of roast lamb in cheesecloth, tied a leather water bottle to her belt, and set off for the forest's edge.

After a steady hour, the dogwood-choked path left the woods, becoming a grassy track drawn golden by the sun. Firya shed her shawl and breathed deep of the thin air. A thrum of breath and heartbeat filled her ears.

"Your daughter will never fulfill your hopes for her," said a voice at her side.

Firya's toes gripped the rock through her sheepskin boots. "No," she said. She'd grown stronger at refusing the dryad's first offer, but defiance still hindered her breath. *A daughter, after all this time?*

The woman whispered into view at the corner of her vision. Over the years, Firya had stolen sight of her in sidelong glances and still pools. She was lovely, bronze-haired and green-eyed. Her skin was deep burnished brown; her skirts and her cloak were grey. Her name she'd given with Firya's second sacrifice, blood of her body. Kirel.

Firya had once been nearly as comely, before Lerene accepted Jonnah's bride price. Before he'd set her to breeding sons. And after all her wrenching pain, all four of them were Jonnah's boys clean through. When they were babes, Jonnah would chuck them under the chin and let them pull his beard, or tumble with them like sheepdog pups. They were only real to him once they could ride after him to the fields. Yet they took to him like goslings after a goose. "No more children," she insisted. "What of the freedom you promised me?"

Only the wind, whistling down from the crags, answered her. Firya turned back to her climb. The path mounted to a dip between high hill tops, and then Firya was among the groves. Needles carpeted the mountain rock, bright oranges and softer browns woven into the rich warm earth. Firya settled on a root reaching over a tiny spring-fed pool. "Kirel," she said, and Kirel was there.

The dryad gathered rising mist from the pool and wove it into grey yarn on her fingers. "Jonnah cares for his own appetites, his own adventures," she said with a moue of scorn.

How she sounded like Lerene. Firya shrugged her shawl open. "He had to go," she said. The farm's profits depended on the spring wool fairs.

Kirel lifted her hands and considered her scarf of grey wool. Its length grew from her hands like thunderheads in summer, then disappeared on a breeze. "You'll work yourself thin forgiving him," she said. "He left you with the boys, a baby coming, your mother in her illness."

Jonnah must have seen Lerene's blue lips before he went. Dropsy thickened her legs until the flesh overflowed her thin feet. But he'd left to cross the straits with a jaunty wave. Firya's eyes heated with tears. "Kirel . . . is my mother dying?"

"Ah, little one." Kirel shifted without moving, and pressed Firya's shoulders, encouraging her to lay her head down. Her lap was cool as clean sheets rescued from the line in the moments before a bursting rain.

"I think she might be drowning," Firya murmured. Wishes lasted as long as a woman's strength. Lerene must once have promised too much. Now the mark of Firya's grip printed Lerene's soft arm long after she'd helped her from the privy.

"Your mother never had a biddable daughter, did she?" Kirel's cool fingers carded through Firya's fresh-trimmed hair. "You deserve better."

Grasshoppers trilled beyond the grove. Firya never should have left Lerene. The boys would be back from the pastures, clattering about the kitchen, disturbing their grandmama's rest. She needed to return.

"You walked too far with the child," Kirel said. She spread her cloak woven of cool air over Firya's shoulders.

A tremble in her belly made Firya draw a dizzy breath. She could feel a tickle inside like a young trout flashing silver in the stream. "She's quick," she murmured, and her tears flowed harder. A girl child, soft as a kitten. Obedient to Firya's wishes. But oh, how she hated the tear and pull of bearing, the endless *need* of a suckling babe.

"Let me ease her way," Kirel said.

Would Jonnah look the other way if Firya lost the babe? Women did, at her age. But— "I can't." Even if the loss was an ordinary sorrow, Jonnah would neither believe her nor forgive her. He didn't hope for a daughter, or even another son. He believed Firya would spite him for his ill-timed gift.

"The air's thin here," Kirel asked. "Let me take your burden."

No. "I've brought no offering," Firya said, and wept. There was too much debt between them. She'd keep the babe, to stem Jonnah's contempt, and to hold fast to the gifts Kirel had already given.

"Your promise holds true." Kirel's voice whispered beneath the hissing wind. Her skirts were soft as spring moss, warm as dark earth.

Firya closed her eyes and leaned into the lap of the mountain.

When she woke, her fingers curled loosely around a ripe fir cone, freshly fallen from the summer tree.

3.

Firya lifted the heavy swath of her daughter's hair in her hands, then let it spill back, like a Herrow draper showing off his finest wares. "How short then, for a girl reaching womanhood?" she asked. The shining mass, straight and dark, reached to Narene's waist, more silken by far than Firya's dull crop. "Do you think you'll cling to the earth, if I take it all?"

"Don't," Narene said quickly, then turned with a smile. "How much did you ask Grandmama to take?"

"Oh, your grandmama wouldn't listen to me," Firya said. She touched her own hair, the nut-brown strewn with silver strands. Narene had never known her grandmama, and so Lerene's memory was sweeter, and still more bitter. Narene's heart loved where Firya's could only rankle.

But then, Narene's love lighted as easily as a butterfly on rich vetch. Firya ran her brushes through her daughter's hair until it sparked. She'd woken Narene with a palm curved to her forehead and a whispered word, at dawn. They'd bathed together in the stream beyond the flax fields, far from Iden's eyes. While her hair was still wet, Firya plaited her hopes for Narene, her own lost daughter-dreams, into a strong braid tied with a ribbon of grey silk.

"For your future," she said. "Are there any young men you want to beguile? A Herrow man, a trader maybe? A sailor from beyond the straits?"

Narene laughed and shook her head.

"Don't move about so, child."

"I'm not a child!"

"No," Firya said. Narene was a starling in autumn, ready for her journey south. Each new beat of her wings wrenched Firya's breath. The boys were married and grown, but Firya had never had more than their obedience, their good-natured fondness; for this one, this last, Firya had always had her heart. "Indeed." She stroked a few wisps from Narene's forehead. "You'll have the dryads dancing for your desires."

Narene held the scissors up with both hands and opened the jaws. She'd polished the rust from the old blades, but the iron handles were black with years. Even if Lerene had shaved Firya to the skin, Firya would never have grown light enough to fly.

"I want . . . hearthfires and sheep in the fold. I want . . ." Here she giggled again, more girl than woman. "I want Alun Blacksmith."

"What?" Firya dropped Narene's braid. "That stupid boy?" She remembered Lerene's cold disbelief after she'd shared her own childish hopes. They had none of them come true, anyway.

"Mother, you're ruining it." Narene twisted around to frown at her. "Here."

"Oh, little one . . ." Firya took the scissors and set the blades to the top of the plait. Too low would leave Narene no room for joy, and Firya loved her daughter's dauntless joy. Too high would make her capricious, but Narene was already so steady, brimful of earnest trust. Firya chose a length, then moved her hand a fraction higher, and made the cut. Narene's shoulders rounded under the sound, then she squealed and leapt off her stool.

"Where's the plate, Mother?" She danced about, tossing her head like a filly.

"Here," Firya said, holding up the circle of bright bronze. "Here, and let me finish." Narene settled long enough to let Firya snip an even fringe around her lovely face. The dryads could never resist her. "There," she said. "You're ready for the groves."

"Oh, Mother. I'll find the dryads where I look for them."

Firya's heart squeezed against her smile. Narene would never tame a dryad with such artless hope. "Wishes aren't scattered like seeds, where any woman walks . . ."

"I want to go and show Magun." She whipped her hair back and forth to sting her cheeks. "She's got a month yet."

A woman, and yet such a child. Narene needed all her strength to cling to the ground. "You're a mist who wants to be a cloud," Firya said. She'd meant to speak tenderly, but taut anxiety filled her voice.

Narene admired herself in the bronze plate, then handed it back to Firya. "I'll be back for the milking. I promise."

"Surely you do. Will you get supper on for your father?" Jonnah would rather taste a silent pipe by the grate than hear Firya's talk.

Narene sighed. "Yes, Mother."

"Thank you, then." Firya cupped Narene's chin. Her eyes were dark as good ale, and her cheekbones had a saucy tilt. Yes, with her new-cut hair tickling her chin, Narene could draw better men than Alun Blacksmith—if she went looking, instead of waiting to be found. "You could have such magic, love. I've never been prouder."

Narene reached up to kiss Firya's cheek. "It's the best day in all the world." She skipped down the cart path to Iden, one hand stealing up to touch the curling ends of her hair. Before she reached the first turn, she was singing.

Firya rubbed her thumb over the strands of hair from Narene's forgotten braid. Narene had always lived in Jonnah's wide stone farmhouse, always run wild with four brothers to mind her. Firya gathered up the stool and scissors, returning them to the undercroft. Narene was so used to plenty that she hadn't even thought to ask for her own womanhood braid.

Firya laid a hand on the worn cushion of the rocking chair in the chimney corner. She should have Jan break the chair for kindling, the wood was so old and dry.

As long as supper was on the table, she wouldn't be missed.

Sun glared down on the hills as Firya left the woods. Her skirts thrashed around her thighs, slowing her. Sweat pooled under her empty breasts. She'd once leapt up the hills as easily as the young goats she could see playing on the crags far above. But her tides had been slowing this past year. The slope steepened each time she brought her paltry offerings to bury. The way was open now, but in deep winter? In next year's empty spring?

Narene could have fluttered to the height in an hour. A whispered wind might pluck her from the earth. Better for Firya to struggle, rather than turn Narene loose where she did not know the way.

Firya's legs burned when she came to the grove, panting. The evergreen branches arched above her, the splay of needles hiding the sky. "Kirel," she gasped, but no answer came.

Firya touched the nearest tree. Its trunk split in long seams, rough as an old woman's face. Firya leaned against the trunk and pressed her cheek to the hoary bark. Witches' hair drooped from the branches and caressed her shoulders.

The tiny spring was no more than a trickle in the heat. Moss clung to the rocks around its edges, a gentle pad to rest her hands against. Firya dipped her lips to its crystal water. Winter rain cooled her throat.

When she lifted her head, Kirel lounged in front of her. Her feet were bare beneath skirts of ripe hay. "Firya, the impatient."

Firya eased herself back on her ankles. She kept her eyes on the spring, rather than meet Kirel's glacier eyes. "That girl," she said, playing out honesty like a line. "She's such a stay-at-home."

Kirel let one shapely foot trail in the spring. "Oh?"

"She wasn't born in a scrubwoman's cot. She can read and factor and sing like a lady, and she'd rather spend every spare moment spinning. And Alun . . ."

Kirel's smile curled. "She wants the blacksmith's boy?"

"Alun is worse than Jonnah was at his age," Firya said. With each offering, her stoppered mouth had loosened with Kirel. This once she let every word she held back from Iden's ears come pouring out. "I gave her every freedom and she wants to chain herself to a rock." Firya slipped Narene's braid from her pocket and stroked the tip. A worm for her hook.

Kirel picked a single strand from her skirt and twined it around her fingers in a cat's cradle. She offered it across the spring to Firya. "Who will be good enough for your daughter to love?"

Firya lay the loosened plait on the moss between them. "I wanted so much when I was her age." She pinched the grey strands of Kirel's cat's cradle between thumb and forefinger. The touch of Kirel's yarn was deliciously cold under the heavy sun. Firya turned her hands under Kirel's, and she held a snowstorm in her cupped palms. "She'll want it someday. Something more than Iden town."

Kirel's fingers brushed across hers like frost. She looped the cradle easily. "And when Narene comes home from her adventures, from ships and cities, will you be satisfied at last?"

"She follows that boy wherever he goes." Firya frowned over the criss-crossing yarn. She'd come to barter for Narene's dreams, but her daughter deserved so much more. "She hangs about his father's forge like every silly Iden girl."

"Were you never a silly Iden girl?"

"No."

"Not for Jonnah?"

"I made the best of my gifts." With a deft twist, Firya took the cradle. She offered her hands, bound in Kirel's foggy threads.

Instead of taking the cradle, Kirel touched a sprig of heather clinging to a rock above the pool. The tiny pink flowers crinkled beneath a memory of ice. "I could turn Narene's heart from Alun."

A hedgerow dryad couldn't offer better. "She'd leave Iden, then? And safely?"

"Oh, yes." Kirel's yarn tightened about her fingers.

Her eyes on the cradle wrapping her hands, Firya spoke slowly. "You promised me freedom once." There was green sea to the north, white cities across the straits, and golden lands softening to the south, and Firya had seen none of it. "But I've been no further from Iden than your grove."

Kirel pinched the yarn between slender fingers, and turned the cradle.

She chose wrong. The cradle fell into knots, leaving Firya's hands wrapped in yarn so cold it burned.

Firya reached for Narene's braid but her hands wouldn't close around it. Dead white patches spread across her knuckles. "Kirel, I can't. It's— it's not mine to wish." Fumbling with fingers trussed into claws, Firya finally managed to tuck the plait beneath her skirts. Cold locked her jaw but she pushed until her silence broke. "Narene will come when she's ready."

Kirel's eyes were pale as a reflection of clouds, but she shrugged as if Firya had interrupted their game for her own pique. "Ah, Firya. Bring me sweet milk from your babe's lips, the blood of your body, or your own daughter's unwanted braid; but do not waste my time." The threads loosened into mist and drifted away.

Firya's hands were her own, brown and wrinkled as fallen leaves.

4.

Firya hefted the churn, heavy with cream, to her hip. She settled her stool behind the barn, where the last of the morning's shade would cool her. The new butter was nearly finished when she heard footsteps creaking the barn's old planks.

"Old Mannon wanted to pay a silver penny less, as I'm an apprentice still, but Da' said, show me one flaw, and I'll charge nothing at all."

Alun's voice, strutting and smug. Firya dropped her dasher. Narene must have seen the empty kitchen and assumed she was up in the groves. Firya strode around to the barn door, prepared to send Alun yapping back to Iden town, but stopped when she saw the two of them. Narene leaned against the gelding's stall, holding up a handful of oats to his eager lips. Alun stood in front of her, hands tucked in his wide leather belt. Motes of hay dust swam in the sun seeping into the barn through the old chinking, limning the two of them gold as larches.

"Were you worried, Alun?" Narene asked. She stroked the horse's velvet nose. "He might have found something wrong with it."

"'Course not." Alun threw back his shoulders. "He couldn't find a thing. If he had, Da' would've taken it out of my hide."

Firya snorted. How could Narene think a young rooster was worth her heart?

The gelding tossed his head, seeking more oats, and Narene laughed. No longer a girl's laugh, but low and inviting. She kept her eyelashes low, her lips curved.

"Narene . . ." Alun reached out and caught her fingers between his rough hands. "It's been three months, hasn't it?"

Narene turned slightly, her skirts flaring around her ankles. "Nearly."

Alun shifted like a plough-ox chewing cud. "What I mean is, you're a good lass. My Da' wouldn't mind another woman's hands around the place . . ."

Even Jonnah had more words, and better, all those years ago. Firya had heard enough of such clumsy love-making. Narene would stand there all day besotted if Firya didn't intervene. She thrust the door open. "Narene."

Narene started and took her hands back from Alun. "Yes, Mother."

"Have you forgotten your chores? And your poor father, starving in the fields without his dinner?" Firya stared at Alun, and he met her eyes directly. Impudent snip. Narene ducked her head and sidled past Firya to the farmhouse.

After too long, the boy touched his forelock. "I'll be going, then, ma'am."

Firya watched him until he was well on his way. How easily a boy could trap a girl, with no more than promises and a ready smile.

Narene stormed from the kitchen carrying Jonnah's dinner basket. She crossed to Firya, looking ready to stomp her foot like a watchful ewe. "You were hateful to Alun."

"Narene, he's a lump of dirt. You're a flying bird." If only Narene knew what price her womanhood braid could command in the groves. She so badly needed a dryad's guidance. "You're going to hurt so, someday, if you tie yourself to him."

"I love him." Narene shook her head. "You're the only one who's tied, when you're so certain that you're free."

———•———

Rain drummed on the blacksmith's roof and seeped through the window-shutters. The kitchen was filled to bursting with every relative and neighbour who thought they'd earned a taste of the betrothal toasts. Firya sat tight against Alun's old grandmama at one elbow and Jonnah's wide-spread satisfaction at the other. "Thanks be, Thom," Jonnah said as Alun's father mulled his ale with a hot poker. "It's good to have Narene settled at last."

Thom passed along the steaming ale and shoved the hissing poker back in the hearth. "And all it took was a season's silver!"

Jonnah laughed, too loudly. Well, Thom had been eager in the bargaining. And Jonnah had already paid four good bride prices. Maybe he deserved to gloat over the silver clinking in his purse.

Firya shook away Thom's offer of another mug. At the head of the wide trestle table, Narene tucked her hair back, as though it had fallen into her eyes by all innocence. She'd never been so shameless as a child. Beside her, Alun leaned down to whisper some crudeness in her ear, and she blushed. Had Firya cut her hair too high after all?

"Aye, but Alun has her promise now," Jonnah said. "It'd take a dryad's wish to free her."

Thom shared a smile with his wife, Lizal. "Narene, you wouldn't witch our Alun, would you?"

Jonnah grinned. "Mayhap she already has!"

Firya pressed her lips together. Despite the fire crackling in the grate and the mulled ale in front of her, she couldn't rub warmth into her fingers. The men's boastful jokes proved they knew nothing of magic.

"Better for Narene to wish for children." Thom raised his mug to Narene.

"Healthy children," Lizal amended, with a hasty look over her shoulder. She at least had the sense the dryads had given her.

The guests raised their drinks with a glad murmur. Alun took the deepest swallow. His cheerful face was pink with ale. "Best we ask Firya for wishes," he said. "Narene needn't seek the groves, not when *she's* half-dryad already."

Anger filled Firya's stomach with sour milk. No wonder Narene held so close to Iden with Alun feeding her such poison. Her spurned braid still lay tucked at the back of her bureau drawer.

Jonnah's hand fell on her knee and squeezed. His quiet warning galled worse than Alun's ignorance. "Narene knows well enough where to lay her wishes," Firya said sweetly. Keeping a rein on her fool beloved, for one.

Jonnah heaved to his feet. "The night's growing dark," he said. "We've a ways home, and the rain's coming. Firya?"

Firya bared her teeth in a flat smile. "Our thanks for your hospitality. Narene's chosen the best of Iden town." Grass-snake words, hissing but harmless.

Jonnah wrapped her in her wool cloak, and they stepped out into the wet street. Laughter lifted in their wake.

"He'll make her hate the dryads, going on as he does," she griped, with no hope of Jonnah hearing her. Firya would warrant Lizal and Thom expected Narene's bride price to pay for itself in the good fortune she'd bring them. Firya's reputation had loosened their lockbox.

Jonnah shrugged. "Narene's a good girl, and she knows her mind." He tramped across to the saddlery where they'd left the cart. When he returned, leading the gelding, his breath wreathed his head like pipe-smoke. "It's not Alun will make Narene neglect the groves," he said at last.

Moonlight glimmered through the clouds. Firya turned her face up into the cold damp. Rain slid down her bare neck and under her collar. No, Alun wouldn't forbid Narene the groves. No one wanted to offend a dryad. But even if Narene struggled to the heights, she'd be choosing Alun's ridicule, his resentment. Firya knew those choices well enough.

Jonnah cupped her elbow, and she climbed to the cart bench. After lighting the lanterns, he joined her, slumped from his years in the fields. "It's just life, is all, Firya. The dryads are for young girls' dreaming. Not for women years married, with a home and all."

"A home I worked for." Firya hated the sound of Lerene in her voice, the waspish anger, but it broke through despite herself. "One I sacrificed for."

Jonnah turned to study her—whatever he could see in the gloom. He'd never seen much, less when it suited him not to. "You're hurting her, being like this. Nor just her."

When she didn't answer, Jonnah flicked the reins and the horse set off. The wheels sucked free of the mud. Back to the freedom of the farm and the bounded fields. The freedom of every day the same, unending, for years.

The kitchen was black as pitch when they arrived. Jonnah lay a log on the dim coals, but the house was never warm enough, no matter how the hearth blazed. "I'm chilled clean through," Firya said. "It's winter already."

"A month yet," Jonnah said. "My bed will warm you, if you ever come to it." He left the kitchen, his bones creaking as loudly as the house in the wind.

Firya curled under a threadbare wrap in the chimney corner and let the fire die in the grate. Narene did not come home.

———•———

High white clouds ran before a dry wind. The day would be clear, the breeze perfect for winnowing. Sheaves of new wheat were stacked by the threshing floor. Firya had been up before the cockerel, cooking by lantern light. Jonnah had invited half of Iden town to the threshing. More hands to work the flails; more mouths to feed.

"Have you another barrel of ale, Firya?"

"None fit for Iden town to drown themselves in." At sunset they'd lose Narene, and Jonnah wanted Firya to host the rabble while she watched her daughter disappear. Lerene was right. The only pride Iden recognized was standing up and spitting when the wishes turned.

"I'll send Cade for it."

Firya dropped her knife to the board. Her swollen knuckles bent at odd angles. She'd given up on spinning and knitting these past months. The wool chafed so. Even slicing old carrots into the stew left her joints throbbing.

"Why don't you rest, Mother?" Bellen's wife, herself with three boys . . . always boys, in their family. She took up Firya's knife with heedless skill.

Firya drifted to the kitchen door. By eventide the swept floor would be mud to her ankles, the washing-up piled to the ceiling. But beyond the yard and the fields were the hills, a tapestry of evergreens.

The eastern horizon gleamed gold. In this late season, the light wouldn't reach the steep-sided groves until nearly noon. Firya's back ached to think of tossing the wheat baskets, again and again, faces coated in rough hay-dust, choking on the chaff. The wedding feast would be eaten by torchlight and by candle. She could be gone and home again long before then.

Firya walked out the door without reaching for her shawl. Bellen's wife didn't notice her leave. Firya passed among the men setting up the flapping canvas tents and shifting the bales of wheat without a glance, and floated across the stubbled fields. Only the mice, scurrying after the gleanings, saw her go. Cold gusts wafted her upward and softened her steps, until Firya came to the grove on feet lighter than a doe's.

Kirel stood over the pool. The water was warm enough to steam in the chill air, mingling with Kirel's mist-grey cloak. "Are those bells I hear, down Iden way?"

The spreading branches of the ancient firs stirred in the day's wind. Firya went to the closest. She pressed her palm into the bark to feel the pain bloom in her old hands. "She's lost to me."

"You want Narene to fight for her magic."

Kirel's scree-sharp voice caught on her desire like a barb. Narene had never intended to make her sacrifice. She'd thrown away her power, and every comfort Firya had tried to offer. "She'll marry Alun," Firya told the old tree. The tree whispered comfort to her, but she couldn't hear the words. "She loves him."

"No," Kirel said tenderly. She lifted a hand to touch Firya's cheek. Her palm was as soft as dew. "She'll be bound to him. I hear bells on the wind, Firya. I hear a girl weeping because her mother isn't there."

The mourning wind wailed through the trees. Firya's breath fluttered in her chest like a sparrow netted in a wicker basket. The golden light filling the grove slanted in from the west. Sunset. The wedding. "Narene!"

"She doesn't need you now." Kirel smiled, and it was the smile of an ancient woman, skin rough as bark, fingers as powerful as roots gripping the mountain. "Freedom's price is wide, Firya. I gave you everything. Five children living. A husband who loved you. A daughter who adored you."

Firya's feet splayed against the living rock. The mountain heaved beneath her. Kirel brought her other hand to Firya's head and the press of her cold hands rooted deep in Firya's skull. "These are my trees around you. Every one of them took wishes, and paid in full."

The old fir behind her was knotted with years, stronger than the mourning wind. Firya clawed for the trunk and held fast. Lerene's lips had been blue when Firya, heavy with her daughter, walked at her side to the high groves. It had taken all day, with Lerene's eyes rolling like a panicked horse as her lungs filled. But they'd come at twilight to the grove, and Lerene's last breath had been full and clear as a dawn breeze. Lerene hadn't come for sacrifice, or for power; only for the rest Kirel had promised. "You're wrong," Firya said. "My mother *gifted* you her bones."

Kirel's mouth opened wide around an avalanche of laughter. "Ah, then gift me yours, Firya, and rest with her now."

No sacrifice would satisfy Kirel, no payment stand as a final settlement. "No," Firya said, and closed her eyes. "I will gift you my magic." Every wish, every mastery bought and paid for, she would return. Let her be a scrubwoman like her mother before her, if she could return to Narene. "That for my price. That for my daughter's heart."

————·————

She came from the hills as if from a far greater height. She limped until she could go no further, and sank down to rest in the long shadow of a hedgerow willow.

When she looked up, a young girl sat across from her. She was dressed in white linen and a green woollen cloak. Her dark hair was cut short and even above her ears. "Narene," Firya said.

"Mother." Narene laughed. Her eyes were bright with tears. "Mother, you came."

Firya smiled. Her old bones pained her, as they always did, but the deep cold of the groves had gone. "You should be with Alun." But no, the light was wrong. It was no later than mid-afternoon. She could hear the rhythmic calls of the men threshing, the women tossing the grain into the windy air.

"I found the dryads, Mother, when I looked at last."

Firya spoke against a thickness in her throat which threatened to stop her breath. "There was never any need to ask *them* for your happiness," she said. Kirel had claimed her bones and given her no joy she might not have found for herself.

Narene ran a thread of grey silk ribbon through her fingers. The ribbon Firya had used to knot her womanhood braid. "What wish could I ask for, on an autumn day?" Narene said, her eyes bright with teasing. "What wish for a girl about to wed?"

Frost chilled Firya's breath. The braid was gone. Narene had called on the dryads at last, when she had no need for worthless wishes. The dryads could pluck at her now, cozen her with promises. Unless she'd begged for no more than what she already held dear, her heart's home. "A fire in the hearth," Firya begged, "and a husband returning."

Narene shook her head. "She's given you to me." She took Firya's bent and broken hands, and raised them to her lips to kiss. "I wished for a grandmother for my daughter," she said, "a grandmother I can tell her tales of, when I hold the scissors to her hair."

Author's Notes to My Younger Self: I want you to know that it's okay to be ambitious. It's worth struggling or striving even when things are going well and there's no apparent need for effort. Dedication and drive toward a goal are wonderful things that will pay off later.

ROBOCARE

Rich Larson

Maud was doubled over clipping his gnarled toenails—which was a real job, what with the rods in his hip, a kink in his back, and eighty-eight years' worth of general wear and tear—when the goddamn carebot showed up again.

Three precise knocks, then: "Good morning, Maud! It's Berg, and I'm just here to check in with you." The electronic voice was clear and soothing, enunciating perfectly for all the seniors without cochlear implants, and altogether too happy. "The weather is overcast, fifteen degrees Celsius, and . . ." There was a brief data retrieval pause. "The Chicago Bulls lost to the Seattle Satellites last night by a score of 128 to 111. I'm sorry! I know your favourite team is the Chicago Bulls."

"I have a phone," Maud growled from his chair. "I know the weather. I know they lost."

"The Chicago Bulls now have a record of 0–8 to start the season," Berg said. "I'm sorry!"

"I bet." Maud clacked the nail clipper shut and stuffed it into his pyjama pocket. He didn't want the carebot seeing him all hunched over moaning and groaning trying to reach his feet. "Well, come on in. Do your thing. And then get out."

The carebot opened the door and walked in, a smooth ambling gait on flexy pneumatic joints, and it was painful to see a robot moving so much easier than he could. They'd come a long way since the herky-jerky Boston Dynamics days. This one was more-or-less humanoid, with a squat and sturdy frame softened by doughy white silicate pads. The big emoji display screen on its front was nearly always smiling.

"Let's start with your blood pressure," Berg said. "May I touch your upper arm?"

Maud grunted, pulled his sleeve up, and the carebot wrapped one soft manipulator around his biceps.

"They've planted new rhododendron bushes in the garden. Do you enjoy gardening, Maud? I noticed you have a . . ." Berg paused, swiveling one camera. "Aloe vera plant by the window."

"It was a gift," Maud said. "I'm not a gardener. Got a black thumb."

The carebot hummed for a moment, processing, before it spoke again. "Is your thumb black because you left it in the toaster too long, Maud? Ha! Ha! Ha!"

Maud narrowed his eyes. "Are you trying to make a joke? Or are you glitching?"

"I have made improvisatory jokes since Tuesday," Berg said. "I'll stop if you flag the behaviour as inappropriate."

"You got a long ways to go. Just finish the checkup."

Berg obliged, taking a blood sample and a bacterial swab as it babbled through world news items: Korea's reunification, the migrant barrier debate, an announcement that seven percent of the oceans were now officially covered in reflective foam.

"That'll go wrong," Maud said. "Guarantee that'll go wrong somehow."

"You made the same prediction about coral reef restoration," Berg said. "That initiative is widely considered to have been a success, Maud." It paused. "I can see your sleep cycle is still irregular."

"Of course it's irregular," Maud said sourly. He jabbed his thumb at the window, past the spiky aloe vera in its scuttling sun-seeking pot, toward the abandoned house on the lot across the street. "Those kids were at it again. Having a fucking party over there in the old house."

"Did their fucking party prevent you from sleeping, Maud?"

"Don't say that. Sounds bizarre when you say it." Maud rubbed his bristly scalp. "They're trashing the place. I saw them sneaking in with spray paint canisters Thursday night."

"Did you alert the authorities?" Berg asked.

"Very first night it happened, yeah," Maud said. "They sent a drone, showed up about an hour and a half later, and of course the kids had already scarpered. Useless. Then they came again last night, being all quiet about it."

"Did their being all quiet about it prevent you from sleeping?"

Maud ignored that. "They've got no respect for old things," he said. "They think they can do whatever they want. They think they can do whatever they want, and there's no consequences. Someone needs to put a good scare in them."

"Maybe you could ask them to stop, Maud," Berg suggested.

"What, me hobble out of bed in the middle of the night to shake my fist at a bunch of teenagers? They'd laugh their asses off." A thought struck him, and he peered at Berg. "You know, in the dark, you'd pass for a security bot. One of those Taser-toters, the kind they always got prowling around the downtown. Probably outside your programming, though."

"What is outside my programming?"

"Putting a scare in those kids," Maud said. "Me, they'd laugh at. You, they'd get the hell away from."

Berg paused to process the information. "You are requesting that I accompany you off the property on a walk early tomorrow morning to frighten adolescents."

"Well. Sounds stupid when you put it that way."

"I accept," Berg said. "Please send me an alert when you are ready. Have a good day, Maud!"

The carebot marched out of his apartment and closed the door before Maud could tell it he'd only been joking.

———•———

The day, like most days at the Wildrose Court assisted living facility, passed at a trickle. Maud had his routines, of course. Lunch was half an avocado and fried egg on toast, which he could make in the kitchenette of his own suite. While he did the washing up—everything was slow now, everything took time—he listened to his usual astronomy podcast. It wasn't quite the same, now that Milo wasn't listening at the same time and messaging him about it.

The hosts' voices were smug as they talked about the artificial moons in China finally being dismantled for being ridiculously cost-inefficient, and normally Maud would feel smug too, but Milo had always had a soft spot for the big silvery satellites—thought they were romantic—so Maud felt peculiarly guilty imagining them all controlled-falling out of the sky.

After soaping and rinsing his few dishes, he slept on the foam couch. He used to set an alarm on his phone, but lately being unconscious was his preferred state, so he slept as much as he could. No aches, no pains, no memories. He woke up groggy about two hours later and read for a while, old French poetry because working both languages supposedly kept the Alzheimer's away. He knew, vaguely, that he was reading the same stain-covered book of poems over and over, but he liked them so he did it anyway.

He turned the pages with his left hand because he had no feeling in the right, none at all, and maybe if he'd gone in for surgery all those years ago it would be different, but now he was too old to have them open up his wrist and fix his tendons. The anaesthesia wouldn't play nice with his weak heart or the medications he took for it.

He only looked up from his book when the aloe vera started stomping. The little white legs that let the pot trundle back and forth under the window, following the sun, were now tapping impatiently. Maud had taken the aloe vera because it was the one plant of Milo's he was sure he wouldn't be able to kill, and he'd bought the smart pot as an extra measure. Now he hauled himself off the couch and over to the window.

The read-out on the pot showed a rainshower icon; watering instructions scrolled underneath. Maud shuffled back to the kitchen and filled up a kettle with water, then shuffled back.

"No more mini-moons for Shanghai," he said, in the plant's general direction. "Told you that would never last. Maintaining that low an orbit is a big old money-sink."

The aloe vera's pot gave a chirp when enough water had been poured into the dirt, and Maud set the kettle down, rubbing his knotted wrist. Through the window he could see the old house, overgrown lawn rippling in the dusk breeze. Whenever Milo had come over to his place for a beer, he'd lamented about the old house, about how it was going to waste and what a shame.

And now a bunch of little pricks were spray-painting the walls and probably smashing the windows next, getting high on opioid derivatives or whatever kids were using these days. Maud decided then and there that he would do something about it, whether Berg came along or not. He found a black woollen sweater in his closet and put it on, along with a black cap.

In the mirror he tried to puff out his chest and look grizzled—a grizzled old security guard. He practiced waving an old solar flashlight from the drawer as he scowled. That helped a little, so long as nobody noticed it was blue with tiny cartoon birds on it.

Prepared, Maud guided his couch over to the window and settled in to wait.

———·———

Supper came by delivery, since Maud had been avoiding the dining hall for the past three weeks, but he ignored it. He didn't seem to really get hungry anymore. Food was mostly something he took with his medications.

He watched. He waited. He had the book of poems in his lap but never managed to focus on it for more than a few stanzas. It was possible the kids weren't going to show up. It was possible they'd never show up again, and Maud was keeping watch over an abandoned house for no reason at all. But at least he was doing something.

And finally, just before midnight, they showed up. A gaggle of kids in puffy recycled jackets, most of them wearing backpacks, too. No laughing or shouting this time, but they loped off the sidewalk and into the overgrown grass like they owned the place. Maud watched one of them scale the splintering wooden fence to the backyard and open the door for the rest.

Maud grabbed his phone off the couch beside him, slipping the once-begrudged loop over his wrist out of habit, and flipped past the aid icon to the direct contact line for the Wildrose Court's carebot. Berg showed up about five minutes later, knocking just as loudly as it did during the day. Maud struggled up off the couch and opened the door.

"Good evening, Maud," Berg said. "I see that the adolescents are preventing you from sleeping."

"Damn right," Maud said.

"Why do they make you angry?" Berg asked.

Maud stared. Blinked. "Because they think they can do whatever they want," he finally said. "But you can't." He gritted his teeth. Berg was right. He was angry. "You can't," Maud repeated. "The bad stuff just happens and you can't do anything."

"Bad stuff, Maud?"

Berg's calm voice made him feel even angrier. "Your life goes to shit and you lose all your friends one by one and you can't *do* anything because you can barely fucking *dress yourself.*"

He could feel a whine in the back of his throat, which made him feel pathetic as well, and his pulse was squeezing fast, thudding in his wrists and neck. His blood pressure was probably skyrocketing.

"We are doing something right now, Maud," Berg said. "We are leaving the property in order to frighten adolescents."

"Yeah," Maud muttered. He swallowed. Composed himself. "Let's get on with it, then."

He tugged the black cap a little lower on his forehead as they left. The hallway was dim and empty. He could hear faint media sounds from half the doors he passed, insomniacs holed up for the night with their screen-delivered opium. That was him most nights. But not tonight. Tonight, he was doing something.

Berg slowed its walk to match his hobble, so they got to the elevator at the same time. Maud jabbed the button with a shaky finger.

"It is only four degrees Celsius outside," Berg said. "I am so glad you are wearing a hat, Maud." Its emoji display was grinning with blocky white teeth.

"You need to be a lot more intimidating when we get over there," Maud said. "Can you do a siren noise, maybe? That'd do the trick."

"I can do a siren noise," Berg confirmed.

Downstairs was empty too. Maud paused to look around the dining hall, lingering at the table by the window where he and Milo had always sat for supper or for hand-and-foot canasta. Then he made for the exit with Berg in tow. There was nobody around to ask what they were doing so late, and the doors buzzed open at their approach.

Maud knew he was free to leave whenever he wanted—his son had been real insistent on that point, how he was a resident and not a prisoner—but right now he couldn't actually remember the last time he'd stepped outside. He pulled the collar of his coat up against the cold, and they walked out into the parking lot, past the electric stalls and around the corner of the building.

Maud froze when he saw the yellow curb where Milo had tripped and fallen three weeks ago, a trip and fall that should have been a bruise and a laugh but instead cracked his dumb old skull open and sent him to the hospital to die with plastic tubes all over him like a hungry squid. There was no stain on the cement. No evidence it ever happened at all, even though Benny and Rhoda and what's-his-face on the veranda had all seen it and chattered about it for a week straight.

"It has been twenty-three days," Berg said.

"What?" Maud snapped.

"It has been twenty-three days since you left your room," Berg said. "Fresh air is delightful, Maud."

Maud shook his head and soldiered on, hobbling across the empty street. Berg glided along beside him. They passed from the pooled bluish light of LED street lamps into the shadow of the old house. Maud could hear the sounds of casual conversation, a muffled laugh, as he stepped onto the overgrown lawn. The dandelions were up to his calves.

This was it. He took out his flashlight, cleared his throat, and stomped through the open gate. "Hey!" he barked. "What the hell do you think you're doing?"

Four teens spun around, eyes startled wide, and he figured he'd nailed it, gotten the inflection right and everything. He strobed his flashlight from one face to the next, noting with disappointment that one of the vandals was wearing a Bulls hat, then directed it to the ground where their backpacks were open and the contents spread out. He didn't see the pipes and beer cans he'd been expecting.

"Hey," said the nearest girl. "Hi. We're growing sink-moss."

Maud blinked. "What?"

She pointed to the back of the house, and he followed her finger with his flashlight. Clinging to the old wood of the veranda and the walls were long swathes of moss, so deep green it was nearly black. He frowned and shone the light on the ground again, where there was a lantern set up and the metal canisters he'd taken for spray paint a few nights ago were hooked to some kind of tube and pump.

"You know, the kind that eats CO_2," she said. "Hopefully. This is our first trial with a cellulose-bonding variety." She peered behind him. "Hey, it's the bot from the seniors' place. Berg? Hi, Berg."

Maud's mouth fished open and shut. He turned in time to see the carebot wave one manipulator.

"Good evening, Tasha," Berg said. "Is your project going well?"

"You know each other?" Maud demanded.

"Do you live at Wildrose too?" the girl asked. "It's really nice, right? I love shuffleboard. They have such a great table."

"I hate shuffleboard," Maud said, more to mask his confusion than due to any strong opinion on the game.

"Oh." The girl shrugged. "Yeah, so we met Berg when we came over to do a demonstration and explain about the Greenhouse Project. Maybe you missed it? Basically we got a grant to try out this new batch of urban sink-moss on a couple places around town. But it can't handle sunlight until it bonds with the wood, which is why we're spraying at night. It was all in the presentation. I could link you the video."

Maud had definitely missed the presentation, the same way he'd missed all the dinners and Friday films and orthoyoga and poker nights and therapy sessions. Twenty-three days since he'd left his room. He'd been hoping to find kids smashing the windows and spray-painting the walls so he could be righteously angry at someone, but here they were doing something Milo the gardener would have loved.

"You knew they weren't vandalizing the place," he croaked to Berg, feeling his face heating up. "Why didn't you say something?"

"Fresh air is delightful, Maud," Berg said. "And I was worried you were becoming despondent. It has been twenty-one days since Milo Kepler's accident. I'm sorry."

Maud switched his flashlight off and rubbed his face with his sleeve. "Twenty-one days," he mumbled. "Still feels like fucking yesterday."

"May I touch your upper back, arms, and shoulders?" Berg asked.

Maud snorted. "What?"

"To facilitate a hug," Berg explained. "The physical contact will help you release endorphins."

Maud figured he already looked like a total idiot, hobbling around playing cop in the middle of the night and interrupting environmental initiatives, so he gave the carebot a grudging nod. Its arms flexed around him and tightened like a weird, soft socket wrench. Maud bit back a big sob.

The kids looked awkwardly at each other. One of them started fiddling with the canisters.

"Thanks," Maud said, when the carebot let go. He gave it a tentative pat on the arm. "You're all right, Berg." He turned to the kids. "I'm sorry. For interrupting. It was stupid of me. Your generation tries to do something good, my generation tries to shit on it. Or else just me, I guess."

The girl scratched at her head. "No big," she said. "And, you know, the whole concept of generations is kind of nebulous? And is mostly used to create in-groups and out-groups?" She held out a metal nozzle. "I know it's sort of late. But you can help Denny with nutrient delivery, if you want. Point and spray."

Maud took the nozzle, and the boy with the Bulls hat gave him a slightly suspicious look before he shrugged and motioned him over to the veranda. Maud glanced back at Berg. "Think I'll stay for a bit," he said. "As penance for being an old asshole. I know you've got to get back to the residence."

Berg's smiling emoji bobbed in a nod.

"See you next checkup, I guess," Maud said.

"See you next checkup, Maud," Berg said, and padded off.

Maud went to the veranda, where Denny was already spraying away. "So," he said. "Those Bulls."

"Oh, man." The kid shook his head. "They're terrible."

Maud pointed the spray. "Goddamn terrible," he agreed.

Author's Notes to My Younger Self: I'm sure the list of things I wish I could tell my younger self will be growing and changing as I age, but for right now I wish I could tell him to shoulder less blame and guilt for things outside his control, and to shoulder more responsibility for the things within his control. And to drink less.

DRESS OF ASH

Y.M. Pang

There is an Etossarn tale about a girl who became a servant in her own house.

After her mother passed away, her father remarried. Her stepmother, a woman of high status but little wealth, banished the girl to the servants' quarters, where she cooked meals, scrubbed floors, and lit kindling. The girl's face became covered in soot, and she wore a dress of ash.

The story came from a book of translated Northerner legends Father had given me. Mother scoffed at it. "Why read boneskin tales? Our own legends are the ones that matter."

She had a point. What use were Northerner stories to a Swordbearer of Keja?

Yet during that late summer sunset, as Kaya's form disappeared into the trees, all I could think about was that girl in the dress of ash. Unlike her, no prince came for Kaya.

Kaya, my dearest sister. Whatever else, I loved you. I loved you.

———•———

I lost my father in a duel between a wooden sword and a sheath.

On a breezy spring day, I emerged from the training room of our residence at the capital to see him striding across the courtyard, a bag of tied cloth slung across his back. My mother, aunt, and cousin were not home. It was only me and the servants in the compound.

Even at eight years old, I understood.

I placed myself between Father and the front gates. "Where do you think you're going?"

His face registered a brief surprise, then reverted to his usual carefree smile. "To the market, little flower. I was thinking of buying your mother a . . . fan."

A lie. He'd sooner buy her a poisoned chalice.

"With that?" I eyed his bag.

He knelt so we'd be at eye level. "You got me, little flower. I'll be going a little farther than the market. But I'll be back soon."

"You're leaving us. You're running away." It hurt, saying those words, because they meant Mother was right about him. I'd heard their voices at night—Mother calling him useless, an unworthy Swordbearer.

"There is something I must do. I'd stay if I could."

I pointed my wooden practice sword at him. "Then fight me. If you win, I'll let you go."

He chuckled. "Don't be ridiculous, little flower."

"I'm not your little flower! I'm the heir to the Marin clan and a Swordbearer of the Kejalin Empire. Defeat me, or you shall not pass through those gates."

Sighing, Father stood and shrugged off the cloth bag. He untied his sword from his hip and drew it—then threw it aside, holding the empty sheath.

The top of my head barely reached his waist. But I'd learned five of the Seven Forms faster than anyone Master Ouwi could remember. I'd never seen Father set foot in the training room, and Mother's comments didn't make me think highly of his swordsmanship.

"Shall we begin, Yulina?"

"Your duty is here, Father. I will not let you go."

I thrust my wooden sword at his knee. I half-expected him to step around me and leap over the compound walls. I would be in the trouble then, for I had not yet mastered lightness, a fundamental Swordbearer ability.

But he didn't. He deflected my blow. And the next. With at least one foot on the ground the whole time, following the rules of a sword duel.

I barely blocked his first counter-attack. His next strike sent me staggering back toward a budding bush.

I swung my sword again. How could a man of such middling reputation deflect all my blows? How could I become First Sword, if I couldn't defeat this . . . weak . . . foe?

His sheath caught me on the back of the hand, so hard I loosened my grip on the sword. His next blow sent my practice sword flying. He tapped his sheath against my shoulder, near my neck.

My defeat, no matter how one looked at it.

His eyes held sadness as he picked up his discarded sword and bag. "That was impressive, Yulina. You will make an excellent Swordbearer someday." He stepped past me, toward the gates.

Wait! I wanted to yell. I wanted to turn around, grab his robes, beg him to stay. But I'd set out the rules. He'd stay if I defeated him, and go if I did not.

A creak as the compound gates opened. A slam as they closed.

I knelt in the grass, biting my lip. Refusing to cry. I was Marin Yulina, daughter of Marin Reina, Swordbearer of the Kejalin Empire. Even in defeat, I couldn't forget that.

———•———

Mother embraced me that evening, when I told her what had happened. I couldn't remember her embracing me so tightly, before or since. I cried then, my tears soaking the lavender of her robes into purple. "I'm sorry," I said. "I couldn't stop him."

"You did well, my daughter. Give you two years, and you could've beaten him."

"But I didn't have two years. I needed to beat him today."

"And what difference would that make? His mind was set on leaving. He would've simply left on a day you weren't there. You cannot force your love upon someone. You cannot make them stay."

"If only you were there."

Mother laughed. She brushed away my tears with a callused thumb. "I don't need him," she said. "You're all I need, Yulina. Never forget that."

I leaned back. No more tears. "I won't, Mother. I'll make you proud. I promise."

———•———

Mother remarried when I was ten. She might need nothing but me, but our finances needed more than that. Father had departed with most of the gold and silver in the compound. Our alliance with the Takosa clan, Father's family, fell apart. We still needed to maintain the compound, pay off the debts incurred by my great-uncle, and pay for my lessons with Master Ouwi.

On their wedding day, Mother's new husband gifted her a blue fan decorated with swallows. She gifted him a barrel of the finest *hishu* wine. I had no idea where she had procured the *hishu*. It was only made in the palace, and our clan did not exactly have status there anymore.

My stepfather was a commoner. A merchant with voluminous amounts of money, ambitions, a dead wife, and an eight-year-old daughter.

Her name was Kaya. I'd always wanted a little sister. I loved her immediately.

———

"No, like this."

I stood behind Kaya, adjusting her grip on the practice sword. Then I stepped back.

She took an experimental swing.

"Not yet." I smiled. I'd done the same thing during my first lesson with Master Ouwi. "For now, just hold it. Feel the shape of the hilt. Understand what it means to bear this weight."

Her arms had already begun to tremble. The practice swords were made with the same weight and balance as real swords. "For how long?" she asked.

Master Ouwi had made me stand there for two hours, but I saw no reason to force Kaya do the same. I contemplated for a second—and at that moment the door slid open and Mother walked in.

Her lips thinned. "What do you think you're doing?"

"Teaching Kaya. I know I'm not qualified for proper instruction, but—"

"What do you think you're doing, teaching a girl of commoner blood to hold a sword?"

I heard a clatter. Kaya, dropping the sword as if it burned her.

"She is my sister now. She is part of the Marin clan. Would you have her embarrass us?"

I could see fire dancing in Mother's eyes. "Commoners do not hold the sword, Yulina. Do you want her to lose her head?"

"But Hokina Sohei—"

"Commoners do not hold the sword unless the Emperor says so! As I am still your mother and the head of your clan, you will listen to me."

I clenched my teeth to hold back the retort. After a long moment, I hung my head. "Yes, Mother."

"Good." She glanced at my sister. "Kaya, the south storage room is getting dusty. Go clean it."

———

On the second evening of the Five Moons Festival, I returned home from a gathering at the Inyara compound. Mother had taken me, my aunt and cousin, and even my stepfather. But not Kaya.

I found my sister kneeling in the courtyard, ripping leaves from a fallen zelkova branch. The moon hung thick and fat in the sky. In its light, my sister's grey robes looked almost regal, almost like the Emperor's silver-threaded ceremonial garments.

I ran toward Kaya. "Hey, you're still awake?"

She looked up. The corner of her lips drooped when she saw Mother and Stepfather behind me.

"Yulina!" Mother called. "Inside. It's time to sleep."

"We'll be just a few minutes," I said.

Mother hesitated, then went into the south building with her husband. I was left alone with Kaya. I suddenly didn't know what to say.

She continued ripping off leaves. When the branch was bare, she looked up and said, "So, was it fun?"

The poetry competitions were fun to watch, but that probably wasn't what she needed to hear right now. I grabbed Kaya's hand as she reached for a stalk of stubborn weed.

"Hey," I said, "I'll speak with Mother. I'll see if you can go to the gathering on the Fourth Day."

Kaya shook her head. "Don't. It's . . . not your mother who told me not to go."

I blinked.

"It's my father. He said I'll be a burden, and the last thing he needs is Swordbearers seeing him dragging around a commoner child." The silver moon gazed out from Kaya's dark eyes. "He says he doesn't need me. He needs another child, a child with your mother. A child who can cement his place in a Swordbearer family and be an heir to the Marin name."

She tugged her hand away from me. I let my grip slacken, let her slip away, even though I was Swordbearer and could've clung too tight for her to escape. So fragile, my commoner sister. So little, I could do for her.

———•———

I broached the subject of a new sibling with Mother.

She laughed. "Rest assured, Yulina, I will not have another child, least of all with that commoner. You are my only child, my only heir."

"But at night . . . do you not . . ."

"Oh, I am not wearing the *komi* charm. I don't need to. Because that one will never make me pregnant. I've made sure of it."

I was almost afraid to ask further. Maybe things would've turned out differently if I hadn't. But I was heir to the Marin clan. I wanted to become like my great-grandfather, the Chancellor who crafted the Reunion Treaty. I wanted to become like my grandmother, who'd reclaimed the northern Ancestral Lands. How could I live up to their legacy if I couldn't face my own mother?

"Mother . . . what did you do?"

———•———

It was the wine, of course. Mother had laced it with black yew extract, which slowly crippled virility. Normally the spice of black yew was easily detected, but the aftertaste of *hishu* covered it up. And my stepfather, commoner as he was, hardly knew how *hishu* should have tasted anyway.

Mother trusted me to not say a word, and I didn't betray her trust. Not that time.

———•———

When I was thirteen, I defeated Master Ouwi in a match for the first time. Maybe he'd let his guard down. Maybe he'd gone easy on me. Still . . .

The sun sunk below the compound walls. Master Ouwi congratulated me and departed, but I remained in the courtyard, practicing. Waiting for Mother. I wanted a match with her, but she'd gone out that morning and still hadn't returned.

The wind sent the leaves of the zelkova tree swirling down, and I sliced them with my sword. Sliced the pieces again, before they hit the ground. Mother still did not allow me to touch the Marin sword, but she'd handed me this one, which she had used in her youth.

I lowered my sword and transferred it to my left hand. Stared down at the palm of my right. If only the present me had faced my father that day, I would have defeated him. But then, I would have never met Kaya.

The doors of the compound opened. I looked up and expected to find my father standing in the doorway. Why did I think that? Thirteen was too old for such daydreams.

My stepfather stepped inside—and almost immediately stumbled off the path. The wind blew his scent across the courtyard, but I could tell from his gait alone that he had been drinking.

He froze when he saw me. "You here to kill me?"

I blinked. I'd last seen him that morning, as he left the compound muttering about needing to find an answer. I didn't know what his question was, but apparently the answer made him return crazy.

Then I realized I had transferred my sword back into my right hand, unthinkingly. Maybe that explained his words.

He threw his head back and laughed. "Kill me then! Kill me, kill me!"

The door of the southern building opened, and Kaya rushed outside. "Father!"

He turned his bloodshot eyes on her. "You!"

Kaya grabbed his arm. "Come in, Father. I—I'll make some tea for you."

He shoved her aside so hard she almost fell. I took a step forward.

Kaya met my eyes. She shook her head. "No, Yulina." She took hold of her father's arm again, and this time he did not shake her off.

She led him up the veranda and through the sliding doors of the building. I lingered at the bottom of the steps. I hated how my stepfather treated Kaya. And in his current state, I didn't trust him.

But Kaya had told me not to interfere. I remembered Mother's words: *You cannot force your love upon someone.*

———•———

I was asleep by the time Mother returned. That did not stop her from lighting a lamp and opening the door to my room.

I woke, caught sight of her face, and relaxed.

"Yulina," she said, "I've been appointed Governor of Dari."

I took her hand. "That's . . ." I fumbled for words, speaking nonsense for five seconds. "That's wonderful! I knew the Emperor would not forget the debt he owes to Grandmother."

Mother's lips thinned at the mention of my grandmother. She said, "I want to leave as soon as possible. We cannot let the temporary Governor become too comfortable."

———•———

Three days later, we trundled down Yutai Road, four of us in one carriage.

Mother had wanted a second carriage, but Stepfather had ended that plan. "Do you think my money is limitless?" he'd yelled through a mouthful of rice roll.

In truth, Mother hadn't even wanted to bring him or Kaya along. But she didn't want to leave them in the capital either, where she could not keep an eye on them.

In the confined space of the carriage, Mother poured wine for Stepfather and showered him with compliments. It was rather unnerving to hear her speak sweet words, knowing how she spoke about him with me, knowing what she had done.

Kaya and I tried to play Crossed Swords, but the jolting of the carriage kept sending our pieces sliding from the board. Kaya finally swept all the pieces back into the box and snapped it closed with a sigh of frustration. "You always beat me anyway," she said.

"I've been playing longer. You'll become good if you keep practicing." I raised the board. "Also, you forgot this."

She snatched it from me and struggled to pry the box open again. The carriage must have hit a rock at that moment, for the pieces flew out of the box and spilled everywhere.

Mother looked up in the middle of pouring wine. "What are you doing? I thought you were playing Crossed Swords, not skipping stones. Is there anything you do well?"

My stepfather chortled. "Clean it up, Kaya. You're pretty good at cleaning, aren't you?"

Kaya knelt on the floor of the carriage, retrieving the pieces. I joined her.

Our eyes met across the gap between benches. "I don't need your help," she snapped.

"By the way," Mother said, "I think one piece flew out the window."

I rose. I couldn't stand all the way up; I was now tall enough for my head to hit the ceiling. "It's the carriage's fault, not Kaya's."

Mother lifted the wine pitcher. "I was pouring wine at that exact moment. I did not spill any."

"Kaya isn't Swordbearer. Weren't you the one who said that? You shouldn't set such standards for her."

"Yulina. Please, just stop."

I looked down to find Kaya with her hands pressed against her ears. "You're not helping," she said. "Just, say nothing, okay? And sit down. Please."

I obeyed, more in shock than anything. Kaya finished gathering the pieces, at least the ones in the carriage. We never found out if Mother was right about one piece flying away, because neither of us played with that set again.

Mother continued fawning on Stepfather and pouring the occasional drink for him. I wondered if her plan was to keep him permanently intoxicated during her tenure as Governor.

Kaya pulled a book from the stack we'd brought. My mouth went dry when I realized it was the book of Northerner legends.

I glanced at her discreetly as she read, trying to think of a diversion before she reached the story about the girl in the dress of ash. But three pages in, Kaya rubbed her head and stowed the book away.

"Not interesting?" I ventured.

"It's not that. It's just, reading in this carriage makes me dizzy."

"Oh. I get it. It'd make me dizzy too."

"Really?"

"Really. That's why I'm not reading right now."

Kaya's mouth turned in the beginnings of a smile. "Aren't you Swordbearer? Aren't you supposed to be stronger than that?"

I shrugged. "I doubt being unable to read on a carriage will stop me from becoming First Sword."

The rest of the morning passed without incident. Kaya's anger toward me cooled as we talked about our favourite stories. I was careful to not mention *Way of the Swordbearer*, despite having read it more times than I'd read anything else. Whatever misfortune her father's remarriage had brought her, at least it gave her the opportunity to read all the books in the Marin compound.

Green forests marched past outside the window. Around noon, we turned off Yutai Road.

"Where are we going?" I asked.

"You'll see," Mother said with a smile.

Soon the path grew too narrow for the carriage. We climbed out, my stepfather strapping on his wine jug. Mother bade goodbye to the servants and led the way deeper into the forest.

Kaya and Stepfather clung to each other, looking around anxiously.

I breathed deep, inhaling the scent of earth, and listened. "Water," I said.

Mother smiled again.

I envisioned Hokina Kura's map of the Kejalin Empire which I'd studied many times. Estimated how far a carriage could travel in half a day, tried to match that with a spot on the map. "Are we going to the White Jade Falls?"

"Correct," Mother said.

"I didn't realize it was so close to Yutai Road."

"It is. I thought it would be a good place for us to pray, since we are passing by regardless."

The path straightened and the trees thinned. I caught sight of the Jade River and turbulent falls.

The White Jade Falls resembled a sword: tall, narrow, and blinding in the midday sun. It plunged into a deep pool, and along its shores, white water rushed over stones glazed green by moss. I had seen depictions of waterfalls, even of this one, but the strokes of those paintings resembled torn shreds of old cloth compared to reality. And nothing could bottle the sound, or the misting of water on my skin, even from far away.

I spotted no other visitors on the banks, or on the rocks leading to the top of the plunge. Mother pulled brown packages from her sack and handed one to each of us. "Rice rolls," she said, before walking closer to the waterfall with Stepfather. Kaya and I lingered by the riverbank, marvelling at the entire scene: falls and river and forest.

"The Battle of Divided Jade took place here." I raised my voice a little, though thankfully we were not close enough to the falls to warrant shouting. "That's why Swordbearers visit this place."

"I *do* know that much," Kaya said, but her tone was more playful than annoyed. "It's one of our great victories."

"Actually, the Ravagers won the battle. They just lost so many in the process, it damaged them for the war."

"Huh. Lone Eye described it as a victory."

"He was writing two hundred years after. Tiga Suwin was at the battle, and he described the Ancients and Swordbearers retreating." I chuckled. "His account isn't very popular, since it's half lost and reads like an ogre's scribblings compared to Lone Eye. But if you're interested, I'll see if I can find a copy in Dari."

Kaya sat down, feet dangling above the water. I joined her. We unwrapped our rice rolls and bit into them. Beyond today, it would be flatbread and pickled radish, except when we stopped in towns.

"You know, when I first met you, I was surprised you liked reading," she said.

I huffed. "A Swordbearer should be well versed in all arts. Not just the blade, but words as well. Plus, my father really encouraged the words side, just as my mother valued the blade."

I rarely spoke about my father to Kaya. Mother wouldn't be pleased. But she was all the way at the foot of the falls, and the crashing water drowned out our voices.

"Did he teach you to read?" Kaya asked. "No, never mind, you probably had a tutor, like you had Master Ouwi."

"No, my father taught me. Mother thought he was good enough for that, at least."

"Ah. I was taught by my mother. I'm not sure how good a job she did."

"Considering how much you've read already, I'm sure she taught you well."

I felt a gentle weight on my shoulder. Kaya, leaning against me as we watched the falls. Maybe, after four years, she was finally ready to accept me as her sister.

"Yulina!"

I turned at the sound of Mother's voice, close behind me.

"It's time for us to go into the White Jade Cave," Mother shouted.

Kaya and I stood. We followed Mother to the foot of the falls, where Stepfather waited. Here the spraying water became more than a gentle mist, but summer had not yet ended, and I welcomed the scratch of cold fingers against my face.

Mother and I edged as close to the falls as we could. I peered at the curtain of white water, but even my Swordbearer eyes could not see beyond it.

"You can jump directly," Mother said. "Or you can jump there first, then toward the falls." She pointed to a large rock protruding from the middle of the river. "It's your choice."

"I can jump directly." I no longer had misgivings about my mastery of lightness. I could leap to the top of the Central Shrine faster than Master Ouwi.

Mother nodded. She didn't question me, didn't doubt my ability to evaluate myself. This was what I loved about her.

A small voice said behind us, "Can I come?"

Mother turned. My stepfather clapped a hand over his mouth. Kaya's face showed immediate regret.

"You, come?" Mother said. "Don't you know where this is?"

Kaya shrank back. Her voice was barely audible against the crash of water. "It's the site of the Battle of Divided Jade. That's why I wanted to come."

"The cave is sacred. Commoners should not even think of entering. How would you make the jump anyway?"

I stepped between them. "I'll carry her."

Mother looked torn between shouting and laughing. "The White Jade Cave was crafted from the bones of the first Swordbearers, who sacrificed themselves upon these waters. A commoner should not step inside."

"I'm sorry," Kaya whispered. "I didn't know."

"Kaya isn't a mere commoner," I said. "Sure, she may not have Swordbearer blood, may not hold the gifts of the Ancients. But she is a daughter of the Marin clan now. Others who married into Swordbearer clans became tutors, palace guards, even Governors. Kaya should have those opportunities too. Wasn't that the promise you made when you married h—married Father?"

I couldn't say whose face held the most shock. I had never called my stepfather Father before, always using polite but undescriptive pronouns or refusing to refer to him altogether.

My stepfather recovered first. He seized Kaya's arm, then spoke in slightly slurred tones. "Sorry for the girl's ignorance. We'll wait here."

"You don't need to wait." Mother gestured at the flatter rocks running along the side of the falls, which could serve as stairs. "The White Jade Falls are magnificent, even if you may not enter the cave. Why not climb to the top, for the view there? We'll find you afterward."

My stepfather nodded. Kaya mouthed something to me. I thought she said, "It's all right."

"Ready?" Mother said.

I wanted to argue further, but if Kaya said it was all right, what could I say? "Ready."

Mother went first. She barely needed a running start before leaping. Her deep purple robes trailed behind her as she hit the falls, then disappeared.

I took a deep breath. Gave myself a slightly longer running start, just in case. Jumped.

The moment of floating was breathless, exhilarating. No wonder some Northerner writers said we Swordbearers could fly. This was little different. Then I hit the water.

A heartbeat of thunder and cold. Then I burst out from the other side, my knees bending as I hit the wet cave floor. Not quite light as a feather, but close.

Though it had been impossible to see from outside in, the cave was not dark. Some light still reached through the waterfall, and my Swordbearer eyes were already adjusting.

The White Jade Cave was . . . white, as the legends told and as the name indicated. I pressed a hand against the cave wall. It felt more like bone than jade. "Do you think it's true?" I said. "That the Ancients made these walls from the bones of fallen Swordbearers?"

"Who knows? Some say it's not just their bones here. It's their souls too, guarding this river forever instead of moving on."

"That's sad. Wouldn't they be happier in the Reclaimed Realm?"

"I don't know. Maybe you should ask them."

Keeping one hand against the wall, I dropped to my knees. Mother did the same. The cave floor was wet, but I was already soaked from the jump, so it made little difference. Closing my eyes, I prayed. Prayed I would become First Sword one day and restore the glory of the Marin clan. Prayed I would make Mother proud. Prayed I could protect Kaya, even if it was from Mother or Stepfather. How, though, when much of the damage was already done?

The voices of my ancestors did not speak to me, no matter how I tried to tease speech from the roar of water. My mind began wandering away from prayer. What was Kaya doing at this moment? Hopefully Stepfather wouldn't reprimand her too harshly for asking to come to the cave.

A shuffle told me Mother had risen to her feet. I opened my eyes. Faint patterns covered the bone walls, but I couldn't make out any messages, just lines that resembled rivers.

"It's time to go," Mother said.

I stood. "Did our ancestors speak to you?"

Mother marched to the curtain of water without responding.

Leaping out of the cave was harder than in, for I could not see the banks as I jumped. I succeeded, however, landing on a moss-covered rock by the riverbank. We must have prayed for longer than I thought, for the sun had sunk almost to the treetops. Kaya and my stepfather were not at the riverbank.

We climbed the stones with lightness, with rhythmic leaps, toes barely brushing the rock. Near the top, my stepfather's voice blasted my ears like the whack of a practice sword. He and Kaya stood close to the mouth of the falls. His face was twisted like an ogre mask, his arm arcing viciously as he shoved Kaya away. She fell, crashing against a rock, almost slipping into the water.

My next leap took me right to Kaya. I grabbed her shoulder, helped her sit up. I glared at my stepfather. "What do you think you're doing?"

"Took you long enough getting out of that ratty cave," he spat. I noticed his wine jug some distance away, smashed to pieces.

"Are you okay?" I asked Kaya. She nodded and tried to push my hand away.

"Who do you think you are, telling me what to do?" Stepfather growled. At first, I thought he was talking to me, but then I realized his beady eyes were trained on his daughter.

"The wine, Father." Kaya climbed to her feet and shook me off, facing her father. "It's not good for you."

He laughed. "Not good for me? Nothing in this stupid place is good for me! I thought I'd find myself a better life, find you a better life." His gaze found Mother. "A child with Swordbearer blood. That would have . . ."

"Husband, let us head back to the carriage," Mother placated him, wringing the sleeves of her damp robes. "You are not thinking straight."

"It's over! I've known it was over even before we set out on this damned journey!" He jabbed a finger at Kaya. "Now even this brat wants to control me!"

"She's your daughter," I said. "She cares about you."

"Is she? Is she really?" Stepfather's voice dripped sarcasm. "Or has everyone been lying to me this whole time?" He lunged at Kaya.

My body . . . moved. I was Swordbearer, and my words had all failed. My sword flashed into my hand.

Stepfather stumbled to a stop, staring at the blade. It was a finger-width from his throat.

"Yulina, no!" Kaya screamed.

My stepfather laughed. "Yes, kill me! Kill me!"

"Ignore him, Yulina," Mother said. "He's gone insane."

I took a deep breath. Replayed his words in my head. His words from today, from that day. "No." I sheathed my sword. "He knows."

I pulled Kaya back with me. "Sorry," I said. "I should not have done that. I have forgotten my vows as Swordbearer—to protect the weak. Including you, Father."

My stepfather looked more frightened now than when I'd pointed my sword at him. As if he finally understood what he'd said. As if he were calculating whether he still had something to lose, something he'd forgotten.

I had been torn between two vows. My loyalty to Mother, and my Swordbearer principles.

Way of the Swordbearer, Part Five. A Swordbearer shall strive for truth. Not veiling her own eyes to the truth, not uttering falsehoods to others.

I kept a firm grip on Kaya's arm and felt her tremble. I met my stepfather's bloodshot eyes. "You went to a doctor, did you not? Before we left?" I pitched my voice to carry above the river's rumble. "You know you are sterile."

The air weighed upon me like a mountain. I dared not look at Mother, for then I would stop.

"Do you know why that is?" I asked. "You don't, do you? I promise you, whatever else, Kaya is your daughter."

Kaya began to sob. I couldn't look at her either.

"It was the *hishu*, the wine Mother gave you as a wedding present," I said. "She laced it with black yew extract."

I didn't know if he knew what black yew extract was. But he didn't need to. I had said enough for him to understand what it had done. What Mother had done.

My stepfather took a step back. "Reina . . . you . . ."

Mother's face was stone. "What a fool you are. Your ambitions would've amounted to nothing regardless, as no child of yours could have done much. But they would have been . . . unnecessary."

"So from the beginning, you've never given me a chance?"

"Should I? You, a commoner?" She shook her head in disbelief. "Who thought a simple marriage could raise him above his abilities? A man who would throw away his own daughter if she dragged him down?"

My stepfather looked at Kaya. His face, previously red with anger, was now pale as the rushing waterfall. "This was a mistake from the beginning," he said. "Kaya, I'm sorry. I'm sorry."

He leaned back over the edge. Let himself fall.

"No!" Kaya screamed.

I leapt off the cliff after my stepfather, stretching out an arm, snatching for him. But I hadn't reacted fast enough. He was already plummeting to the bottom of the falls, and this wasn't how lightness worked. It couldn't make me fall faster.

My stepfather hit the large rock in the middle of the river, the same one I'd refused to use as a stepping stone earlier. It wouldn't have mattered if he'd hit water; he was not Swordbearer, and he would not have survived either way. He left a smear of blood before sliding off the rock. I landed a moment after, just in time to see the water swallow him.

"Father!" Kaya's scream came from the top of the falls, but it felt so close.

I dove into the water. Despite the afternoon sun, it ran mercilessly cold. The stories said the first Swordbearers could dance on water, but I'd never heard of any present-day ones doing so, and I certainly hadn't that ability. So I swam, cutting through the water in desperate strokes, chasing the pine green robes of my stepfather.

I caught his ankle. Rose for a gasp of air. Towed him toward shore. It was difficult to keep both him and myself afloat, but I did it. I had to.

Mother had already leapt down the steps and stood at the river's edge, looking fearful and livid. She stretched out a hand, which I ignored as I clawed my way up the muddy bank. My eyes were fixed on Kaya, who stumbled down the last steps of the falls, tears shining in the late afternoon light.

I laid my stepfather on the riverbank. He was dead. His neck was broken, and half his head had caved in where it hit the rock. The water had washed away the worst of the blood.

Kaya fell to her knees and buried her face in his chest, sobbing. I stared down at my hands, riverbank mud almost hiding my stepfather's blood.

The sky turned the gold of sunset. Mother stepped around Kaya and bent over her husband's body. "This was . . . an unfortunate accident. Understand?" she said. And she shoved my stepfather's body back into the river.

Kaya lunged at Mother, teeth bared, a jagged rock in her hand. I mustered a shout, a half step, then Kaya's rock was flying through the air and she with it. My sister landed in a heap some eight paces away.

Mother dusted off her hands. "That was a foolish thing to do, girl. I will be generous and pretend it never happened."

I ran to Kaya. Stretched out a hand as she sat up, but she flinched away.

"I'm sorry," I said.

She groaned, coughed. Climbed to her feet.

"I know nothing I say matters anymore," I tried. "Not after . . . not after all that's happened. But . . ."

Kaya turned her back on me and started walking. Not quite steady yet from Mother's blow, shoulders shaking as she continued to sob.

"Kaya, please. I'm sorry. I'm so sorry!"

She ran, then, weaving toward the trees. I caught up, wrapped my arms around her.

She fought me like a wildcat, her nails ripping bloody scratches down my arms. "Let me go! Why can't you let me do what I want for once?"

My grip slackened, not from her attacks but her words. She broke free and walked into the trees.

I followed, at a distance now. "Please, Kaya. Don't go."

"Why? It's not like you care!"

"I do care. You're my sister."

"I was never your sister! I've never thought of you that way, not once!"

I stopped. My heart pounded harder than when I'd leapt from the waterfall after my stepfather. Tears blurred my vision. "You can't go, Kaya."

"Let me go! If you care, if you really care, then listen to me!"

I took one step. Another. Stopped. What could I do? My actions had only led to this. I was useless. Maybe I should trust Kaya this time.

Trust her. Which meant standing there, frozen, as my eleven-year-old sister walked off in the bloody glow of a late summer sunset.

You cannot force your love upon someone. You cannot make them stay.

The trees soon shielded Kaya from view. I wandered back to the riverbank and sank to my knees. Mother stood over me.

"She'll be back," I muttered. Even if we had killed her father. She was an eleven-year-old child with no family, nowhere else to go.

Mother didn't speak, didn't come close but didn't walk away either.

Sunset turned to nightfall.

"We need to leave," Mother said.

"No."

"Kaya isn't coming back. You know that."

"I'm not leaving."

"We need to get to Dari. We've already spent half a day longer here than planned."

"I'm not leaving without Kaya. You can . . . you can leave without me."

"Don't be ridiculous, Yulina."

"I'm serious. If you want to go, go. I'm not going." I swallowed a lump in my throat. Whatever else I'd lost, I had never considered losing Mother. But now those words were spoken, and I could not take them back. I was Swordbearer.

Ten heartbeats of silence.

"I'm going back to the carriage," Mother said. "I need to speak with the servants. They've probably taken off without us now, and I can hardly blame them."

I doubted that. Kiei's family had served mine for seven generations. I trusted him, if no one else.

"You're staying here?" Mother said. I nodded.

I was left alone by the riverbank, listening to the evening song of cicadas, watching stars slowly blink into view. My mistakes were truly irreversible this time. Even Mother had left me.

After an eternity, I heard footsteps. I looked up to find Mother holding an armful of twigs.

"You're back," I said. Surprised.

"If you're not leaving," she said, "I'm not leaving either."

"But you need to get to Dari . . ."

"I told you," she said, "I need you. It's foolish of you to wait for that girl, but if you stay, I'll stay too."

Later, by the crackling fire, I said the words I should have said all along. "If Kaya comes back, can you not treat her better? After all you've done to her, to her father . . ."

Mother's lips thinned. "I had no idea you cared so much about that girl."

———•———

We waited for ten days. We waited until our rations ran low, as we supplemented our supplies with fish from the Jade River, roasted over a sputtering fire.

Kaya did not return. I'd hoped she would, but I knew she would not. After ten days, even I admitted there was no point in waiting any longer.

We rode north along Yutai Road. Mother was terribly late for her anticipated starting date as Governor. The Emperor was probably worried or enraged—if he had even been the one to appoint Mother. If we were even important enough for him to care about. After all, no search parties had been sent to look for us.

Mother's tenure as Governor of Dari was short and disastrous. I could not say it improved our clan's standing. I could only hope it wasn't memorable enough to be a hindrance.

I would fix all this, when I become First Sword.

I can now defeat Mother ten matches out of ten. I plan to enter the Imperial Tournament next spring. Perhaps I am not yet ready to win, but I need to cross swords with Princess Eda, with First Sword Okowo, to see how far I have to go.

As for Kaya, my dearest sister, my greatest failure . . .

I loved you. I hope you are alive, and that you found your prince.

But I don't know if I'll continue looking for you. I've seen the hatred in your eyes, heard the accusation in your voice. I know if we meet again, we will meet as enemies. As is my fate as the ash girl's sister.

Author's Notes to My Younger Self: To my teenage self: I see, you've gotten in trouble again. You're wondering if you can ever become a functional member of society. It's all right. It's better to be dysfunctional with a passion, rather than functional without one. Trust me, I've been on the other side. Sometimes I still wish I could become you again.

HOPE TO SEE THE GHOST TONIGHT

Patrick Swenson

We're ten years out of high school. It's too damned soon to be reliving those years, in my opinion, but I've survived the hastily-planned class reunion, caught up with my old buddies I'd never expected to run into again, and now the August weekend is over.

Except for this.

An impromptu run with friends to the lake.

We're jammed into Scott's red pickup, all ten of us, and this is *exactly* how I felt all weekend. Cramped. Forced. Squeezed into a tight spot. The Flathead Lake cabin belongs to Marcy's grandparents, but they only come to Montana from Arizona in June and July.

Scott drives, and my elbows are in tight because Judy is so close to me. I smell the vodka martinis she's been drinking all night. It's ten miles from town to the lake, and here we are, ready for an overdose of honest-to-goodness nostalgia. Marcy keeps reminding me it'll be fun.

We arrive and Marcy doesn't have a key to the house. It's a two-story cabin, but it's so dark I can't see anything but featureless walls and a few boarded-up windows. I wonder what happens if an animal gets in there and dies. I realize I'm just fine staying outside.

Marcy remembers the padlock combination to the pumphouse down by the dock, and we pull out lawn chairs, blankets, lighter fluid and dry matches. Scott and Judy start a campfire down on the beach, and it snaps and pops like amplified Rice Krispies. We huddle around the campfire, enjoying the beach, happy for the flickering light. The campfire marks a point halfway between the dark expanse of the lake and the silent cabin that looms behind us like an obsidian wall.

I wrap a blanket around Vickie Brady and me to keep out the evening chill. A shimmering moonpath crosses the water from the beach to the far mountains, and it seems as if the wind is using the path to bring the threat of rain.

I'm not that old, but I feel like a bit of my life slips away each passing year. My father and mother are gone, killed in a horrible car accident. Once I graduated high school, I withdrew from everything. Who could understand what I'd been through? Who cared? It's a failing: I don't know how to be around people, but at the same time I'm terrified at the prospect of being alone forever. At least the gang saw fit to touch base with me; otherwise, I'd never have come to the reunion.

I thank the soft flicker of the fire, for at least it gives me a sense of security, its heat and light a kind of oasis between the black lake and the empty cabin and surrounding woods behind us. It's not very adult of me, but I've never liked the dark.

We sit quietly. I might've felt out of sorts all weekend, and even tonight, but this moment with old friends seems right.

"I've got an idea," Paul says suddenly. "Let's play a game."

Well. The evening *had* seemed right, for a few minutes anyway. "Oh no," I say. "I don't *think* so. At midnight?"

"Why not?" Paul says.

"Play what?" I ask. "A game of cards?" I throw a rock out as high as I can over the lake, and five seconds later it splashes the water with a *ssshoook*. A perfect chugger. "Go Fish, maybe?"

"How about," Paul says, "we play Hope to See the Ghost Tonight?"

We're all quiet for a few moments. Scott, who's put on about thirty pounds since high school, is still breathing hard from the walk down to the beach. "Jesus," he says, "I haven't played that since the sixth grade."

"You and the rest of us," I say. "We outgrew that game."

"Hey," Henry says. "*I* never played it before."

"Don't worry, Henry," Paul says. "We'll teach you the rules." He glances around the campfire. "Well? What's it going to be? If we do it, we *all* do it. Right, James?"

"Look," I say, staring straight at Paul. "We played it when we were kids, after suppertime, in town. You know: a big fenced yard, parents in the house, neighbours on every side. It's now midnight. Does the word 'civilization' mean anything to you?"

"Yeah," Paul drawls. "Boring. C'mon, James. You're not afraid of *ghosts*, are you?"

"I'm for it," Vickie says, next to me.

"Me too," Dusty Sherwood says, standing up as if his statement has decided it for the entire group. "It'll be fun, right?"

Everyone stands, one by one. Everyone that is, except me, but I know I'll give in. I'll play the game because the gang's always done everything together, right? In our old age, when we can barely walk, we'll all be wondering: Why is it we never spent that one last night playing Hope to See the Ghost Tonight with each other?

I stand.

Everyone else runs to the cabin, to the dimly lit porch, which is wooden and big enough for all of us. It's covered with a shake roof. I *walk* to the porch, though, trying to act indifferent. When I step up, I announce, "Fine, let's do it. But I'm not going to be the ghost. No fucking way in hell."

"James, you big *baby*," Judy says, patting my head. I brush her off and smooth out my hair. She laughs. "Don't freak out. *Jesus*."

"I'll be the ghost," Paul says.

"So how do you play?" Henry asks again.

"I'll go hide while you explain it to him," Paul says, and without waiting to see if we all agree, he jumps off the porch, dashes around the corner of the cabin, and is gone.

Marcy explains the rules to Henry. "Paul hides while we count, then we all try and make it around the cabin without getting touched by the ghost. You can go any direction, but you have to make a complete trip. No going halfway and backtracking, unless it's to start around the other side. The porch is Base. Anyone the ghost touches stays behind to help in the next round. The next round, you now have more people hiding wherever they want around the house. You never know when someone's going to jump out at you! We go until everyone's been touched. Last one touched is the winner."

Henry shrugs. "Sounds easy."

I shake my head wearily but keep my mouth shut. I don't want them to know any more than they already do how dead-set I am against this, because they'll tease me about it, like they did when we were kids.

I was in third grade when my parents were killed in that car accident. They'd had too much to drink, my dad especially, and he swerved into the oncoming traffic. I played the game for the first time four weeks later with my friends.

Playing the game as a kid, engulfed in the darkness, I felt so terribly alone, even with my friends around. I missed my parents. The rest of the gang never showed much sympathy about it, pushing me to play the game, making fun of my reluctance. We've all outgrown those cruel childhood days, but why do I feel like they've returned? I always hated playing the damn game as a kid, and I hate the idea of playing it as an adult even more, here in unfamiliar territory, with my parents even further away in my memory.

Now, in a singsong voice, Marcy starts the chant, and everyone but me joins in.

"One o'clock, two o'clock, three o'clock, four o'clock, five o'clock, six o'clock, seven o'clock, eight o'clock, nine o'clock, ten o'clock, eleven o'clock, twelve o'clock midnight, HOPE TO SEE THE GHOST TONIGHT!"

We scatter, jogging toward the corners of the cabin.

Vickie leads a pack toward the right side, but I set off counterclockwise, keeping the cabin on my left. I follow Scott, because he's the slowest, and if we flush Paul out of hiding, he's likely to go after Scott, and I can sneak by. Judy and Dusty are ahead of us—even better—and the rest have disappeared around the other side of the house.

Once I round the corner of the cabin, darkness surrounds me like a blanket. I slow to a walk. The crunch of footsteps on twigs and pine cones, and the dim outline of the cabin on my left, keeps me headed in the right direction on a path between the cabin and the looming trees. The shadows of Scott, Judy, and Dusty trudge up the slight hill leading to the back, and instinctively I veer toward the cabin, staying close to the wall.

Someone screams from the other side of the cabin. It's Vickie's high pitched yell, no question about it. I run to the next corner, then frantically search for Paul's position. I hope I can get by while he's busy with Vickie and the others.

Black shapes run toward me, and I freeze.

Jesus. I can't tell who's who, whether or not these are the others, or if one of them is Paul. I crouch, poised to take off into the woods, or even backtrack and run all the way around the other direction. Doing that would be risky. Longer, because I'd have to keep going around the other way. More of a chance for Paul to catch me, and I'd be stranded out here, just him and me with the others safe on Base.

"He's behind us somewhere!" Marcy yells, and she runs by me with a *whoop*, because she knows she's made it—she's going to get to Base without being tagged. Three others pass by and I still haven't moved. *Stupid*.

I run. Speed might just get me through this round.

Go.

The wall of the cabin brushes my left side all the way around. I hear the sounds of pursuit, and I don't know if it's Paul, or others trying to keep up with me, hoping to follow on my coattails and avoid being caught.

"Damn it, who *is* that?" I yell over my shoulder.

"Shut up and run, James me boy." It's Dusty. "We're dead meat if you don't *hurry* your ass!"

I smile, concentrate on rounding the last corner, and there's Base, a bunch of the gang already on the porch, a couple of others rounding the far corner at the same time.

I reach the porch and turn to look behind me. Dusty and Judy make a big show of pouncing on the porch and yelling, "Safe!"

We're all panting, and we wait for possible stragglers to come in. Scott lumbers in last minute, and we take inventory of those on base. Only Vickie is missing.

"Not bad, Henry," Dan says. "Your inaugural run, and you made it around without being caught."

Henry doesn't say anything, but his hands are shaking, trembling like an alcoholic at his first A.A. meeting.

"So who even saw Paul?" I ask. Heads turn toward me in unison. Their faces show they don't understand what I mean, so I pick out Marcy from the crowd. "You ran by me," I say. "You said he was behind you, right?"

"Sure," she says. "Right." She looks down, then away toward the left corner. "Okay, so I didn't *see* him, but it was him, I'm positive. Huffing and puffing, grunting like an idiot. You know Paul." She squeaks a smile. "He can be a real animal sometimes."

I turn to Dusty.

"Don't look at me," Dusty says. "I didn't see him; I was too busy running behind *you*."

"I didn't see him either," Scott says, still breathing hard.

"C'mon, let's start counting," Judy says. "Paul and Vickie are probably getting restless out there."

Then why aren't they yelling out? Egging us on? *What's the hold up, guys? Let's go, let's go!*

The chant begins. "One o'clock, two o'clock, three o'clock . . ."

Once again, I don't participate in the chant. I'm looking at Henry, who's looking warily toward one corner of the cabin, mumbling the words half-heartedly.

"... twelve o'clock midnight, HOPE TO SEE THE GHOST TONIGHT!"

The best offense is defense in this game, so everyone hangs back, almost crouching toward opposite corners, hoping someone else will go first. Sometimes a ghost will ambush you right around the first corner, so everyone swings wide to get a good angle of escape. I take the same route as last time, along with Dan and Judy.

Again, it starts on the other side of the house.

I hear a muffled shout—it sounds like Dusty—and a short piercing scream, which has to be Marcy. Dan takes off running, but I listen to the sounds from the other side.

"James," Judy whispers harshly, making me jump. "What're you going to do?"

Cheat. Go back to Base and stay there. I say, "Let's go," and we jog around the corner and up the hill to the back.

"Was it Paul or Vickie tagged them, you think?" Judy asks.

I hazard a guess. "Paul. Sweet Vickie would hardly cause that much commotion."

No more shouts come from the opposite side of the cabin. I expect to find Vickie waiting around the back, but no, she isn't there when I turn the corner. I don't see anyone else, either, not for sure—I want to look for them and reassure myself, but I can't find *anyone*—even though, staring into the night, I'm convinced I see movement in the forest.

The vision spurs me on, and I run ahead of Judy, once again staying close to the cabin. *I'm not familiar with the woods around me,* I tell myself, but I realize I'm just plain scared of going anywhere but straight ahead.

Another shadow coalesces in the woods, wraith-like, standing there stock still, and I wonder who it is. Paul or Vickie? Someone they've already caught, waiting it out? Someone just tagged, who can't participate until the next round?

Or is it something else?

A chill runs through me, as if someone has just run a knuckle down the spine of my back. Looking behind me doesn't help, because now I can't see Judy at all, and I'm alone. *Alone.* I'm shivering uncontrollably.

The wind eddies around the cabin, and now I smell smoke from the dying fire, and there's another odor, sickly sweet. My imagination desperately tries to place it. Did someone fart? Maybe it's someone's cologne. Or—

A dead animal in the woods, the scent of hot blood mixing with the humus of the forest floor.

In my mind, I see my dad at my first T-ball game. He's the umpire, and supposedly impartial, but he's behind the plate, crouching a little, waving me in from third base. As I run toward home, he crouches lower, smiling. "You can make it, James, you can make it!"

The memory fades, and I sprint toward the last corner. I think of Dad as a ghost now, a comforting presence, pushing me past the unknown. The wind whistles in my ears, but it doesn't block out the sounds behind me: the clomping of footsteps and gasps of wheezing breath.

"Who's *following*?" I yell, which is the same thing I said the first round, at almost the same spot Dusty told me to move my ass.

No one answers, but the breathing sounds different now. It could be someone's breath catching, maybe, but to me it sounds like a snarl.

God, I want to take a quick look over my shoulder, see who it is. It might be Judy after all, though I can't imagine she's kept up with me. Dan or Dusty, maybe. If that's the case, I'm safe; I'll just kept running and we'll all make it to Base. If not—

If it's Paul or Vicky, I decide at this point to thank the stars and join them out in the woods. But I don't stop, I *fly*. I leave whoever—or what-ever—it is behind me.

The final corner.

Henry and Marcy are on Base, and I sigh, relieved. I force myself to slow to a jog, trying to look nonchalant as I step onto the wooden porch.

"About time," Marcy says.

"Shut up," I say. "I made it, didn't I?"

"Barely."

I don't care. "Are we all that made it?"

"Looks like."

I glance at Henry. "You have any problems?"

Henry is shaking visibly from head to toe. I mean, I've heard people say that before, as a general description, but this is for real. It's as if he's suffering from a bout of hypothermia.

"Henry?" Marcy asks. "What's wrong?"

He shakes his head. "Nothing."

I look at my hands and swear. They're shaking too.

Marcy sees it. "Oh Christ."

"Look," I say. "Who did you see on your way around? Paul? Vickie? Scott? *Who*?"

"*Je*-sus, lighten *up*," she says, but a hint of something crosses her face before she looks away. She pulls at something stuck in her hair. "Cobweb," she explains. "I ran into the trees to avoid—someone—and I ran into a fucking cobweb."

"You don't know who you saw," I say. "You don't *know*."

"I don't know," she repeats. "It was one of them. Christ, James, it's too fucking dark to *see* anyone."

"Henry?" I ask again.

"I don't know either," he whispers.

I don't believe him. I mutter an oath under my breath, turn to Marcy again. "You screamed. I heard you from the other side of the cabin."

"Oh. Yeah. Someone ambushed Dusty and me—you know, scared the shit out of us. Couldn't just jump out, oh no. They had to growl and carry on. Dusty fell. I kept going."

"So who was it?"

"Goddamn it, I don't *know*!"

"They're waiting," Henry says softly.

I look at him, momentarily confused. Waiting? *Who's* waiting?

He glances up, and a new determination is there, set in the hard line of his jaw. He isn't shaking so bad anymore. "They're waiting for us," he says again, and unbelievably, he starts the chant in a soft monotone. "One o'clock, two o'clock, three o'clock—c'mon you guys—four o'clock, five o'clock . . ."

Marcy joins in. "Six o'clock, seven o'clock, eight o'clock . . ."

I still refuse to say the chant, even when Marcy punches me lightly in the ribs. *I will never say that goddamn thing again.*

Then it's eleven o'clock, twelve o'clock midnight, Hope to See the Ghost Tonight. No exclamation mark. Marcy and Henry don't shout the final words. If I'd been standing at the corner of the cabin, I wouldn't have heard a single word.

Marcy and Henry run in opposite directions. It was a lucky choice twice before, so I head the same way as the first two rounds, counterclockwise, following Henry. I turn left around the first corner and nearly fall, but I catch myself and look up to track Henry. Only—

He is already out of sight.

Shit. I stop. *Already?*

I grit my teeth. Look out into the trees. The swaying limbs look like skeletal arms, the dense foliage like rotting flesh. I see movement, not from the wind, but from bodies, converging on me.

There are too many. Oh god, there are just too *many*, and I'm by myself on this side of the house.

I continue on at a walk, trying to find an opening. A half dozen shapes are poised to strike, waiting like demons at the entrance of Hades. Where is Marcy? Did Henry get by? I imagine the shapes doing more than tagging me: ripping at my flesh like dogs; lapping at my spilled blood like mindless vampires; I close my eyes a moment to rid myself of the image. There is no way I'm going to get around. I'm going to get tagged, I'm going to get—

I turn and race back to Base. I decide to try the other way around. No one is at the porch or anywhere on this side of the house as I pass by and go around to the other side of the cabin. My heart's thudding in my chest, and I press my hand against my sternum. Going around this way, in the opposite direction, the path toward the back of the cabin is almost unrecognizable. New territory.

The shapes are here too. They could be human—*Jesus*, they probably are—I don't know *what* the hell I'm thinking. I run forward anyway, determined to slip by.

Miraculously, I do.

They follow me. Whoever's behind me as I dash around the back, they're doing their best to unnerve me, panting heavily, growling deep in their throats.

Laughter erupts behind me, and alongside the path, out in the trees, short unsympathetic cackles set my teeth on edge. Several shapes await me at the final corner, but I don't stop. I barrel down on them, determined to bowl them over and cause them a little pain in return for my capture.

My eyes are good, for God's sake. I should be able to see who they are when I get close enough, but I'm distracted by a sliver of space between them and the cabin. I juke left, then slip to the right and round the corner. Something slashes at my arm as I go by, and I cry out, momentarily stunned, but no one says "tag!" I might've caught an exposed nail or piece of metal on the cabin's siding. Maybe.

I don't stop. The porch light flares like an airport beacon, and no one else is there. I close in, and I have the most desirable urge to slide, my dad behind home plate, encouraging me to run faster to avoid the infielder's throw. *"You can make it, James, you can make it!"*

I arrive standing. Dad isn't there. Mom isn't in the stands cheering. They're both gone. Gone a long time, something horrible and avoidable taking them away from me.

When my feet hit the porch, I turn and look back in the direction I came from, because suddenly I feel Base isn't all that safe.

No one has followed me. The shapes from the corner are gone. There's blood on my arm. *Fuck*. It's a deep cut.

I crouch, sit down on my haunches, and look out over the lake. As blood dribbles down my arm, I glance back every few seconds to the opposite corners of the cabin. The moonpath to the other side of the lake has nearly vanished, overgrown with the rising waves, choked out by darkness. I'm shivering; I can't stop; my eyes swell with tears. Whether it's from the stinging wind or not, I can't tell, but I know the gnawing at my insides is real: fear through and through. I can't explain what I've seen and heard the last time around the cabin.

I'm alone, but that isn't so unusual. I've been alone a long time. I can't remember the voices of my parents; they aren't anywhere inside me. My friends are gone too. They went so far as to invite me out to this nostalgic, annoying tradition, and now they're adrift somewhere in the night, stolen from me. As far as I'm concerned, only the demons of loneliness and the ghosts of abandonment are out here.

I hate this game, I hate this game, I *hate* this game.

My knees pop when I straighten. We checked the screen door earlier, but I pull on it anyway, hoping to coax it open with a sudden rush of adrenaline and muscle. I'm not at all sure I even want to get inside. Maybe it's worse in there. The screen door jumps off the latch, swings wide, then falls off the hinges. A heavy oak door still blocks my way, though, and the knob doesn't budge when I try to turn it. I lean into the door, trying to bury my head into the wood; maybe I can will my body to pass through it, like a ghost. All I manage to do is smear blood on the door.

I'm done with this game. I won't play any longer.

"Guys?" I turn away from the door. "Hey!" I yell. Then I yell as loud as I dare. "Guys, you out there? Fine. Game's over. Allee, allee, oxen free!"

No one answers me. The wind picks up in defiance.

Toward the head of the lake, lightning spreads itself across the horizon like a sheet waving in the breeze; raindrops patter like little feet on the porch roof.

I don't move from my spot. I *refuse* to move. I stand there, staring at the lake for fifteen minutes. No one comes back. No one shouts, *C'mon, James, you big baby, it's just us out here*. No one chides, *You're not afraid of ghosts, are you?*

I don't believe in ghosts. There are no demons in the woods, no creatures of the night waiting to send me to the land of the dead. But something inside me refuses to agree. I believe in the fear. I believe that if I face it, I'll destroy some of those demons that have hounded me since the loss of Mom and Dad. This stupid game has to end, one way or another. I played it hoping to shake off some of the deep-rooted fears of my childhood. I *forced* myself to play it. What did I think? That I could reclaim what I'd lost? Redefine myself?

Don't freak out, James.

I have just one option; there's only one way to finish the game.

I take a deep breath. As the fear bubbles inside me, something else I haven't felt in a long time joins in. It's a single word, the first word from a childhood game, and what the word means to me is: *You can make it.* I start counting, very slowly, through clenched teeth, and with each tick of the clock, as blood from my arm drips on the porch, I prepare for my run around the cabin and into the unknown.

"One o'clock, two o'clock, three o'clock, four o'clock . . ."

※ ※ ※

Author's Notes to My Younger Self: I published my first novel when I was 55. I would tell my younger self to keep writing and don't put it off for so long. I'd say that the whole "it's a life-long dream to publish a novel some day" goal is admirable, but it doesn't have to be *that* far along in life before it's realized!

LAY DOWN YOUR HEART

Liz Westbrook-Trenholm & Hayden Trenholm

Jeremy inspected the spare bedroom, rearranging the pillows on the double bed. A vase on the night table awaited a fresh bouquet of flowers, and the small desk held a pen set and a sheaf of note paper. A space had been left for a fresh water jug and a glass. A single photograph adorned the wall, from their trip to the jungles of Bechuanaland to see the gorillas in 2007, the year before Lesedi went away.

Lesedi had always needed a retreat, a place to go when the troubles of the day—his or hers—led her in the night to abandon their marriage bed for a place of private repose. After twelve years of sleeping apart, he doubted either of them would easily grow accustomed to sleeping together again, no matter how hard he had worked for and fervently dreamed of that blessed day. She'd need the room more than ever, and it was perfect. He would have to commend Henry for the thoroughness of his preparations. He jotted an aide memoire on the pad he now kept tucked in his jacket pocket.

But wait. Where was the book? He'd told Henry to put it there. Told him he wanted Lesedi to see it. That book, that book about—he scrabbled through his notepad, looking, looking.

No such book exists. His own scrawl, just that sentence and a date. A memory sputtered to life. He'd shouted at Henry, accusing him of stealing the book, and Henry's dark eyes, gentle as he reminded him that they had talked about it before, that he did not own such a book,

that Master Falconbridge himself had searched and found no such book had been published.

Jeremy lurched to the window, leaning on the frame and pulling in deep breaths. Two men stood across the street, watching the house. He leaned closer to the glass, squinting to make them out. They resolved into one figure only, the single hawker who always waited forlornly beneath the palms for someone to buy his fruit cups.

Jeremy's face flushed with sudden heat, and he raised the sash to relieve it. The dry season was well begun and the morning air was cool against his skin, though the wintery July sun promised heat before the day's end.

He thought briefly of a trip he and Lesedi had made on one of the few occasions the Tanzanian Institute of Advanced Physics could spare its assistant director, to the Serengeti highlands, waking to frost on the ground and the duttering rumble of an old bull elephant half hidden in the high grass at the edge of their camp.

Warmer than that here, and the breeze carried the smell of curry from the small restaurant on the corner and, faintly beneath, the honeyed scent of jacaranda trees. Beyond the fruit seller lay Bagamoyo at its most beautiful, the turquoise Indian Ocean lapping languidly on white sand, empty of all but a few of his neighbours, huddled beneath open-sided tents away from the browning rays of the sun. A liveried slave stood to one side, awaiting the whims of his owners. A momentary unease filled him, like the stomach drop in an elevator, and the sand was filled with laughing children—black, brown, and white—playing together under the watchful gaze of their loving parents. Absurd imaginings.

The never-ending hum of traffic was underlaid with the faint rhythm of drumming from the free town of Jijilabure, on the far side of Bagamoyo. Rehearsal for the evening festival which he had promised to let Henry go to. Perhaps he and Lesedi could join him. . . . He turned to ask her.

Jeremy stumbled back to the bed and sank onto its edge. He forced his thoughts into coherence, planting himself firmly in the here and now, Lesedi in prison for twelve years because she would not help the government weaponize her work, and he, expending his dwindling political capital in obtaining her release. This room was the symbol of his success at last, thanks to a regime change that placed some of his carefully nurtured contacts into positions of power in the new government of national unity. This waiting flower vase, this pen set and notepaper, this space ready for water all meant that Lesedi herself was returning. He remembered her here from all those years ago, turned sideways on the desk chair, voluptuous and desirable in her little pink suit as she listened to him expound on the bureaucratic battles he was fighting to bring his colleagues into the twenty-first century and to convince his government that investment in selective breeding, maternal health programmes, and better care were critical to maintaining Tanzania's pre-eminence in the slave trade.

"Feed them, treat them, breed them properly, and Tanzania will have the most valuable stock on the continent," he'd told her.

"And it makes the slaves happy," she smiled, raising an eyebrow.

"Happy workers make for higher productivity," he'd rejoindered. How often they had had that talk, Lesedi his sounding board for justifying better treatment of slaves?

Then it would be her turn to tell him her latest thoughts on the mutable relationship between space and time, translating near incomprehensible physics into thrilling possibilities.

"This science changes everything, even our understanding of time and space. We need to harness it to light the world, perhaps even reach the stars. *Not* use it to blow up our neighbouring countries." Her eyes sparkled with intensity and intelligence he found inspiring and erotic. They would have that life again, they would.

His heart lifted, slowed, and settled. The room was perfect.

It was perfect, except Lesedi was still not home, was still stuck in the halfway house in Zanzibar City. Every promise of her release only led to further delays in their deliverance. For three days now, no word had come at all and he feared the latest shuffle of ministers would provide the Security Minister, a holdover from the previous all-white government, yet another excuse to keep his wife away from him. Should he again contact Curtis Nyere, his former senior advisor-turned-politician, or see what more Doris O'Brian, restored from the limbo of "special projects," could do?

Henry's footsteps pounded on the stairway, presaging his appearance in the doorway, his black face shining with sweat and his mouth split wide in an unaccustomed grin. "She is here, Master Jeremy! She is here. The Mistress has returned to us. She has come home."

A tingle of trepidation lifted in his chest and filled his throat, preventing his voice from releasing the joy he felt. He shuffled past Henry to the top of the stairs, composed himself, and then descended the steps as gracefully as he could, quelling the faint tremor he felt in his thighs, gripping the bannister tightly for fear of falling again.

She was there in the entranceway, a small bag still in one hand, as if she feared to put it down, as if she feared this house, the house they had lived in since they first married, would suddenly vanish, slip away as if it had never existed. Her hair had turned the colour of steel, and lines ringed her eyes and mouth, but it was still the same bright spark of intelligence in her gaze, the same small smile, the same inquisitive tilt to her head. She was so thin! But, he reminded himself, it was the same body he had loved and missed for so long.

He stopped at the foot of the stairs, afraid to move closer, afraid to speak, as if she too might vanish, might slip away to a place he could not reach. His hands slowly reached out. She placed the bag on the floor beside her feet.

"My Jeremy."

"My Lesedi."

She took the first small step; he took the next. They met as they always had, in the middle. He grasped her hands in his, her fingers warm and strong, and then his arms were around her, pulling her face tight against his chest.

"You still smell like you," she whispered to his heart. His breath caught, but he had no words to say in response.

"Should I put the tea on?" Henry's voice came from the top of the stairs.

Jeremy stepped away but did not move his hands from his wife's shoulders.

"Y-yes," he said through the tightness in his throat. "That would be nice."

"Don't we have a maid to do that?" asked Lesedi.

"No," said Jeremy. "I should have told you. This house and Henry are all we own now."

"Well." Lesedi threw up her hands in an old, familiar gesture of impatience. "We'll have to see about that. Henry, take my bag up." She hugged Jeremy. "I'll make the tea. I did learn some things on the prison farm."

———•———

Lesedi paused at the baize door leading to the scullery and kitchen. Jeremy remained where he was, looking faded, like a photo left under sunlight. Henry remained at his side, watching her.

"Look lively, Henry."

He dropped his chin, lids hooding his gaze. Deliberately, he lifted her bag and trudged upstairs with it.

"Jeremy, come with me."

Jeremy nodded then and followed, looking for the tea. "Henry does all that," he said.

Lesedi found it in a battered tin cannister covered with patterns of jacaranda flowers. She sniffed deeply. "Orange pekoe, but not the best." She filled the kettle, plugged it in, found the teapot. "China, *hemele*! I'd forgotten what it's like. Old tin billies for us on the prison farm." She turned. Jeremy was seated at the scrubbed table, leaning against an embroidered pillow she remembered from before her arrest. "While Henry is occupied, we can talk about our plans," she said, pulling out the chair opposite him and sitting.

"That's where Henry sits."

She stared at him, astonished. "You eat with him? You sit at table with a slave?" He dropped his gaze. "Well. We'll be putting an end to all that. When I get my job back at the lab, we'll have enough to get another couple of staff." She shook her head. "Meanwhile, Henry needs to be reminded of his place. And it is not at table with the master."

"You're a force of nature, Lesedi." He reached his hands across the table and took hers. "Let's talk later. Let's just look at each other for awhile."

She was bursting with plans, but she quelled her impatience. She had not remembered him as being so gentle and vague, but twelve years was twelve years, after all. His letters had been sharp and to the point, as much as had survived the sadistic censors, though she had to admit that lately his digressions had increased. And there were his constant references to his increasingly poor memory. No. They were unused to each other. They just needed time. As she gazed into his watery eyes, she felt her own fill, and her impatience fell away. Dear, dear Jeremy.

Lesedi stared at herself in the mirror, her once-favourite pink suit hanging on her like a wilted petunia.

"I was so fat!" she declared. She cinched a belt around the waist, bunching the fabric. "Like a sack!" Hopeless. Her face and neck were as droopy as her skirt, the leathery texture of her skin absurd against the feminine fabric. How could she return to the lab looking like this? Anxiety knotted in her stomach at the thought of running a gauntlet of shiny young colleagues, a haggard old has-been attempting a return to long-lost glory days.

"There must be something." She dug among the mothball stink of her old closet and there it was.

She drew out her white lab coat, flung there the very night they'd come and dragged her from her bed. She slipped her arms into the sleeves and the old thing embraced her as if they had never been parted. It concealed all but the front panel of her suit. It forgave her aged face and hair, indeed, gave it gravitas. "Ah, beloved."

"Are you talking to me, or your lab coat?" Jeremy, from the door. She gazed at him in the mirror as he came up behind her, wrapping his long arms around her waist.

"You are inextricably entwined with my work, my two great loves," she said. "I cannot survive without you both." He hid his face in her shoulder. Hurt? Should she have not . . .?

He raised it again, and his eyes were shining. "I am so proud. So proud of you, to be with you."

———•———

She held that thought to her as she followed the new director of the Institute to the work room where she would be joint supervisor overseeing research, at least—he'd said—until she'd settled in and caught up with developments, a mere formality, given her acknowledged brilliance. Flattery to cover the fact they wanted her mind, but only if it still worked as it had. She didn't care about the demotion; here she could do science without the burden of paperwork her old job entailed. The young fellow who'd been introduced as her partner supervisor seemed innocuous enough, if a bit doughy. Archibald Southwood, pure English establishment, was undoubtedly there to keep her out of trouble or report her if she got into it. She was so nervous at returning she could barely bridle at the inference she might not be up to snuff.

The work room had double doors. The Director and Archibald each pushed open a door onto a room lined with long tables loaded with equipment, so much of it new in the twelve years she'd been locked away. She had requested, though rarely received, the latest research papers in the prison library and had interrogated every new scientist-prisoner for the latest developments, but so much had changed. She had pored over schematics in preparation for her return but still feared she might not recognize some device that had become common place in her absence.

Men and women were bending over equipment—a scanning tunnelling microscope in the corner and the new titanium-sapphire laser used to manipulate atoms—or sitting at one of the desktop computers that had largely replaced the massive machine still sitting idle against the far wall. Others were deep in discussion over a dozen lines of calculus on the blackboard at the far end. As she stepped between the Head and Archibald, they turned toward her, falling into two lines either side of the central corridor between the tables. A gauntlet, indeed.

Lesedi, for the first time in her life, felt an urge to turn and run. Gathering herself, she shoved her hands deep into her lab coat pockets and took the first step toward the large desk at the end of the room where she would do the bulk of her practical work.

They began to clap. First one or two, and then more, and then all of them, clapping, clapping. She took in their faces then, smiling, some whose eyes shone with tears. She choked back her own emotion. Start as you mean to go on, Lesedi, she told herself. She nodded at each, moving between them until she reached the safety of the so-familiar table, from the like of which she had lectured and instructed, and on which she had worked, diagramming experiments, wrestling the maths underlying theories. She turned to look at them. The applause died away. They waited.

"Well," she said. "We'd best get to work."

———·———

Lesedi lifted her face to the moist warmth of the breeze off the Indian Ocean, enjoying the sight of a backward tilted dhow heading to the fish market under full sail. She'd fallen into a routine of walking home from the lab along the beach, shoes off, toes digging into the sand, the line of palms and bush green and whispering on one side, the waves lapping the beach like applause on the other. The journey took her through the fish market with its pungent odours, the sand slippery and oozing with guts—which gave her an excuse to wade in the gentle cleansing waves—but at least she avoided the rough stone slave barracks and hard cobbled streets of central Bagamoyo.

What a change a few weeks had made. No more toiling in the hot sun, fingers stained orange or red from filling cloth bags with turmeric and henna, while overseers waited for any excuse to apply the lash. And her work, finally able to write out her theories and formulae, free to discuss ideas openly with colleagues rather than in whispered exchanges of encrypted phrases. Though openness was a relative term, given that toady, Southwood's, constant spying.

This walk let her transition from work to home, although work never truly left her mind. Nevertheless, she made an effort to give Jeremy her attention, at least during the hours between pre-dinner cocktails and post-dinner brandy. She'd restored some semblance of proper domestic management to the place, now she'd found a cook and a serving girl, both quite skilled, thanks to Jeremy's reforms that provided routine formal training to slaves. Rather revolutionary that had been, but now the skilled ones were all that were available in the market. She had to admit it lifted some of the burden of breaking in new staff. The restoration of a proper routine was good for Jeremy. He appeared to be improving, a little less vague.

She wiped the sand from her feet on the ragged grass marking the boundary between the beach and their home. Could she afford to buy a gardener? The grounds seemed beyond Henry to manage, although surely he had time, now he had the cook and the girl. She passed between the pillars into the cool portico fronting the back of the house. She loved the Moorish fretwork framing the arch and the silken feel of polished tile beneath her feet.

"Henry!" she called. Silence. "Where are you?" He appeared, finally, just when she was about to go in search of him. "What kept you? Here, take these. I shouldn't have to ask." She handed him her shoes and her satchel with the evening's work. "Satchel to my study and shoes clean for morning, Henry. *If* you can manage it." He raised his bowed head with a flash from his yellow-tinged brown eyes. "I see you failed to cut the grass, despite my specific orders."

"Saturday, Ma'am."

"What?" It was Lesedi's turn to be startled. "Today is Thursday."

"Yes, Ma'am. Market Day. Monday, wash day. Tuesday, ironing and dusting. Wednesday . . ."

"What are you babbling about, Henry. Have your wits gone soft?"

"Saturday is outdoors work. I cut the grass then."

"I say when you do things, Henry. The grass needs doing. Now. Go and do it."

He lowered his eyes in a supposed expression of humility, but his shoulders were stiff, rebellious. For a moment she thought he would disobey. Then, slowly, he shuffled off toward the garden, setting her satchel and shoes down on a table by the entrance.

"*Verswarende!*" She scooped them up and carried them to her room herself. Henry needed taking in hand, like a dog that had become accustomed to climbing onto beds and sofas and had to be taught its place on the floor.

She found Jeremy in his study, staring at a pile of papers in front of him, fingers drumming.

"Are you working on something, my love?" she asked, glad to see him engaged. So often she found him staring at something only he could see.

He looked startled for a moment, then smiled, shaking his head. "No. No, just . . . thinking." He brightened, leaning forward. "And you? What about your day?"

"My day! Oh, ho." She threw up her hands. "It takes a deal of effort to keep the Head's lacky out from under my feet." She paced. "I do not trust that Englishman. Not at all. Always peering, poking, wanting to know about 'applications' of the research. And Jeremy, Jeremy, the research! At last, no longer imaginings projected onto the brick walls of my cell, eidetic tricks to fix them in my brain, but true, mathematical crunching and, my darling, it works!"

Jeremy smiled, admiring, encouraging, silent.

She knelt in front of him, her knees complaining only a little. In lowered voice, she said, "Time, space—I have found the key."

"That's good?" Jeremy asked.

"Jeremy, darling one, if the next cycle of experiments works, it opens up the possibility of manipulating time and space, even, theoretically, opening gateways into alternate worlds, or alternate versions of this one, at the very least. Imagine it, Jeremy."

He leaned forward, seizing her hands. "I know! I know! I've seen one of those worlds."

She sat back on her heels. "It's theoretical, Jeremy. You couldn't . . ." She checked herself as his face fell. She seized his hands. "What have you seen, dear? Tell me all about it."

"A world where all are free. No slaves. Equality among all peoples."

Gently, she cradled his cheek in her palm. "People are not equal, my dear one. How can they be? Slaves, lowly workers, the uneducated."

"Yes," he insisted. "I have seen it, as real as you. Machines doing menial tasks slaves do here. Computers so small they fit in the palm of your hand. Everything so advanced—as if freedom had released all of our potential. Our *human* potential."

"Jeremy," she hesitated. "The theory only postulates other realities; it hardly predicts something so . . . specific. You mustn't think that—"

He seized her hands. "It means everything to me. I want this to be. I know it can be. I have seen it, Lesedi. Seen it!"

She squeezed his hands, folded them in his lap, and rose. She had a fair idea how this idea had got planted in his head. "Jeremy, you've let Henry run amok. He's verging on rebellious."

"Who?" Jeremy frowned at her in confusion. Worse and worse.

"Our head slave, Henry. Jeremy, you—"

His expression cleared. "Oh. Roli." He chuckled. "Rolihlahla, in fact. But I confess I find that a bit difficult to get my tongue around. He's all right with Roli."

"He's all right. . . . Jeremy, what is this Roli-whatever nonsense? He's a slave. His name is Henry."

Jeremy's gaze on her was gentle. "His slave name is Henry, darling. His true name, the one given to him at birth, is Rolihlahla. He prefers it."

"He prefers. A slave *prefers*! A slave does not *prefer*, Jeremy. You've let this reform business get completely out of hand. We actually have them doing calculations in the lab, albeit in a separate room, but, *groote hemele*! Slaves? Doing master work?"

"Doing work of which they are capable," Jeremy remonstrated. "They are people, Lesedi. Surely you would sympathize with their plight."

She stared at him, uncomprehending.

"You were a prisoner. You were required to do forced labour, at the whim of the overseers."

Lesedi's arms felt heavy, hanging at her sides. Energy surged within her chest and gut. Words rushed to the surface, choking on each other in her throat. He compared her, Professor Lesedi van Dyck, to a slave? To Henry? Twelve years in prison for the crime of standing up for her right to manage her own research, to refuse to have it suborned to the evil will of their totalitarian government, and he compared that to the abject resignation of an inferior menial? Who was he? What had become of her Jeremy? All those years she survived torture, fought for her sanity and psychological integrity, and he consorted with slaves, a slave, with Henry. Henry.

Henry had done this, rebellious, sly, underhanded *schurk*.

"I will sell that one to the mines," she muttered. Turning her back on Jeremy's alarmed face, she retreated to her study. Work. She would work. Then she would think about this, this appalling travesty.

———

The central problem was the nature of space. Was it empty or was it full or was it both simultaneously? One could imagine empty space but immediately, it filled with something. Lesedi had taken to calling the particles that popped into existence—there were more than one—condensates. Quarks and anti-quarks flashing into and out of existence, a kind of quantum field to match those that Maxwell and Faraday had described for electro-magnetism. Without empty space, the ruptures her calculations predicted could not come into being. But if two sufficiently heavy particles, say, two gold nuclei, could be smashed together at high enough energies . . .

As soon as she thought it, she saw how it could be done. She would need the synchrotron housed in the basement of the lab, or, maybe later, the new larger particle accelerator in the mountains. She hunched over her desk, writing notes, formulae, as the light outside the window began to fade.

She may have heard the dinner gong; she couldn't be sure. Sometime later, Henry's soft voice penetrated the door to her sanctum. "Master Jeremy awaits you at dinner, Madam."

She strode across the room and flung the door open. "You. You will be gone as soon as I can find a buyer for you. Until then, you will stay away from the Master."

Henry staggered back, as if she'd physically struck him. His mahogany skin greyed and his nostrils flared. "I know what you are doing in that lab. The government man does not know. But I do."

She turned on him. "You. You know nothing about anything."

He trembled, shoulders hunched, and arms crossed protectively across his body, but he met her gaze. "I know. You think this government is soft. They are waiting, like hyenas watching an old buffalo. They will drag you down and tear you apart while you bleat."

Struck dumb, by his insolence as much as by his expression of her worst fears, she could do nothing but stare at him.

"You will destroy him. You will destroy everything, with that quantum gravity science of yours."

Astonished, she said, "How do you know about this? Who has told you? Answer me, at once!"

He looked evasive, eyes glancing down and away, but then he raised them again, shining with fierce brown light. "While you were gone, I wrote his letters to you, in the last years. I deciphered that code, and I put what he wanted to say to you into the code. Then you came back. But again, you are gone, all day, all day. While you are gone, at that lab where you play with our lives, I wash him. I dress him. I calm him when he grows angry or sad. I listen to him, and I bring him back to this world when he wanders too far into that other. No, I did not get the grass cut. I was keeping Master Jeremy safe. As I kept him safe, when you were in prison, fighting against the world. I kept him happy."

Lesedi felt a tearing turn in her gut, as if she'd discovered a fatal error in a long piece of mathematics, some flaw that tore the whole delicate construct apart.

"Henry . . ."

"My mother named me Rolihlahla. That is the name I will use when I am free, as Master Jeremy has promised."

They were standing thus, face to face, as Jeremy's frail figure drifted into view at the top of the stairs. His mouth was loose, and his eyes frightened as he looked from one to the other. Lesedi saw now what she would not see before.

She nodded once. "I come to dinner."

She took Jeremy's arm, then paused, waiting until Henry— Rolihlahla—took his other. They descended the broad staircase together.

———•———

Jeremy stood in the doorway of Lesedi's study. It was not a place he normally went, as she left him to his own inner sanctum. But this evening, he remembered the papers he'd kept hidden under a loose floorboard in the garden shed, the papers he'd meant to give her on her return months ago. A simple bundle of a few dozen sheets, wrapped in waxed paper and tied with a blue ribbon, now faded to grey. Everything fades to grey, he thought, even the things we most dearly love. He tapped lightly on the door frame with his other hand, his fingers marking the same rhythm that had been haunting him for nearly a year. He heard himself humming a few slow notes.

Lesedi looked up from her work, shaking her head slightly, as if, like him, she sometimes needed time to come back to this moment. To this place. "What is that?"

"I'm not sure. A hymn maybe, from when I was a boy. It seems so familiar, but I can't recall the words."

"I don't know it," she said. "But I meant that bundle."

Jeremy held it out to her, wanting her to simply take it without need for explanation. His wife did not stir from her desk. "Those papers. From before they took you."

"My papers? You were to have burned them. If the government knew, even now, they would take me again." She stood up suddenly, her chair tipping to the floor, like a door slamming. Her eyes widened at the proffered gift as if the grey ribbon had transformed into a puff adder.

"I know. I meant to do it. You'll see, some of the pages are even scorched. But they were all I had of you, the only link between the life before and the life after. In that first year, when they wouldn't let us even write, I wasn't sure you were still alive, I was glad to have them." The words, long suppressed, poured out of him. "I read them through, time and again, though I don't pretend to understand much of what they contained, the math not at all. But it was like having you with me, your spirit filling my empty spaces."

Lesedi said nothing but took the bundle from his hands, tugging away the ribbon and letting it fall to the floor. Her fingers stoked the pages, lingering over the promised scorch marks.

"This is why they arrested me," she said to him as if he didn't already know every detail of her arrest, the show trial that followed, and the constant badgering of government agents, seeking some clue to her breakthrough ideas. Some traitor in the lab—like her doughy Southwood now—had learned enough to know the possibilities. That had been enough to take her from him, been enough to nearly destroy them.

He could not, would not let them destroy her work as well. "I grasped enough to know that what you were doing is more important than the ambitions of some petty dictator. More than the ambitions of any dictator, any government across this benighted world. What you were doing— what I hope and pray you are doing again—can change the world."

"More like destroy it." Lesedi put the papers on the desk and laid one hand protectively over them.

"But is what you wrote possible? Are there other worlds, other universes, lying next to ours, like membranes, almost, but never touching? And if they did touch could we move between them, could we even merge one into the other?"

"Theoretically, yes, yes, but practically, that is different. The probabilities make the outcome entirely uncertain, unpredictable. Jeremy, even if it were practicable, the energy required is non-trivial to say the least, and the results . . . well, it'd be like throwing a dice with thousands, maybe millions of sides. One can't know what will turn up."

"A pity you can't weight the dice," Jeremy said, "like that fellow we encountered on the ship during our honeymoon."

Lesedi tilted her face up to him, laughing at the memory. "What a rogue! He might as well have had a die with only sixes on every side." Her smile faded and her eyes grew unfocussed, no longer looking into his eyes but growing distant, as if seeing other worlds, the way he sometimes did. If he could imagine it, she could realize it, of that he was sure.

"Perhaps . . . no. No, it is too dangerous. If the government knew, they would try to weaponize it. And, suppose I could accomplish this thing, it could well destroy everything we know as real."

"Not everyone would think that was a bad thing."

Her stricken look cut into him, but he knew from years of operating the machinery of government that sometimes you had to completely break a thing before you could see a way to fix it. And her hand still rested on those papers; she had not asked him again to see them burnt.

Jeremy turned to leave Lesedi to her work.

"Oh," he said. "I've remembered a bit of that song. Something 'will lead us home.' Perhaps you will find what that something is."

———

Lesedi paced indecisively up and down the dark back corridor where the Institute had assigned rooms for the slaves who undertook the onerous calculations of quantum electrodynamics and the translation of theories into precise formulae for testing, tasks still better done by human brains. Jeremy's faith was touching, she supposed, but he'd no idea of the complexities involved. The problem of maintaining emptiness, even for the briefest of intervals, was the most subtle, elusive and multi-faceted one she'd ever tackled. She had divided it into segments, assigning each to a different team and never discussing one team's results with another. It was an unwieldy methodology and the results reflected its flaws, but she was afraid to let anyone know the true scope of what she was trying to achieve, at least until she herself understood it better.

There were few enough at the institute who could follow her reasoning. Fewer yet with sufficient understanding to devise the mathematics needed to test her intuitions. Of those few, whom could she trust to keep *shtum* about it until they knew for sure what they were dealing with?

She trusted no one. That was a conundrum. How could she trust any of those who'd remained and advanced the military applications for her work in particle physics when she had been hounded, tortured, and imprisoned for refusing to do so? How could she be sure the new, young scientists were untainted?

In her wakeful nights, she'd gone around and around with it. She needed good minds to help her collate and coordinate the puzzle pieces into a coherent whole, and she needed them to be discreet. And so, she paced outside the slave calculators' work room, hesitating at its swinging door each time she passed it, yet never entering.

The work coming from this room was excellent, with one calculator in particular, Calc 23, showing flashes of sheer, intuitive brilliance. Calc 23 was a slave. Lesedi should be pleased at that. It solved her concern about discretion, because slaves could go nowhere and talk to no one without express permission from their masters. So, it was logical. Use the calculators to test her theories.

But. Slaves? Doing the work of free people? As intellectual equals? Or, if she admitted it, as intellectual superiors?

Yes, she had reached détente with Henry, Rolihlahla, she corrected herself. And snorted. The slave who preferred . . . anything. Still, she saw how crucial Rolihlahla was to Jeremy's equilibrium, and to the equilibrium of their home life, indeed. He had shown himself to be something more than dutiful and loyal. He had shown himself to be fierce and loving and extraordinarily insightful. He had wrung respect from her, against all her prejudices. Still, his remained a domestic role. He was no scientist. But the calculators—this was a leap across the socio-cultural chasm between enslaved and free that confounded her.

Damn. Was she a person of intellect, or nothing more than a product of her conditioning? Jeremy himself had pointed out the absurdity of her position. But it *was* how she felt. Slaves were slaves.

But.

Lesedi wanted to meet Calculator 23. She wanted to know if this room held the members of the team that would move the coordinated problem forward, without tipping off her colleagues, and especially the head and his toady, Archibald Southwood. Her conditioning also made her hate Englishmen, who had so devastated her beloved home in South Africa.

She pushed open the door.

It did not take long for Lesedi's reliance on slave calculators to cause comment. Archibald Southwood oiled up to her at a post-work sherry party and probed her about what could require so much calculation.

"Oh, crunching, crunching, you know how it is, Archie," she said. He hated being called Archie.

"You seem to consult with Calc 23 a great deal," he persisted, ignoring the poke. "It seems unusual."

"I have to explain everything four times, you know how it is with them," she said, and felt a stab of guilt. Calc 23 was quick, quicker than any other calculator, and more insightful and intelligent than most of the colleagues she could think of.

"But whatever is the focus?" Southwood would not give up.

Lesedi knew she'd have to give him something to head him off. "You know Team 5 is focussing on confirming our understanding of the theory underlying deviations from the expected constants in the field interactions of the . . . am I boring you?" More administrator than mathematician, Southwood's eyes had instantly glazed over. "I am not explaining well," she apologized. "If you talk to Professor McLaren, he'll be able to clarify it more concisely, as head of Team 5." McLaren, a rather second-rate intellect in Lesedi's opinion, was convinced of the huge importance of the busywork she'd given his team, double-checking the calculations on established areas of Quantum Mechanics where few surprises remained. He was also the most verbose being on the planet. Let Archie lose himself in the labyrinth of McLaren's verbiage while she considered how to cover her tracks better.

Later that very day it was Jeremy who came to her rescue.

"Do you need to work at the Institute quite so much, Darling?" he'd asked, sounding elderly and plaintive. "I miss you." Henry added a long, reproachful look to the complaint, compounding her guilt.

"My husband is unwell," she told the Director next day. "I need to work at home a few days a week. My nearness reassures him." The great Lesedi van Dyck need only ask. "I'll want to borrow a calculator," she said. "23 is pretty good. I'll take her."

"I'm afraid that is against Institute rules. Calculators are valuable property. We cannot risk them being damaged. Or escaping."

"She can be fed and lodged with my household staff, freeing up Institute resources, and our security is good. I'll see she's returned in good condition." When he continued to hesitate, she nodded. "Very well, perhaps you would consider selling her to me."

The director named a figure—an outrageous one—and Lesedi wrote a cheque, hoping the overdraft would cover it until she come up with the cash.

She and Calc 23 walked home along the seafront in something akin to a holiday mood. At last they could talk frankly about the theories and problems facing them in working them out, without lowering their voices or glancing over their shoulders.

"We should have a name for this, Calc 23," Lesedi said. "Quantum gravimetrical transference field theory is so cumbersome."

"Barika?" the young woman suggested. "In Swahili, it means bloom or success."

"As the theory will bloom and succeed," Lesedi said. "That's splendid."

"It is also my given name, from my mother and father," Calc 23 said hesitantly, eyes not meeting hers. "Although my nickname is Bari. Shorter that way."

Lesedi stopped in her tracks to gaze at the forward girl, eyes cast downward with such unconvincing modesty. She was surprised to find that she wanted to laugh.

"Certainly shorter than 'Calc 23', Bari. Though how will we tell theory and girl apart?"

"I think sometimes I am the theory and it is me," Bari said.

Lesedi clapped her hands to her breast. "Hah! I know this feeling!" How strange that the girl's round skull with its tight curls, so different from her own on the outside, should be so like hers within.

When they arrived home, she called Rolihlahla as usual. He materialized under the portico promptly, which boded well for Jeremy's condition that day. However, when his eye fell on Bari, his heavy-lidded calm gave way to bug-eyed astonishment.

"What are you doing here?" he demanded.

"I live here, Rolihlahla," Lesedi said dryly.

"I will be assisting Professor van Dyck, Father," Bari said.

——————

Jeremy slipped from the bed and reached for his robe. Lesedi turned but didn't waken, though she mumbled a little. Blurred with sleep, her words were little more than murmurs. When they were younger, Lesedi's sleeping conversations with herself had driven him to find rest in the spare bed, but now he liked to stand in the dark and listen to the sound of her voice. She spoke again. The words, "chromodynamics" and "negative spin variance," might as well have been a foreign language for all they meant to him. But he knew that, sometimes, she found the solutions she was seeking in her dreams.

As do I. The curtains stirred and the sweet smell of tulbaghia mingled with the sharper scent of jasmine. Beyond the window, the white froth of the surf marked a line between the darkness of the shore and the darker water beyond. Dawn would come soon; already the voices of the fisherman preparing the dhows rose and fell above the steady shush of the waves. Time for work while his mind still held its morning freshness.

He finished the letter to Curtis Nyere, whose spotless credentials in collecting slave stock from the interior had led, step by step, to his appointment as the first black Minister in the new Tanzanian government. He was even being touted by progressives as a possible future President. While Jeremy had his doubts—whites still held most of the votes, and despite recent reforms, the old guard waited in the wings ready to seize control if the opportunity arose—he knew an ally when he saw one and knew, too, a time might come when they would need every friend they could get. He had dutifully praised the Minister's latest initiatives in managing the slave imports from the central highlands and offered a few words of advice that he was fairly certain would resonate with Nyere's thinking. He sealed it and placed it on top of a pile of other correspondence to old friends and colleagues, not the least of whom was Doris O'Brian, whose star was also rising and who, it turned out, had worked behind the scenes to shorten Lesedi's time in the halfway house. *Thank yous* could soon be turned into *pleases*. For the last few days, he had written to everyone in his contact list, seeking assurances that Lesedi's work could continue without interference.

A faint tap on his office door drew him from his reverie. He'd been staring at an old photograph of Stone Town's Christ Church Cathedral beside the former slave market where he had begun his career so many years before. Of course, the trade commission was now housed in a gleaming glass-and-steel tower in Dar es Salaam but the market still functioned—modernized and, he liked to think, humanized—as a processing centre for manual workers destined for the spice farms or the plantations of Indonesia. In his mind, he had stood once again beneath the vaulting apse listening to the choir sing the old hymns: "All Praise to Thee, my God, this Night"; "Rock of Ages, Cleft for Me"; and, what was it?

The words came back to him and he sang them, his voice clear but wavering:

> Through many dangers, toils, and snares
> I have already come
> 'Tis grace that brought me safe thus far
> And grace will lead me home

The tap came again and a young woman peeked around the door. "Master Jeremy? Are you all right?"

Fear stabbed at him. Who was this? What was she doing in his house?

"Breakfast is ready in the dining room."

Bari. Henry's, no, Roli's daughter. Come to live with them. No, that was wrong, too. Come to work with Lesedi.

"I'll be down in a minute. Thank you, Bari."

The girl was a blessing, he thought. Roli had been so happy to see her; the old man practically danced as he did his chores. Lesedi, too, seemed transformed by this fresh young presence though he could not quite express what the change might be.

"No matter," he murmured. "Everything is unfolding as it should."

He stood at the top of the stairs, wondering what it was he was forgetting. He glanced down at his feet. They were bare. That would hardly do. He returned to their bedroom. Lesedi had already made the bed—a leftover habit from her years in prison—and his house shoes had been tucked under his dressing table. He slipped them on but then caught sight of himself in the mirror, hair unkempt, face unshaven and still in his robe.

"That will never do."

Dressing took longer without Roli's nimble fingers, but he was determined not to call for help. There had been too much of that lately. He'd let himself go, like old . . . old . . . no matter. He wouldn't go that way. He still had things to do.

Satisfied at last, he made his slow way down the stairs, pausing outside the entrance to the dining room to ensure his shirt was buttoned properly and his morning coat free of lint.

"He's forgotten." Lesedi's voice was exasperated.

"Should I fetch him?" asked Roli.

"He was still in his gown when I called him. Perhaps he is dressing."

"Does he still remember how?" asked Lesedi. "He almost went out without his shoes yesterday."

Jeremy looked down at his feet. His shoes were there, even socks. Had he forgotten anything else?

"It is not so bad," said Roli. "He has good days and bad."

"More bad than anything else. Perhaps it is time to send him . . . there is a hospital I know . . ."

"No, Madam!" Roli's voice was sharp and Jeremy waited for Lesedi's rebuke. "You must not! It would kill him. I will do everything—Bari will help me—to take care of him. To save him and you from embarrassment."

"It's not that," Lesedi's voice caught. "He is drifting away—from us, from the world."

"From this world, yes. But maybe he is on the way to a better world. He is even composing hymns."

"Yes, that song he claims to have heard as a boy . . ."

"Amazing Grace," said Bari. "That's how it starts: 'Amazing Grace, how sweet the sound.'" Her voice was clear and bell-like.

"It doesn't matter if he heard it or if he wrote it—it gives him joy. Just as having my daughter back, if even briefly, has given me joy. Do not send him away. Please . . ."

"I . . . won't. I couldn't. It would kill me, too." Lesedi sobbed slightly. "Thank you. Thank you, Rolihlahla. You are a good . . . friend."

What have you done? You stupid old man, you have made Lesedi cry. Jeremy returned to the stairs and made a show of descending them loudly. *They mustn't know I heard. And maybe by tomorrow,* he thought wryly, *I won't have.*

"Morning all," he said, entering. "Sorry to have kept you. I could hardly come down, looking like a shambling old man. I should really go back to shaving every day. Did I do all right?" He stuck out his chin for Lesedi to stroke. Her touch was as gentle as moonlight.

"You look so handsome today," Lesedi said, leaning forward to kiss his cheek.

Jeremy was surprised, happily so, by this public show of affection. "Let's all sit down, shall we?"

"Yes," said Lesedi. "Bari, would you fetch two more settings? Please." When Bari hesitated, she said, "We can't manage this without you."

Jeremy smiled at the feast Roli had teased out of the cook. Sausages and eggs and fried potatoes, of course, but also grilled kudu, chapattis, a small bowl of ugali and some fried plantains. A steaming pot of tea rested on a trivet by his chair. He waited until Bari had returned with the extra settings before filling his plate.

"You were talking in your sleep last night, Lesedi. Does 'chromodynamics' and 'negative spin variance' mean anything to you?"

Lesedi's fork fell from her hand, and she stood abruptly. "Jeremy. You're a genius. Bari, we must return to the lab at once."

"After breakfast, my dear. Even science needs fuel."

———

It took nearly a week to gain access to the cyclotron located in the basement of the lab. Southwood seemed to have tied the protocols for approval in knots, but eventually he sent her a note saying she could have access for two hours. It had taken most of that time to prepare the gold nuclei for insertion and programme the device for her first experiment. If the theory was right and if the old machine was up to creating the necessary velocities, the colliding particles should create a miniature "big bang" with, at its heart, a real vacuum, a space devoid of particles and fields, though it would last but an instant. The next step, done at the big accelerator, in the hills to the west, would be to pour particles into that space—all containing negative spin—to overwhelm the cancelling effect of quantum probability. The emptiness would be transformed into a gate and then . . . *Enough, Lesedi, one step at a time. It may all be nonsense.*

Lesedi checked the calibrations on the cyclotron, ticking off in her mind each of the protocols for the run-through. This one was crucial, a small first effort to test the scalability of the theory's application. Lesedi didn't glance up as Bari materialized at her side, but she felt the girl's presence, a slim dark shadow that anchored her, made her feel whole, happy, fulfilled.

"Something's wrong," Bari murmured, voice pitched low so only Lesedi could hear.

"Where? What?" Lesedi surveyed the settings, seeing no problem.

"Not the settings," Bari whispered. "Southwood is here with two men."

Lesedi straightened, stretching her back. "Southwood is always parading around with . . ." She stopped herself when she caught sight of Southwood's companions, moving toward them down the room's centre aisle. She'd seen hyenas like these before, been seized by them, beaten by them, and thrown by them into prison. She whirled back to her console and frantically punched keys to cancel the settings and scramble the commands.

"Please step back from the equipment, Professor van Dyck," Archibald Southwood said, his tone smarmy as ever.

"We're busy, Archie, can't you see?" She continued working, desperately entering nonsense, wrecking all her hours and days of work.

An arm clad in crisp white cotton reached in front of her, blocking her view. A small brown stain marred the edge of one cuff, tea, perhaps. Not blood. They rolled up their sleeves when they were working. *She hung by her arms, a bag over her head, waiting, waiting for the next slash of the frond to add its burning cuts to the ones already searing across her naked breasts and belly. No questions, just beatings, layering fresh stinging cuts on the previous day's aching scabs. Please. Please. Ask a question. Talk to me. Tell me what you want. This time I'll tell you. This time I won't lie. Jeremy. Jeremy. Jeremy loves me. Jeremy is waiting for me. Jeremy is working to get me out of here. Jeremy. Jeremy. Beat then. Ask or don't ask. Murderers. Hyenas.*

Lesedi's vision cleared. She stilled her inner screams. She folded her arms to hide her shaking hands and pinned Archie with a glare. He swallowed.

"We need you to come with us." He flicked a glance to the Hyenas at his side. "To answer some questions about your research."

Lesedi turned her attention to Hyena number one. "You and I have not met." Southwood started to speak, but Hyena One overrode him.

"I know you by reputation, Professor Van Dyck."

And I know your kind, as well, she did not say. She merely raised her eyebrows at him and asked, "You're interested in quantum gravimetrical field theory?"

Southwood, sounding exasperated, said, "We are aware that your work has more to it than you've let us believe."

Lesedi gave him the same look she'd offered Hyena One. "My work is an open book, Archie. At least, to minds not too inferior to comprehend it."

Southwood coloured. "We've met with the team leads to discuss that 'open book' of yours," he retorted. "A very interesting discussion. They soon . . ."

"You met with my team leads? Without me?" Lesedi poured her fear into rage, all focussed on the Southwood. "You discussed my research project without my permission?"

Southwood held his ground. "You've been hiding things, Professor van Dyck. It didn't take them long to realize that you've been deliberately keeping them in the dark about the real purpose of their projects."

"That is a preposterous notion! The teams must focus on the work they are assigned, without becoming distracted by what the others are doing. How I run my lab is my concern. How I organize the research, *my* concern. Who are you to question my methods? You, you administrator! Run off, Archie. Go organize another sherry party. Leave the real work to minds sufficient to the task."

"We can discuss this in private," Southwood insisted, flicking a glance at the Hyenas, who remained silent, even mildly amused. Waiting. They knew how to wait.

Lesedi waved a hand at the few inhabitants who hadn't slipped out of the lab already. Some pretended to work; others stared openly. "We'll discuss it here. Since you accuse me of secrecy, let this be an open book."

Southwood opened and shut his mouth.

She plowed over him. "You want to know about my work? My work is, *as* I said, in quantum gravimetrical transference field theory. It is progressing magnificently. The teams have produced good results and, in another five, possibly ten years, we may even begin to see applications beyond laboratory experimentation at the elementary particle level."

"Five to ten years!" Southwood exclaimed.

Hyena One lifted a hand, and the administrator fell silent. "We are told you are on the verge of a world-changing breakthrough. Our government is very interested and concerned for national security. The intrusions by your *former* countrymen on our southern borders . . ." He paused, considering. He said, "Your husband is very proud of you. I am sure he would want you to share your 'important research' to protect your adopted homeland."

Jeremy. Oh God. All those letters he'd been writing. She'd thought they were just busy work. Something to keep him happily occupied. What had he been saying? *Jeremy, oh, my Jeremy.* "My husband is not a scientist," she said. "He is not what he once was." She checked herself. "We are not what we once were." She let herself deflate, droop with feigned fatigue and age. "Yes, I have had the teams working toward a central problem concerning gravity fields. But collating it all is, perhaps, beyond my waning abilities. My memory, you know . . . I can't keep these complicated things in my head anymore."

Southwood said, "We understand, Professor van Dyck. This comes to us all, in time." His patronizing tone made her want to box his ears. With an effort, she maintained her fatigued and vague manner, even when he leaned in so close she could smell his sweat. "Calculator 23, on the other hand, will be able to provide us with a clear picture of what she's worked on with you. The team leads say she's very talented, for a slave."

---·---

"They've taken her! My god, Jeremy, what have you done! The Hyenas have taken Bari."

"Lesedi, Lesedi, what hyenas?" Jeremy plucked feebly at her hands, trying to undo her fists, as if that would lessen her turmoil.

"Madam! Madam! What are you doing?" Roli appeared and patted Jeremy on his shoulder. "Calm, now Master Jeremy, calm now." He helped him to a chair.

"Calm!" Lesedi cried. "We have been betrayed. By one of Jeremy's so-called friends. All I have done to keep the work secret, undone by careless words."

"I didn't tell them what you were doing," Jeremy tried to explain. "Only that it's important and you need to be allowed to work without interference."

"You told them enough. The 'security of the nation' is at stake, according to them. The Institute Head is useless, hiding in his office. I hunted him down anyway and demanded he return her to me. Demanded he let me work without that toady Southwood breathing down my neck. He dared, actually dared to suggest I take time off, to rest my mind. He said I seemed fevered. In fact, that lackey Southwood and his security hyena friends have got him to suspend my privileges again. He admitted as much. Sly, slippery bastard! 'Cooperate with them, Professor van Dyck. How can it hurt?' Tempting me like the devil himself."

"What did you say?" Jeremy asked.

"I almost agreed, right there. But I said I'd think about it."

"No." Jeremy seized her hands, trying to follow the complexities of the situation. "No, you mustn't give them this ability."

"But, mein Gott, Jeremy, what else can I do? They have her!"

"Who?" Roli said. When Lesedi didn't answer immediately, he repeated. "Who do they have?"

Jeremy whispered, "Bari. Your Bari."

Roli shook his head back and forth, wildly, keening, teeth bared in a snarl of rage and heartbreak. "What have you done! My beautiful flower, they will crush her. They will destroy us all. Why did you do this thing?"

SEASONS BETWEEN US

Lesedi clutched his head. "Be still! Be still. I won't let them keep her. I will do what they want."

Roli fell silent, but his chest heaved as he peered into her face, seeking hope.

She seized his hands. Jeremy stared at their intertwined fingers, hers, thin and pale, Roli's, thick, warm and gnarled with the work he'd spent his life doing for him, for Lesedi. "I will cooperate, Roli," Lesedi said. "I won't let them keep our Bari."

He slowly shook his head. "It won't help. Always they will do things like this." He pulled himself straight, head held stiffly to attention, mobile mouth pulling down. "Change the world, Madame Lesedi," he said. "Do that thing you and Bari have been working on. Make it different. Bring her back to me."

Lesedi said, "Even if I could get my privileges back, I need *her* to do it, Roli. She is my mind. She is better than me. The child I could only dream of having. I will do whatever they want to get her back."

"*No.* You mustn't." Jeremy surged to his feet, filled with an emotion he had never felt before. Rage. Rage at Lesedi. Rage at her betrayal. That she would leave him again, fail him again.

A sound like a paddle tenderizing beef. Burst of pain in his fist. A cry and the thump of a body hitting the carpet.

"Master Jeremy, no!" The slave Henry's arms were around him, pulling him off balance. He fell to the carpet beside his wife.

Lesedi dabbed at a trickle of blood on the corner of her mouth but said nothing. Her eyes were filled with tears, but he couldn't tell if her expression was of anger or fear or sorrow. He couldn't tell, when always he'd known how to read her face like a child's primer. What had he become?

"Lesedi." Her name was drawn out of him like a sob. His shoulders shook, the anger draining away as quickly as it had come. Lesedi crawled across the carpet and wrapped her arms around his trembling body, and they lay like that for the longest time; Lesedi and Roli holding him until calmness returned and his mind cleared.

"I will somehow fix this, my darling Jeremy," Lesedi whispered. "Though I don't know how I can."

"Take us away," Jeremy entreated.

"Where could we go? Scotland? America? It is hardly better there."

"No," he said. "Take us to the new world."

"Oh Jeremy. It is only a theory—and a wild one at that. We may not even be able to complete the preliminary experiments. Unless I know what is happening at the quantum level, I can have no idea what will happen at higher energy inputs. Besides, without access to the lab, and without Bari to help me, there is nothing more I can do."

Calmness washed over him, a feeling of control as he had not experienced in countless months. "I created this disaster. It is now my job to fix it. I don't have a lot of clout anymore but I have some. I will contact Curtis Nyere. I'm sure he will help."

Roli shook his head sadly. "He will not. He did not achieve his position by fighting the system."

——·——

Nyere took Jeremy's call but the conversation was brief. "I'd like to help you, Jeremy, for old time's sake. But I am, sadly perhaps, the poster boy for the government's reforms, the first black minister since the repressions of the 1950s. I cannot risk my people's future for the foolishness of an Afrikaners woman. Do not call me again."

He expected nothing more from Doris O'Brian but some loyalties ran deeper than others. Perhaps her own time in the wilderness had prepared her for sacrifice. Jeremy had no doubt her upward rise would once again come to a halt because of this favour. "I can get your property—what was her name, Bari?—returned to you. It's only temporary but maybe long enough to get you all out of the country. I can do nothing about Lesedi's credentials. It's a shame, she was such a brilliant scientist."

He did not report that last remark to Lesedi; she did not need her confidence shaken further. Bari returned to them two hours later to hugs and tears and much relief. Doris had done more than obtain her release; she had obtained travel documents for both her and Roli.

"This is wonderful, Jeremy, but it gets us no closer to changing the world," said Lesedi, smiling ruefully. "Perhaps we should follow Doris's advice and flee the country. If we can get our own documents in order."

"Small steps, my dear." Jeremy descended the narrow steps alone to the sub-basement of their house to his most secret of secret hiding places. He pried away a brick from the wall and reached deep inside to find the small rock that, when pressed, opened a flagstone in the floor. He returned to the kitchen where the other three were sharing a pot of hot tea.

"First things first," he said. "Lesedi, could you call the other staff?" She looked uncertain but did as he'd asked.

The cook, a portly woman in her fifties that they called Sarah, and the serving girl, barely the age of majority, stood with eyes downcast. Perhaps expecting discipline after all the yelling and turmoil of the day. Jeremy stood in front of them, holding two envelopes.

"Sarah, Catherine, these are certificates of manumission. With these you are free to return to your villages or go anywhere within the Republic of Tanzania and Zanzibar. You are free to use whatever name you choose and live the life you elect. These are legal documents, and you must always keep them safe."

For a moment, no one moved. Then Sarah tentatively held out her hand.

"Thank you, Master."

"No," said Catherine, taking her own envelope, "Thank you, Mr. Falconbridge."

When the women had left to fetch their things, Lesedi rested her hand on Jeremy's arm. "When did you obtain those?"

Roli had moved to stand beside his daughter, a look of confusion on his face.

"The day you brought Bari home," he said. He turned to Roli and held up two more envelopes. "Surely you don't think I would have forgotten you, my dear friend? And, by good fortune, your daughter too. I meant to do this earlier but . . . it slipped my—"

"I never doubted your promise, Mas . . . Jeremy." Roli slipped his hand into Bari's. "But I never imagined it would bring me such joy."

"Amazing Grace," said Bari.

"You are now free to come and go as you please," said Lesedi. "You need not risk yourselves for the dreams of two old fools."

Roli smiled gently. "You have been many things in the years I have known you, but fool is not one of them. It is a new world—even if only for the four of us. If the rest is impossible, so be it."

Bari reached out and stroked her father's cheek. "I always had faith I would see you again. And I have faith in Jeremy's vision." She paused, her face momentarily twisted in pain. She had not spoken of her time in detention but, Jeremy knew, the Hyenas, as Lesedi called them, would not have been gentle. He wanted to comfort her as he had wanted to comfort Lesedi all those years she had been taken from him. But he had done all he could; it was up to Rolihlahla now.

"When they were . . . questioning me, I took myself away," Bari said to Lesedi. "I thought of how you created theories and placed them on your prison walls, so I tried to paint the inside of my skull with formulae and, well, I think I have the answer." She recited a series of letters and operators, so quickly Jeremy could barely register them. But the light shining in Lesedi's face told him all he needed to know.

Jeremy held up a fifth envelope. "This will get us wherever you want to go. We need only choose our destination."

He handed it to Lesedi and she scanned the contents, several letters and two photographs. "Where did you get those?"

"What?" Jeremy reached up and straightened Lesedi's collar.

"Never mind that now. These documents . . ."

"Yes, yes." He shook his head. "My mind seems to flit like a butterfly in a flower garden."

"You need to concentrate, my darling."

As if it were in my control, he thought, *as if anything is in my control anymore*. The documents, the documents she was holding, that he had saved all these years, they . . .

"Ah yes, evidence that Security Minister Bryan Smythe is a traitor. A spy for the Russians no less. It was long ago, before *y* replaced *i* in his name, and I doubt he is any longer enamoured of the Tsar but it would still be enough to end his career. I always thought I might need a get-out-of-jail-free card."

"But you didn't use it to get me out of jail," said Lesedi.

"I would have but . . ."

"But it is like a gun with only one bullet," said Roli. "For all his smiles and nice words, *we slaves* know the Minister's true nature. He would have released you only for as long as it took to arrange your deaths."

"Exactly right," said Jeremy. *In another world, Roli would have been a great policy advisor, or perhaps even a political leader.*

"Then there is no question," said Lesedi, "we must use this bullet to get us out of the country. Go somewhere safe."

"There is no place safe in this world, Lesedi," said Bari.

"We must try to go to another one," said her father.

"Or bring that other one here," Jeremy added.

Lesedi flung up her hands. "Have you all taken leave of your senses?"

Jeremy captured her hands in his. "Perhaps we've come to them, my dear."

"Most likely we will all wind up dead!" But she left her hands where they were, in his.

Roli nodded and said nothing. He reached out and laid his hand on top of Jeremy and Lesedi's. After a moment, Bari added her hand to her father's.

"Like in a book," Jeremy said.

"Whose ending we write ourselves and freely choose," said Bari.

"But . . ." Lesedi began, then looked down at their joined hands. Her face relaxed. "We have already written it. We have created a new world, even if we are its only citizens."

"Amazing Grace," sighed Jeremy. "And grace will lead us home."

———•———

It proved surprisingly simple to arrange the exchange. The envelope—sealed and addressed to Smythe's home address—was sent to the American ambassador for safe-keeping and eventual transmittal to the Minister. The Minister delivered Lesedi's credentials and an order she be given full access to the large synchrotron beneath the mountains of Morogoro. He even sent his personal driver to take them.

"They will record everything we do," said Lesedi as she led the three of them down the pristine corridors to the elevator that would take them deep beneath the earth. The facility had a bare complement of technicians who had been ordered to assist them in whatever it was they were there to do. By the looks on their faces, Jeremy thought most of them were eager to do so. Lesedi's name still carried weight among the scientific class—even if it was now Bari who was in charge of the science.

"No matter," he said. "We have already said our goodbyes to this world. What happens next is in other hands."

He and Roli drank coffee and played cards and talked of what they would do if a new world came while the women entered their formulae into the vast bank of computers governing the particle accelerator.

"I will write poetry," said Roli.

"You do that now."

"But in the next world, someone might publish it. And you?"

"I will be a fisherman."

"You can't swim."

"Well, I'll use a boat."

They were interrupted by Lesedi rapping on the door of the small office. "It's time." She led them down to a glassed-in platform above the massive machine, most of it disappearing into tunnels on the left and right.

"What will we see?" asked Roli.

"What will we remember?" asked Jeremy.

"I don't know." Lesedi nodded to Bari, who typed the last few commands into the input. "Only good things," Bari said and turned a key on the control. A low hum built around them. "Everything is nominal."

Jeremy closed his eyes and began to hum in tune to the machine beneath them. The voices of his family—his *family*—rose around him. Singing his song.

There was a flash of light, burning through his eyelids, and everything became clear.

No better world except that we make it.

※ ※ ※

General Information: A note from Liz and Hayden about *Lay Down Your Heart*: We have co-written short stories before, usually of a comedic sort, but this collaboration was an adventure into fresh territory. Inspired by the beauty of Tanzania and the heartbreak engendered by the Slave Chambers in Stone Town, Zanzibar, we evolved the narrative of *Lay Down Your Heart*, exchanging processes, ideas, and drafts until we no longer truly know who wrote what.

※ ※ ※

Author's Notes to My Younger Self: Liz Westbrook-Trenholm: Heed advice from those with experience; it's useful. However, decisions are yours to make, and yours to live with. Make them boldly and independently, don't second-guess them and have confidence in your abilities. You will land on your feet. Equally, be supportive and kind to others enduring their own struggles.

Hayden Trenholm: Practice perseverance. The best results often come from a long slow effort and the decisions made in haste will govern your existence for longer than you think. Be wise rather than clever—use all your faculties to guide your life, not just your intellect. Above all, live your values and make sure the most important value is kindness.

THE VEIL BETWEEN

Karin Lowachee

The first word between us is madness. We chase each other through every life in every universe but only I remember. Is this a form of hell? If so, there are more than nine. I know this because they're impossible to forget. This isn't a turn of phrase.

These hells are *impossible* to forget. So are the moments of heaven. They're in my memory and in my notebooks, the writings of a madman. The writings of an old man. Yet the writing is the only thing that keeps me here, tethered to our story. Keeps me with you through time and the universes between us.

I am this old man with a black notebook and three pens: black, red, and blue.

I am the boy you met in the hospital.

I am the man on the run with you in the desert.

I am the one you call Love, after the crash.

We are so many other names and other lives, coma patients suspended in worlds without dates and years. None of that matters. The month is cold or it's warm. The people are friendly or they're not. The doors are open or they are closed. I close my eyes and see you in one world, I open my eyes to love you in another. Sometimes something as simple as the flutter from the pages of a book conjures the memory and casts me sideways, Alice through a portal. I write it all down to hold onto some semblance of sanity. What I see, what I feel. Who we are.

These worlds begin as fragments in a mosaic and collect into shape. The shape of my life, the shape of our lives. I write it all down and wish

somehow the words can jump from here to there so I can show you in every world.

I want to show you that no matter how many lives we run to ruin together, what matters is we are together.

What matters is we are running together.

———•———

I am this old man with yet another doctor in yet another hospital, this doctor and her notes, asking questions.

How old were you when you started to remember everything?

How old were you when you met Allen in the asylum?

The same age as when I met Tristan in the desert town.

And Billy on the road before the crash.

You are Allen and Tristan and Billy.

I am always Caleb.

If there is any continuity in these millions of lives it is us, you and I. Young and old. Hate and love, not opposite but entwined.

In the beginning I was so angry that you always died.

In the beginning I didn't understand death, not when I could remember every life.

If you were here, you'd say, *Don't tell her anything*. Not only because it sounds crazy, but because it's not hers to know. But I'm an old man and all I have left are these memories.

And maybe that's all we ever have; maybe that is what we're made of.

———•———

In one life we met in the asylum where the walls wept in the summer and outside in the yard you offered me a contraband cigarette. We were both crazy and knew it; unlike what everybody says, it is possible to question your sanity and be batshit. Like criminals, we ask each other why we are inside and both of us lie about it and we smoke and crouch against the wall and watch the birds flit in and out, launching from the lawn into the sky.

That's what freedom looks like, you tell me, and I think I fell in love. So simple and so ignorant but love is that, isn't it, the unacknowledged ignorance of another person through which we convince ourselves we know, we see, we understand. But I understood nothing and so it was deep, this love, and I was young and barely remembered the other lives.

We are fifteen and abandoned but we find each other in that asylum where the walls wept in the summer a kind of acid rain green.

I had my notebook, even then. The first time in my room, you open it and begin to read and I sit on my hands on the squeaking bed and rock back and forth like a metronome. And you ask, *Is this why you're in here?* Even though you know because in group they asked and we weren't supposed to lie, even though everybody lies, especially to doctors, and all I talked about were my dreams and how they began when I was thirteen and they crowded my head and sometimes I couldn't hear anything so my parents thought I needed mental help. Put him away where somebody can fix him, he thinks he lives in another country, he's speaking in tongues, he talks about wars he's never fought and people he's never met and skies that don't look like ours.

You smile and murmur, *That's cool,* and I love you a little more, I love the way your back looks in that t-shirt, like muscled wings, I love the length of your arms and your broad shoulders and the cherry blossom tattooed on your wrist. You say it means that everything dies, nothing lasts forever or even for very long.

I let you read my notebook because in it I remembered everything. *Everything?* Yes everything, every minute every second of every day since I was thirteen and sometimes it's not even my life here, this life, this body and these walls. I don't know how to keep it all separate in my head so that's why I'm here.

You say, *I want to know more.* You say, *Tell me about all of your worlds.*

Where do I start? I'm never going to forget you and that's not hyper-bole, it's not even romantic, I am never going to forget every detail of you and you might even be remembered in another world.

I was fifteen and felt it. How our lives ran together like rivers from different seas.

Every day they chase us from the yard and into the hall and they take away your cigarettes but we find ways around the corners and the pills and we collect pebbles of them in the palms of our hands, pink and blue and yellow, and you tell me about the river you used to sit beside in the summers when your family went to the country and the smooth rocks at the shore and then your words stop because some memory catches you and you turn away.

Don't you want to forget some things?

Of course, but I have no choice. There is no choice. You said you were in the asylum because you tried to kill yourself, Allen. More than once. Why?

But that isn't something you will ever tell me. Not in this life or any other. And there is no choice about forgetting or remembering. You forget to survive and I remember as a part of life I can't separate from death. I remember every single one of your deaths, the hell that chased us through our lives.

————.————

It feels like a western, Tristan, all hot round sun and the earthy barn scent of horses and dust and desert vegetation like cactus and tumbleweeds, and we're watering the horses in a shallow ravine with some remembrance of a storm from the night before. The long equine heads drop to slurp the muddy water and they flick their ears and the reins shake and flies pick at their soft spotted hides and their grey tails swish. We sit with our hats pulled low and there's a tear in your trousers. There's a bullet wound gaping in the tear in your trousers and the bullet went clean through. Last night I had to burn it through with the heated steel of my knife and you cursed me out so hard it carved into the stars and I used my second shirt to tie your leg and we drank whiskey and listened for approach. But there's no approach and now the sun is burning and the sky is more blue than the brown water the horses drink and you ask if we'll ever get to the end of the Earth.

I don't know but that's the only place for us, we've been riding for five days straight and I tell you about my dreams, the one where the walls are weeping in a strange big building and instead of pebbles in the ravine there are small coloured stones, so small we can swallow them. One's supposed to put us to sleep and one's supposed to keep us calm and the other one makes it hard to dream. We're running because I can't keep any of it in my head and I'm sorry, I know it's dangerous and there's no helping it, my father said I should be put down like a dog and now here we are with your shot-up leg taking rest with the snakes and the spiders.

Ain't nobody at fault if your head's a little sideways.

Doesn't it feel like we've known each other all our lives? Doesn't it feel like it's been twenty winters?

We ride headlong. Your leg won't stop bleeding. Your face grows pale. We stop on the mesa and the desert drops its cold weight on our backs. The horses breathe smoke like dragons, our breath curling out from our lungs and wrapping together and I wrap you up in my coat and my arms and build a fire through which I can see your eyes and how damp they grow like they are sweating even as we shiver. In the morning, there is frost along the flats and I have to help you up onto the horse. I ride behind you cradling you like a madonna and the back of your hair smells like the air and it is burning. I press my nose into it anyway and press my hand to the wound on your leg and though the blood is thick and slow like lava it stains my fingers and you tell me to burn it again, the first time didn't take.

It goes on like this for days, you're slowly bleeding and I'm trying to stop it. I talk to you to keep you awake until my voice sounds raw. I tell you what your names are in these other lives. The big building with the coloured pebbles: I call you Allen.

The one where you crash: your name is Billy.

Through every life, I am Caleb. You call me Caleb and I answer.

————•————

Billy, how's your head? This is a regular question between us after the crash. You ask me too. *How's your head, Caleb? What other lives do you remember?* At first it was a kind of mocking, a tease because you didn't believe me. But through the years when I write down these memories and let you read them in my notebook, the consistency of the fragments tells another story.

Are you sure you're not just telling stories?

No, because if they're stories I should be able to put them away, manipulate them, forget about them for a while. Instead these pieces come to me with such power and clarity, provoked by some scene or word, whether it's on television or in conversation. The summer sun flashes a kind of hallucination across my eyes, you and I riding through a desert on horseback, the scent of blood in my mouth. The first time I ran into the hospital after your crash, the emergency room melded for a moment with another room, one with bars on the windows and doors that lock from the outside. I stood beside your bed, held your hand, and saw birds in my mind. I heard you say, *That's what freedom looks like.* But it wasn't a memory from this time, this life. We knew already how freedom felt.

Racing down a desert road together, the deep and steady thunder of the wheels beneath us.

The first time we see each other in that rundown town, two travellers at the frayed ends of the world.

Immediate recognition and not understanding how.

Not even time can hold us.

Are we always together?

Yes, always.

I don't tell you about the dying.

In this timeline, after the crash and all the hours spent outside physiotherapy rooms, I meet a doctor and she tells me about total recall. We talk about the chaotic nature of memories while I watch through the glass as you learn how to walk again. Some people can recall everything in their lives, she says. Not many, but it exists for a few. She is one of the doctors that documents such things. I thought that shit was just in science fiction.

I thought for most of my life I was just crazy, because in other lives I am crazy or I'm told that I'm crazy. It's easy to believe it when everyone around you says it.

Then I just accepted I'm crazy and that's when I met you, Billy. Eyes so black they hold the crazy in. They take all the crazy in the universe and suck it down into nothing. I fell in.

The doctor says, *Temporal recall.*

That's what the doctor tells me eventually, that her particular group has discovered this thing, this phenomenon. Temporal recall, like telekinesis or something psychic and psychic means crazy, doesn't it? I don't know how she knows there is something about me, maybe it's the distraction in my eyes but that could be because I'm worried about you. Maybe she sees the lives lined in my features, each stroke a memory.

Eventually I show her my notebook.

That's when our arguments start because you don't want anyone to know our secret, Billy.

They'll put you away. I hear you. I can't claim to listen to a hundred lives I'm leading in other planes of existence, or whatever they call it, and think they won't come for me. The ever-present "they."

They'll put you away and then where will I be?

You and I made a pact to never leave each other and if one of us goes (it will always be you but I don't say that) then the other has to immediately kill himself. Was this ever a joke? It wasn't for me. Don't call it romantic, it's just practical.

There is no life without you and I've seen it a million times.

———•———

Back in the asylum we play checkers in the TV room. Your name is Allen. I'm still Caleb. There's someone in the corner, facing the corner, talking to herself. There's someone else in front of the TV arguing with the TV. Outside, snow falls. The cold and wind howl at the window-pane. For minutes, I am caught in the cadence of the winter storm, flung and flurried like the snowflakes into a vortex of other memories. They feel like a blizzard in my mind, impossible to catch just one and examine the crystalline perfection of pattern. Instead, I am trudging along a glacier, spike-heeled with crampons and mittens that make my hands sweat. Above, a sky so blue it feels endless, like night will never fall. A permanent day for a permanent memory, and in a blink the white disappears with the cold and I am staring at the edges of a window, and I look back at you, Allen, and you are looking at me over the red and black pieces of our checkerboard.

Again?

Yes, more than again. Always. We are in winter and I am pulling you on a travois, you're buried under furs and your hands have turned blue, more blue than the sky, and your dark eyes show nothing of the day, just night.

My headache feels like a sun expanding behind my eyes. Going supernova.

Caleb. You pull me back. Again. *Am I there?* you ask.

Of course you are, you're always there.

We're on a glacier and I'm trying to keep you alive. Always trying to keep you alive against the perpetual fall of night.

At night in the asylum the restless spirits wail like the wind, up and down our wing of the hospital. In our room we stare at the shadow the window bars make on the blank wall.

Do you think we'll ever get out of here?

You will before me. I'm permanently crazy. They just want to see that you won't harm yourself again.

Except I will.

Except you will.

So maybe I'll stay in here with you.

But the thought of that cuts through me like a wound and I look across the gap of space between our beds and the cold of the glacier yawns beneath my feet and it changes in a blink to a desert, a winter desert dusted with new snow. The horse's breath plumes in front of us. You can't stay. You shouldn't stay. Maybe you need to be out there so I can follow you.

This is the only pattern that matters. You're hurt and I try to fix you and you keep hurting yourself.

I'm old with it, even in our asylum. I feel the years lined along my bones, stringing my muscles together. Sometimes when I write in my notebook my hand changes into a shape of thin skin and thick blue veins, the gnarl of an ancient tree.

Since one of us can't leave and the other doesn't want to stay, we make a pact to both get out together.

No matter what, we run together.

The memory tells me you're dying in the desert, Tristan, but it doesn't come to me chronologically. Time doesn't work that way and neither do our minds. Birds outside our barred window remind me of desert crows and I see myself shooing them away from the blood on your leg while you sleep, the mercy of sleep. The horses hoof the ground and snort. The moon is a round white eye in the night, a cyclopean indifference to how alone we are, running from our families because they think I'm mad, possibly demonic, and you're a deviant.

Something's different about this memory, though.

I'm also bleeding. Or is it your blood?

On the palms of my hands there's blood.

On the front of my shirt is blood.

The sticky mass in my hair is blood and we're both cold, shivering like we're trying to throw off a bad spirit.

I hold tighter. The crows come again, a flutter of black wings and black eyes darting in every direction where they smell death.

In a blink we're riding again, the horse takes the brunt of this weight with its head lowered and you're too weak to even grasp the reins so I hold them and hold you. The winter sun blurs overhead like a sulphur disc and I feel that this is later, much later, that this isn't the first few days when we ran from the town. It's your other leg bleeding, and along your ribs where I cauterized and it didn't take. Again. Always.

Why are you always dying?

It screams in my head like a crow's call.

Why are you always at the end of your life?

Show me another life. The tears seep out the corners of my eyes, a cold burn. Show me something else so we're not just this, the universe can't be this cruel, it isn't a god.

Our bodies on the ground with the snow falling on them, dusting your eyelashes. I can't even build a fire, I just hold your hand.

Word travelled through the towns. There's that witch and his deviant. Sinful creatures, sons of perdition.

They shoot me first. And as I'm stumbling down the street, I hear you running toward me, shouting, your gun out.

But it's too late.

———•———

Why don't you just lie to them?

Three months in the asylum, Allen, and I know you're going to leave me. You can't take it anymore, you want to be free, all of our promises sound like lies now and I should've known better. A pact to run together, who are we fooling? When you go back to your life it's to the country homes by the river and the gilded lights and good education. Why don't I lie so I can leave too? So we can have a life outside of this big building, one without pills and bars on the window and locked doors and wistful birds?

There's nothing out there for me. Except you. And I can't have you. We leave here and you hurt yourself.

That's the pills talking.

Because you don't see your own deaths and I'm old from the sight of it, the constant fucking reality of it.

The only reality in worlds of crazy.

All the worlds of crazy in my head.

———•———

Billy, how's your head?

A hospital at night feels like a morgue. I sit beside your bed. It's right after the crash and you're bandaged around your head like a mummy, like a burn victim, white gauze and stitches holding your face together, holding your skull together so you don't spill all over the pillow like an egg. I hold your hand but it's like holding a corpse's.

I came to the hospital before your crash.

This is the concussive force of a memory, felt in delay.

I used to come here long before your crash.

I lay in bed, or on a tray. Yes, a tray like a meal in a cafeteria and they put me inside a big drum and told me not to move as they took pictures of my head. Inside my head.

Caleb, how's your head?

I've been inside this hospital, in and out, for weeks. Weeks stretching to months and so many tests, studying to be a doctor doesn't come with this many tests. Being a student doesn't inflict this many tests. Tests of my memory and tests of my cognition and tests of my vision. Something is wrong with my head and it's always been wrong and they tell me some weeks in, some weeks after all of these damn tests that there's a part of my brain that doesn't want to play with the other parts and now it's rebelling. It's malignant, like resentment, like some form of hate that's embedded in love and the only one it hurts is you.

The doctor who tells me about temporal recall is my doctor.

I didn't meet her outside your physiotherapy room. I met her months ago, but she visits me when I'm outside your physiotherapy room.

This is the thing about memory—it's a mosaic, not a list. Not a timeline you can open out and stretch from here to eternity.

Memory is what happens when you tear up a whole book of paper and toss the bits and pieces into the air.

She tells me this ability to cross universes comes with a price. Like everything. Like love.

You're going to die.

But everybody dies.

You're going to die sooner than others.

Sooner than Billy.

Billy, how's your head?

When you open your eyes. When they remove the bandages. When your raw dark eyes look into mine.

How's yours? you ask.

Because we made a pact. We have a deal. If one of us dies, the other one follows.

You're the one following me through time, after all. Through all of our millions of lives. My millions of memories of us, dying.

———•———

It eats into my brain in every life, this madness. Maybe I shouldn't be surprised. You can't hold so many memories and lives in your head and not overflow, or be eaten. My brain is eating itself to make room for more. Every life just chewing on the grey squishy bits, synapses snapping between my teeth, creating little jolts of electricity. And with each bite I make space for another life.

I make space for you, Billy. Allen. Tristan. Love.

So many names. I write them all in my notebook in the hope that one day you might find it, somehow, through time. And you will recognize yourself. Like I recognize you in every life.

We recognize each other.

The body dies, over and over, but the soul untethered becomes caught in certain gravity. This gravity is you, pulling the disparate parts of my matter to a cohesive whole.

Here we are through all scenescapes of time.

An asylum.

A desert.

A hospital after a crash.

(On a glacier.)

In rooms, fighting.

On the road, racing.

I write it all down, too many pages to count. Tear them up when you're finished reading. Throw all of the pieces into the air and let's start again. At the same time. Again. When I'm old and you're young. When I'm dying and you're alive. When you chase my death because we promised. You'll die again too. We'll run together toward the other side of life. Through each veil of waiting memories. They wait for us to find them.

Are we always together?

Yes, always.

Again and always, running together.

Author's Notes to My Younger Self: Be kind to yourself and cultivate a love of learning and connection. Human beings grow, develop, and become compassionate through honest introspection and connection to others. Rein in the ego, attempt a wider perspective to balance too much self-involvement. Seek joy and recognize pain as a part of the whole. Life is a spectrum of experiences.

SYMPATHÉTIQUE

Alvaro Zinos-Amaro

When we arrive at the *parador* in the early evening I should be pleased, for it's been a long journey, but instead anxiety snakes through my mind as an unfamiliar silence descends within. The guiding voice I've relied on all these years is gone.

The incandescent Andalusian sun even at this late hour only grudgingly relinquishes its seemingly indomitable hold on the sky, a golden furnace shimmering with orange hues streaked with blood. My grey tee clings to my armpits and tugs at my skin as I insist on manual driving while hunting for a parking spot. After finding one, I refrain from picking at the dried sweat crusted on the back of what I suspect is a now sunburned neck, irritated at myself for having forgotten to apply sunscreen. Maybe I can blame Dr. Linares back home, who threatens me each time I postpone my big four-oh checkup, and who warned me to go easy on salty foods and booze during this trip but failed to mention anything as banal as sun protector.

Jann and I unload our suitcases with few words. I tell myself the tingling in my forehead, which has been intensifying with each mile that's brought us closer to the coast, is simply fatigue.

I know this is not true.

Jann, with her fresh tilted frisette haircut and breezy chiffon overlay blouse, appears just as cool and prim as when we boarded our flight from Toronto to Madrid. I observe her with admiration and maybe a dash of jealousy. Despite our two-hour, delay she was her usual cheery self on the plane, finding distraction in movies and games while I groused about our lost time. Even when the AC of the bright

red Volkswagen Polo rental we picked up in Madrid began to falter five hours into our cross-country road trip, her spirits—though not her back—remained undampened. The AC unpleasantness coincided with our hitting noxious traffic in the vicinity of El Chaparral, Granada, one of the freeway's few non-gridded interchanges, and I came close to calling it quits. But Hydrargyros had whispered to me about a poor outcome for such a deviation, and I decided not to risk it. Jann's encouragement may have helped me stay on track too.

"Our drive was longer than the flight," I remark, puffing at the weight of our bags as we traipse toward the *parador*'s ah, snug, entrance. I'd forgotten how small things feel in Europe. "Cozy" is Jann's preferred term.

"But we're here now." She pauses. "You can smell the Mediterranean."

As I approach the young man with slicked-back hair behind the front desk, I sense Jann basking in our new surroundings. Her relaxation is an almost perceptible phenomenon to me, little currents of satisfaction that mingle with the breeze coming off the sea. Six years of marriage and I still don't know how she does it, this process of effortless adaptation, immersion. It's like a magic trick, a spiritual osmosis that allows her to dialogue with the environment while the environment in turn converses with her, a two-way convergence of energies. The clerk returns my credit card and hands me our keys. As we enter the hall, a yawning sense of loss at my broken connection hits me—hard.

I stagger forward.

"Hey," Jann says, offering her arm.

"I'm fine," I mumble, but I hold on to her until the metaphysical dizzy spell has passed.

I knew this was a bad idea, I think. Ninety-two percent probability of lost connection, Hydrargyros had predicted. Fool that I am, I chose to ignore the odds. We haven't been here all of ten minutes, and I'm already starting to regret the trip.

"Maybe I'm dehydrated," I say as we head to the elevator, attempting to salvage respectability, to hide the severity of my inner defeat.

"Maybe," Jann says.

Once inside the room, I fall asleep almost immediately. Around midnight Jann tugs at my shoulder and offers me a snack. I shake my head. She proffers a pill for my headache, and I swallow. In the dim moonlight I see her on the balcony, sipping wine, a mere few feet from me, yet in a different universe. I groan, turn over, and return to the darkness.

Except that I don't settle back into the depths of my initial slumber, caught instead in the churning dregs of semi-consciousness. I'm self-aware enough to know I haven't dreamt—and that I won't dream, not tonight, not for the next ten nights of our coastal sojourn. When I was a teen, I discovered that large bodies of water, even medium-sized lakes, cause interference. I wanted to believe that this might have changed since my last such experience, that whatever invisible muscle permits my linkage might have become strong enough over time to overcome the signal interruption. Clearly, that was wishful thinking.

In the dark, Jann's soft breathing is a welcome, familiar mantle, but ultimately not comforting enough. I listen intently to the nothingness of the room, as though it might have something to say.

I turn to face the balcony, then turn back again, pull the pillow over my head.

My body tenses.

Adrenaline flows.

I haven't experienced an absence of connection this profound in years.

It terrifies me.

Lack of oneiric contact means no new information for Hydrargyros, and no new data for my quicksilver companion means no reliable guidance for tomorrow. No tips on what best to say, where best to go—how best to be. Each dreamless night that passes I'll become increasingly stranded, more and more cut off from the only reliable source of information about my own well-being: my future-self.

———•———

In the morning I wake up late to find Jann showering. I blink and retinal-access the latest model predictions, which I downloaded via Hydrargyros the night before we left Toronto. According to the most recent model iteration, a light breakfast is the way to go, followed by a jaunt to the convenience store, and then our first expedition to Fuengirola's beach. Eighty-nine percent odds that these events will lead to a pleasant lunch and a superior evening, with a small margin of error. But it all starts going wrong almost immediately. First, Jann seems to be taking forever, and nothing I do imparts upon her a sense of urgency.

"I'm sorry you didn't get good rest," she says, slathering sunblock on her legs, "but don't take it out on me. Here, do my back, please."

She's right about the effects of my sleeplessness. My headache has worsened. A distinct rumbling in my stomach lets me know a skimpy breakfast will be unsatisfying. And my body's torpor undermines my verbal attempts to encourage swiftness.

"I'm going to clean up," I mutter. It helps. After a cool shower and shave, I refocus my thoughts. By now Jann is in a higher gear too. We zip through toast and coffee, grab some items at the food-and-fruit bazaar next door, and then march down Calle Miguel de Cervantes for two blocks until we hit the main beach walkway, the Paseo Marítimo Rey de España. Far busier than I expected, we find ourselves jostling among crowds, mostly German- and English- and Portuguese-speaking families with rambunctious children whose unstable trajectories seem designed to cut us off at every turn.

The beach itself is also crowded, a plague of mushroomed yellow and watermelon-red *sombriyas de playa*, as they call beach umbrellas here. Jann finds us a decent spot. I plop down the cooler and set up our stuff. We have a difficult time entering into relaxed conversation. She makes a few attempts, as do I, but nothing seems reciprocally satisfying. At one point Jann asks me a question twice, only it's not a question, but her telling me she's going for a walk. I grunt acknowledgement, annoyed at my own distraction. Is this really the best possible version of this day? Beneath my shades, I close my eyes. I try to give myself up to the moment. Instead, memories of conversations with my future-self surface. This has been happening with increasing frequency. The more solitude I seek, the more I run into myself.

———·———

"Maybe it's time to call it quits," future-me is saying.

This conversation occurred on campus during my first semester as an assistant prof. I locked my office door.

By this time my future-self and I had perfected something approximating real-time communication—whatever the word *real-time* means when you're talking about signals that instantaneously leap across decades—but we didn't have a system in place to measure what we were doing.

"You've got to be kidding me," I say. "Clearly, I'm benefitting from your knowledge, and don't tell me your retirement isn't being enlivened by an influx of ever-new memories."

"Ever-new yet evergreen, is that it?"

His sarcasm is impossible to miss, but I choose not to respond to it.

"If this arrangement is really so peachy," he continues, "shouldn't we be, I dunno, happier by now? We're investing a lot of time into something with no clear payoff."

"Investing time?" I mock. "Is that a joke?"

But he's managed to get to me. Why must my older-self insist on reducing our conversations to emotional, ultimately un-shareable subjectivities like happiness? It's been almost a year since our initial contact, but his grindingly skeptical attitude is truly wearying. Am I really destined to become this negative?

"We *are* happier," I say with an authority I don't feel. For a moment, I wonder who I'm trying to convince. "Problem is, we're losing track of all the changes, so our baseline keeps shifting. Without a fixed standard, we can't appreciate how much better off we are now than we used to be. It's all about incremental well-being."

"I don't know, kid," he says.

"Would you have enjoyed being called kid when you were my age?"

"Oh, get over yourself," he scoffs. "That fancy university title doesn't mean crap. You know I had it worse than you."

According to what he's told me, his life at this point was considerably messier than mine. A bitter break-up with Jann, failure to secure a position at the University, depression. That alone, I think, should be enough to convince him that we should stick together.

"You did," I say. "Which is why you should be thankful I'm course-correcting—for *both* of us."

"For all I know, what we have here is the existentially blind leading the existentially blind," he says. "Double the misery, half the fun. You remake my reality, but how do I know it's improving?"

I could have argued or poked holes in the simplistic analogy, but the bottom line was that he was right. When I began making decisions directly related to future-me's knowledge, we wondered how his experience of reality would be affected. It turned out to be anticlimactic. Even major ripples caused him no physical sensation at all: one instant his memories aligned with the world and the next they simply didn't. No vertigo or sense of discontinuity. When we connected, the link somehow reached inside his head and his memories shifted. Most changes—the ones not absorbed by time's inherent inelasticity—were subtle and required little readjustment. Still, we needed version control. We needed a way to measure how my altered behaviour in the present translated for him downstream. We needed to be able to map specific actions to specific consequences. As good a mathematician as I was, there were far too many variables for me to track. I didn't even know how to define the parameters of the problem, a realization I'd found overwhelming.

But when I considered it that day, I had an insight. I realized I didn't just have *my* resources on hand, but his too—

———•———

Jann returns from her walk, interrupting my reverie. She looks satisfied. Peaceful. Or perhaps distant? I'm tempted to blame the fact that the combo of my sunglasses and hers makes it hard for me to read her eyes, but the truth is that I've never been great at guessing her moods. "Hey." I look up at her and smile. "Nice walk?"

She sits on the empty foldable chair beside me, dabs at sweat on her forehead. "Hotter than I expected," she says. "You sure you don't want to go into the water?"

I survey the scene. Up ahead parents are doing their best to teach their children how to paddle on their comically-shaped inflatable contraptions—with limited success. There's much splashing, laughing, and tumbling about. My head hurts at the very notion of getting closer to the boisterousness.

"You go on," I say.

Jann's head falls in disappointment. She purses her lips, about to speak, stops herself.

Something inside me sags.

I push it away.

I look again at the water, which now appears a deeper, more enticing blue. The gentle lapping wavelets, with their white frills, offer a tantalizing glimpse of tranquillity, of refreshed perspective. But I hold my ground.

After reapplying sunscreen and sipping one of our diet beverages, she heads out.

I sit back and close my eyes.

———•———

During that conversation with future-me I realized I'd been think-ing about our problem in too limited a fashion. Even if our worlds were separated by forty years, what was stopping us from using *both* of our technologies rather than just mine?

"How far has AI advanced in your time?" I ask future-me. "Give me specifics."

That he does. We deep geek for about twenty minutes, and when we're done I feel the inklings of an answer to our version control challenge.

"Walk me through the schematics of a Feigenbaum AI," I say, "and I promise you you'll start seeing the dividends soon."

A pause. Has my ambition scared him off? Maybe he's not looking for this kind of intensity, for this level of committed entanglement. More than once I've pictured my own retirement as a placid affair with little pressure or responsibility, a time to enjoy the fruits of youth's labour. But after having come to know future-me, I realized this fantasy was foolish. Who we are, and the world we inhabit, always become more complex, never less so. Having now studied both sides of the equation, I'm convinced our labours never end but merely adapt themselves to our ebbing abilities.

To my relief, he breaks the mental silence. "I think I see where you're going. Like Wordsworth said all along: the Child is Father of the man. Engrams," he guesses.

"Yes," I say. "Every memory and sense perception your brain stores. Your AI codifies the data and then you shunt it via neural interface to me. Then I pass it on to an AI on my side, and presto. If there are any patterns, we'll find them."

"You might get overloaded," he says.

"We can limit the transfers to once a day," I propose. "We'll do it while I sleep. That way my brain will have more bandwidth to assim-ilate whatever you send. And if it becomes too much, we'll stop and come up with a new plan."

Another pause, thankfully more short-lived. "You're signing up for some weird dreams, my friend," future-me says.

"No stranger than your rearranging memories," I counter.

"Who says that dreams aren't just another type of memory?" he replies.

It's not the first time he indulges in an attempt at poetry, and as usual it leaves me cold. I chalk it up to the eccentricities of old age: floaty thoughts, less efficient neurons, and so on.

"One more thing," he says. "What are we going to call the system?"

"Hmm. I suppose Version Control is a little on-the-nose?"

"Dreams are . . ." He drifts off, then completes the thought: ". . . like mercury."

Somehow, this makes perfect sense to me. "That's it," I say. "Our AIs will be Quicksilvers."

"I like it," he replies. "But I've got a thing for Latin. How about Hydrargyros?"

"Now I've got a headache too," Jann says upon returning from her swim. "Too much sun."

"I'm so sorry, babe," I say. "I think we have medicine." I lean forward and start rummaging in our bag, but she holds up her hand.

"I'm a little dehydrated, that's all. I'm going to go back to the room and take a nap. I'll be fine."

"Oh," I say, abandoning my clumsy effort to find the medicine. I sit back, unsure what to do to offer further consolation. "Is there anything I can—"

"I've got it," she says, and smoothly swoops up the room key.

I picture myself sitting here during the next hour, maybe the next two, surrounded by these loud children, cowering in our artificial island of shade, which offers only a partial reprieve from the castigating heat. The ice in our cooler is half-melted, and I lack the concentration to read. My forehead feels sickly warm to the touch. I could use some quiet time too.

"I think I'll join you," I say. "This is probably enough beach for the first day."

She grimaces. "I'd like the room to myself if you don't mind."

This I didn't expect. "Uh?"

"You snore," Jann says. The laugh that follows is humourless.

"I won't sleep," I say. "I promise," I add, frustrating myself by offering a level of commitment I think is unreasonably conciliatory.

"But I want to come back here in a bit, and we'll lose our spot," she counters.

"Okay, fine." I settle into the chair, entrenching myself and making it harder for her to bend down and kiss me, which proves a futile gesture on my part because she makes no such attempt.

"I'll be here," I say as she ambles away.

As soon as she's gone, I revisit forecasts for the day. Despite my hewing as close as possible to my optimized actions, everything seems to be going wrong, possibilities wilting before my eyes. I wish I could contact future-me. Even a little guidance could help. What is Hydrargyros missing, I wonder? Given the sensitivity of its models, even a trickle of new data could send me off in a completely new direction. If I could reach future-me, maybe we could arrange for an emergency download.

I try to redirect my frustration regarding today's skewedness toward positive action. My options are limited, but not zero. When Jann comes back, I'll ask her to return the favour and hold down the fort while I make up some reason to step away. Then I'll drive inland several kilometres and hope to escape the sea's interference. I start anticipating each step, calculating how long it'll take to re-adjust our plans and start having a better trip.

After about an hour I text Jann, but there's no response. Half an hour later I try again. Should I call her? No, I think. She's just asleep, recovering from jetlag. She clearly had a hard time nodding off last night, possibly due to my snoring. But how long am I expected to wait here? I could pack up our stuff and return to the *parador*, but it's a bit much for one person to carry, and she'll probably be upset that I lost our spot, and won't appreciate being woken up.

No. There's a better alternative. I perform a quick inventory of our belongings and decide, once I fish out a couple of high-tech items, that there's nothing so valuable it can't stay unsupervised for an hour or so.

Amped up by a sense of urgency commingled with purpose, I half-jog to the car. There's no traffic at all, and in record time I'm ten kilometres away from the coast. Engaging manual override I pull off the side of the A-7053 and temporarily activate the car's diagnostic mode, which automatically triggers privacy nets and will buy me enough time for my needs. Windows polarizing, I initiate my neural interface's encrypted contact protocol and wait for an answer.

Nothing.

I try again.

Nada de nada.

Again.

No sirree.

And then, just as I'm about to give up, a faint response. The message is garbled but not beyond my ability to decipher: *Need—closer—*

I cancel diagnostic mode and manually drive another ten kilometres inland, reaching Cerro la Esparta, in Mijas.

Our connection is much better now, not as seamlessly intimate as I'm used to, but miraculously stronger than I had a right to expect this close to the sea.

I decide to skip all pleasantries. "This trip is all screwed up," I say.

"You're on sabbatical in the south of Spain with Jann," future-me replies. "How bad could it be?"

"Remember that petty bickering you mentioned back when you were applying for associate professorship?"

"I see," he says. "Probably just travel grouchiness. Give it another day or so."

"No, no," I say, perplexed at his lack of understanding. "You're not hearing me. I'm doing the right things, but nothing's working out the way it should." The connection goes dead for a time. "You still there?"

"I'm here," comes the reply, tepid, measured.

"What's the deal?" I ask.

"I know my timing isn't good," he says. "But it's never going to be ideal, so I may as well lay it on the line now. I've got bad news. I'm pulling out."

This again? It's been about ten months since the last time future-me intimated he was dissatisfied with our arrangement. He goes through this periodically, a restlessness that makes him reconsider all of his life choices, including his partnership with me. God, when I get to his age I hope I remember this and can stop myself from having a midlife crisis every year. At any rate, I remind myself not to take it personally, and to focus on the quantifiable.

Hydrargyros solved our fundamental conundrum. We have measurable proof now of the improvements in both our lives; that's unshifting ground, to which I cling on this occasion as I have during each of his previous crises of faith. "What could possibly be the problem?" I challenge.

"Nothing to do with you," he says. "You're doing a good job, kid. Better than I would have. I mean, better than I did."

"Then why are you talking about quitting on me?" I insist. "On *us*?"

I listen hard. His next words, bullet-like, arrive silvered with melancholy. "An end is approaching. It's simply best to quit while we're ahead."

I dial up the car's AC, before remembering that it fritzed out on us yesterday. I hold my palm up to my head and rest it there for a moment.

"*You're* deciding that?" I say. "Right now?"

"If it's any consolation," he says, "please know that I've thought it through."

"What would provide some actual fucking consolation would be to know *why* your holiness is bailing."

Energy shifts on the other end of our bond. I don't know how I know this, but I do. Barometric pressures of the soul building, a vortex inside swirling black clouds. I'm simultaneously pulled in and pushed out. I lower the car's windows, afraid my ears are going to pop and my brain melt. I breathe. I count the times we've been here before, on the edge of this precipice, and remind myself that even when it feels hopeless, there's always a way back to safety. The mental storm activity channeled in from the future begins to dissipate. I should be reassured, or at least appeased, by the downshift. And yet I'm not, for the fading storm system is not replaced by the familiar presence of future-me. He's still there, yes, but he's attenuated somehow. We are separated by something more than time now.

"Have you ever considered the possibility," he says softly, "that I may have been feeding you lies all this time? Maybe I'm not you from the future. Or maybe I am, but it's from some other world, some other timeline. I could have made everything up, kid, amused myself by having you lap up absurd fantasies."

Away from the cliff, I tell myself. Turn around. The voice inside my head is hoarse, cracked in all the worse ways. "I trust you," I say, "because I trust myself."

"I think if that was true," he says, "you'd have no use for me."

And that's when I know I've been shoved over the edge and am plunging down. I feel like the fall may last a lifetime. "You can't—" I begin.

"I have to," he says. "This is going to be your last download from me. I hope things work out for you. I really do. Goodbye, kid."

Before I have the chance to respond, the link snaps. I have a hundred things I want to think across time to him and can't. Before I'm able to consider the implications of my loss, Hydrargyros kicks in with future-me's latest data. I lose all sense of time during the transfer, and yet I know when it has ended. I feel completely voided, achingly emptied of myself. This is it. Whatever sympathetic resonance joined us, it's vanished. He's truly gone now.

Inaccessible—

Forever.

I sit in silence. In time the car alerts me that the diagnostic is complete. I dismiss the results with a limp flick of the wrist and notice my mouth is hanging open. I touch my lips, which I discover are parched.

The car's privacy screens deactivate, and I'm once more reachable to the world at large. Messages, held until now, spitfire at me. They're all from Jann. Concern first, then vexation, then deeper concern, then the sort of stoic resignation that can cloak something disastrous. Shit. Have I really been gone two hours? I dictate a quick reply telling her I'll be back shortly and programme the car accordingly.

By the time I make it back to our beach umbrella, now mocked by the sunset, the core of my body has pretzeled itself into an impossible geometry. I've become an impostor of myself. My legs feel disconcertingly light and thin, like stalks; my steps seem to hardly leave an impression on the afternoon-kilned sand.

"I'm so sorry," I say, plopping myself down next to the folding chair currently occupied by Jann.

I observe her features. A faraway gaze reassembles her face into a stranger's.

"Let's pack up," she says.

"Um. Okay."

Her movements are quick and efficient. Minutes later, she marches toward the hotel without a backwards glance, and despite her greater load I struggle to keep up. By the time we reach the main street, I'm at least ten feet behind. When we reach the room, she unpacks methodically and steps into the bathroom.

"Aren't we going to talk about this?" I say.

"You apologized already," she says. The shower begins to run.

"Right," I say. "But you didn't accept my apology. And you're not curious to know what happened?"

Moving in and out of the bathroom as she performs various tasks, she chuckles. "So this is somehow my failing, right? I'm the deficient one here. Let's see: lacks inquisitiveness. I'll add it to the list."

"Seriously. Come on. All I'm saying is, let's talk for a minute and clear the air."

Now she stops, studies me from the lip of the door. "It would take a lot longer than a minute to clear the air."

"However long it takes, then."

"You really want to do this now?"

"Yeah," I say. "I *am* sorry."

She dips into the bathroom, turns off the water, and remerges with a certain tightness in her frame, as though her centre of gravity has been displaced to some realm beyond my ability to experience. She sits on the edge of the bed, her back ramrod straight. "What are you apologizing for?"

"You told me to look after our stuff, and instead I took off and didn't answer your messages for hours."

She smiles. "You can do better than that."

Desperate, I tap into the final download from future-me. It offers nothing useful—I'm way too far off course for any of its data to be applicable. So I delete it all and brace myself. "What do you mean?"

"Awww," she croons. "Really?"

"Really what?"

She sighs, then nods. "Fine, fine. This is not the first time you've behaved this way. It's been going on for months. Actually, now that I think back—" She squints—"it's been years. I told myself I was being paranoid. That I had trust issues, which I did. But I've done the work and things haven't improved. I've gone along with it far too long. Not anymore. Not anymore."

"Gone along with what? What are you talking about exactly?"

"Do you think that by forcing me to spell it out you're somehow going to gain the upper hand?"

"Let me get this straight," I say, and now I find myself pacing. The room is far too hot, and sand sticks in between my toes even though I've already cleaned my feet twice. "You're saying I'm having an affair."

"And the prize goes to the brilliant mathematician with the mistress," she says.

"I swear to you," I say, voice deepening. "I haven't been with anyone but you since the day we met."

She snorts. "That's a convenient way of redefining terms so that you don't actually have to admit culpability. I never said you were *sleeping* with someone. I don't know if you're talking to a gal or a guy. Honestly, I don't care. Your focus and your heart aren't in this relationship—*that's* what matters. You're not here, with *me*. And I'm not doing it anymore."

I look at Jann. Her head tilts down, and I want to close the distance between us and hold her. I want to stroke her hair, cup her face in mine and kiss her. I want so many impossible things.

Most impossible of all, and most fervently desired, I wish I had data, concreteness, precision, specificity. I want to talk to myself. I don't even care what future-me says. The inaudible sound of my mind reaching back through time would be enough to soothe me, to steer me, to provide hope.

Old people, future-me once told me, are simply regular people who happen to be old. At this most inappropriate moment, I marvel at the wisdom of that declaration.

"If I tried to explain, Jann, you wouldn't believe—" I begin.

"You're right," she interjects. "And it would be silly of you to expect me to. So let's skip it."

Other words from remembered conversations with a me who doesn't yet exist drift into my consciousness, as though underlining Jann's worst fears about me. Though I don't read much fiction, future-me will apparently fall in love with the classics when he enters his sixties. He once remarked to me that the bildungsroman should be supplanted with the *reifungsroman*—the novel of "ripening." That's where life takes us these days, he said, if we're lucky. Is this what luck looks like? Is this maturation?

I say something to Jann, largely because the silence is unbearable, and she replies, and we continue expending words without advancing meaning. I sense myself detach. I'm watching an actor, now, putting on some kitchen-sink melodrama. It's not a bad performance at first, though admittedly a little stiff, but it soon teeters over into histrionics. The female lead maintains a more disciplined approach, projecting a sense of injured pride precisely by dint of the emotions she chooses not to reveal. The actors proceed to delve into several meaty pages of dialogue. They visibly enjoy each fresh salvo of delicately chosen words of injury, but truly what they relish are the implied, rather than the explicit, accusations. Eventually, though, both actors grow weary of the script, and of the kind of shadowy sordidness that seems to have swamped the production—where is the director? Is there no one at the helm?—and finally they retreat into obdurate silence. The woman, after a sorrowful glance at the man she once loved, leaves the room. The man lies down on the bed, his eyes open, his hands still, barely moving through the night. He is transfixed by something the audience will never understand. When she returns, during the pre-dawn, only curt gestures and logistical words are exchanged. The vacation has come to an end. Everything is finished. Many struggles lie ahead, and terrible darknesses. The bedraggled actors contend also with a different, megalithic truth: they who never created life have on this night and day co-authored a spectacularly bathetic death, one from whose grip they will never be free.

—·—

On the return flight to Toronto, Jann and I soar over the Atlantic, the last time we will travel anywhere together. I feel forsaken not only by future-me, but also by past-me. I become immaterial and exist nowhere, suspended between water and sky, between who I was and who I'll never be.

There is something truly sad about the idea that I couldn't keep myself interested even in me.

Or is *this* what I wanted all along?

———•———

On the appointed day, I take the time to make myself an elaborate breakfast involving steel cut oats with cinnamon pears, and coconut and cardamom filled crepes. I savour each bite of this impromptu feast, making it last as long as possible.

Then I enter my self-driving car and observe the late September chestnut foliage on the twenty-minute drive. I reflect on cycles of death and renewal. Maybe, I ponder as I enter the medical centre's parking structure, I had it wrong. Maybe I misjudged future-me. Perhaps he didn't cut me off voluntarily, but was diagnosed with an incurable illness, and wanted to spare us both a hopeless, agonizingly disintegrating relationship. Best to quit while we're ahead, isn't that what he said?

Parking near Dr. Linares' office is easy, perhaps more easy than I'd like. I'm almost an hour early for my appointment, and at last, now that I'm here, the situation begins to sink in, weighing me down. My lingering in the car is not so much a conscious decision as an autonomic response to my sudden feeling of extreme inertia. The parking lot looks exactly the same as it did two weeks ago, when I came in for my forty-year exam, and yet I'm the one who's different, completely out of sorts.

Keep it together, I urge. Instinctively I reach toward my pocket for an anti-anxiety pill, but it's been a month since I maxed out the prescription, and my fingers find nothing but lint. *The fact that the doctor scheduled an appointment to review your results doesn't necessarily mean something bad*, I tell myself. But it's difficult to take myself seriously.

Walking with monotone numbness, I make it to the front entrance, enter the elevator that will usher me to the medical office, and take a deep breath.

Again operating from habit, I seek the companionship of Hydrargyros on the ride up. Again I come up empty-handed. It's been a week since I bid my even-keeled companion farewell.

I greet the receptionist, who asks me to repeat my name because I mumble it the first time. With a critical gaze, she checks me in and advises me I'll be called shortly.

I sit and wait.

Memories of previous visits to this office are unavoidable. Except for the most recent one, they all include Jann. Dear, dear Jann. My now ex-wife. It's been six months since the divorce was finalized. Does this deserve a commemoration of some kind, I wonder? Does a divorce warrant an anniversary?

Our separation was almost immediate upon returning home. I made several attempts at reparations, promising that the source of my distraction had been dealt with, but—wily Jann, observant Jann—she sensed I was lying and dutifully rejected my overtures. She was right, but not in the way she thought. It wasn't future-me, that time, that had been consuming my energy, but present-me's obsession with understanding how it all went wrong. I think back to—

My name is called out over the intercom.

I shuffle into Dr. Linares' office.

"How are we today?" she says, looking up from the touchscreen on her desk.

"Huh. Not bad."

"Please, sit."

I do so.

"Thank you for making the time to see me," she says. Her expression is friendly, calm—studied?

As though I really had a choice, I don't say. "Of course."

"Before we proceed to review your results, I'd like to ask you a few questions that'll give me a better context for the data."

"Uh," I say. "Okay. Sure."

"Would it be fair to say that you've experienced several stress-inducing events over the last six months?"

My more morbid side wonders if this is the equivalent of physician's humour. "You could say that," I reply.

Prompted by the doctor's question, the last half year plays out before me with startling clarity. Obsessive day after obsessive day, compulsive week after compulsive week, I directed Hydrargyros to analyze the problem of *why* my system had broken down, and all the while the rest of my life fell into disrepair: my remissness at the University provoked my dismissal, the divorce papers came in, I took to drink and medication, ghosted on the few remaining friends who reached out to offer moral support, defaulted on my mortgage, and had to move into a small apartment. None of it mattered. I just wanted an explanation. Hydrargyros and I segmented my life into chapters using clustering algorithms, ran every manner of stochastic retro-predictive analyses, parsed countless causal chains. And at last, on a crisp fall day in the late afternoon, with the pent-up sugar in the sap of the maple trees in my new neighbourhood causing their leaves to blaze auburn-red with the declining sun, at last, we arrived at an answer.

Of course.

So obvious, in hindsight.

The false assumption of personality matrix cohesion.

In other words, I *changed*.

Each decision I had made based on foreknowledge of how things were to turn out altered me, shaped me into a different person, so the way I responded to circumstances *itself* changed. A vast model of non-linear concatenations centred around an endlessly self-refracting variable—me.

It was bound to collapse.

"And how would you say you've coped?" Dr. Linares says, bringing me back to the present. She leans forward.

Once I possessed the knowledge I'd sought, I had expected to find relief, liberation. Instead, I'd felt barren, completely bereft of closure, thoroughly un-enlightened.

"For a while, it was a bit of a struggle." I recline back in my chair.

She nods. "Your insurance benefits include counselling, if that's something you'd like to explore."

Counselling. I close my eyes, wondering if this is the fate that befell future-me. Did he succumb to despair? An end is approaching, he said. A voluntary end, perhaps? "I appreciate the offer," I say vaguely.

And then unexpectedly her face relaxes and her eyes smile. An invisible wall has come down. "I can see something is bothering you," she says. "Try to take a deep breath and let it out. I'm here to help, if only you'll let me."

I hear warmth in those words, genuine caring. I want to tell her of my fears, of my sense of being marooned. But how can I explain to someone who's never had the advantage of future knowledge? "I . . ." I lose myself, thinking about future-me, somewhere up there in the timeline, always knowing more than I do, always several steps ahead.

"It's okay," she reassures. "Just being here in the moment with me is enough for now. You don't have to speak if you don't wish."

Those words do something to me. A part of me still wonders about the news that she's leading me toward, the prognosis we're building up to, but my mood is curiously altered. I pass from anxiety to genuine calm. Naturally, I'm skeptical at first, since someone in my situation might well rollercoaster from glumness to elation and back again, but something about this feels different—like it's a new type of happiness that's here to stay. With every part of my being, I want it to stick. I believe it will.

And then it dawns on me.

I'm thinking about *my* future now, rather than being preoccupied with future-me.

He doesn't matter. He never did. Future-me is beyond my reach—and in the most important sense, even when I could talk to him, always was.

"Good," Dr. Linares says, as though sensing the shift in my demeanour. "Are you ready to review your results?"

This moment, this present, is all I have to work with.

I decide it's enough, and so it is.

Let the work begin.

"Yes," I say.

———— ☀ ☀ ☀ ————

Author's Notes to My Younger Self: Control won't pre-empt regrets, so relax, and use that energy to forge deeper connections with those around you. Make yourself vulnerable. Do your best to be worthy of the love in your life always, rather than taking it for granted. Remember: panta rei. Therefore: amor fati.

THE SELKIE'S SKIN

Bev Geddes

I was with friends the day it began. We had come ashore on a sandy stretch of beach protected by a headland of jutting rocks. Waves broke wildly against them, sending flumes of water skyward. No human came to this beach for there were few limpets to collect for bait and the tide was strong, not easily navigated by the small coracles the villagers used for fishing.

We dove through emerald waters, laughing as the sun sparkled silver discs across the surface. We shouldn't have come ashore during the day. It was forbidden. Only when night stretched shadows along the sand was it truly safe for us to leave the sea. The villagers were a superstitious lot. They feared the darkness and things that blossomed along with the full moon. That suited us fine. Most days. But today was free of clouds and rain and I longed to feel the sun against my skin. We had lingered on the rocks for hours until the bone-white beach beckoned. It didn't take much to convince my friends to accompany me.

Six of us dragged ourselves out of the water onto that warm shore and shrugged out of our skins. I heard it said once by a villager, when he didn't know I rested just beyond sight, that selkies are fallen angels, forgiven by God, but forever cast out of Heaven. This was foolishness, of course, but such is the belief of those who care only for their own small ways.

We delighted in the warmth of the sun on our naked forms. Human skin is much thinner than seal pelt and the wind tickles soft bellies and sand scrunches beneath toes in the most delightful of ways. We danced in a circle and sang as daylight faded on the horizon, unaware that we had been heard and were no longer alone on that beach.

The first warning something was amiss came from the sky. The gulls, which had been flying high like scraps of cloud, swooped toward the earth and circled above our seal skins piled next to a rock pool on the headland.

Awareness stirred. A scent on the wind. A dark energy. I cried out, sending everyone scrambling for their skins. One by one, they slipped beneath the waves and were gone without a backward glance. I reached the rock last, stumbling through the sand on two legs that wouldn't move as I wanted them to, salt tears sheeting my cheeks.

"No. No. No," I cried.

There was nothing there. My beautiful skin, silver-grey and soft, was gone.

I looked up into the pale blue eyes of a human man. He took in my form hungrily and, for the first time, I covered myself, ashamed of what I was. His judgment hung in the air. So too, did his lust.

He held my selkie skin in one hand.

"Please," I wept, my tongue awkward around human words. "Please, give me back my skin. I can't return home beneath the waves without it. My family is there. Have pity. Give me back my skin."

The man's eyes softened with kindness for a moment, and my heart leapt at the sight, but they quickly clouded over with desire. He turned away and began marching up the beach, his broad shoulders set.

"I will nae give ye back yer skin," he said. "Ye'll come wi' me and be my wife. I'll treat ye kind enough and not abuse ye, but ye'll take on my ways and do as I say." He glanced back at where I stood. "I'll call ye Ailish. 'Twas my wife's name afore she died in childbirth, taking our bairn with her."

The man's eyes darkened and he frowned as though angry with himself for saying so much.

"Tis an honour, and ye'll do well to remember tha'." He strode away from me as though nothing else needed to be said.

I watched his steady progress up the beach and onto the rocks, heading inland. My heart wilted like seaweed on the shore. But the body doesn't always die when the heart is broken and I couldn't return to the sea as I was. I followed, weeping.

The man led me to a small croft nestled between two hills close to the beach. I took in the simple walls made of fieldstone and the ratty thatched roof. A few chickens scratched by the door. I heard the lowing of a nearby cow, but little else, save the chirr of crickets. A thin ribbon of smoke trailed from the chimney pot and light glowed in the windows as night dropped down.

I willed myself forward, legs trembling from the unaccustomed walking, as the man pushed open the front door and waved me through impatiently. I noticed one eye twitching as he did so, and his fingers tightened on the seal skin in his hands. I stumbled through, feeling the pelt brush against my arm as I passed. Tingling. Begging to be donned once more.

"Wha's this, then?"

An old woman dragged herself up from a chair perched close to the hearth, dropping the ladle she had been using to stir whatever was bubbling in the pot above the peat fire.

"Dinna fesh yerself, Mam. 'Tis a selkie lass I found down on the beach jus' now when I was searching for driftwood fer the fence."

The man looked down at his feet and shifted back and forth beneath his mother's black stare.

"And I'm keeping her," he added belligerently.

The old woman narrowed her eyes and stepped forward, drawing the shawl from her shoulders and draping it across mine. "Ye've never had enough sense to lick up a spill, Willy-boy. Ye've taken wha' is nae yours and against her will, if I'm nae mistaking the tears. There'll be hell to pay for it. Give her back her skin and let her return to the sea where she belongs afore she curses ye."

"She's but a lass. There's nowt she can do. I will take her as my wife and you'll teach her to be one of us. She'll forget who she once was, soon enough."

"A lassie doesna forget her soul, William. Ye may take her selkie ways from her, by ye canna touch her soul."

"She's a selkie, old woman. She hasn't a soul."

The woman just stared sadly at me, shaking her head. "That I dunna believe, son," she said. "But ye will have yer way, I ken well enough. I'll teach her what I know, but there is heartbreak here for all, mark my words." And with that, the woman took my hands in her own and led me back behind a curtain to the sleeping area of the tiny croft.

True to her word, the woman taught me to spin and cook and mend. She helped me with the human words that scratched and grated as they left my lips, and how to dress modestly, and to look down rather than gaze directly into the eyes of another. Their ways were not my ways, but I learned.

The man didn't touch me. I'm not sure if the old woman forbade it, but I think that must be so, for early each morning he would leave in a right temper and storm off to spend the days fishing in his boat and the evenings drinking with the men of the village.

Many a curious neighbour came to call, for word spreads quickly in such a place. The old woman sent them off with a curt hand, muttering to herself how this was no good for anyone.

She was strict with me and frowned at my clumsiness. She wouldn't allow me to sing in my own tongue as I battled with the prickly skeins of wool or stirred the watery seaweed soups.

"Ungrateful," she hissed as I pushed away plates of fish cooked until tasteless, so unlike the fresh mouthfuls of juicy raw cod I was used to. I nibbled on a piece of oat cake, not because hunger drove me, but because the woman sat glaring at me until I choked down a few mouthfuls.

Over time, I felt my shoulders bow beneath the demands of donning human ways. All that was light and breezy in me disappeared to a place I could no longer reach. I walked wrong. I spoke oddly. My hands fumbled and my movements were too slow.

But at night, when the moon silvered the surface of the ocean, I slipped out of the croft and away from my snoring captors and crept to the sandy beach. Standing by the shore, I listened to the water purl against the stones and sand and breathed in the salty air. The weight of what I had become lightened and lifted.

I sighed, calling out for my family until sleek heads popped up from beneath the waves, their almond eyes shining in the moonlight.

"Take me with you," I begged in selkie tongue as they swam closer. "Take me home."

Each night, their answer was the same. "Find your skin and we will come for you. It is the only way."

I dropped my head into my hands for, although I had looked endlessly, I couldn't find where it had been hidden.

"There must be another way. For even if I do find my skin, I'm not sure it will fit anymore. A sadness dwells inside me. It prickles and sticks and its roots have pierced my soul. I do not belong here."

My selkie friends would nod sadly and slide beneath the waves.

"Neither, it seems, do I belong with you, my *anam cara.*"

I stood and stumbled away from the ocean, certain I was consigned to walk between the worlds forever and belong nowhere.

On that endless night, I sat with the wind and the stars and gave over to the thought of throwing myself off the headland. Death whispered in my ear. Death's voice was gentle and I believe, even now, that it was simply lonely for the touch of a friendly hand.

What stopped me from following its persuasions, I'm not sure. All I know is a light flickered somewhere deep in my heart, plucking at my resolve. It spoke, faded, then gathered itself and spoke again. It was not my time. Not yet.

I wandered back to the croft in the bruised silence of night and crept behind the curtain onto my cot, pulling the thin blanket over me. And slept.

I awoke early, for there was rain on the roof and a chill wind rattled the window panes and scurried down the chimney, causing the fire to lap in on itself with a muffled roar. The old woman was already up pulling a bannock from the pan. William was nowhere to be seen.

"Up, lazy girl. There's much to be done today and ye've slept long enough."

I rubbed the sleep from my eyes and pulled the shawl around my shoulders, shivering in the damp air.

"Where's William?" I asked, accepting the proffered cup of tea from the woman's blue-veined hands.

The woman glanced back at the fire, her shoulders stiffening. "He's gone to the kirk to talk to the minister." Turning, she glared at me. "To set a date for yer marriage, girl. He says he's waited long enough and he would have ye to wife sooner than later. I've tried, ye ken. Tried to talk him away from this, to send ye back where ye belong, but he will nae have it."

"I cannot," I whispered hoarsely. "I cannot be married."

The old woman nodded. "*They* will nae have it either. Ye'll have ta be baptized first. But they say ye hae no soul. The minister would put his eyes out afore he does such a thing. And if ye canna marry, William will have ye anyways and then both will be properly shunned by the village. I'll nae have that."

She looked down at me, not unkindly I will say, and continued, "Ye'll have ta leave, and quickly. I've made a wee bundle for ye with bannock and the few scraps I can spare. Head south along the coast. Dunna stop for anything and dunna let William catch ye."

"How will I live? What will I do? Can you not give me back my seal skin? I will disappear beneath the waves and never return. I promise."

"I would ifn I could, Ailish, to be done with you and this sorry business. I dunna ken where William has stowed it. He's a stubborn man. Life has made him bitter and mean. I canna ask him. There's nowt to be done. Here." She stuffed a worn-out piece of cloth bulging with provisions at me. "Be gone, so tha' I might have me life back."

I took the bundle and retreated behind the curtain, dressing quickly. I needed time before William returned home and discovered I was gone.

I yanked open the door to the croft and pulled the shawl tight over my head. Rain peppered my feet. I don't know if sending me out into that wild weather softened her heart, but the woman's parting words provided direction in my terror.

"The wise woman from the glen yonder told me that if a lass was to shed seven tears in the ocean at midnight on a full moon, the FinFolk will come from the depths to give aid. I dunna ken if they will help one of yer kind but tonight the moon is ripe. Ye must avoid William 'til then."

I nodded and stepped out into the swirling rain, and made my way toward the ocean and the place where I had first lost myself, unsure how the FinFolk might help when my own kind could not.

The storm blew itself out after soaking me thoroughly, frustrating all attempts by William of finding me in the fog and rain. Finally, the clouds parted and the moon shone brightly in the star-strewn sky.

I let seven tears fall, and waited.

Something began to stir out in the bay, a gentle ripple across the still water, moving toward me. Breath halted in my throat and I dug my fingers into the pebbled sand.

The water erupted where my tears had met the sea and the figure of a man drew upward, fully clothed and dry. His hair was as dark as his eyes. Although he was tall and handsome, his face was solemn. Not one to be trifled with, I feared.

"Who has called me from my home?" His voice sounded like a bell across the water, deep and sonorous, enchanting.

"I have called you, FinMan, to come to my aid. I am in danger. There are those who would harm me."

The FinMan narrowed his eyes, his nostrils flaring as though he was scenting the air around me.

"You are not what you seem," he observed.

"No. I'm a selkie whose pelt has been stolen. I cannot return to the sea."

"How would you have me help you with that?" The FinMan made for land and came to stand towering above me.

I scrambled to my feet, remembering who I once was, and replied, "I cannot stay here on land or I will be destroyed. I cannot find my skin, but I wish to return to the place where I was once whole."

"This is not possible."

"So, I will die."

"You have cried seven tears and the spell is woven. I must help you. But you do not belong beneath the waves anymore. You hold the stench of what you have become. You will drown if I return you to your home."

"What can be done?" I cried.

The FinMan crossed his burly arms and stood a long moment gazing across the ocean as if the waves themselves would lend a solution to the woman who walked between two worlds.

"There is one thing that can be done," he said finally. "You cannot live in the human world. Nor can you live in ours. But there is a place for one such as you." He glanced down at me, sadness gleaming from his thunderous eyes.

"Do you trust me?"

I did not trust him. I trusted no one. All brought harm. Fear sounded deep within me, clattering against my ribs. There was nothing to be done for it. I nodded.

He gestured for me to stand back from the water's edge, drew thick fingers to his lips and gave a piercing whistle. The water on the bay began to boil and kick up spray. A majestic horse-like creature emerged from the depths, black as night, and trotted across the waves toward us.

"A kelpie," I hissed. I had heard of the magical underwater creatures but had never seen one.

The FinMan tousled the kelpie's mane and whispered in its ear. The creature nodded and turned its dark eyes on me.

"He will take you to a place far from here. There is a cave on a small spit of shoreline to keep you warm and dry. Our kind will make sure you never hunger or thirst. Perhaps some of your kind will not fear to come ashore there to keep you company while you live out a mortal life. It is the best I can do."

His hand rested on my shoulder and I knew this was the only way for one such as myself. I would have sanctuary. My heart ached, but there was no choice.

"I agree," I whispered. "It is better than living as I have done."

The FinMan nodded to the kelpie and the great beast knelt before me so I could scramble onto its back. He lifted up over the waves, galloping into the sky until the world of humans faded into shadow. Wind streamed through my hair. I didn't want the flight to end. There is a freedom in the wind that stiffens the sails and turns the boat once more to sea. A heartening. The whisper that, although things have changed, there is still possibility. That was how it felt, high above all that had happened to me.

Finally, the kelpie dropped from the sky and a tiny cove opened up through the shreds of mist and cloud. It slowed, touching down gently on a rock-strewn beach. I clambered from its back, my body trembling and heart thudding wildly. The kelpie nodded to me, then launched upwards into the waiting night. He left behind a silence that echoed louder than any thunder I'd ever heard.

———•———

I learned from my selkie friends that the villagers believed me dead by my own hand; toppled from the cliff in the storm. I had hoped William believed it too and that he might toss my seal skin out over the ocean for my friends to find and return to me. Canny and clever, he did not. Instead, I was told, he took the skin and buried it in St. Olrig's Kirkyard, where he knew I could never go. Tales arose through the years that nothing grew atop that grave, but water puddled along its surface and, on nights when the moon hid its face behind the clouds, the cry of a seal could be heard above the wind, mourning for its missing soul.

I, too, felt the loss.

———•———

There is a hole within me the shape of my selkie skin. I topple into the loneliness of that shape as the days pass. It murmurs to me of what might have been.

I am a patchwork person. Made of bits and pieces retrieved from the wreckage of who I once was. But each day I learn to move with this new skin and find ways to dive through the water. Although I can no longer swim as I once did and must come up for air, the water's freshness slides along my skin and I remember that my life has texture, although rough and rimmed with sadness.

I have chosen my own path. Different from what I imagined. Still mine. My needs have been few; my dreams extend only as far as the water and as high as the cliffs that protect me. The seasons turn, as they must, and my memories fold into themselves.

Time polishes loss, grinding down the sharp edges, binding up the wounds. But always there is a scar. It pulls and pinches when I move just so, or when a scrap of remembrance brushes too close.

My eyes dim now; hands shaking so I cannot bring food or water to my lips. The time has come. I drag myself from my snug cave to the shoreline. The sun traces warm fingers through my hair and salt air sits on my tongue. Above me, the gulls call in a blue, cloudless sky. Such a sight I must be to them, no more than a ragged bundle of bones tossed up on the sand by the tides.

It is enough. A life lived is enough. I have made something of my days, however small.

"I've kept faith. I have held," I tell the misty horizon. "The waiting time is over."

The sea whispers against the land. There is a stillness beneath the sound. As I pull a last breath into my body, I see the loving eyes of the ones lost to me.

"Home. Finally, home."

I smile as a grey pelt velvets my shoulders.

"Be at peace," the sea murmurs.

We return to ourselves in the end.

Author's Notes to My Younger Self: Life breaks you; whittles away cherished dreams, blasts your world apart. Playing by the rules won't prevent loss. And when life roars through, draw yourself up, gather the scattered pieces, and crawl out of that dark place. Search for the light and don't give up. You will return to yourself, made of stardust and steel.

For Colin, Luc, and Matt. Always.

MESSAGES LEFT IN TRANSIT, DEVICES OUT OF SYNC

S.B. Divya

On the day of my husband's launch, I stood in the viewing area with the other families, my hand over the squirmy thing in my abdomen. Thumba Equatorial Rocket Launching Station sprawled near Thiruvananthapuram, the capital city of Kerala. Lazy blue water meandered behind us. Rich green foliage contrasted with the brilliant white of cement and deep azure of the sky. Fans whirred from the awning above, stirring the warm, humid air and the scents of humanity. They did little to stop the sweat beading all over my body.

Would the baby feel the earth-shaking rocket? Would this moment embed into their subconscious somehow, leading to a life of . . . *I don't know* . . . a reckless pursuit of adrenaline-fueled sports? Every decision felt more fraught as I entered my third trimester of pregnancy. Envy, pride, and tension warred as the rocket carrying the lunar base's second crew soared into the great beyond.

I didn't want to give birth to our first child while my husband went to the moon. Not only would he miss the delivery, but he wouldn't get to hold the baby for months. A newborn is an amazing feeling—the warmth, the fragility, the scent. I experienced it with my sister's first child, and nothing can compare. But he had history to make. Important work to do. A mission to accomplish.

My mother's hand clutched mine. My in-laws stood behind us. They'd been so happy when I got pregnant.

"Mangal's father was absent when he was born," my mother-in-law said, after the noise faded. She winked. "We don't really need the men at that time."

I held back my objections: that India had changed in the intervening decades; that men were expected to participate in raising their children *from birth*. I did my best to balance being a good daughter-in-law with my natural ambitions. It got easier after the Indian Space Research Organization disqualified me from the astronaut programme. Mangal and I had met during ISRO's interview process. We thought we'd be the first couple in space.

———•———

We received the news on the same day: Mangal's acceptance and my rejection. His expression kept oscillating from elation to apology and back again.

I straightened my shoulders, cupped his face, and looked deep into his eyes. "I'm so proud and happy for you. Truly," I said and meant it.

"You can apply again in a year or two," he said. "You're just as qualified as I am."

We both had flight time from our air force days. We had advanced degrees. My eyesight was better than his. But I would never be an astronaut.

"It's my blood work," I said, forcing a detached calm. "Low hemoglobin counts." Of all the stupid things that could disqualify me, it seemed like the least important.

His shoulders drooped long enough to look genuinely sad, but then the excitement of his success overwhelmed it.

"Let's go celebrate," I said, so I could drown my sorrows while toasting his happiness.

———•———

I put my mechanical engineering degree to good use after that. The Chandra project needed skills like mine, and it allowed me to live in Thiruvananthapuram with my husband. The Vikram Sarabhai Space Centre—VSSC—had grown since its inception, now rivaling those of the US, Russia, and China. If I couldn't train as an astronaut, at least I could participate in space exploration from the ground. And much to the joy of our parents, it also meant that we could start a family sooner.

We tried for two years, but in this too, I was disappointed. The doctors recommended IVF, but then ISRO selected Mangal for the Lunar Research Programme. It seemed prudent to wait until after his mission to conceive. I should have switched back to birth control then, but the professionals said we'd need help. I didn't expect it to happen naturally.

We'd intended to walk hand-in-hand on the moon. Instead, he'd be analyzing lunar soil while I completed the most ordinary miracle of all—bringing new life into the world.

———·———

"Priyanka, record a message," I said into my phone.

Hi, it's me. Bedrest is torture. You know how terrible I am at sitting still? They won't even let me do basic housework. Here I am, dealing with back pain and bleeding and boredom while you get to play in lunar gravity. I can't even have wine to go with my whine.

Amma has taken a month's leave from her job to help me. Two more weeks and they'll let me up, and then the baby can come any time.

I've been sorting through our pictures. I'm making an album of Life-Before-Baby, the years we've had to ourselves. I've put in photos from our wedding and honeymoon, and I'm thinking of making it a scrapbook—pasting in the receipt from our car, your acceptance letter, things like that. What do you think?

I've told you how proud I am that you're an astronaut, right? And now you're on the Moon! I miss you.

Maybe I should include my job offer letter in the album. Something I can be proud of for myself. God knows I've tried to hide my disappointment—

I stopped, breathed, and leaned my head back.

"Priyanka, don't send. Save draft message to my journal, locked to private."

———·———

The RCEMP, or Remote Control Electro-Mechanical Person, was my first baby. No matter how much we streamlined spacesuits, they remained awkward and risky, but human beings have to interact with their environment to understand it. The subconscious wants all five senses engaged. We needed a way to let our astronauts explore the moon and keep themselves safe at the same time. The RCEMP was our solution.

One unit went to the lunar base, but like any device sent to space, we had a replica on Earth to help with troubleshooting. A week after the launch, my doctor put me on bedrest. I did what I could from home, but I had to see the machine, to feel it under my hands for my best work to happen. No amount of pleading would budge the doctor's opinion.

Before my mechanical baby took its first steps on lunar soil, I snuck out to mission control so I could cheer along with everyone else. I kept out of sight of the cameras. Our project manager personally took me home afterwards. It was worth every minute of risk.

———•———

When I went into labour, my mother stood by my side, pressed wash-cloths onto my forehead, and massaged my aching back and hips. Mangal could only watch from afar.

"I feel so useless," he said via video-link. "Are you okay? Is the baby okay?"

"Hah, now you know how I've felt the last few weeks," I crowed. And then gasped as the muscles beneath my navel tightened.

We had asked the doctor not to tell us the baby's sex.

"I want to name them Chandra," I'd said before Mangal left.

He'd laughed. "Come on, isn't that too obvious?"

"It's the project that brought us together. Plus, it will work regardless of the baby's gender."

After a few attempts at terrible name ideas, he'd capitulated to my cleverness and agreed.

As I breathed through the contractions, he fretted.

"Kavitha is doing well," my mother reassured him. She wiped my forehead. "Chandra will be okay, too."

People tell you all kinds of things about babies, but they rarely disclose the indignities of labour and its consequences. Only after you've experienced it are you allowed into those conversations, though by then it's often too little, too late.

I held Chandra in my arms as my mother brought the camera in for a close-up.

Mangal blotted tears from his eyes. "You're amazing."

"So are you," I choked out.

"I wish I could be there right now."

Exhausted and crashing from hormones, I would've traded places with him in a heartbeat. Chandra was gorgeous, but millions of people gave birth to babies every day. How many have stood on the moon?

———•———

Will I ever forgive you for missing the birth of our child?

Yes, of course I will. I'm not that much of a hypocrite, to wish I could trade places with you in one minute and hate you for your achievements in the next. But damn you for skipping the worst of it. The soreness. The uncontrollable crying jags. The messes—mine and the baby's.

Maybe you'll be around for the next one, if that happens, but there's nothing like the first time. When she opens her brilliant eyes or grasps my thumb with her mighty little hand, I go dizzy with wonder. You're missing all of that, too.

———•———

I watched Sahana Agarwal's space news channel on the hospital's TV. She showed a clip of the RCEMP in action, side-by-side with footage from inside the lunar base. She explained that the unit had a shape and size similar to an average human and a lunar weight between that of an average male and female on Earth. It provided three sensory modalities: sight, sound, and touch.

My contribution had improved the third—a novel material with a large dynamic range that could sense pressure differentials from fine textures to bulk weight. She didn't mention that technical detail.

Mangal piloted the unit. A virtual reality helmet covered his head. A special suit wrapped his body almost like an EVA suit, and an omnidirectional treadmill moved beneath his feet. On the split screen, when he knelt, the unit knelt. When he grasped at an invisible pebble and lifted it gently, the RCEMP picked up the real object from the moon's regolith.

If I had become an astronaut, would the unit have had that feature? Could some other engineer have made the same breakthrough? *Yes, of course. What hubris to think I'm that special.* Dozens of people helped to build the RCEMP. Only a handful would operate it on the Moon.

———•———

The moment I entered our flat with a baby, everything seemed so strange, like my life had splintered in two and I was me but also someone entirely new. Where would I put Chandra when I wanted to sit in my favourite chair? What if I dropped her on our hard tile floor? Could I watch TV with her nearby, or would she become addicted to the screen as an infant?

When my mother left for her job the next day, I felt more alone than ever in my life. I needed someone to experience this new parental feeling with me. I needed my husband, and I couldn't even call him.

People at ISRO were sympathetic to our situation, but our new baby couldn't overrule the limited communications channel between the lunar research base and Earth. Having a live feed during the birth had been a massive concession.

I dictated more messages, long-winded and rambling, while the baby slept on my lap. In those raw thoughts of lonely moments were words I would say to Mangal's face. I kept those locked away in my private journal, a safety deposit box of bile I needed to expel, and transmitted only partial, positive truths across the void of space.

During our allotted five minutes of video chat, Mangal gazed at Chandra with soft eyes and said, "I wish I could hold her."

I inhaled near Chandra's head. "I wish you could smell her, too. She is so warm and delicious."

On my lap, Chandra smacked her tiny lips and sighed. She warmed me, the weight of her enough to be soothing but not uncomfortable. I stroked her cheek, and an idea penetrated my sleep-deprived brain fog.

"You can," I said, thinking and nodding. "You can hold her."

His eyes lit as he understood. "The delay—"

"It's less than three seconds roundtrip. We can make it work as long as ISRO allows us to use the RCEMP."

———·———

Three days later, while Chandra napped, I bathed, donned a brand new sari, and carefully placed a red bindi between my brows.

The tech crew arrived from VSSC in the late afternoon. They moved the sofa behind the swing and the armchairs to the balcony to clear space in the centre of our hall, but that's because our flat was so small, not because the RCEMP was bulky. It was an identical model to the one on the lunar base. I helped the crew connect it to the power and internet and then ran the systems check.

Sahana Agarwal stood discreetly in a corner of the room to film the whole thing. Her hair fell in perfect waves, and her makeup and clothes were as fashionable as my sari wasn't. The publicity aspect was the only reason VSSC allowed this to happen. At first, they asked me to come into the facility, but Public Relations thought the optics were better from a house, so there we all were, crammed into this tiny space as Mangal's face appeared on the TV screen.

"My brilliant wife," he said with a big grin. "Are you ready?"

I nodded and bounced Chandra in my arms. She'd started to fuss. It was silly, but I wanted her to make a good first impression on the world. Or maybe I wanted the world to judge me as a good mother.

On the monitor, Mangal disappeared under the VR helmet.

A second and a quarter later, the time it took for the signal to reach the earth, the arms of the RCEMP bent at the elbows. I walked over to it and placed Chandra in its arms, keeping mine underneath just in case. How foolish that I didn't trust my own work.

"Do you feel her?" I asked.

Three seconds later, he replied, "Yes," in a husky voice. "I have her."

I held my breath and released our baby into his arms.

The RCEMP cradled Chandra and rocked her back and forth while Mangal, on the screen, completed the same motion on nothing but air. Unlike their interaction on the moon, he and this RCEMP didn't move synchronously, but the physics of a few seconds delay wouldn't matter if we were careful. The unit adjusted one arm to support Chandra's entire body and head. The other arm moved, and its fingertips stroked her dark curls.

Chandra stared up at the RCEMP's "face," which had the same shape and size as the helmet. She blinked, sighed, and then closed her eyes. You could have heard a pin drop in the hush of the room.

"She's so small," he marvelled. "And warm, too."

I hadn't realized the RCEMP temperature feedback was enabled. It wasn't a necessary feature for this mission. I bit my lower lip as my heart beat faster, and then I gave in to the urge and wrapped my arms around Mangal and our child, cameras be damned.

"I love you both so very much," he said, his voice breaking on the last word.

"You must feel wonderful to make space history like this," Sahana said softly from her corner.

On the screen, Mangal nodded, and seconds later, the unit nodded.

"You too, Doctor Varma," the reporter said.

I looked back at her, startled. Nobody had called me that since my post-graduate teaching days. A small smile curved the reporter's lips.

———◆———

The whole world celebrates your accomplishments, but they don't know the names of those who made your journey possible. Hundreds of engineers designed and built your vehicles. Physicists plotted your course. Chemists gave your rocket the power to escape Earth. Doctors made sure you stayed healthy during a three month stint on the moon.

They didn't know the name of the person who kept you safe while a facsimile explored craters. The person who loves you, who's gazing at an adorable and lovely child sleeping on her lap.

They didn't, but now they do.

It wasn't your fault, their not knowing. Nor was my resentment, mostly, but I forgive you anyway. My feet may never leave the Earth, but tonight, I feel lighter than air.

Author's Notes to My Younger Self: Persistence is more important than perfection, and if you stick with something long enough, you will improve at it.

JOE

Vanessa Cardui

The details of my parents' lives are not well documented,
But eight boys and one baby girl were born and soon lamented.
But ten was more tenacious, and once born, refused to die,
So Mátyás József Farkas lived, and that boy who lived was I.

I made it.

I'm not sure that they wanted me, and I didn't know them long,
I was on my own when our little home began crackling with bombs.
I packed a bag, I locked the house, I gave away the key,
And I crossed into my parents' homeland as a refugee.

I made it . . . but I didn't stay long.
I made it . . . but I was only fifteen,
And no help on a farm or in a restaurant.
But I did find work that would take me far,
And keep me busy to the end of the war,
Helping out the German army with their horses and their carts.

My clothes got tight and I saw I'd grown,
I was given some black garb in place of my own,
The war ended in May, I was on my way, I had *made it!*
Now I'd never really been a patient kid,
Which should partly explain the next thing that I did:
I started home without getting rid
Of my black and damning clothes,
And they scooped me up with their other fallen foes.

It was a two-week march,
They only fed us once,
One loaf of bread, and some meat that I ate half raw.
You could get shot if you took too long to shit,
And we drank from the ditch,
The same water that soaked the corpses of men like me.

Men just like me.

Three months in camp was a little like life,
I met the father of my future wife,
We needed a chess set, so I found a knife, and I made it.
I kept the knife and I didn't get caught,
I didn't get sick, and I didn't get shot,
I guess some are lucky and some are not, but I made it.

I made it!
I made it!
They let us go, and I went where they spoke my tongue.
And I did what a good man does:
I supported a wife and kids,
And for once, my life became about more than just me.

No, not just me.

The fall of 1956 was turbulence and fear,
The slaughter in our streets needs no elaboration here.
Our muddy trek to freedom was the hardest of my life,
I made it only goaded by my strong, beloved wife.

There was one moment when we might have died,
The machine gun sprayed when our baby cried,
And we bit the mud, and if they'd really tried,
Then there would be no song.
Some thieves took a chance then to rob us blind,
We were crossing a border, they crossed a line,
But we crossed in time, and when I read a sign in German . . .

I knew we'd *made it!*
We made it!
My children and my grandchildren are Canucks.

'Cause I chose not to live in fear,
And had some amazing luck.
(And in all my life, I never buried one kid.
They all survived, like none of my siblings did.)

Kedves nagypapa, I hope you don't mind,
I told your story as though it was mine,
It might have been wrong that I made this song, but I made it.
You brought us here, and some of us died,
But a dozen of us are still alive,
A dozen descendants with shining lives, we made it!

We made it!
We made it!
Your love and courage pulled us from the abyss.
And I thank you, for all of this,
The opportunity to exist.
I'll remember you and honour all that you did.
The loving man I knew when I was a kid.

⁂

Author's Notes: Joe was my grandfather. When he was dying of cancer, he wrote an autobiography for the benefit of his children and grandchildren. He escaped death in Europe many times before coming to Canada, and in his book, whenever he survived a dangerous situation, he wrote "I MADE IT!" in bold capital letters. When I first read it in 2018, more than 25 years after his death, those words exploded in my mind as a cry of triumph and became the chorus to this song. I wrote it to honour him, and my grandmother, and all of the parents and grandparents who have fled their homelands to make a better life for their children.

Editors' Notes: This song had its world premiere during the Calgary book launch of *Shades Within Us: Tales of Migrations and Fractured Borders.* How appropriate it is also for this anthology on memories and identities.

≈≈ ≈≈ ≈≈

Author's Notes to Younger Self: Hush, child. Your life is a miracle. Great dictatorships were formed and broken, and men and women bloodied, to bring you into being. Your parents, born to improbable enough circumstances themselves, were catapulted from their homes to find each another and concoct you. Your heritage is strife and triumph. By your own strife and triumph, you will consecrate their grief.

SUMMER OF OUR DISCONTENT

Tyler Keevil

Alan had taken the night shift in their family look-out atop Bryn Y Fan mountain. It had been a struggle to stay awake. Recently the emissaries had rarely appeared before dawn but the Paradigm had changed its patterns before, so they couldn't afford to be slack.

He peered through the telescope at regular intervals, scanning the valley in the direction from which the emissaries always appeared. His son Bran had jury-rigged an infrared sensor that they attached at night, using an old thermal imager. It was basic but effective. Through it, Alan saw the orange glow of a few sheep and cows, but no humanoid shapes. No emissaries.

When the sky paled and an edge of sun slit the clouds on the horizon, he turned from his post and spotted his daughter Summer scrambling up the shale slope behind the lookout. On time. Summer was always on time. She moved efficiently over the uneven terrain, far more agile than him now. Alan was only in his early forties and should still have been in his prime, but around her and Bran he felt increasingly old, and outmoded.

He opened the door for her. Summer was wearing a wide-brimmed hat that had belonged to her mother and a loose leather jacket. The way it flapped around her made her look like a cowgirl. She glanced at his face and said, "You look tired."

"I'm knackered."

She crossed the lookout and took up the rifle, which he'd left leaning against the wall. It was a basic Thompson .270, with a retro wooden stock, completing her Western look. She opened it to check the cartridges—as if not trusting him to have loaded it correctly—and snapped it shut. She laid it flat on the table and peered through the telescope, then set about removing Bran's infrared add-on.

"You better get some sleep," she said.

"If you see anything . . ."

"I'll signal."

"Before you shoot."

"I'm not that trigger-happy, Dad."

"I just have a feeling."

She looked back at him, curious. Not understanding his impulses—his inexplicable hunches. His children were both rationalists, like Olwen.

"It's the solstice," he said. "The Paradigm might change its methods."

"Okay, sensei," Summer said.

He let himself out and began the descent to their cottage, Hafod, at the head of the valley, half a mile away. From the base of the shale slope it was easier going—the path well-trodden, an old sheep-track they'd worn in further by trekking to and from the lookout. The cottage was built from traditional stone, with a slate roof typical of Mid Wales. Hafod was Welsh for "summer house" and centuries before it would have been where the farming family lived during the summer months—near the upper pastures where their herd grazed. A thread of smoke leaked from the chimney: they used the Rayburn for cooking and heating, and saved the solar panels and wind turbine for electricity. Much of the work had been done before the Shift. It was just serendipitous that Olwen and he had made their place largely self-sufficient. The reason they'd bought a smallholding in such a remote part of Wales was to live off-grid, get back to basics, at a time when the world was increasingly plugged-in, on-line, wireless, and fused.

They hadn't expected their lifestyle to protect them from what happened.

In front of the cottage, slate flagstones formed a rustic patio, where they'd set up a picnic table. Summer had left their steel coffee bodem there, knowing Alan wouldn't sleep right away, knowing he had his rituals, his ways of coping. The solstice had always struck him as a particularly melancholy time of year, arriving earlier than expected, at the end of June: summer had barely started, and yet the passing of the longest day meant it was also already over, that autumn was on its way.

Alan poured himself a mug and cradled it, the warmth through the ceramic seeping into his palms. Sitting out there was something he and

Olwen had always done: for morning coffee, or evening wine. Watching the sunlight roll down one valley wall at dawn, as it was doing now, or scroll up the other at dusk. It had been routine since they'd moved out there, just before having the kids, nearly twenty years ago. It seemed an impossible length of time—too long and too short. It didn't feel so long ago, in terms of his memories, his life with Ol. And yet it seemed too short for everything that had happened: for the world to change, for most of humanity to be lost—and then for Olwen to be lost, too.

That felt too recent, and raw. Not a scar, but a wound: 171 days old, but still painful. And their lives were divided into the time before, and the time after. In the time after, he sipped his coffee alone. Tasting it sweet and creamy, with fresh milk from their cows. Gazing down the valley, at the ribbon of river below. And patches of mist on the hills, which were rounded and ancient—very different to the Rockies he'd grown up around.

Wales had always seemed mystical, and partly mythical to him: his first experience of it having come through reading the Arthurian legends as a kid, and later, as a teenager, Susan Cooper's fantasy novels. When he'd met Olwen, and moved out here, it felt partly as if he'd entered that story landscape, or dreamscape.

Now life did feel like a dream, or nightmare: a world taken over. Only pockets of individuals left. Maybe he and Summer and Bran were the last. Maybe that was why the Paradigm was in no rush—was content to send its benevolent, non-aggressive emissaries. No matter how many they turned away, forced back, or shot down. They could only wait for the next, and the next. They pretended they were waiting for one thing, but with each passing day it seemed increasingly futile.

Alan feared what he was really waiting for was an end, any ending. Even if it meant converting: a truth he would never admit to Summer and Bran. They were young, and hurt, and full of fury. The loss of their mother had made them all the more adamant: they would resist and fight till the last.

Losing her had affected him differently. All the fight had gone out of him. All the fire. Olwen had carried that with her, carried it away. But he still had to pretend, for Bran's sake. For Summer's. He could still maintain appearances for a while.

"Ol," he said to the emptiness around him. "Where did you go?'

He sat for another half hour and was beginning to nod off when he saw the signal from the lookout. The signal wasn't unexpected: emissaries often showed up just after dawn or just before dusk. The first few they had cautiously engaged with, from a safe distance. But once the emissaries' single-minded purpose had become apparent, the family had kept them at bay with warning shots or—when necessary—taken them out. Summer, in particular, was a crack shot. But no matter how many they warded off or put down another always approached the next day, and the next. The Paradigm appreciated patterns and was, if nothing else, persistent and punctual.

So a signal at that time of morning was not unexpected. But the type of signal made Alan stand up: Summer had raised a red flag, not yellow. Not their "business-as-usual" sign, but something new. A change. The Paradigm did this, occasionally. Trying out a new tactic. Methodical as an old Cray computer learning to play chess. If one strategy or pawn sacrifice failed consistently, it made adjustments: it changed the form of the emissary, or its route or manner of approach. They had encountered awkward, robotic-looking scouts mimicking the shape of humans; carbon copies of the deceased that had been somehow reconstructed; and real people, flesh-and-blood, that had been converted to the cause. They arrived on foot, or horseback, or four-wheeler. Cars weren't an option: he'd made the track that had once been their drive impassable.

This time Alan felt unaccountably thrilled, even elated by the sight of the flag: anything to disrupt the agonizing stasis. Anything to break the stalemate, end the endgame. He swigged what remained of his coffee and ducked inside. Near the entrance, they had a small side table with an old-fashioned telephone Bran had rigged for them: a landline that ran from the cottage to the lookout and wasn't connected to any other network. Just a two-way system, impervious to hijacking by the Paradigm. They also had three handheld radios that ran on an ultra-high bandwidth, but they tried not to use those unless necessary. They didn't think the Paradigm monitored them but couldn't be sure. It had used radio transmissions in other parts of the world: rural and remote areas where it couldn't reach people via their computers, or tablets, or phones, or implants. That's what they'd heard, before they'd switched off entirely. Speculation that it could hypnotize and manipulate, using patterns and frequencies. Coax people to come to a centre, where they would be fully converted, with so many others.

Of course, how much of that was truth, how much paranoia, they had no way of knowing. But still. He wondered about their handheld radios. He wondered if the Paradigm had somehow seeped into Olwen that way. Embedded the idea that she should leave, check out the town.

He switched on the telephone and hailed Summer. "I told you I had a feeling," he said, then cringed at how much he sounded like a smug father, and added, "Something new?"

"Not new exactly."

"You put up the red flag."

A pause. A crackle of static. It wasn't like Summer to be reticent, unforthcoming. That was Bran's area.

"It's her. It's Mum."

Alan felt a jolt—as if his heart had been stopped and then restarted. The fluttering double-beat. And a quickening, sickening rush.

"You're sure."

"I'm looking right at her, through my scope."

"Don't shoot."

"No shit, Dad."

"Don't swear, either."

He put a hand to his brow. Squeezed his temples with thumb and forefinger. Pinching his skull like a vice. It was what they'd hoped for, and feared, for so long.

He asked, "How far away is she?"

"Far side of Llawryglyn, slopes of Bryn Crugog."

"From the north."

"On foot. Should be here in a couple of hours."

"You better come down," he said. "I'll wake Bran."

He signed off, but for a time he stood with his hand on the mouthpiece, staring at the ridge that obscured his view of Bryn Crugog, where Olwen would be. Or a version of her.

———·———

He went to wake Bran who, it turned out, was already awake. Bran was fourteen—two years younger than his sister—and should have been entering the lazy and messy phase typical of teenage boys. But of course their life was not typical, and neither was the world they inhabited—and his children had grown up accordingly. Bran's room was spartan and spotless: swept hardwood floor, no stray clothing in sight, no frivolous decorations. The walls were adorned with charts: some recognizable, such as star charts and tide graphs, and others inscrutable, beyond Alan's grasp.

When Alan knocked and entered, Bran was on his chin-up bar, doing rapid lifts. He managed this easily: he still had the body of a youth—lean and wiry and hairless—and could pull himself up without any of the flailing or cheating Alan would have needed. Bran had become obsessed with improving himself, physically and mentally. Striving for a kind of impossible perfection.

Such obsessiveness had always been in him and had increased since they'd lost Olwen. His mother had understood him best: Olwen had seen from early on that Bran had a knack for math, physics, and technology that matched her own. In the previous world, he would have been called gifted. Olwen had worked with him closely, cultivated that, probably pushing him too hard—but since they'd lost her, he'd pushed himself even harder. He'd said to Alan once: "We're just a machine, too. A bio-organic machine, developed over hundreds of thousands of years, refined by evolution. But we got sloppy. We got reckless. We can still beat it. We just have to be better than it."

Bran did not stop his set when Alan entered. Opposite his chin-up bar and weight set was his work desk: the only part of the room that ever looked moderately untidy. He had a university-level physics text open on it, next to a box-like contraption that he had been tinkering with for several months. He was vague and evasive when asked about it. He just said it was one of Mum's ideas, which he was trying to complete. For her sake. Sometimes it looked like a jack-in-the-box: sprung wires and cables sprouting out all over the place. This morning it looked neat, sealed, nearly complete.

Alan asked, "How much sleep did you get?"

"Enough," Bran said. His tone was sharp, breathless. As if to say, *don't bug me, Dad.* Bran dropped from his bar and fell immediately into a set of push-ups.

Alan said, "I need you alert. At your best."

"Don't you realize?" Bran lowered his voice, making it comically husky, to sound like an action hero. "I'm-always-at-my-best."

"We're having a family meeting."

"That's going to be tricky without the whole family."

"Maybe it will be with the whole family."

Bran stopped, mid push-up, his muscles taut, his arms quivering.

Alan said, "She's come back."

Bran shook his head, muttered something to himself. It was another habit—a worrying one. He'd begun talking to himself in short asides. They were all too cooped up, spent too much time on their own, together, without any other social contact. Alan tried not to pay much attention, since sometimes his utterances took the form of insults: "Shut up, Dad," or "You don't know anything." But this time he thought he'd heard Bran saying, "So this is it." But he couldn't be sure.

Bran exhaled loudly and continued his push-ups—more slowly, as if thinking at the same time. Considering multiple angles. As in the graphs on his wall, charting spectrums and vectors. Space and time broken into lines, edges, parabolic arcs.

His son said, "I'll be out when I'm done this set."

He flipped himself over and began a series of rapid crunches. His face tense, his jaw taut, his teeth gritted. His expression as impassive as a machine.

———·———

They met outside at the picnic table. Alan made a pot of tea and that formed a centrepiece: a clear glass teapot, faintly steaming from its spout. At first the three of them sat staring at it, watching the leaves swirl and settle, as if it was a crystal ball that could make predictions.

Alan reached for it, poured Summer's cup, then Bran's, then his own. He imagined pouring a fourth, opposite himself, for Olwen. That possibility. It was too painful to hope.

"I admit," Summer said, "I thought about putting her down, like any other emissary."

"Without consulting us?" Alan said.

"Without *telling* you. You'd never have known."

Bran shook his head, muttered inscrutably. Then, more clearly: "You could have ruined everything."

"Would have spared us this."

"We don't know what this is," Alan said.

They sat, tense and silent, considering that. Alan caught a flicker of movement in his peripheral vision. Above them, ghosting on invisible currents, hung a red kite—the bird so emblematic of Mid Wales it had featured on the logo of the county council, before that had been altered to the stark white emblem of the Paradigm: three concentric circles. This bird hadn't made a sound, and rather than scanning the hillside for prey, it was watching them.

"Kite," he said.

Summer walked to the edge of the patio, reached for her rifle, and raised it to her shoulder, sighting through the scope.

"Don't miss," her brother said, taunting.

"I won't."

She breathed in, steadying her hands, and on the exhale pulled the trigger. The report was deafening, and rolled down the valley in echoing waves. The bird jerked and dropped, spiralling earthward. Alan worried she was taking a little too much satisfaction in such kills, but it wasn't just bloodthirsty paranoia. They'd salvaged carcasses and found signs of the Paradigm: nanotech, implants, chipwork. Nature adopted, or co-opted, to the cause.

"There'll be more," Bran said.

"I'll shoot more."

Alan didn't know how much difference it made; it seemed as futile and useless as killing the emissaries. The supply was endless, and the Paradigm had time they didn't. If it could use red kites, why not squirrels, badgers, mice? Why not anything? But thinking like that was self-defeating. They had to believe its resources were limited, for the moment, and that their small, broken family on a mountain-top in Mid Wales wasn't a priority.

Summer slid the safety back on, leaned the rifle against the patio wall, and re-took her seat. The silence that followed the gunshot felt fresh and clean. It had given Alan time to consider things.

"What did she look like?" he asked.

"Like Mum."

"What was she wearing?"

Summer tipped back her hat, squinted skyward, searching her own memory. "Light jacket. Hiking boots. A rucksack. What she would have worn for a trek."

Alan took a sip of tea. "Hat?"

Summer looked at him like he was speaking in tongues. "Dad . . ."

"Was she wearing a hat?"

"Yeah—I think so."

"*Her* hat?"

Summer and Bran exchanged a look, as if concerned about his mental health.

"If it's the exact same hat," he said, tapping the brim of the one on Summer's head, "it means she's a carbon copy."

"Whatever she is, she's not Mum."

"You don't know that," Bran said.

"Sure. She's been working undercover for six months, somehow evading the Paradigm's conversion techniques, and hasn't bothered to let us know."

Alan said, guardedly, "There are other possibilities. We've talked about this."

"I knew you two would get lured in," Summer said, palming the table. "I should have just shot her."

Bran glared at her, his hands gripping his tea cup so tightly Alan thought it might shatter in his hands, in a burst of china shards and hot liquid. Summer glared back, then laughed it off, shrugged—whatever, right?

"It wasn't," she said, turning to Alan. "The same hat, I mean."

Bran muttered again—something Alan couldn't hear.

"Didn't catch that," Summer said. "Care to share, Branflake?"

Bran shrugged, looked uncomfortable. "No thanks, Summer of Discontent."

Their childhood nicknames—either insulting or affectionate, depending on the situation. Branflake not just because of the cereal, but since Bran was sensitive, flighty—flaky. Summer of Discontent not just punning on Shakespeare, but because she was the surly one, the cynical one, the one to find fault with every little thing.

Before the bickering elevated, Alan intervened. He said it was worth going over it, to make sure they hadn't missed anything. It was possible Olwen had died, or been killed, and the approaching figure was merely a carbon copy, lab-bred and quick-grown, without any of her memories. A puppet mocked-up to trick them. If that was the case, it would be evident quickly. But if Olwen had been captured, taken alive first, the Paradigm could have absorbed her, used her memories, knowledge, and experience to create a version of her—cybernetic or bio-organic—that would be able to play the role more convincingly, while still being nothing more than an extension of the Paradigm. And a real danger to the three of them.

"But if she was converted," Alan said slowly, choosing his words, "there's the chance the process can be reversed. There's the chance we could . . ." He couldn't say it: save her.

Summer lowered her head onto the table, dramatic and typically theatrical—like a poker player who had lost it all in one hand. "That's what the Paradigm wants us to believe."

"It doesn't mean it's not possible."

"That's how it will get you."

"Even if there's a chance," Alan said, "we have to take it. We have to be sure."

Summer sighed and sat back up, adjusted her hat which had gone askew. "If we let her in, if she comes up here, it will leave us open to conversion. We might as well plug into the Paradigm and be done with it. She could slowly convert us without us even realizing."

"She's right, Dad," Bran said.

His quiet certainty seemed ominous. In the distance, a buzzard cried: the sound forlorn and comforting. The Paradigm spies tended toward silence, stealth. The cry seemed genuine, that of a real bird.

Alan took a last sip of tea. It was green tea, and he'd made it too strong. It burnt harsh and bitter on his tongue. He understood their anxieties but had to believe they could still outmanoeuvre the Paradigm. It had all the resources and power, but they had human ingenuity and intuition. And love.

"We can do this," he said. He took their empty cups, began to arrange them on the table, sliding them about as if playing a shell game. "We have the plan. I meet her alone. Out here. In the open."

"The plan won't protect you from her," Bran said.

"I'll have a radio, switched on. You two will have the other handhelds, keeping tabs on me. If it sounds as if she's luring me in, converting me, you do what you have to."

Summer held up her hand, mimed pulling an invisible trigger. "Take her out."

"And me too, if you have to."

She looked at him, startled, then quickly away. The short drop of her fearless act pained him: reminded him how young she was, how young they both were. Or how young they should have been, in a different world. Bran took one of the tea cups, turned it around and around on the spot, considering the plan. Alan felt strangely flattered—that they still gave his voice any credence, that they had any faith in him at all. That he still had something to contribute. After all, he hadn't been able to stop Olwen from leaving: he'd let her convince him, and he'd let her go. And she hadn't come back. Until today.

"I've always been hazy about the next bit," Summer said. "Say she isn't converting you, and you get her talking—what then?"

"I establish how much of her is . . . her."

"And then what? Try to talk her around? Try to undo her conversion?"

"It might be possible. If it's partly implants, and nanotech. If her emotions are strong enough to override whatever work has been done. It's happened. We heard of it happening."

"When the Paradigm was still learning."

Alan held up his hands, signifying helplessness.

"It could work," Bran said. "But not in the way that you think."

Summer frowned at her brother. "What other way is there?"

The question hung in the air, and the buzzard screeched again, as if reiterating it. "There's something else," Bran said—so softly Alan thought at first it was more muttering, an aside they weren't meant to hear. Until Bran added, "She left me instructions."

And that, of course, changed everything.

They stood at Bran's work desk, looking down at the black box—or whatever it was—that he'd been working on for the past few months, alone, and before that with Olwen. The room was cool as a tomb, the old stone walls four feet thick. The window was much smaller than it would have been in a modern house: a narrow rectangle, the light from it falling on the box.

"I think she knew," Bran said, "or even expected it. Being converted, I mean."

"Don't talk rubbish," Summer said, sounding to Alan very Welsh, very like her mother.

Bran twitched his head, muttered, then—seemingly with great effort—elaborated for them, in a rush. "She said it wasn't enough to wait the Paradigm out—it has eternity—we just have this—this lifetime, this life, this family—she said we couldn't sit here forever, that it would find a way to convert us, one by one—so her idea was to find a way to counter that. Something that would enable us to push back against it, or at least live out our lives."

He finished breathlessly, leaning on his table, not able to meet their gaze. The speech was the longest string of words Bran had mustered in recent memory. Alan nodded, hoping he didn't look concerned, wanting to be there for Bran, to be supportive, but also feeling as if he was listening to the eccentric ramblings of a street corner preacher.

"Your mother was a passionate person," he said, inanely.

Summer was less diplomatic. "Bran, you're talking bollocks."

Bran swore, shook his head, and turned away from them. Visibly worked to control himself. Speaking with his back to them, which he sometimes found easier, he said, "Mum knew she was going away—maybe not for this long, but long enough—and she left me instructions, for the project we'd been working on. How to finish it. When to finish it."

"Right," Summer said. "Your VHS machine."

By way of answer, Bran forcibly cleared everything else from the table—his physics and engineering books, his pencils and screwdrivers and soldering irons and spools of copper coil and tin solder and wire—all the tools and components he used. Bran and Olwen had gutted random bits of tech from around the cottage—old computers, radios, laptops, tablets—and salvaged further components from neighbouring farms, abandoned now that the previous residents had been converted.

Bran shoved all that to the floor, giving the box centre stage. He ran his hands over it, as if checking it for tampering or damage. The box's interface was simple: a chrome on-off switch, a black and white LCD display, currently blank, and a dial that could have been a volume knob. Beside it sat a simple remote control.

Bran inhaled, steadying himself. "Mum had her theories about the conversions. The different ways The Paradigm gets to people. Or into people."

Alan clapped his hands, rubbed them vigorously, acting the part of foolish father. The role he once thought he'd never play, but which he seemed to play constantly. "I know the basics," he said. "There may be some devotees who converted of their own free will— having been convinced by the broadcasts and media saturation and misinformation . . ."

At this, Summer just scoffed, as if unable or unwilling to accept that there were people that pathetic, that spineless. But religious and polit- ical systems had used those tactics for thousands of years, long before the Paradigm had manifested itself. All the Paradigm had to do was draw on that knowledge, refine it, and re-deploy it in newer and better ways.

"Hypnosis was probably part of it too," Alan said, "Subtle and subliminal."

"Sure," Summer said, "it dangled a watch in front of five billion faces."

"Summer," Alan said.

Summer guffawed. "You just used your stern-dad voice."

"Look," Alan said, "it probably had methods we haven't thought of. The point is, no matter how refined, non-invasive conversion tech- niques would only work for some people."

"And not Mum," Summer said.

"We might assume."

"She's right, Dad," Bran said. "Mum would've had to be forcibly converted."

Alan crossed his arms, uncrossed them again. He went to Bran's little window and looked out. He didn't want to say it, didn't want to think it, but somebody had to. "So she's been altered. Was somehow tricked or lured to a conversion centre. Is being controlled via RFID or microchip or nanoparticles or some similar combination of technologies we hadn't quite developed yet, but the Paradigm has."

"Why hasn't it done the same to us, then?" Summer said.

"Same reason it doesn't send a dozen emissaries, armed, to drag us to a conversion centre. It has its own code," Alan said. "Vaguely Christian ideals: it wants true believers that submit to it of their own free will."

"Free will my ass," Summer said.

"It's a grey area."

"Sure," Bran said. "Grey matter."

They looked at him.

"Like, brain matter."

"Bran just made a joke," Summer said, not quite believing it.

Bran stammered back at her, embarrassed and angry, but then Summer did something unexpected. She crossed to him and put her arms around his neck and whispered something, like his mother might have done. When Summer stepped back, Bran seemed calmer, more capable of explaining. He said, "If Mum is carrying implants—whatever kind—you're not going to be able to talk her around, Dad."

"That depends," Alan said, without saying on what. He felt out of his depth. He'd never had a head for technology, even before the Shift. It was why he'd wanted to live way out here, offline and off-grid. Olwen was the opposite: she had PhD in electrical engineering and knew as much about it as anybody—more than enough to foresee what was coming.

"Whatever implants the Paradigm's using," Bran was saying, "it has to communicate with them wirelessly. And in all of human history we've only ever devised one way to do that: via radio waves. Whether its old-school wireless, FM radio, digital radio, wifi, GPS—it's all various forms of radio waves. So unless the Paradigm has developed something totally new, it's using some form of radio waves. Probably with our old infrastructure."

Bran's eyes had a shine to them now. He went over to his chin-up bar and did five quick reps, as if needing to channel his nervous energy into something physical.

Summer asked him, "I get that this is important, but how?"

When he dropped, he landed light and breathless. He went back over to the box.

"Mum figured if you could eliminate the signal, you could neutralize the Paradigm's influence. Temporarily. She designed this and left me to build it." Then, quietly and wondrously, he added, "By the summer solstice."

That startled Alan. That she'd predicted a specific date. As if she'd had a plan.

"And you didn't tell us?" Summer said.

"I told you I was working on her project."

"But not why."

Bran mumbled and picked up the remote control, fiddling with it. "I didn't know if I could do it without her. I thought I would fail her. But I haven't. It's ready. Just in time."

"And if she is carrying implants," Alan said, "this will disrupt them?"

"For as long as we can power it." Bran smiled, both shy and proud. "She called it the Yadaraf Box." When Alan and Summer just looked at him, he added hurriedly: "You know—like the reverse of a Faraday Cage—it does the same thing—blocks and obliterates radio waves—but is a lot more convenient."

Summer patted him affectionately. "If you say so, Branflake."

Bran muttered, rolled his eyes, flicked his head.

"Whatever it is," Alan said. "It increases our chances."

———·———

Two hours later, Alan sat at the patio table, alone. The table was set just as it would have been when he and Olwen had evenings together. If she'd been converted, he thought using memory triggers might help bring her back to herself. So he'd dressed in a familiar shirt, uncorked a bottle of their homemade dandelion wine, and brought out the short bodega tumblers they'd bought in Tarragona on their honeymoon. He'd poured the wine to let it breathe, and sat waiting, hoping. He remembered taking these measures on more typical nights, when the stakes weren't so high, when he'd hoped they could just grab a little time together, once the kids were down, and they were both tired, or melancholy, or outright depressed. Maintaining a relationship after the end of the world was not easy. But they had tried. They had managed. They had found moments—even if some of those moments were partially an act, a performance.

Now he felt on the cusp of his most important performance.

He reached for the handheld radio in front of him on the table, made sure it was on. They'd experimented with hiding it but it needed to be in the open to pick up their voices. And it was a good decoy: its presence obscured the thing they really wanted to hide—the Yadaraf Box, mounted beneath the table, just in front of his knees.

He leaned to speak into the radio. "Check two-one," he said. "Testing."

"I read you," Bran said.

A crackle of static, then: "You guys sound like kids playing army."

"Thanks, Summer."

Summer was monitoring from the lookout, watching Olwen's approach. Bran was closer to hand, in the attic of the cottage, from where he could activate the Yadaraf Box with the remote. Both had a clear view of the patio.

"How far is she?" Alan asked.

"At the property line," Summer said.

"I guess I'll leave this on now."

A pause. More static. Then, Bran asked, "What are you going to do?'

"Talk to her. Try to figure out how much of her is left."

Bran said, "I'll hold off using the box until we know, to save juice."

Bran figured if they used all the energy stored from their solar panels and turbine, they could charge the box for about ten minutes. They had to use it right.

"If it sounds like she's converting you," Summer said, "I'm going to shoot."

"Summer."

"I'm just saying."

Bran said, "We need to know first, or you may be killing Mum."

"Quiet," Summer said. "She's at the gate."

It went silent for a few seconds, and Alan thought they'd both signed off, but Summer added in a whisper: "Don't bottle it, Dad."

That peculiar British saying. Don't bottle it. Don't choke.

"I won't," he said.

The wind was blowing, as it always seemed to do in Wales. He closed his eyes, felt the sun on his face, the air at his shirt collar. Heard the rustle of the leaves in the beech trees lining the gravel track that served as their drive. Smelled the gorse and heather. Pictured the dream of his life, this life he had fallen into, in Wales—the strangeness of being here, with his children, his family, at the world's end near the end of the world.

And he exhaled and opened his eyes, and saw Olwen.

Walking up the drive, smiling, grateful to be home. And it did feel like a dream. The moment he had imagined for days and weeks and months. Just this. The same: she looked exactly the same. Wearing a wide-brimmed hat like the one she'd given Summer, but a darker shade of beige. Blonde hair tucked behind her ears. Her face red, sweaty from the hike. It was her. It had to be her. He stood up, feeling mesmerized already, and feeling as well the real danger of it. A glimpse of how the Paradigm worked.

If it could offer you this, how could anybody resist?

But he had already decided: he would not resist. He would play along. He would embrace this homecoming, welcome the prodigal mother back. That seemed better than suspicion. So long as he did not lose himself in it and forget that it was a ploy.

He went to her. He intended to walk at first but found himself running. She picked up her pace in return and they met at the edge of the patio, and it would have been like a sentimental reunion in some film except for the fact he stumbled a bit at the last minute, nearly knocked her over. Then, laughing, hugged her, held her fiercely, her hat falling back into the dirt, the outdoor smell of her making him giddy. And pulling back to kiss her, repeatedly, talking to her between kisses.

"You came home. You came back. You're here."

"I've missed you so much," she said.

And if it was somewhat unnatural, it didn't matter. It was her voice, saying what he wanted to hear. He took her by the hand and led her to the table, laid out and waiting for her, for this.

He said, "You must be exhausted."

"I am—but so happy, Alan. So happy."

As they sat, he didn't release her hand—holding it across the table, while with the other he offered her the glass of wine he'd prepared. She took it and admired it. "Our wine! Which year is this?" A comment that seemed deliberate—designed to show her knowledge and understanding of the dandelion wine's significance. Or was he being paranoid?

"The best vintage—the year Bran was born."

They touched glasses, drank deeply, and Olwen sat back, letting go of his hand to fan herself. "Where is Bran? And Summer?"

"They're here, nearby, getting things ready for you."

She nodded, accepting that, even though it was completely unnatural, that the kids hadn't rushed out with him to greet her and welcome her. She looked about, as if taking in the setting, not quite believing she was really back. Her eyes passing over the radio on the table between them. The fact she didn't comment on that seemed suspicious in itself.

"I have so much to tell you all," she said.

"Tell me," he said, "tell me everything you can."

"I'm sorry I've been gone so long. I couldn't get word to you guys. It was too risky. The Paradigm could have used it, made me a route in."

At the mention of it, Alan felt a prickling along his forearms—a sickening sense of hope and dread. He told himself whatever was coming, whatever she said, couldn't be true. It would be a lie. A very cunning lie.

"You went to scope out Llanidloes," he said. "See what had happened."

She nodded. "It was stupid. I know that now."

"I tried to tell you."

"I remember." She was smiling fondly as she said it. "But you know me: I can't stand waiting. I couldn't take being cooped up. We had to take initiative. At least find out what was going on. We'd been cut off for too long. You wanted to stay hidden indefinitely."

He let the dig slide. It was very much like Olwen. "What did you find?" he asked.

She reached for her wine again, knocked it back. He topped up her glass. It was one of the more convincing aspects of her act—the thirsty exuberance. For some reason, it felt all too human, at odds with what he expected of a Paradigm disciple. He found himself drinking to match her, the sweet wine making him happy-headed in the heat.

She shook her head. "So much. So much. I camped outside and watched the town from Pencincoed for days. At a distance, it's a functional, regular town. Everyone is simply going about their business. Saturday is still market day. People shop, have lunch and coffee, chat in the street. The only visible difference is the worship. The amount they're called to prayer and congregate. Three times a day."

Alan nodded, intrigued and caught up in the story. "We'd heard something about that before we switched off. The Paradigm feels humanity lost something, that sense of unity and community, when we abandoned religion and moved toward a secular society."

"All the churches and chapels are in use now, and united. I imagine mosques and synagogues are the same, and any places of worship. All hung with those white banners, worshipping the Paradigm." She grinned, sardonically, convincingly, and put air quotes around what she said next: "Celebrating its glory and what it's given to humanity."

"What about the conversion centres?" he asked. They'd heard a lot about them in the early days. And the treatment. The forced conversions.

"They used the community centre for that, on Oak Street. But it wasn't very busy. I guess because most people are converted. Maybe at the start the Paradigm needed to take more drastic and heavy-handed measures. The horror stories we heard about. But not so much now."

Alan grimaced. "Now it can afford to take its time like it's doing with us."

"The funny thing is, Al," she said, putting her hand over his again. "In watching the town I didn't feel as hopeless as I thought I would. I mean, people aren't walking around like robots or zombies. They're the same as they always were. Bev is still running the bakery. John Davis's garage and MOT centre is still just as busy. Everything's a little more subdued, that's all. People live in a pleasant daze: no tension, no arguments, no fights. Just peace. I guess we can take it as an example of what's now happening everywhere. I thought if this is the new world, it's not as bad as all that."

"Is that why you stayed for so long?"

He couldn't help it. It came out too sly, too insinuating. Clearly an attempt to catch her off-guard: prove she'd been converted. But Olwen threw back her head and laughed.

"God, no. I knew you'd think that. You and the kids. They're listening, right?" She gestured casually at the radio with her wine glass, slopping a little in the process—a very convincing way of seeming tipsy. "Hello, my darlings."

After a moment, Bran said, "Hi Mum."

Nothing from Summer. Not yet.

"You miss me?"

A crackle of static. Alan wondered if Bran was choked up. "Every day," he said.

"I was just telling your father I knew you'd think I'd been converted. Why else would I have stayed away for so long, right? Get this. It turns out there are others like us—others who've held on. They've found ways to survive. Some came from the traveller and Roma communities, that were living largely off-grid like us when the Paradigm manifested."

Alan was studying her carefully. The sweat on her cheeks, the soft glow of alcohol and excitement, seemed so real, so genuine. But he could imagine Summer, listening and watching—and knew what she would say.

"That's amazing," he said, too brightly. "How'd you find out?"

"While I was camping up on Pencincoed, a group raided town. Made off with food and supplies. It's not hard. It's easy, in fact. The Paradigm has a policy of non-violence and non-intervention. So the raiders were allowed to take what they wanted, as far as I could tell. Though one or two remained behind—were somehow convinced, or converted, in the midst of the raid. I guess the ones more susceptible to the Paradigm's methods."

"So it takes its tribute," Alan said.

Olwen explained she'd followed the raiders, approached their camp. They had distrusted her at first—thought her an emissary—but she'd managed to convince them by explaining she'd seen the raid, had been living ten miles away, in isolation with her family. The raiders were moving on—they never raided the same town twice—and they were heading north, to Newtown, in convoy. For a gathering of other groups like theirs. Calling it a resistance was too grandiose. But it was the start of something.

"I had to go, Alan," she said. "It's what I've been waiting for, what we've been waiting for. I'm sorry I couldn't get word to you guys, but if I'd spent four days hiking here and back the raiders would have been long gone." She linked her fingers with his. "I'm so sorry I worried you."

He could feel her wedding ring. Ran his thumb over her knuckle. An old habit. Feeling the scar there, from where she'd skinned it to the bone, climbing with him in Pembrokeshire. He felt the heat of the sun on his neck, the haziness of the day, the soft fog of the dandelion wine. It seemed to make sense. It did make sense. It was such a convincing and plausible story, and very like Olwen.

"It's okay," he said. "We knew you'd come back." He held her hand a while longer, held the feeling awhile longer. He was tearing up. Olwen's face blurring as if from heat ripples. It almost had him. But not quite. Not yet.

Then he said, "Bran—it's time."

Olwen frowned, not understanding.

There was no sound as Bran turned the box on. No obvious change to the patio air or atmosphere. But Alan saw it spread across her face: a relaxation, a realization. And her eyes. They seemed to come into focus. A brief dilation of the pupils. It was in the eyes after all, that he could see her coming back to herself.

"Olwen," he said.

"Alan."

Her grip on his hand now was fierce, desperate. Real.

"How did you know?" she asked.

"Your accent. It was too crisp. You always sound more Welsh after a few glasses of wine. The Paradigm had everything right except that."

"It allows drinking," she said. "But never to excess."

"How much do you remember?"

"Of what we just said? Everything. It's not that it blacks you out. It's more like . . . it's like a drug, I guess. You sense it affecting you, changing you. You don't have as much control. But you don't care. You're perfectly happy. And I was genuinely happy to be back, to see you."

She shook herself, as if still emerging from the dream of the Paradigm's influence. She looked beneath the table, guessing where they'd hidden her Yadaraf Box.

"Bran finished it," she said.

"He's a genius."

"He is, you know."

"He comes by it honestly."

Alan remembered: Bran wouldn't be able to hear any longer, now that the box was activated, since it would disrupt their radio signals as well as the Paradigm's. He turned in his seat, saw Bran watching through the curtains in the attic window, motioned him down. Summer was too far away, up in the lookout. But he stood and waved.

As Bran ran down the stairs, Olwen said, "We don't have much time."

"Bran said ten minutes."

"I'd hoped for a bit more."

"But we have enough time to save you," Alan said. "Right?"

Olwen looked past him, over his shoulder, to where Bran was coming out the front door. She released Alan's hand and scrubbed tears from her cheeks and stood, letting Bran run into her arms, grabbing him, holding him, whispering to him, "My beautiful, wonderful boy."

Bran was not sobbing or even crying. But he was shaking, his arms locked behind his mother's back, his expression frighteningly intense. He looked utterly shell-shocked. Still holding him, Olwen looked back at Alan and asked, "What about Summer?"

"In the lookout."

"I have to see her."

Leaving Olwen and Bran, Alan went inside to the telephone, which wouldn't be affected by the box. Summer was waiting on the line when he picked up.

"It's working," he said.

"How can you be sure?"

Alan looked out the window, to where Olwen was holding Bran, whispering to him. Soothing and consoling him, presumably. Not converting him. She had to be herself. It had to be working.

"I saw the change. She wasn't quite herself, and then she was."

"Or the Paradigm faked the change."

"We have to believe, Summer."

"Believe in what, Dad? Has it got you, too?"

He shook his head, even though she couldn't have seen him from her vantage point.

"If you want to see your mother, you have to come down."

"I'm fine where I am, thanks. I can see the reunion through my scope."

"Summer . . ."

"Get out there, Dad. Don't leave Bran alone with her."

Alan put down the receiver and stepped back outside—on edge, watchful, but not even quite knowing what he was watching for. Whatever Olwen had said to Bran seemed to have had the desired effect; he was calming down. They were talking about the situation, about what could be done.

"As soon as the power goes," she was saying, "I'll go too. I'll be back under its influence, and it will know what you did. Will store that information. Save it. Use it."

"We can save you," Bran said.

Olwen touched his face, his cheek—as if not quite believing the reality of him.

"It didn't take any chances with me, Bran. There's no way we can remove the nano-particles. They're fused to my cells—all through my body." She held up a hand, spread the fingers. From Alan's perspective, the evening sun was directly behind, so it looked as if she held it in her palm. "The Paradigm isn't just in me," she said sadly, "it's part of me now."

"Ol," Alan said, took a faltering step toward her.

She went over to the table, poured herself more dandelion wine.

"But then what's the point of the box, Mum?" Bran said, his voice cracking. "I built it because you told me to. I built it so we could save you."

She took a sip. "I didn't know enough about the Paradigm," she said. "How it works, how it converts. How invasive its control mechanisms are. But we got the chance to say goodbye, didn't we?" Then she looked up at the look out, frowning. "Where's Summer?"

"She's coming, I think," Alan said. Worried, now.

Bran muttered something, shook his head. "Where's the implant?" he asked Olwen.

She looked at her son, curious.

"It must have put a transceiver in you. Something to receive and transmit information, feed it back to the Paradigm, and locally control the nanoparticles."

She smiled. "My clever boy."

"We could remove that," Bran said, in his rapid-patter way, "Cut it out—even when the Yadaraf Box fails—the Paradigm's signals resume—you won't have anything in you to respond—the nano-particles will be useless to it without the transceiver."

"It's a wonderful idea, Bran," she said, sounding sad, "but the implant is here"—she tapped her chest—"near my heart. About the size of a pacemaker. We don't have the means or time to remove it, and there's a failsafe."

Bran made a frustrated, enraged sound. Clenched his fists, turned away.

"So what do we do, Ol?" Alan asked.

Olwen went to embrace him again. "Just enjoy it. Enjoy the few minutes we have, to be us, to be a family." She looked again to the lookout. "If only Summer were here, too."

Alan felt a tingling, then—that prickling of the forearms. Was it Olwen or wasn't it?

"I'll double-check," was what he said.

He returned to the telephone inside, picked it up. Summer was still there.

"Summer, listen. I want you to look at her through Bran's infrared sensor."

"What am I looking for?"

"The implant. She said it's in her chest, near her heart. It will show up as a cold patch in her heat signature. A piece of metal, like the ones we find in birds, but bigger."

There was a pause and a clatter as she put the phone down, then rustling and sounds of movement. Soon after, Summer picked up again. "I see something," she said. "But not near her heart. Higher up. Beneath the collar bone."

"She might have been wrong about where they put it."

"Or she might be lying."

A pause. Alan watched Olwen talking to Bran, the silent movement of her mouth. Away from her, shielded by a pane of glass, Alan more readily sensed the strangeness of her—the not-quite-right impression. Her voice—so soothing—had veiled it. And his desire to believe in her, and Bran's invention. He didn't doubt it worked. But she'd mentioned a failsafe—maybe that was deliberate? Maybe there *was* a failsafe: something that kicked in when the implant got cut-off from the Paradigm's transmissions. A localized control mechanism. Meaning she would be closer to her real self right now, but not fully herself.

"Could you shoot it?" he said. "The transmitter?"

A pause, as Summer considered. Then, she said, "Yes. But I need her with her back to me, and still. Preferably sitting."

"I'll get her in the chair."

Then, realizing what he was asking of her, he said, "Summer . . ."

"Just do it. I won't miss."

Alan put down the phone, his hand trembling. Tried to get his face together before heading back out. A final performance. A last act. From beneath the sink, he grabbed another bottle of their wine: by chance taking one from the year Summer was born. Bran had scratched out the year and added "Discontent" instead, so the label read "Summer of Discontent." Carrying the bottle in one hand and a glass for Bran in the other, Alan strode out, smiling tearfully, feeling hopeless and desperate, having tasked his daughter with the impossible, and exposed his son to possible conversion, and convinced now his wife was lost. And having to pretend otherwise—to pretend it was all okay, it would be okay. But then, that was what fatherhood had been for him, from the beginning—and all the more so since the Paradigm Shift. Forced optimism, painful joviality.

And now for the finale, it came to him easily: well-practiced and well-rehearsed. Uncapping the bottle, announcing grandly that he'd had a eureka moment and solved their predicament, while Bran looked at him worriedly and Olwen stared at him with what might have been wariness. But on her part, or the Paradigm's?

"I have a plan," he declared.

"Dad," Bran said. "No offence—but you don't know enough about the tech."

"He's right, cariad," Olwen said gently. "If Bran and I can't figure it out . . ."

"Skeptics!" Alan said, planting the extra glass for Bran, and liberally pouring a drink for his son, before topping up his and Olwen's glasses. He raised his, as if making a toast. "You haven't even heard what I have in mind, and already you're doubting. That's just like you—just like this whole family. I'm only the bumbling father who holds it all together."

"Dad," Bran said, "are you okay?"

"I know this is hard," Olwen added. "But we don't have much time."

"We don't have any time," he said. He went around the table, pulled back her chair—acting the part of host, while ensuring that it was angled, as near as he could tell, toward the lookout. "So you need to listen to me.

Sit down and let me lay it all out."

She sat, and he moved her chair in, and then—to make it seamless—circled the table to do the same for Bran. Sitting, Bran reached for his wine and took a sip and immediately coughed. Alan laughed heartily, patted his son on the back. "It's your sister's vintage," he said, in his joking voice, "astringent and bitter."

"Speaking of Summer . . ." Olwen said.

"She's hurrying down now, cariad. She'll need to hear this too."

Bran shifted in his seat, restless. "What's the deal, Dad?"

"The deal is, son, that life is short, time is precious. Before we save your mother, I just wanted us to sit together. Now close your eyes, both of you." He did so, then peeked at them—knowing they wouldn't follow suit immediately. "Close them! Good. Now, listen. Hear that?" In the distance, coincidentally, a buzzard shrieked. "Now breathe in deeply."

"Dad . . ."

"Okay—open them. Here's my plan. We just sit like this, together, and wait."

Bran frowned. "Wait for what?"

The shot rang out, and Olwen jerked and a spatter of blood sprayed across the table. Her wine glass shattered like a light bulb. The bullet had gone clean through. Bran screamed and Alan staggered up, circling the table to catch Olwen as she slumped sideways, fearing his idea had been insane, that Summer had missed, that he'd unwittingly tasked her with killing her mother, that this truly was the end of everything.

Until he felt Olwen's panting, knew she was alive—for now, at least—and turned her over to lie her down. She put a hand to his face. "Alan—it's you."

"And it's you."

And it was. For the first time since she'd returned, she was fully herself.

Bran knelt on the other side of her. "Summer tried to kill her."

"No," he said, "I told her to shoot."

Alan was tearing open the collar of Olwen's shirt, exposing the bullet hole. The exit wound was just below her collar bone, and not clean; it had burst outwards, most likely due to the shrapnel caused by hitting the implant. It was bleeding profusely. But no organs and no major arteries. Summer's shot was as perfect as could be, as perfect as always.

Olwen clung to him. "The implant," she said, wonderingly.

"That was the idea. Now we've got to make sure you don't bleed out. Bran, get me towels, boiled water, a pan. The First Aid kit. We need to clean and disinfect the wound."

His son stared at him blankly, mutely.

"Bran—now!"

Bran went. Alan couldn't do anything related to technology, but he could do this. He gripped her hand fiercely, feeling the slippery heat of her blood between their palms, told her repeatedly they were going to save her. In the middle of that, he realized she was trying to tell him something too: that the Paradigm didn't just learn from its converts; it worked both ways. She had learned from it. She knew what it was, how it functioned.

"We have a chance," she said. "We've got a chance here."

Whether true or a delirium he couldn't tell, not then. Bran came back with the towels first and Alan grabbed one and held it to the wound, staunching the flow of blood. There was a scrambling sound from the slope behind the cottage. Summer was coming down, leaping over the cascading shale like some mountain goat, the rifle slung over her shoulder.

Seeing her, Olwen's face lit up, her eyes shining with tears and pain and love. "Summer's finally here," she said, in wonder.

And their daughter descended, reckless and hell for leather, landing on the grass at the base of the shale slope and shucking her rifle and running straight to them, demanding to know what she could do to help—not even asking if the bullet had been on the mark, so confident in her own abilities. And Bran came rushing out with the water and pan and First Aid kit and it was only when they were all there, working together, that Alan truly believe they could save her, they *would* save her, and they would fight this thing, they would be a family again—even if only for a short time, even if one of the last in history.

⁂

Author's Notes to My Younger Self: My story contribution is largely about being a parent, and being a parent has really taught me that we are simply a biological organism: miraculous, extraordinary, and constantly changing—from fetus to baby to toddler to child to youth, and further. So I think that's what I'd tell my younger self: life is a series of stages of growth, and all we can do is embrace the stage we're in, relinquish the ones we've outgrown, and prepare for the ones ahead—right up until the last. And to be kind, of course. To everybody. Including yourself.

A GRAVE BETWEEN THEM

Karina Sumner-Smith

The man in the black mask says this is what he has heard: that it must be her hand on the shovel, her breath and her earth; so no, he won't help her dig. He won't fall for her tricks.

He's wrong in the details—wrong in the head—but there's blood on his hands, more with each passing moment, and he has the gist of it close enough.

Avery nods, quick and afraid. "I'll do it," she says. "Whatever you want. Just let my family go."

He doesn't, of course. Instead he binds them tight and locks them in the basement, then bars the door while Avery watches, trembling. Her mom and Aunt Jenny she doesn't worry about as much—they're bound, but beneath the duct tape and bruises their anger burns hot. They'll have themselves free by morning, one way or another. No, it's the kids that concern her: Katie with her head held defiant, little Matthew sobbing into his stuffed dog, Lucas so silent and still that Avery knows he's hidden himself away in the dark corners of his mind. She wonders how long it'll be before she can coax him to return.

"You can let them out yourself," the man tells her. He adjusts the ski mask over his face, then bends down to pick up the blanket-wrapped body he brought to their door, struggling with the weight. "When you're done."

He's lying, but maybe she needs the lie.

"This way." Avery clasps her hands tight so she can't do anything she'd regret, and leads him into the backyard.

———·———

When the doorbell rang—when Aunt Jenny opened the door to a black-clad figure with a dead body in his arms—this is how Avery thought it would go: they'd invite him in, send the children upstairs to bed, then put on the kettle for tea.

There's a small cot in the room adjoining the kitchen, sheeted discretely with plastic, where they would have left the body while they spoke; while seldom used, the cot is there for just such occasions. They would've discussed terms—or, rather, her mother and Aunt Jenny would have told the man Avery's terms, while Avery herself appeared aloof or sympathetic or absented herself from the conversation entirely, as best suited the situation. There would have been a decision—and if the man agreed?

Then, and only then, would she have dug the grave.

But when Aunt Jenny invited the man inside, he'd taken a step and then just . . . stopped. He'd gone statue-still—staring, Avery thought, at her. Then he'd carefully lowered his bloody burden to the welcome mat and drawn the knit mask over his face.

That's when the gun had come out. That's when the shouting had begun.

It should have gone differently—but it didn't and here they were.

Avery had been tired when that knock came, struggling through the last few math problems Aunt Jenny had assigned, and watching the much-erased pencil lines blur as her aching eyes struggled to focus. Now she feels very awake, and very, very alive.

Outside, the night is cool and dark, no streetlights for kilometres, and the stars' brilliance doing little to illuminate the poorly mown yard. The only light comes from the porch, the old bulb haloed in spider's webs and dusty moths' wings.

Avery takes a step, another. She could scream, she knows. She could scream and cry for help, and no one would hear her. The closest neighbours are more than a half-hour walk through the woods, and it's farther still to the nearest town. The house is isolated—intentionally so—and this is the first moment that Avery regrets it.

"Here," the man says when she's taken a few strides into the darkness. "This is far enough."

Here is not nearly far enough. So close to the house Avery can still see the bonfire lights of her family in the basement, five lives burning strong and bright and so close it seems she could touch them without reaching. But she can't tell him that.

"I can't have a grave in the middle of the yard," she says instead, trying to keep her voice steady and mostly succeeding. She's not wrong.

"Not my problem." He places the blanket-wrapped body on the grass so very gently.

He accompanies her as she fetches a shovel from the shed at the corner of the cleared section of the property, watching to make sure she doesn't make a break for the trees. He's bigger than her, taller, and smells of sweat and blood; yet it's only from so close that Avery realizes that he's not quite as large as she first thought. His bulk comes more from layered clothing a few sizes too big than it does from muscle.

He's bigger, stronger, faster than her—but even so, she thinks about escape. No one needs to be hurt. The night is dark, but within the forested part of their land it's darker still, the canopy of leaves so thick that not even starlight can fall within. Avery knows this land and has walked its pathways at all hours since she was ten years old. She knows how to run here, how to move swiftly and quietly, how to use the bush to hide.

But then there's her family.

But then there's the gun.

So she goes into the shed and chooses a well-worn shovel, then walks back to the body to start digging.

———•———

The ground is rocky and dry. Benign neglect is not the only reason for the condition of their yard.

Avery's first strike of the shovel pulls up a heap of grass and soil no bigger than her palm; the second attempt is much the same. The third she hits a buried stone, the shovel's blade making a *ting!* as it rebounds.

The man is, of course, watching her. "No games," he says. "Just dig."

"No games," she agrees, tossing aside a shovelful of stones.

Five minutes pass, ten, and the man starts pacing and still Avery digs. Her hole is shallow, a mere scratching in the dirt. She widens that hole, removing the layer of grass and topsoil bit by bit until a long rectangle emerges.

"You have to dig deeper," the man snaps. "It's a grave, not a fucking flower bed."

"Yes," she says, only that, and continues widening the hole.

It was, it seems, not the response he expects. From the corner of her eye, she sees his hand holding the gun twitch as if trying to rise on its own; his mouth works as if her answer must be chewed to be understood. His anger is almost a physical thing, filling the darkness between them, and Avery all but holds her breath as she tosses aside another shovelful of stony earth, and another.

At last he makes a sound of dismissal and turns away.

There's a rhythm to digging and Avery tries to lose herself in it, in the lift of the shovel, the bunch and stretch of the muscles in her shoulders and arms, the bend of her knees. She's dug graves before—here, on this land. Some were in use for only a span of hours, but some few remain, close, toward the treeline; though unmarked, she knows every one.

This is not the first grave she's dug, only the first she's dug without the steadying presence of her mom or Aunt Jenny. The first she's dug with a man standing over her with a gun, watching her every move as if he's waiting for her to fail.

After an hour of digging, Avery pauses to lean on the shovel.

"What are you doing?" he asks. "You can't stop."

"I need a break." She tries to catch her breath, runs her forearm across her sweaty forehead. Her hand, when she lifts it, shakes from exertion.

"You can't." The command his voice once had is gone; his words, though insistent, instill little fear. He suddenly seems less threatening and more petulant, insistent but out of his depth.

"I am. It takes hours to dig a grave. *Hours*, and I'm tired. I don't know what you expected."

He expected to be gone already, she knows that. He expected her to dig faster, like a machine, not a stressed seventeen-year-old girl who hadn't slept the night before and is up now long past her desired bedtime.

Avery looks toward the treeline, but even so she sees him reach for the gun tucked into the waistband of his pants. Sees him hesitate.

The heat of the moment has gone; whatever fear and anger fueled him when he came to the door has dissipated into the cool night air. It's just the two of them now, the body still and unmoving on the grass, the growing grave like a shadow between them.

A few minutes pass in stiff, uncomfortable silence. Avery catches her breath. Not moving, she's quickly becoming cold, the breeze making her shiver as her sweat cools. Even so, she's in no rush to start digging again.

Instead she looks to the house, shifting her focus to see the burning lights of her family in the basement. They're not still anymore, not sitting where they once were; they're up and moving. One of them has found a way past the duct tape, freed all the others. That, more than resting, lets her take a deeper breath.

They're okay, she thinks. And she knows that, in the end, she can handle herself.

She glances again to the man in the mask—or, as she's come to realize, the boy. She'd first thought he was in his twenties, at least; but now, listening to his voice in the darkness, she realizes he can't be much older than her, if at all. While her first impressions of him were muddled, she thinks now, this can't have been planned, not any of it. He's making this up as he goes along. He feels as scared as she does, and maybe as lost.

And Avery, digging—here, in this rocky earth, where she has dug eight times before—feels more like herself with every moment.

She could have killed him already. She knows it, true and solid as any of the rocks she pulls from the cold soil. Or, at least, she could have hurt him enough to stop him when he came into her house and threatened her family. Incapacitated him. Left him weak and writhing on the floor, for a moment—or, perhaps, forever.

Paralyzed. Blinded. Struggling to breathe without aid, his spasming, fluttering heart fighting to remember how to beat.

No, there was a reason Aunt Jenny had turned to Avery with panic in her eyes when that gun came out; a reason her mom whispered, "Calm, just stay calm, it'll be okay," over and over again. In the end, it wasn't the man—the boy—with the gun that they'd feared most, but Avery losing control.

There are rules to what she can do, rules and ritual, and if they are self-imposed they are no less necessary. There must be a need, there must be a grave, and there must, in the end, be permission. No accidental deaths, no murders. Not ever again.

"You can take the mask off, you know," Avery says then. "I've already seen your face."

It's true, even if she remembers only impressions—pale skin, dark hair, darker eyes. Yet it's the wrong thing to say. She sees fear and panic grow in him, and the anger he uses to cover both.

"Look," she says hurriedly. "I'm not going to call the cops, okay? That's not what this is about."

"Yeah?" Hard, accusing. "Why's that?"

"I'm the one with a grave in my yard. How you think I'm going to explain that?"

"But there'll be no one in it when you're done."

Avery huffs out a breath. "My mom has already been arrested and charged for fraud because of what I can do," she says. "Years ago." She'd only been a child, and none of them, not least of all Avery herself, had realized the full extent of her abilities. She'd been called the girl with divine healing powers, at least in a few online features and new age magazines.

The first big accident—when they'd ended up with a little girl who was no longer dead and no longer had cancer but had two very dead parents—had brought the eyes of the law upon them. Avery had been protected, given into her aunt's care, while her mother had taken the fall. Fraud. Reckless endangerment. Manslaughter. Murder. The list had been long; the charges the prosecutor had been able to make stick, less so.

But prison time had been no less than she'd deserved, her mother had since said more times than Avery could count. She should have kept her child's gift a secret, should have sheltered and protected her, and let that be that.

They'd been in hiding ever since—both from the law and from those who would come to her for healing, to bring back those they'd lost. Yet the desperate still make their way to her. On underground forums, rumours of her existence and whereabouts remain: the girl so powerful she can cure even death.

"I don't need the attention, okay? There are questions I don't want to have to answer."

At last he says, "Fair enough." Even so, it's a long moment before he draws off the knit mask.

His skin is pale but flushed; cool as the wind feels, it's far too warm to be wearing a winter hat. His hair is a sweaty tangle that falls long over his ears and forehead, the uneven ends speaking more of the time since his last haircut than any attempt at style. The bravado is entirely gone now from his posture and expression. Dark eyes look at her, strangely hesitant. Questioning.

"Hey," she says softly. She holds out one dirty hand. "I'm Avery."

He clears his throat, hesitates, then quickly takes her hand—and just as quickly drops it. His palms are clammy. "Jesse."

"Nice to meet you, Jesse."
Then Avery takes the shovel and begins to dig once more.

———·———

Perhaps an hour passes before Jesse speaks again.

In that time, the grave has grown deeper; Avery stands now in a long, rectangular hole deeper than her knees, and when she digs her shovel strikes thick, hard clay that's even worse than the stones. There were farmers in this area once, but not many and never terribly prosperous. She's never had trouble understanding why.

Jesse's voice comes out of the darkness.

"Are they the same, the people you bring back? After they rise?"

She pauses, grateful for the reprieve. Her shoulders burn, and her mouth is dry, and she almost feels tired enough to curl up in the cool, dark grave to rest.

Avery thinks about that very first time, when she'd fallen on the playground in grade school and cracked her head on the way down, that blaze of white and pain and then *reaching*—

She isn't the same; she'll never be the same. It isn't what he means, but still she says, "Of course not." Feeling that ache again as if it were new, physical pain vanishing and sick guilt taking its place. Remembering her friend who hadn't slipped, hadn't fallen, but was suddenly down on the ground unmoving. She takes a breath and pushes the memory away.

Yet the answer is honest, no matter that the sharpest memories don't have anything to do with the people who've come to her for help, or the state of the living when they leave.

She looks up at him. He sits on the ground, the pile of dirt to his one side, the body on the other. His legs are crossed, and the gun and the mask have been tossed aside. Even so, he will not meet her gaze.

"They're not zombies, if that's what you're asking. Not damaged. They're still themselves, but . . ." Avery lets out a heavy breath. "Raising them, healing them, it doesn't change what happened. Doesn't change that they died."

Jesse stares at the bloody blanket and the concealed figure beneath, his expression blank.

"Will he remember what happened?"

He. Not his mother then, not a girlfriend. Boyfriend, perhaps? A brother, a friend?

"If he was conscious for his death, then yes, he'll remember."

Now Jesse looks at her, his dark gaze intense. "But he might not know that he . . . that he died, right? He might think that we just helped him, patched him up . . ."

Avery shakes her head. "He won't be injured anymore, Jesse. Not at all. He's going to wake up here, in my back yard, covered in blood and earth without so much as a scratch on him." He would be weak and headachy, confused and disoriented—but very, very alive.

The blood, the dirty clothes—those, too, could have been different. Upstairs they keep a supply of clean clothing; and usually they bathed the bodies before . . .

But here they are. She sets the thoughts aside.

"Oh," Jesse says. "I just . . . I wish he didn't have to know."

"Who is he?" Avery asks softly. "May I see his face?"

Jesse nods, and at that gesture Avery sets the shovel aside. She makes her way to the body, then kneels, looking down at the blanket. Jesse doesn't move. Slowly, she draws the blanket back.

The body is easily as large as she is, yet the face is of someone far younger. A boy, no more than twelve or thirteen, no matter his stature. His skin is darker than Jesse's—olive, or perhaps light brown—yet the similarities between them are easy to see. The dark hair, the sharp line of the nose, the softened curve of the lips.

"My brother, Nathan."

There's blood smeared across the boy's—Nathan's—cheek, and blood on his mouth, but no wounds that she can see. No head trauma, no obvious bruising. Carefully, she draws the blanket farther back.

At first, it's hard to see the hole in the fabric of his sweatshirt; there is only blood, black in the dim light, sodden, shining. Despite the time since his death and the swaddling of the blanket, he's drenched in it. Carefully, Avery probes for the wound. There it is: a small hole, no larger than a fingertip, low along his right ribs.

Bullet hole, she thinks. A collapsed lung, for sure—and who knows what other damage the bullet did, rattling around inside him? Enough to bring death, swift and sure.

She nods and pulls the blanket back over the boy's face.

"He shouldn't be dead," Jesse says.

Maybe she should say what her mom might have said: that no one should die young, that death wasn't fair, that everyone should have a life full of opportunities for happiness and growth and change. Something, Avery thinks sourly, best stitched on a pillow.

She knows death the way few others can. She has seen the dead and the dying, the critically injured and the desperately ill. She has died herself once, and dragged herself back to life; she has caused death. Over and over, she has caused death, at first accidentally and then with permission, and it never, ever gets easier.

"He should," she says in bland counter. "He was shot. He bled out. That's how it works." Carefully she stands and rolls her shoulders, wishing the movement did anything to ease the pain. She looks back to Jesse. "My helping him, raising him, it doesn't change what happened, you know. It doesn't make him any less dead *now*."

There is silence—angry, uncomfortable silence, broken only by the sound of her climbing back into the grave, of the shovel striking dirt. She shouldn't push; she knows it, and yet . . .

And yet.

"I know," Jesse says. There is so much anger in the words, so much hatred, and every bit of it is turned inward.

Her voice is softer when she asks, "How did he die?"

The pause is longer this time; Avery can feel him assessing her, gauging her intent or her trustworthiness, she knows not which. At last he looks away, runs a hand through his hair.

"It was an accident. He was . . . he was shot." As if that hadn't been obvious.

Another shovel of clay and stone. Another. Then she asks, "Will you tell me what happened?"

The silence stretches, weighted, heavy. A minute passes, then a second and a third—long enough that she thinks he won't answer.

And then, suddenly, he does.

———•———

Nathan, Jesse tells her, is his half-brother, and the boy that he'd raised nearly on his own while their mother was still alive. Yet, on her death a few years before, Jesse had been sent to juvenile hall while Nathan had gone into foster care.

"Prison?" she asks. "For what?"

"Something stupid. Tried to steal a car right out of a neighbour's driveway, thinking I could sell it at the scrapyard. Didn't even know how to drive."

Avery nods as if she understands, or has any idea how much cash you can get for a scrap car.

Jesse shrugs. "They wouldn't have let me be Nathan's guardian anyway. Too young. But maybe we could have been fostered together, you know?"

Instead, it was more than a year before he found where Nathan had gone, and longer until he could see his brother. Even then, Nathan's foster parents—a decent couple clearly interested in adopting the boy—showed little enthusiasm for Jesse in the boy's life. A bad influence they said, and the last thing Nathan needed when he was just starting to settle down. Even so, Jesse persisted, talking to his brother on social media, stopping by when he could, sending Nathan gifts when he had the cash.

All the while, Jesse made a plan for their combined futures.

"His foster parents did their best for him, y'know? But I'm blood. They couldn't care for him the way I . . ."

At this Jesse goes silent, clearly struggling not to look at Nathan's body. At last he clears his throat and continues.

Jesse was planning to move across the country, head to B.C., maybe get work in construction or at one of the resorts. The plan was that in a couple of years Nathan would follow—they'd share an apartment, Jesse could help Nathan go to university, maybe connect him with a job.

Except, it seemed, Nathan couldn't wait a couple of years. The day Jesse set out, Nathan was there too, bag in hand, and nothing Jesse said could make boy turn around. So Jesse used half his money to buy another bus ticket, and when the cash ran out before the highways did, they started hitchhiking.

"Nathan's big for his age," Jesse explains. "I put a ball cap on him and told him to keep his head down. No one noticed."

No one said anything was more like it, Avery thinks, but keeps the words to herself.

They'd gone some distance—and had a few free meals—when everything went wrong. A ride gone bad. A trucker got ideas, there was a scuffle, and then *bang*. Just like that.

But there's something in his voice, something in the way he says it.

"Did you try to rob the driver?"

"No, why would you—"

"The gun. The knit mask. It's September, Jesse, not February."

He shrugs, then, awkwardly. "It's not loaded," he says. "I don't even have bullets."

But the driver, it seems, did. Jesse was the one with the weapon, the one demanding cash—but Nathan was big for his age, and he wore a mask too, and in the struggle he was the one hit. The one who fell to his knees at the side of the road, blood bubbling on his lips. The one who lay unmoving as the truck sped away.

"My fault," Jesse whispers. "All of it."

Avery isn't interested in his guilt, not really. "And so you came to me."

It's a moment before he says, "I heard a story about you once, you know. The girl who could heal the dead. Eyes so pale they're almost white and a scar across one cheek. Girl I knew in juvie—Sascha—said she'd died from cancer once, but that you brought her back. I didn't believe it. Not until I saw you standing there, older, but looking just like she'd said." He hesitates, then shrugs uncomfortably. "It's not so hard to find your address online, if you know where to look. And Nathan . . . he died not so far from here."

Avery closes her eyes. She remembers Sascha—remembers the healing that had sent her own mother to prison. But she doesn't say anything, and this time Jesse doesn't notice, too lost in his own thoughts.

"I've never told anyone that," he says. "About stuff that happened when I was a kid. Didn't think I could ever tell anyone what happened to Nathan."

"It's easier in the dark when no one can see your face. It's like . . . no one's judging you. You can say what you need to say." At least, that's the way it's always felt to Avery.

"I guess so," comes the reply. A moment, then quietly: "I've never been able to talk to anyone like this, though. Like, not at all."

Or maybe, Avery thinks, it's only that he never had anyone to listen.

But then, how long has it been since she's had anyone to talk to?

"You're a good storyteller," she tells him without looking up. "It's like you're my own personal podcast. Any other stories to tell?"

But Jesse's shaking his head, turning away.

"What about him?" Avery asks, not wanting the moment to end. Not wanting that silence to return. "Nathan. What was he like as a little boy?"

Jesse lets out a breath that tries and fails to become a laugh. "Oh, man. He's always been the funniest kid. And smart, y'know? Super smart. Must've got it from his dad, whoever he was." He looks up at the night sky, all that stretching black, and it's like he wants to vanish into the darkness. His Adam's apple bobs in his neck, and he brushes away a tear, and another.

She pretends she doesn't see either, head down, digging. Another shovel of dirt onto the pile, and another.

Then Jesse's voice comes again, lighter somehow, despite his swallowing back tears. "Okay, so this once when he was like four or five, right, Nathan came home from the playground . . ."

For a time Avery doesn't think about the hole that she's digging or why, doesn't let herself remember that the little boy in the tales is lying dead only feet away, all his stories ended. She just listens.

————

"Okay, enough," Jesse says some time later, when he's found a pause in his stories. "Is what Sascha told me true, about your ability? With it being you who needs to dig?"

She shakes her head. "No, not really. It's just—"

"Then it's my turn." He reaches for the shovel.

For a moment, Avery is caught speechless. If they'd done this the proper way, Aunt Jenny would have explained—

He would have *known*—

But they didn't and he doesn't, and even so, the offer is genuine. Jesse is, it seems, slowly realizing what he's doing and what he's done, and though he thinks he can't let her family out of the basement he can at least do this.

And she is so very tired.

She nods once, quickly, then leans the shovel on the side of the grave. It is not so high that she needs a ladder to climb out, but it gives her a place to sit, legs dangling, and catch her breath.

In one easy motion, he's risen and leapt down into the hole. It's the thoughtless agility of a person to whom athleticism comes easy. He could have been a soccer player, she thinks, or a cross-country runner. Maybe he could have been a swimmer or taken up mountain biking in the back-country hills or—

Well. Perhaps in another life.

Even so, she's suddenly aware of the closeness of him, the heat of him in the cold night, the easy way he lifts the shovel and begins to dig.

"Rocky," he says at last, as if he has to say something. As if she had not told him this very thing and then dug a hole more than three feet down while he stood and watched, dirt and stones and pale clay piling up beside him.

She snorts. "I know."

Perhaps it's just the dim light, the way the porch light throws his face into shadow, but it looks like he flushes. Flushes and then, almost in spite of himself, laughs.

It's not a sound she's heard from him—not a sound she expected to hear, ever. It is, like his motion, easy, comfortable. She wishes—and it's a foolish wish—that she could hear him laugh again.

She likes him. It's stupid and she knows it, but in spite of everything he's done, everything he's said, she finds she likes the sound of his voice and the movement of his hands. Likes, maybe, the person he could be.

She looks to her hand, dirt-blackened and callused; she looks to her feet, hanging into the grave, and then closes her eyes against a wave of sorrow and regret.

In another life, she tells herself, and wishes the words didn't feel so hollow.

———·———

For a time, Jesse digs in silence. Avery watches as the last of the grave is dug, down and down until it's done.

"That's enough," she tells him. She doesn't know the depth, doesn't need measurements; her heart and gut tell her they're done.

Or maybe it's only that she can't have him tell her more stories, can't keep fighting the stupid thought that they could have another night—not like this, but somewhere. Sitting on a porch, maybe, the night like a veil around them. Just talking.

She has her family, whom she loves more than anything; she has her little brothers and sister. It's just that she can't remember the last time she had a friend.

Jesse takes her offered hand as she helps him climb from the grave. He dusts his hands on his pants and looks around. Already, the night sky is lightening. On the far horizon, Avery can see a hint of blue.

Jesse looks at her, and for the first time the only thing between them is air.

"Is there anything . . .?" He fumbles for what to say. "I mean, before you can do your thing, is there anything else that I can—uh—"

"You could let my family out," she says. Only that.

He doesn't know what she's known for hours: that her mom and Aunt Jenny got themselves free, that they locked and barred the doors, that they took the kids up to bed in the dark and silence, and watch now from the upstairs windows. That they could have come to her rescue, only she has waved them off once, twice, three times with a quick shake of her head that could be mistaken for brushing away sweat.

She'll see this through, if that's what Jesse wants.

He says, "You can let them out when you're done." The same words he said at the start of the night, mere hours and forever ago. Except this time, he sounds uncertain.

"Yes," she agrees softly. "But so could you. No mask. No gun."

You could apologize. The words hang unspoken between them. Unspoken—but heard.

She sees it in his face, that twist of guilt and regret, as he remembers what he's done. He looks at the gun, long discarded on the ground, and then at the blanket-wrapped body. Something hardens in him then, like a mask coming down over his features.

"Let's just get this over with."

He doesn't know how to be afraid, she realizes, or how to deal with his fear. Anger he knows. Anger is fuel, anger is productive—even if, truly, that anger has nowhere to go. Nothing to do but hurt.

She wants to tell him—again, this final time—that it doesn't have to be this way. That he can make amends, and ease hurt with kindness, and if he cannot undo what he's done, cannot unmake his choices, he can at least choose different things. Here, now. While he still can.

But there are words, it seems, that she too cannot say.

He goes to the body, kneels down. Nathan's face is covered again, and Jesse does not draw that blanket back, only makes to lift this burden a final time.

"Here," he says. "Help me lower him down."

He's come that far at least. Willing to ask for help; just comfortable enough to think that she might grant it. But she does not move, only comes to stand across the grave from him.

There are tears in her eyes. She didn't expect that. How long has it been since she last cried? Years, she thinks. Years that feel like decades, even to someone as young as her.

Here, now, she feels her youth. Feels all her choices, made and unmade, and wishes she could be someone, anyone, but who she is. But *what* she is.

Wishes, truly, that this boy had come to her any way but this.

"Avery?" It is, she realizes, the first time he's said her name. The first and, perhaps, the last. "A hand?"

She shakes her head.

"Jesse." His name, so gently spoken. "Jesse, no."

He's annoyed at her refusal but brushes it away. "Fine, whatever, I can lift him myself."

She raises a hand. He sees the motion and hesitates. Stops.

"Jesse," Avery says again, and her heart is breaking. She takes a deep breath before she can continue. "Jesse," and her voice is a whisper now, barely that. "The grave isn't for him. It isn't for Nathan."

All the long night she's wished for more light—for the moon to come out, for a brightening of stars. In this moment, she wishes she could see nothing. Then she wouldn't have to watch as his confused expression changes. As understanding comes into his face, that rush of realization.

She expected anger. She expected hurt and denial. She has, over and over, seen all these and more.

Yet he says only, "Oh." It's a quiet sound, nearly a whimper. She watches as he goes to his knees as if he doesn't quite have the strength to stand. As his arms fall, empty, to his sides.

He stares at the grave, that yawning black hole they dug together, side by side. His grave, waiting for him.

"I cannot make life," she tells him softly. "I can only . . . relocate it."

"A life for a life."

"Yes."

He looks to the house once, briefly; looks toward the five lives he knows are inside. But he does not ask that of her, does not even try. Only bows his head, his hair falling across his face like a dark curtain.

Silence between them, heavy, weighted. Silence as all-encompassing as the black.

She does not break it, only lowers herself to the ground and kneels as he is kneeling, the grave and his brother's body between them. She wishes she could go to him, wrap her arms around his shoulders—

No, truly, she wishes they had *time*. That she could become someone whose hand he'd accept in comfort. That she could see him smile. That she could hear that laugh again.

Foolish hopes, all. She lets them go, one by one, and breathes until her eyes are dry.

At last he looks up. For a moment she wonders whether he's going to try to leave. Some do. Even those who understand the necessary sacrifice ahead of time, sometimes at this moment they break. They change their minds. It's no terrible thing, choosing to live; it's not selfish to not give all of one's self, all of one's futures, for one who has already died, even if it might feel that way.

But perhaps she doesn't truly know him, because when he looks at her face she sees only determination. Only thoughts of his brother.

"Okay," Jesse says. "What do I have to do?"

———•———

Other deaths have been wrapped in ritual. Sometimes there's a ceremony if that's what the family wants. Sometimes there are words spoken, or prayers read. Once the sacrifice sang a song before she went into her grave, and her face had been glorious then, transcendent, as bright as her voice had been sweet.

Now there is only the two of them. Avery watches as Jesse climbs into the grave.

"Do you want a blanket?" she asks. Not the bloody blanket that wraps Nathan, but there are others, inside. She could get the blanket from the end of her bed, the blue one with the green stripes.

"Would it make any difference?"

"Only to you." And, maybe, to her. More things she cannot say.

"Then leave it. It won't matter for long, right?"

He crouches, sits, then slowly stretches himself out. The grave is long enough for him, but only just. His hair brushes against the top wall, the toes of his sneakers against the other. He lays his head back, then shifts to get more comfortable.

"Really is rocky," he says then, and lets out a breath that is not quite a laugh.

Her lips turn up in a hint of a smile. "Told you."

She comes to sit beside the grave, looking down at his face, his brother's body on her other side. There should be something else she can say, if not words of comfort, then—*something*. But if there is, she does not know the words.

"Are you ready?" she asks. As if anyone could ever be ready.

He stares up at her from the dark and shadow, eyes wide.

"Will it hurt?" he whispers.

"No. I promise."

"Okay." His throat moves as he swallows. "Okay, whatever you're going to do . . ."

She reaches toward him with one hand, toward his brother's body with the other.

"Wait," he says, voice cracking. She almost expects him to sit, to climb out, but he only takes a shuddering breath and says, "Tell him, tell Nathan . . . it's not his fault. None of this is his fault, okay? And that I . . . that I'll see him on the other side one day. A very, very long time from now. And that I want him to have a happy life, a *good* life. I want him to see the world and get married and get that dog he's always wanted and, and . . ."

He's weeping now; the tears drown out the words.

"I'll tell him."

A long moment, then: "Avery?"

She looks back down into that darkness, even though it's hard. Even though she wishes it was already over, wishes she didn't have to do this at all—that they could all three of them be here, her and Jesse and Nathan, and they could go inside and see her family, and see that her siblings were okay, and then Aunt Jenny would sit them down and they'd have pancakes for breakfast and—

"It's not your fault either," he says. "Look out for my little brother for me, okay?"

"Okay," she agrees softly. "He can stay with us here for a while, you know. If he wants." Another brother for her to love; it's not the worst thing, no matter how she feels right now.

Jesse nods and closes his eyes.

"Thank you."

Then because there is nothing else to say, she closes her eyes, too, and *reaches.*

Below her, Jesse is a bonfire light, white-hot touched with gold and green. She gathers that light in her hand softly, gently, prising away the tangles that keep it clinging to flesh the way ivy clings to a wall. She breathes in, and that light flows into her, warm and bright and flashing like a kaleidoscope; she exhales and the light flows through her, pouring through her heart and down her arm and into the waiting flesh.

The body has gone cold and stiff; it's been hours since Nathan died, and there's the wound that killed him in the first place. One life is not enough. She did not tell this to Jesse because this part doesn't matter, not to him; this part is her sacrifice. She *reaches* for a little bit of her own light and the lights of the world around her: the green sparks of the growing grass, the little mice that tunnel through the earth near the far garden, the worms and insects in the ground around them. She *reaches* farther and farther still, and she can just grasp the farthest lights that are the trees growing at the edges of the clearing, their roots dug deep into the soil, their branches grasping at the sky.

Not her own family, safe in the house—those bright lights she shies from—but everything else.

The rocks aren't the only reason their lawn is so bare, their gardens so sad and sparse. And the clearing that surrounds their house, a wide perfect ring where no tree grows? They did not cut the trees down—not living, anyway.

Every fire needs its fuel. Even this.

She feels more than sees Nathan's wound knit together, as the congealed blood liquifies and drains from where it has pooled in his lungs, at the bottoms of his legs, along his back. She pours the light into him, more and more, feeling every bit of it, every leaf and branch, every blade of grass, every insect and mouse and—Jesse. The brightest light of all, passing through her like a wildfire, hot and fierce and then gone.

Jesse.

———

When Avery opens her eyes, dawn is near. All around her, the grass has turned crisp and yellow, and the trees at the edges of the clearing have gone red as if to welcome autumn early. Soon, the leaves will fall.

In the grave, Jesse is still, silent, unmoving. She cannot look at him, cannot imagine piling all that stone and soil on top of him.

Beside her the bloodstained blanket twitches and shifts—then Nathan inhales.

Avery draws the blanket back. His face is unnaturally pale, his lips near purple from cold, the flesh around his eyes so dark it seems bruised. Soon, she knows, the shivers will begin as his muscles try to quiver their way back to warmth and life.

She tries not to resent him for that life; for being himself and not his brother. What Jesse told her is true: it's not Nathan's fault, not any of it. It will be a few weeks until he feels fully well again, but she'll be there to care for him, just like she promised. And maybe she'll come to care for him too, or maybe he'll leave, but either way he'll live.

In the house, Avery sees movement. Her mom, she knows, will have put on the kettle for tea, and Aunt Jenny will be rustling through the cupboards, mixing ingredients by eye for her famous buttermilk pancakes. She wants nothing more than to go to them, to have them hold her in their arms.

But for now, she'll wait until Nathan wakes. She'll wait to welcome him home.

※　※　※

Author's Notes to My Younger Self: Always be learning something; always be making something. Yeah, sure, your life may be on fire, but this way at the end *you'll have ashes and a cool craft.*

BLUE KUEH

Joyce Chng

Madam Kong passed away last night.

It was bizarre. We'd just visited her in that morning. She was cheerful, even chatty. She even gave us her famous blue kueh she made daily for sale at the market. We laughed, glad to see she was well. Her flat in Katong was immaculately kept and clean. Madam Kong was one of our more at-risk cases because she lived alone. Her sons only visited her on weekends, but her next-door neighbour, Lim Ah Soh, checked on her once a day.

Gladdened, we left her flat. The sun was shining, hot, and the sky was a breathtaking blue. Everything felt good. Then, that evening, her eldest son called to inform me his mother had suffered a stroke and was unconscious. By midnight, she was dead. Ah Soh had found her lying in the middle of the living room. It was already too late.

Our centre manager tried to shrug it off, saying that "it happens." The cluster we served was ninety-percent elderly from sixty-five onwards. Yet, a pall of sadness hung over the office while we tried to process what had actually occurred. All the social workers and volunteers attended the funeral wake in the evening. It felt surreal. The sons were weeping their eyes out, their children playing hide-and-seek among the tables, their giggles an odd counterpoint to the atonal chanting of the Buddhist monks. A strong breeze made the plastic sheets covering the table tops billow but failed to cool the humid Singapore night. One paper plate of nuts and sweets went flying. A small white butterfly perched on the picture frame with Madam Kong's portrait for the entire evening.

The same sadness followed me home. I recalled Madam Kong's positive attitude, her can-do spirit, and her delicious savoury kueh. They were desserts made with love and care. She grew her own butterfly pea vine where she harvested the flowers to make the vivid blue dye for the desserts. I helped her water it once or twice when her arthritis made it too painful for her to walk. Madam Kong showed us the dried flowers once. The vine grew lush and thick, tendrils curling around the metal railings. It bloomed profusely. Now she was gone, nobody was going to water her plants. To make the matter even sadder, her sons had decided to sell their mother's flat.

As I walked along the pathway leading up to the apartment block where I lived, I came across rows of lit red candles and plates of sweets and fruits. One or two people were throwing paper money into a metallic burner, and the smell of burning was intense. Fire roared. Embers swirled about. It was then I remembered it was the start of Seventh Month or the Chinese Hungry Ghost Festival. I was not the superstitious sort and I simply continued on my journey home.

My house was quiet. The rooms were dark. My daughters, Celeste and Jolene, weren't back yet from school. They had projects. I went about dusting the surfaces before going into the kitchen to prepare a late dinner at 8 p.m. I turned my phone on, and it pinged with a message from earlier in the day. The sound was unnaturally loud, and I jumped.

It was a text from Mr. Lim, my optometrist, to collect my contact lenses. After thirty-odd years of refusing to get contacts, I was finally doing it.

Celeste rolled her eyes when I told her about the contacts. She thought I wasn't fashionable enough. I was "too auntie" for her. Since when did being in my forties mean old age? I was still fit and healthy. I watched my diet and exercised diligently. Was I *old*? To the elderly at the centre, I was still very young. Some of the ladies called me "girl."

The contact lenses were a newfangled product heralded as the next best thing in eye care. The lenses combined everything: progressive, bifocals, and anti-astigmatism. Called NewSight™, they were designed to give wearers a better quality of life. Reading would be a breeze now. Besides, customers got to choose the colour too. Mr. Lim was practically waxing lyrical about the lenses.

They were also expensive.

"Aiyah," Mr. Lim was saying, "Not expensive. You get three-in-one! Four, if you include the colour!"

I stared at the contact lenses in their clear solution. They looked small and delicate. The fragility was what turned me off in the first place. "What if they fall out or break? What if they break in my eyes?" I questioned Mr. Lim relentlessly before I made my decision.

"You just have to keep a strict hygiene routine," he told me. "Clean, clean, clean."

I had somewhat managed to get past my fear of hurting my eyes. Wearing the contact lenses under Mr. Lim's supervision felt simple. I could do it. It didn't hurt at all. When I blinked and stared at my reflection in the mirror, I saw my eyes—*blue* eyes—looking back at me. I looked *good*.

Armed with boxes of saline and new confidence, I stepped out of the shop. It took some time to get used to everything looking sharp and clear. I could *see*. I could read the small print on the receipt. I felt brand new all over again, like when I was a teenager. Glasses no more!

When I got home, the elevators were all occupied. I waited, fiddling with the plastic bag. I felt someone walk up to me, a presence behind my back. Thinking it was one of my neighbours, I glanced over my shoulder—

—And I saw Madam Kong. Bright as day. She was wearing her favourite t-shirt with pink flowers and her blue denim shorts. She was carrying a box filled with her blue desserts. Her famous kueh. Her smile was the same cheerful smile I saw two days ago.

Before she died.

"For you," she said in her husky voice and handed the box of kueh to me. "You must be hungry."

Reflexively, I held out my hand. . . . Then I stopped myself. She was *dead*.

The elevator chose this moment to open its door. The box dropped. Madam Kong disappeared. I blinked. Twice. There was the box, its contents spilled out, the kueh squished.

Confused, I fled into the lift and stabbed the button for the twelfth floor. I tried to rationalize what I had just seen. It was a trick of the light. The box of kueh had already been there, left behind by some inconsiderate neighbour.

Madam Kong was *dead. I attended her wake one day ago. Her sons were crying their hearts out.*

Celeste and Jolene didn't question me when I rushed into our apartment. They were busy with their schoolwork; Jolene had her headphones stuck in her ears, lost in her own world, busy sketching on her tablet, Celeste trying to complete a report on her laptop, frowning away as she typed.

I couldn't sleep that night.

———•———

"Wah, stylo milo," Beng, one of the social workers, commented as I stepped into the office, and Wei Ling glanced my way. My head throbbed. I hadn't slept well. I boiled my experience down to wearing new contact lenses. My eyes were sti ll trying to get used to them.

"Aww, thank you," I said, placing my bag on my worktable. The office looked sharper. I winced at the cobwebs hiding behind the air-conditioning unit. Miniscule cracks in the wall. "What's on today?"

"The usual. Daily exercise and home visits," Beng said, checking the schedule on the whiteboard.

"Hey, did you dream of Madam Kong last night?" Wei Ling chimed in. "I did. It was weird. She gave me a box of her kueh." Wei Ling was also close to Madam Kong. Madam Kong affectionately termed Wei Ling 'goddaughter.' Wei Ling would sit next to Madam Kong and listen to her talk about her sons and her grandchildren. She did that with many of the elderly residents. She was kind and patient.

But I froze, the memory of seeing Madam Kong flooding back again. For me, it hadn't been a dream. The office was suddenly very cold.

"It's also Seventh Month lah. Hungry Ghost Festival, you know?" Beng chuckled nervously. "They are all visiting their loved ones lah."

Wei Ling laughed it off, but Beng crossed himself when he thought nobody was looking.

Shaking the rush of fear, I stood in the office doorway and watched the elderly arriving for their daily exercise. Some walked in slowly with their canes. Some were in wheelchairs pushed by their carers. Attendance normally fluctuated. Mondays and Fridays were usually packed. Tuesdays, Wednesdays, and Thursdays were quieter. Sometimes, attendance was poor because of medical check-ups and doctor's appointments. The centre was okay with that, because we were a non-profit organization, but we still worried when we noted unexplained absences. However, there seemed to be more people today.

It was a Tuesday.

Wasn't that Uncle Rahid? He passed two months ago. Did Mrs. Santhi just sit beside Madam Maisarah?

Mrs. Santhi died last year.

I shook myself and my vision cleared. No. The only elderly here were the expected ones. The living.

The rest of the day was a struggle. I kept seeing past faces at the centre. People with whom I'd sat, paid visits, spoken, chatted, and held hands—who had long since passed away due to the confluence of old age and illness. Nonplussed, I took out my contact lenses and wore my glasses. Everything went immediately dull. The colours remained the same, but they were not as sharp and crisp as before. Normal. Nothing out of the ordinary happened. The impossible faces disappeared.

I was irate. I called the optometrist on my lunch hour.

"Hey, Mr. Lim," I said, trying not to sound angry. "I think your contact lenses might have side-effects. I am seeing things."

"Aiyah, the product doesn't make people see things," he said. "You might be stressed from work. I will call you back later." The call went dead.

Annoyed, I flung the phone back into my bag and flopped back into my armchair. It squeaked alarmingly. Still uneasy, I decided to make myself a mug of hot jasmine tea. The office was quiet. Most of the social workers and volunteers were out on afternoon home visits. I was the only one left to man the centre.

A plastic box of blue kueh sat on the staff pantry table. Suresh, the administrative officer, was quietly working on a spreadsheet at his table.

The cover of the box was lightly coated with condensation, as if the kueh were warm. Some of the senior citizens occasionally gave us food as a way of saying thank you. Only last week, Madam Maisarah made us mee siam, spicy rice vermicelli noodles sprinkled with chopped chives and fried bean curd.

"Hey, Suresh, did anyone buy kueh for the team?" I asked. We often bought food to share with each other. Suresh looked up from the spreadsheet and shook his head slowly.

Horrified, I stared back at the box of blue kueh, the blue of the butterfly pea flower.

———•———

I wore the contact lenses again.

This time, I saw more ghosts. More than I wished for.

I saw the old man whom we tried to help a while back, a quiet gentleman who, the residents complained, was a hoarder. He collected newspapers and old glass bottles. He was hanging mobiles of broken glass on the fruit trees planted in the communal garden area. The glass shards spun in the sun: emerald green, dark amber gold, and glowing ruby red.

He'd died at home, surrounded by squalor and broken glass shards.

The old gentleman was laughing joyfully, his mien totally different from his reticent self. Tiny figures flew about him. They . . . they looked like birds, like brown Eurasian sparrows, but not really. Fairies?

Fairies?

Somewhere, monks chanted Buddhist sutras. Another funeral wake. I walked on.

Mr. Gan, playing with his beloved toy terrier.

Mrs. Viknesh, feeding the pigeons cooked rice.

Gloria, talking to the community cats.

Mrs. Dorothy, holding hands with her husband, her beaming face turned to him as if they were madly in love with each other.

Mr. Zarid, just taking a stroll.

So many, so many.

Even shadows huddling together under the large angsana tree. I caught glimpses of faces, hands, feet.

All dead.

These were couples, singles, widows, and widowers, whom the centre had known and come to love. For many, the centre served as a home away from home, a place they could socialize and make friends. Many were lonely and lived alone. Our case files attested to this sad fact. They would tell us stories about their lives, their dreams, their lost hopes and sacrifices, their children, their wishes.

Is there life after death? Why are they appearing to me?

Why do I see them?

Why can I see them?

I touched my eyes, my hands shaking.

It was too much. My world spun. Fleeing back into the office, I removed the contact lenses and packed them in their saline solution.

———•———

"Should I stop wearing the contact lenses?" I asked Celeste idly that evening.

"What for? You just got them." Celeste rolled her eyes. She thought Mummy was nuts.

"I am seeing things," I said, and stopped myself from continuing.

Celeste was back at whatever she was doing, sketching on her tablet. She wanted to be an artist when she graduated. Jolene was in the kitchen, cutting cucumbers for dinner. It was her turn to cook. They were managing well without their dad. A year into the divorce, things seemed to have picked up. They were seeing the counsellor regularly at school. But Celeste and Jolene were generally optimistic and would talk to me if they needed help. It wasn't easy raising two teenagers and working at the same time. I still had to pay their school fees, the house's expenses, and groceries. Luckily, I had help from my parents. Not all were that fortunate. I felt bad for splurging on the contact lenses.

"You mean *ghosts*?" Jolene shouted from the kitchen. "My mum, the psychic! You can have your own show on YouTube, you know. Earn extra money from your fans!" I could see her grinning, a mischievous look on her face. She knew how to push my buttons. "You know, it's Ghost Month, what? They are all around us!"

I shushed her and then burst out laughing at the delicious absurdity. I shouldn't be superstitious.

We spent the night talking about work, school, and our plans for the future. I was determined to be with my daughters as much as I could. I thought of the elderly at the centre. They missed their children. They felt forgotten, neglected, tossed aside. *Would Celeste and Jolene forget about me when I am old? Would they put me in a nursing home?*

Would I walk alone as one of the lost spirits, bereft of home?

There was another box of blue kueh on the staff pantry table.

"Did Madam Kong's sons make this?" Wei Ling said, nibbling into one. "They are delicious!"

"Her sons . . . don't make them," Beng said, frowning as he picked at another kueh. "As far as I know, she didn't teach them how to make kueh. She only started making kueh after her husband died of cancer four years ago."

"Not me," Suresh said from his work desk. "I bought mee rebus. Not the kueh."

Wei Ling almost dropped her half-eaten blue kueh. Her face had turned pale.

———·———

People were burning joss paper. Passersby took care not to step on half-burned paper money as they said it would offend spirits.

Seventh Month was a fretful time. Don't go out at night, don't swim, and don't make fun of the spirits. Unlike Qing Ming Festival where we swept the tombs of our ancestors and loved ones, Seventh Month seemed darker with vicious spirits eager to take advantage of the food and wreak havoc in people's lives. The vicious spirits were hateful because they'd been ill-treated or wronged before they passed, or they committed serious crimes. The stories I heard from my own grandparents and parents were of spirits fighting over the offerings, the bigger and stronger ghosts bullying the weaker ones.

Yet, as I watched, the spirits weren't really offended. Just bemused at the antics of the living and their loved ones who took the utmost care to lay the best offering table with plates of food and drink for them. As a gesture, the centre laid out its own table. We burned joss paper. Non-denominational and interfaith as we were, we respected the various cultures and faiths.

"I hope that will appease them," Wei Ling said. She was still a little spooked by the kueh incident. She actually threw the entire box away out of sheer fright. Suresh cheekily told her off for wasting food.

"If you have only shown them love and care, and have never borne them ill will," I said mildly, "why should you be afraid? Madam Kong came to you in your dreams because you sat with her and held her hands." I patted Wei Ling's shoulder to reassure her. "Don't worry too much."

"We showed them care and concern," Beng said as we walked back into the centre, glad for the air conditioning. The elderly were playing rummy. "We listened to their stories. We tried our best lah. Don't worry!"

———·———

I saw Madam Kong again. Like when I last saw her, she was holding onto a box of blue kueh.

I read up on hauntings a few days ago. Was it a residual haunting, where Madam Kong's emotions lingered so much that they were imprinted in the environment? Was it a memory loop she was stuck in and unable to break free? One website suggested aggressive ways to get rid of persistent hauntings: purification and cleansing rituals by clergy, magical shields, and even moving away. But, Madam Kong wasn't a vicious or malicious spirit, hell-bent on destroying people's lives. The same website also suggested communicating or talking to the spirit since, like us, they wanted the living to listen to their stories.

"Take this," Madam Kong said. She was wearing the same t-shirt and blue shorts as she had been the last time I saw her alive. However, the outline of her figure seemed to blur, as if someone had smudged the edges with an eraser. "You might be hungry."

It was a quiet early evening. Nobody was around. The rush hour hadn't hit yet. In the distance, there was a getai where singers performed for the spirits. Getai was popular during this period. Garishly dressed singers belted out Hokkien and Cantonese favourites.

I reached over and took the box. It felt real. Solid. Warm. "Thank you." I finally found my courage and voice.

Madam Kong turned as if to go. She smiled warmly, her eyes twinkling. "No, I have to thank you, Susan. You visited me before I died."

Tears instantly brimmed in my eyes and spilled, hot and salty. Her words crushed and lifted me at the same time.

"Madam Kong . . ." was all I could say.

"Just remember me." Madam Kong smiled her beautiful smile and faded from view. A soft sigh lingered in the air. I was still holding onto the box of kueh.

I wasn't wearing my NewSight™ contact lenses.

That night, I kept the contact lenses in their little container and left them on my dressing table. I also ate the kueh.

"You, learning how to make kueh?" Beng asked me the next day. He saw me thumbing through a recipe book on Peranakan cooking over the lunch hour. I was reading up on a recipe for lemper udang, a savoury glutinous rice dessert with blue butterfly pea dye added for colour. Made with obvious loving care, the rice wrapped the prawn filling in a neat cylindrical shape within a banana leaf.

"Why not?" I said. "Good to pick up a new skill."

"You are not wearing your contacts." Beng blinked. "Got tired of them?"

I smiled. "I don't need them to see."

Outside the office window, the fairies flew about the sparkling mobiles of broken glass. A wild butterfly pea plant had curled up the white fence surrounding the centre. Blue flowers had already emerged.

Author's Notes to My Younger Self: I will tell my younger self that the one important life's lesson is to be empathetic. Be kind, be compassionate, nothing's black and white.

SECOND THOUGHTS

Eric Choi

"The whole story's out," said Derek Tsai, handing her the tablet.

Elaine Carrington took the device. "Police Shoot Suspect in U. of T. Murder," proclaimed TheGlobeAndMail.com. "Armed Standoff at U. of T. Tied to Military Funded Research," was TheStar.com's lead story.

"How much trouble am *I* in?" she asked.

"You don't want to know."

Elaine sighed heavily, sinking back into the hospital bed, and then . . .

———•———

. . . No. Not before Elaine . . .

———•———

. . . Took a sip of truly disgusting, stone cold coffee.

It was a beautiful Friday afternoon in the middle of July, and Elaine Carrington was alone in her seventh floor office in the Burton Tower of the University of Toronto's McLennan Physical Laboratories. All the other graduate students in the Atmospheric Physics research group had left to get an early start on the weekend.

She stared blankly at her laptop, unable to concentrate on her mathematical models of atmospheric radiative transfer functions. Her mind was instead distracted by thoughts of her idiot boyfriend, a fourth-year Engineering Science student named Derek Tsai. They had just returned the previous week from a disastrous trip to Germany. She wouldn't have believed that a Chinese-Canadian could outdrink the Germans, but Derek somehow managed it. She was beginning to think he had a real problem.

Elaine drained the last of the coffee and powered down her laptop. She briefly considered going to her jujitsu dojo but then decided against it. *Might as well go straight home and get a fresh start on Monday.*

"Excuse me."

She whirled.

"Oh, I'm so sorry," said Maria Alighieri, the summer student. The young woman was dressed in bright orange shorts and a dark green University of Toronto T-shirt. Her long, curly light brown hair was tied in a ponytail. "I didn't mean to startle you."

"What do you want?" Elaine asked.

Maria opened her notebook to a page of handwritten equations. "I was wondering if you could check my derivations. I'd ask Jim, but he's away," she said, referring to their supervisor, Professor James Stafford.

Elaine shook her head. "Electricity and magnetism really aren't my field. Why don't you ask Bill or Ross?" she suggested, referring to Bill O'Leary and Ross McVitie, the doctoral students in Stafford's group.

Maria suddenly frowned, her eyes downcast. "I guess so. Thanks anyway."

Elaine waited for Maria to leave before closing and locking the office door. She made her way to the elevator and pressed the down button. As she waited, she scanned the adjacent bulletin board and saw an announcement:

RESEARCH VOLUNTEERS NEEDED

The Particle Physics and Relativity group is looking for volunteers to participate in a study. The experiment is non-medical in nature; participants will not be required to ingest, inhale, or be injected with any substances. You will be paid a stipend upon completion of the study. If you are interested, please contact Dr. Michiru Takayoshi or his research associate Corey Stadtmauer.

At the bottom of the flyer were the phone number of Professor Takayoshi and the email address of Corey Stadtmauer. Elaine had no interaction with the Particle Physics group, and she knew nothing about Takayoshi or his work. *Maybe I should check this out. It'll give me a chance to see what Takayoshi and his students are up to.*

The following week, Elaine arrived at the door of the designated room a few minutes before the eleven o'clock start time. A group of about twenty people was already waiting in the corridor. She recognized many of them from around the Physics building, but there were also a few strangers who had probably come in off the street.

"Hey, Elaine!"

She turned. "Oh, hi, Bill."

Bill O'Leary approached Elaine with his characteristic duck-like walk from the elevator. He was in his early thirties, of medium height with a long angular face, wearing a red baseball cap from which a few strands of thin, orange-brown hair poked out. He gestured at the door with Takayoshi's sign on it. "You here for this?"

"Uh, huh. You too?"

"Yeah, well, you know me. I like to live," Bill moved his arms like a surfer, *"vicariously.* How about you?"

Elaine wanted to tell Bill she didn't think the word meant what he thought it did, but decided not to. "Just curious, I guess. I've never volunteered for anything like this before, and I'm interested in what Takayoshi's group is up to."

Bill sneered. "Listen, that guy Takayoshi . . . he's very dishonest and weak. Man, do I have dirt on him!"

"You have dirt," Elaine narrowed her eyes, "on Takayoshi?"

"Yup, sure do." Bill crossed his arms. "But it's gonna cost you!"

"Cost me?"

"Oh, come now. I'm not giving out this stuff for free! Don't you know the Law of Conservation of Information? You give me information, I give you dirt."

"I don't have any . . . 'information'."

"Of course, you do. Everybody does. Some skeleton in your closet? One way or another, I'll find out." Bill rubbed his chin. "Say, how are things going with your boyfriend?"

"Uh, fine. Just fine." She changed the subject. "So, how's your wife doing?"

"Excellent, actually. Excellent. Mel just got interviewed for a postdoc at TRIUMF," he said, referring to the Tri-University Meson Facility, a large cyclotron located at the University of British Columbia.

"Congratulations. Do you think she'll get it?"

"Why wouldn't she? She's the very best person for the job, a very stable genius. She knows it, I know it, everybody knows it. I even told her to tell them that."

The door opened, and Professor Takayoshi emerged. He thanked them all for coming, and instructed them to find a desk upon entering the room. There, they would each find an envelope which they were not to open until told to do so.

Elaine spotted a seat by the door, but Bill bolted toward it and sat there himself. She scanned the room for another spot, but with many people still standing it was hard to see.

"Playing musical chairs, are we?" A short, thin man with a prominent chin approached her. His pale, oval face was crowned with slick brown hair. "I'm Corey Stadtmauer. I'm one of Dr. Takayoshi's Ph.D students."

She recognized him immediately. "You were the TA in my second year quantum course!"

Corey smiled. "Yeah, I think I remember you. You're—"

"Elaine Carrington."

"Elaine. Yeah, well, thanks for coming for this." He pointed. "There's a seat over there."

"Thanks."

As Elaine meandered her way to the empty spot, Professor Takayoshi addressed the volunteers. "At exactly quarter past, I will ask each of you to open the envelope on your desk. I want you to read the instructions and follow them *exactly*. It is vitally important that you follow the instructions *to the letter*. It is also crucial that this room be silent. I want you to treat this like an exam." He smiled. "Don't worry, you can't fail. There's going to be a massive bell curve in this 'course'."

Elaine and a few others chuckled.

Professor Takayoshi looked at his watch. "Please open your envelope . . . *now*."

Elaine did so. Inside, she found a single sheet of paper and a USB stick.

    Consider a radioactive decay counter
    that has been used to generate a sequence
    of positive and negative random numbers.
    The numbers produced, which you will not
    see, are stored on the enclosed USB stick.
    Your task is to imagine the case in which
    all the numbers produced are *positive*.

> For the next five minutes, you are to focus
> your concentration and visualize, in your
> mind's eye, the decay counter having
> produced only *positive* numbers.

Elaine read the instructions three times, but the sentences just sounded stranger with each iteration. She finally gave up trying to understand and simply squeezed her eyes shut and pictured in her mind only *positive* numbers stored on the USB stick.

"The experiment is concluded."

Elaine almost jumped. She hadn't realized her concentration had been so total.

"Thanks for coming out this afternoon," Professor Takayoshi continued. "Please give me your mailing address so I can send you the cheque. Talk to Corey if you would prefer electronic payment. Again, thanks for participating."

As she was leaving, Elaine saw Bill in the hall. "What the hell was that all about?"

Bill shrugged. "It was stupid, that's what it was. I can't stand it. No sympathy for stupidity, that's what I say."

"But we're gonna get paid."

"Yeah. Stupid, eh? See ya."

She was almost at the door when another voice called out.

"Hey, Elaine!" Corey Stadtmauer strode up to her. "Thanks again for participating in the experiment."

"No problem," she replied.

"Did I get your email, so I can send your payment?"

"Actually," Elaine said, "I wrote my mailing address on Professor Takayoshi's form so he can send me a cheque. Old school, right?"

"Yeah, sure." Corey seemed disappointed, but then his expression changed. "Hey, um . . . I, ah—I lost my partial differential equations textbook. Hillen and Leonard. Do you have a copy I could borrow?"

Elaine was caught off guard. In fact, she did have a copy of Hillen and Leonard. But after a moment of thought, she shook her head. "No, sorry. But it was nice to meet you, Corey. See you around."

It was now almost noon. She left the McLennan Laboratories and went to her usual summertime lunch spot, a metal park bench on the grass behind the Astronomy and Astrophysics building. As she peeled an orange, she spotted a tall, skinny man emerge from the nearby Lash Miller Chemical Labs.

"Hey, Yegor!"

"Hallo, Elaine."

Yegor Wiśniewski was a third year chemistry major working at Lash Miller for the summer. As always, he was wearing a camouflage-patterned cap and—despite the fact it was July—a Belgian army jacket. He had purchased both from a military surplus store on Yonge Street where, he claimed, he was such a frequent customer the owner gave him discounts.

"How's it going, Yegor?"

"Deed you see da news?"

"No."

"A bomb vent off on a bus en Jeerusalem yesterday."

"That's terrible!"

Yegor shrugged. "It vas a beeg bomb, you know. Beeg bomb. Wery nice."

"Yeah, I'll bet you know all about big bombs, huh?"

"I do."

"Why, you know how to make one?"

"Yes."

Elaine almost choked on her orange. "You're serious, aren't you?"

"Of course."

"Mind if I ask where you learned?"

Yegor took a bite of his apple. *Da Terrorist's Handbook*. I got it off de Dark Web."

Elaine was sorry she asked. "So, anyway, this bombing in Jerusalem. You don't think . . . I mean, you don't think . . .'"

"Tink vat? Dey are freedom fighters."

"Were there soldiers on the bus?"

Yegor paused. "No . . . I tink dey vere yooniversity stoodents."

"What?" Elaine was shocked. "You mean innocent people were slaughtered, and you don't think that's terrible?"

"Dey vere not innocent." He solemnly raised an index finger. "Until de Palestinians are free, no von dere is innocent."

Elaine suddenly lost her appetite.

"You haaf to go?" Yegor asked when she stood.

"Uh, yeah. I, uh . . . I've got a group meeting." She glanced at her phone. "Oh, damn. I'm late already. Gotta go. See ya!"

It was only half-past noon when she returned to the seventh floor offices of the Atmospheric Physics research group, where she shared cubicle offices with Bill, Ross, and Maria. As she approached the door, she could hear Bill O'Leary's loud, cocksure voice.

"—see that, Ross. I mean, we've already bought a house in Vancouver, so it's not as if—oh, torpedo one loaded, sir!"

Elaine entered the office—and gasped as a small white object darted across her path. The spitball ricocheted off the printer and fell to the floor.

"You missed!" Bill barked. "How could you miss?"

"Sorry," sneered Ross McVitie as he put another wad in the straw.

Elaine's eyes tracked to their intended target, the summer intern Maria Alighieri. She was at a computer trying to do a circuit analysis in SPICE but was obviously having difficulty. Elaine could see a few spitballs imbedded in her hair.

"Guys, can you quit it? I have to finish this for Professor Stafford."

"What's going on here?" Elaine asked.

Bill's eyes widened in surprise. "Elaine! You're back early."

"What's going on?" she asked again, turning to Ross.

The chubby Manitoban pulled the straw out of his mouth. "We're just having some fun with Maria."

"This is fun?" Elaine asked rhetorically.

"It's just a joke," Ross whined. "Don't you think it's funny?"

"I guess this was a real knee-slapper back in Manawaka, eh?"

Ross flashed a gap-toothed grin.

Elaine's eyes scanned from Ross to Bill and back again. She had pegged them as juvenile jokers from the moment she joined Stafford's research group, and initially she had brushed aside their childish antics. In recent months, however, she'd begun to seriously question whether their behaviour was acceptable. She wondered if what she had just seen might actually constitute harassment, in which case she should probably say something. But she was stuck working with them for at least another year, and she wanted to maintain a cordial working relationship.

She hesitated, unsure of what to do.

Maybe spitballs are going a little too far.

She turned to Ross and looked him straight in the eye. "Ross?"

"Yes?"

"June 28th."

The gap-toothed grin abruptly vanished.

"'Bubbles'," Elaine continued. "'Doing the turtle' . . . 'There's always room in my bed' . . ."

Ross threw the straw and paper into the recycling bin, whirled in his seat, and turned on his computer.

"Wait a minute!" Bill pointed at Elaine. "You have dirt—" he pointed at Ross "—on *him*?" He pulled up his chair. "Hey Ross, do you know the Law of Conservation of Information?"

"Thank you," Maria whispered.

Elaine spent an hour working out at her jujitsu dojo, then went to Chinatown for groceries before returning to her apartment at the Village by the Grange. As she slid her key into the lock, she heard a noise from inside.

She opened the door. As her eyes adjusted to the darkness she discerned a silhouette. She lunged for the light switch.

"Derek!"

An inebriated, semiconscious Derek Tsai was sprawled on her sofa, moaning loudly. "Elaine? Aw, Elaine . . ."

"Oh, for God's sake!" Elaine navigated around a minefield of empty beer cans. She grabbed Derek and pulled him to his feet.

"Aw, gee . . . S-sorry, Elaine. Had ta . . . ta feel? Okay? Gotta, I dunno . . . crash it down . . ."

She endured his slurred, incomprehensible speech all the way to the door. Without ceremony, she dumped him into the hall. He hit the floor like a sack of potatoes.

"The last time . . ." she muttered. "This is the *last time*." Elaine rummaged through his pockets, found the key chain, and removed her apartment key from the lot. "I've had it with you, Derek! I don't ever want to see your stinking hide again!"

"But—"

Elaine slammed the door. *Why the hell do I always end up with guys like Derek?* She leaned against the door, closed her eyes, and slowly breathed in and out a few times. After a while, she picked herself up and made her way to the kitchen, and then . . .

———·———

. . . No. Not before Elaine . . .

———·———

. . . Was almost at the door when Corey Stadtmauer called out to her.

"Hey Elaine, thanks again for participating in the experiment," he said. "Did I get your email, so that I can send you payment?"

"Actually," she replied, "I wrote my mailing address on Professor Takayoshi's form so that he can send me a cheque. Old school, right?"

"Yeah, sure. Hey, um . . . I, ah—I lost my partial differential equations textbook. Hillen and Leonard. Do you maybe have a copy I could borrow?"

Elaine was caught off guard. In fact, she did have a copy of Hillen and Leonard. After a moment of thought, she nodded. "Sure, no problem. Are you around next week? I'll bring it by your office."

Corey smiled. "Thanks so much. I'll be here. Please drop by."

The following week, Elaine went up to the eighth floor of Burton Tower to find Corey. As she approached the office door, a frisson passed over her. She'd finally broken up with Derek Tsai after finding him passed out drunk on her couch. *I really don't know anything about Corey, and I don't know what this all means, or even if it means anything at all, but it'll be good just to get to know him.*

Elaine entered the office and found her way to Corey's cubicle. He wasn't there. Another student was at a nearby desk. He was dark and muscular, dressed in a faded old tank top and track pants. The name tag on his cubicle said "Ibrahim Zaher".

"Excuse me, Ibrahim?"

He was holding a pen in one hand while staring at his laptop with a blank expression. After a moment, he looked up. His obsidian eyes gave Elaine a piercing, suspicious look.

"Is Corey around?" she asked.

"Corey is not here!" he snapped.

"Uh . . . I can see that. Do you know where he is?"

Ibrahim slammed the pen down. "Corey is supervising another volunteer experiment for Takayoshi."

"Again? Really?"

"Yes, really!" Ibrahim balled his large, calloused hands into fists. "Takayoshi spends all his time on Corey's project. He has left me nothing but odd jobs. I am but his slave boy!"

Elaine was immediately tired of his whining. "If you hate Takayoshi so much and you hate it here so much, why don't you just quit?"

Leaving the brooding young man, Elaine went back to Corey's cubicle and put the book on his desk. As she turned to leave, she scanned the whiteboard on which a series of mathematical derivations was scrawled. One formula in particular caught her eye. It was the Hamiltonian function, one of the equations of quantum mechanics. Another equation was derived from the Hamiltonian by allowing the matrix H to be dependent on z and z*, the state vector and its complex conjugate for some unique quantum state Ψ. But that made the new equation nonlinear, which didn't make sense to Elaine because from what she understood of quantum theory the behaviour of atomic systems should be linear.

"Elaine!"

She jumped.

Corey laughed. "Sorry, I didn't mean to startle you."

"It's okay." She smiled sheepishly, then gestured at his desk. "Here's the book. Sorry it took so long to get it to you. I don't need it back anytime soon, so take your time."

"Thanks a lot. I really appreciate this."

Elaine pointed to the equations on the white board. "This is pretty neat. I'm surprised you need anything from Hillen and Leonard."

"Oh, no," Corey said. "The textbook's for an undergraduate course I'm tutoring."

"Right . . ." Elaine said slowly. "Anyway, like I said, I don't need it back anytime soon." She started to leave. "Well, have a nice day."

Corey picked up the book, hefting it. "Hey, um . . . Elaine?"

She turned.

"I'm really grateful for your help, and I was wondering if . . . would you, maybe, like to have dinner with me sometime?"

Elaine blinked, but she quickly pulled herself together. "Sure. Are you doing anything on Friday?"

"Friday would be great," he replied.

"Where would you like to go?"

His head swayed, as if he were trying to shake an answer out of his brain. "Ever been to that market restaurant place?"

"You mean Marché Mövenpick?"

"Yeah. Would that be all right?"

"Sure," Elaine said. "My email address is my initials 'emc' with the number two and the usual UofT Atmospheric Physics domain."

"Great! I'll drop you an email with my phone number and details."

As she left the office, Elaine glanced over his shoulder and caught Ibrahim's hard stare.

On Friday night, Elaine met Corey at the fountain near the entrance to the Marché Mövenpick restaurant in Brookfield Place. After posing for selfies with the green and white cow sculptures by the restaurant entrance, they went inside. Instead of ordering from a menu, they went "shopping" for their meals in an old European food market setting.

"How's your dinner?" Corey asked.

"It's good," Elaine replied. "How's yours?"

"Not great," Corey grinned, "and I'm guessing neither is yours, really."

They looked at each other for a moment, then burst out laughing.

"They used way too much oil," Elaine said, poking her chopsticks into the Asian stir-fry rice noodles with tofu and mixed vegetables.

"Mine's supposed to be seafood bouillabaisse, but it's smothered in tomato sauce," Corey said. "Who uses tomato sauce in bouillabaisse? Isn't it supposed to be a clear or white broth?"

"I didn't know you were such a foodie," Elaine said.

Corey smiled. "Anything else you'd like to know about me?"

She put down her chopsticks. "Tell me about your research."

Corey's eyes widened. "My research?"

"Sure. What is it exactly that you've been working on with Takayoshi? I mean, is it some secret project or something?"

Corey chuckled, perhaps a little nervously. "Oh, no. Goodness, no. It's no secret. Well . . . not *very* secret, anyway."

She stared him down.

"So you do want to hear."

Elaine nodded sweetly.

"All right." Corey leaned back in his chair. "But before I let you in on the conspiracy, you need to do something for me."

"What is it?" she asked.

"Would you be willing to do the experiment again? I've set up a new online version I'd like you to try."

Elaine shrugged. "Sure, I can do that."

"Great." Corey's thumbs flew over his phone. "I just sent you the link." He put the phone down, took a swig of water, and looked at Elaine. "You know Maxwell's equations, right?"

She began to recite. "Del dot B equals zero. Del dot E equals q over epsilon. Curl of B equals—"

"All right, all right. Anyway, the weird thing about Maxwell's equations is that if you do the math there are actually *two* sets of solutions for the effect of a moving electric charge. One describes an EM wave moving out from the particle for time greater than or equal to zero. We call these the 'retarded' waves."

"Okay . . ."

"But there's also another set of solutions."

Elaine pursed her lips. "You mean . . . the solutions for time *less than* zero?"

Corey nodded. "That's exactly what I mean. They're called the 'advanced' solutions, and the math—" At that moment, his phone rang. He looked at the number and frowned. "Hello, this is Corey. Yes . . . uh, huh . . . What? Oh, my God! When . . ."

Elaine furrowed her brow in concern.

"Right . . . uh, okay. Right. Uh, t-thank, thank you." Corey put down the phone, then buried his face in his hands. "Oh, my God."

"What? What is it? What's wrong?"

"It's Professor Takayoshi. He's been . . . murdered."

Elaine gasped.

Corey struggled to stand up. "I'm so sorry. We've . . . we've got to go."

While standing in line to pay, Corey told Elaine what little he knew. The campus police believed Professor Takayoshi had surprised an intruder in his office. There was a violent struggle, during which Takayoshi managed to hit the police call button on his desk phone. But by the time the cops reached the office, the old physicist was already dead. He had suffered a severe beating, and at some point in the assault, his neck had been broken.

The funeral for Professor Michiru Takayoshi took place a week later. He was laid to rest at the Mount Pleasant Cemetery in North York. A large delegation of family and friends as well as colleagues from the Physics Department were there to pay their respects. Elaine accompanied Corey to the funeral, but he seemed uncomfortable with her presence. She skipped the reception and went to work out at her dojo before going home.

Alone in her apartment, she heated a plate of leftovers and sat in front of the TV. Flipping through the online library, she selected retro films and started streaming *Back to the Future*. By the time she reached the scene where George McFly tells Marty about the science fiction stories he was writing, she'd lost interest in the movie. She turned off the TV, went to her computer, and opened the email from Corey with the invitation to the online version of the experiment. After a brief moment of hesitation, she clicked on the link.

```
Consider a radioactive decay counter
that has been used to generate a sequence
of positive and negative random numbers.
The numbers produced, which you will
not see, are stored on a secure remote
```

server. Your task is to imagine the case
in which all the numbers are *positive*.

Elaine got a curt email from Corey the next day, thanking her for doing the online experiment. She wrote back right away, saying she was thinking of him and offering to help in any way she could. There was no acknowledgement. Later in the afternoon, she texted and then called, but again there was no response.

The clack of furious typing shook her out of her thoughts. Elaine peered around the partition of her cubicle office. Bill O'Leary was working on his computer.

"Hey Bill, what are you doing?" She squinted, at first not quite believing her eyes. "Oh, my God! Are you reading other people's *email*?"

"Will you keep it down? Yes, I'm reading people's email."

"How do you do that?"

"Somebody sitting on their bed that weighs 400 pounds told me," he said sarcastically.

Elaine didn't understand the reference and decided not to pursue it further. But another idea came to her. "Bill, did you read Takayoshi's stuff?"

"No."

"No?"

"Takayoshi was a dinosaur, a weird old dinosaur," Bill explained. "The guy didn't have a smart phone, refused to use his university email account . . . basically, he never used the network. The sum total of his wisdom was on this ancient Windows NT computer in his office that didn't even have a network card. All his stuff was on that museum piece."

Elaine thought aloud. "So, the only way for someone to access Takayoshi's computer is . . . by breaking into his office." She glanced at her phone. The Physics Graduate Students Association served free coffee and cookies on the first floor lounge every Thursday afternoon at five o'clock, but she decided to go up to Corey's office instead.

Corey wasn't there. The only person in the room was Ibrahim Zaher. He was cleaning out his desk.

"Ibrahim?"

He looked up. "Oh. You are . . ."

"Elaine."

"Yes, of course. Elaine. I saw you at the funeral."

She nodded. "What are you doing?"

Ibrahim tossed a pile of paper into the recycling bin. "I am quitting the Physics Department. Takayoshi is dead, but I should have done this a long time ago. I should never have agreed to be his accessory!"

"What are you talking about?"

"Takayoshi's research," Ibrahim breathed. "That project he was working on with Corey? It is funded by the United States Department of Energy."

"DOE?" Elaine snapped. "You have proof of this?"

"I saw a letter in his office."

"In his office . . ." Elaine narrowed her eyes.

Ibrahim resumed packing. "I cannot—*will not*—be associated with research that is in any way associated with the American death machine!"

Elaine was moved by the intensity of his emotion. "Why?"

Ibrahim clenched his fists, and the muscles in his arms rippled. "Our family was from Hodeidah. The Saudis launched an air strike against the hospital and the fish market. The *hospital* and the *fish market!* Who would do such a thing? My entire family was killed! Only I survived because I was in Sana'a that day. The Saudis pulled the trigger, but the Americans gave them the gun. Those were *American* planes, with *American* bombs." He was shrieking now. "How could they do this? *How?*"

"Ibrahim, I'm . . . I'm sorry. I didn't know you—"

"No, you do not know me." His eyes burned. "Nobody knows me. Nobody *wants* to know me. They sneer and laugh at me behind my back. You think I do not know?"

Elaine reached out to touch Ibrahim's shoulder, but he pulled away.

"What's going on here?"

Elaine turned and found herself face-to-face with Corey Stadtmauer.

Their eyes briefly locked, and the colour drained from Corey's face. "What are you doing here?" he stammered.

"Looking for you," she said. "I was thinking of you and wanted to know if you're okay."

"Yeah, well . . . please *don't*—You don't have to 'think' of me, all right?"

"Corey, what's got into you?" Elaine asked. "Why haven't you responded to any of my messages?"

"I've been busy, *really* busy, since Takayoshi died." He was now avoiding eye contact with her. "Listen, it would really be best if we didn't see each other anymore."

Anger welled up in her. "Well that's going to be hard, since we all work in the same building." A bizarre thought crossed her mind. "Are you breaking up with me?"

Corey laughed sardonically. "One dinner and one funeral do not make a relationship, Elaine." He still would not look her in the eye.

Elaine bit her tongue to keep any of a dozen retorts from snapping forth. Finally, she just turned away and stormed out of the office, her hands balled into fists.

She left the McLennan Laboratories and sat alone on the metal park bench on the grass outside. Her mind churned, unsure of what to do. *The U.S. military is funding research at the University of Toronto. The public needs to know. But what I can do? Should I even be involved?* She thought about Professor Takayoshi, and Ibrahim Zaher, and the Saudi atrocities in Yemen. *The only access to Takayoshi's research is the standalone computer in his office. Someone wanted it badly enough to break in . . . and to kill.*

Elaine took a deep breath and stood, her mind made up. She walked over to the Lash Miller Chemical Labs and went inside to look for someone.

"Yegor!"

"Hallo, Elaine," said Yegor Wiśniewski.

"I need your help."

"Hokay."

"Do you know how to pick locks?"

"Ya."

"Okay. Uh . . . may I ask where you learned?"

"Sure. *Da Terrorist's Handbook.* I got it off de Dark Web."

"And?"

"Vell, de best ting is Army issue lockpicks. But I do not have deez . . . yet. Instead, you can use perhaps dental tools, aluminum can, steef metal vire, a credeet caard—"

"Got it. Yegor, can you teach me?" She told him about Corey and Professor Takayoshi, and how their work was funded by an agency supporting the U.S. military.

Yegor looked at her for a moment, then shook his head. "No. I vill not teach you how to pick locks."

"Why not?" Elaine asked, annoyed.

Yegor reached into a pocket of his Belgian army jacket and pulled something out. "Because I have copy of janitor's key."

"How did you get—" Elaine shook her head. "Oh, never mind."

Elaine returned to the McLennan Physical Laboratories that night. She took the elevator to the eighth floor of Burton Tower and went directly to Professor Takayoshi's office. *Is this really such a good idea?* She shook away the momentary hesitation, slid Yegor's copy of the janitor's key into the lock, and opened the door. Taking a deep breath, she entered the office and closed the door behind her. Activating the flashlight function on her phone, she swept the beam over the mounds of papers, journals, and books strewn about the room. It was obviously a waste of time to try and sift through the mess. *Whatever answers there are, they've got to be on his computer.*

She booted Takayoshi's ancient PC from a USB stick provided by Yegor with a program that exploited a security flaw in Windows NT to decipher the password. It took several minutes, but she finally got in. Scanning the contents of the hard drive, she found in the "Conference Papers" folder a file called "CAP_Mockery" and opened it:

A MOCKERY OF TIME

Stadtmauer, C.J., Takayoshi, M.K.

Department of Physics, University of Toronto

It was a draft manuscript for an upcoming conference of the Canadian Association of Physicists. Elaine smiled at the title, knowing it would not survive peer review. But as she read the document, her amusement changed to fascination, and then, to wonder.

. . . The orthodox quantum theory is a linear approximation of a more adequate nonlinear model. This work is based on the introduction of such nonlinear terms to the standard equations of quantum mechanics.

Consider, for example, the nonlinear Hamiltonian function, derived independently by S. Weinberg of the University of Texas (Austin) [9] and C. Stadtmauer of the University of Toronto. The nonlinear contributions of the kind indicated in (42) may exist in nature. Maxwell's equations allow for two valid solution sets. One describes an electromagnetic wave propagating from a moving electric charge for t≥0, while the other describes waves converging on the particle for t<0. The latter are known as the advanced wave solutions.

The advanced solutions of Maxwell's equations would provide a mechanism for the possibility that our minds can influence the past. It is common knowledge that neurons in the human brain transmit electrochemical impulses . . .

She blinked in amazement. Was the past not supposed to be permanent and unchangeable? *We can regret, but never change, the decisions we've made—or can we?*

. . . In a series of experiments conducted at the University of Toronto, a radioactive decay counter was used to produce a sequence of positive and negative random numbers that were unobserved at the time of generation. Several days later, a group of volunteers was asked to mentally influence the statistics of these numbers to favour the output of positive values. In every case, subsequent analyses revealed a minimum 2-sigma correlation between the actions of the volunteers and the statistical bias in the data. Particularly noteworthy was a 5-sigma correlation resulting from the action of ElCa, a 23-year-old female volunteer in the University of Toronto experiments [Note: 5-sigma outlier requires secondary verification. Identifying information to be redacted in published paper].

A chill went down Elaine's spine as she recognized the reference to herself and its disturbing implications. Corey's strange behaviour suddenly made terrible sense. She took a deep breath and skipped to the end of the paper.

> . . . The nonlinear terms can lead to causal anomalies of the Einstein-Podolsky-Rosen (EPR) type[3]. Furthermore, since the correspondence principle states that classical and quantum predictions should agree in the limit of large quantum numbers n, these results may also apply to the macroworld. It is therefore possible that our own minds may be able to influence things that have already happened. Present actions may only appear not to have influenced past actions because the past has already taken into account what we are doing. The common wisdom that the past cannot be altered by the present may therefore be a fallacy, a mere projection of our own temporal asymmetry.

Acknowledgements

This research was supported by the Natural Sciences and Engineering Research Council (NSERC) and the Division of High Energy Physics of the United States Department of Energy (DOE).

The door flew open.

Elaine whirled.

A man of medium height burst into the room. The intruder lunged at her, knocking the phone from her hand. It landed on the floor, its screen cracked.

"Elaine Carrington," Bill O'Leary sneered. "What the hell are you doing here?"

"I could ask you the same thing." Elaine's surprise and fear hardened into resolve. "But I have a pretty good idea already."

"Oh, you do, eh?"

"Uh, huh. Tell me, Bill. Did Mel get that postdoc at TRIUMF?"

"Not yet." He stood between her and the door.

"But you don't expect her *not* to, right?" The puzzle was coming together. "After all, she's your wife, so she's obviously the best person for the job." Elaine's voice dripped with sarcasm. "I'll bet you've even bought a house in Vancouver already. It's a sure thing."

"TRIUMF. Don't you just love these cool acronyms?" Bill laughed, closing the door behind him. "Is that how you feel, Elaine? Triumphant? You've got me all figured out, haven't you?"

"Maybe." Her fingers grazed a hardcover book on the desk behind her.

"Just maybe? What, are you *stupid* or something?" Bill snapped his fingers. "Oh, I get it. This must be the part of the movie where the good guy—or girl—confronts the bad guy, and the bad guy spills the beans on everything." He stepped closer. "Do you think I'm a bad guy?"

"Absolutely." Elaine nodded at the computer screen. "This is what you were after. Takayoshi's work . . . and Corey's. You wanted to wipe their files, slow them down just enough so Mel could publish her work on nonlinear quantum mechanics first." Her fingers closed on the book. "Except it wasn't entirely *her* work, was it Bill?"

"Shut up. You don't know anything."

"Corey's emails were helpful but incomplete, so you still needed Takayoshi's files. But you didn't get very far, did you? Takayoshi was working late. Surprised you. So, being the big *man* that you are—"

"*Shut up!*" He pulled something out from under his windbreaker.

Elaine gasped. She didn't need Yegor to tell her the .38-calibre pistol was no toy. "Oh my God, Bill! What the hell are you doing with a gun?" She forced herself to speak calmly. "Are you crazy?" She looked into his eyes, and gulped.

Bill O'Leary *was* crazy.

Got to keep talking—stall him until I figure something out. "You panicked. Fled when you realized you'd killed him. Didn't touch the computer. I'm surprised at you, Bill. It took you this long to come back and finish the job?"

He waved the gun erratically, his eyes wide and face pale.

He doesn't know what to do, Elaine thought. *Maybe I can use that.* "If you shoot, someone will hear," Elaine warned. "The cops will be here in no time."

Bill howled maniacally, his eyes snapping in to focus on her. "My dear Elaine, there is *nobody* in the building at this hour. Even those extraordinarily low IQ cleaning ladies are gone. The only person who ever came in here was Takayoshi."

The hardcover book was now in her hand. She threw it.

Bill raised his arms to shield his face.

She launched herself off the desk and slammed him into the wall, trying to pin his arms and grapple for the gun.

A shot rang out. Elaine fell to the floor.

Bill trembled and panted like a rabid dog. "Oh, my God! Elaine, you feckless cunt! Look what you made me do. *Look what you made me do!*"

Elaine lay on the floor, clutching her abdomen, pain radiating out from her belly. Warm blood seeped through her fingers. *If only I hadn't been so stupid. If only I'd just copied the files and read them later instead of sticking around. If only I'd told someone where I was.*

If only I'd asked Yegor to come with me.

Her fragmented and agonized thoughts drifted to Takayoshi's theories. *One chance . . . If I concentrated hard enough . . . is it possible?*

But there was a problem: the Butterfly Effect was against her. The smallest fluctuations in initial conditions could cause wild and unpredictable results. Even if she wasn't injured, she doubted her concentration could be so total as to guarantee the outcome she needed.

But she had to try.

Elaine squeezed her eyes shut and tried to concentrate all her remaining strength into focussing her thoughts—

—*of Yegor, of bombs, of Yegor, of* The Terrorist Handbook, *of Yegor, of lockpicks, of Yegor, of spitballs—*

—the superposition of states collapsed, and *then . . .*

———·———

. . . The hardcover book was now in her hand. She threw it.

Bill O'Leary raised his arms to shield his face.

Elaine launched herself off the desk and slammed him into the wall. Frantically, she tried to pin his arms and take the gun away, but Bill was too strong. The barrel of the gun was pressed against her chest.

"Attention! Put down your weapon, release your hostage, and come out peacefully."

He froze. The voice on the megaphone spoke again.

"You are surrounded. This floor has been sealed off. Release your hostage now, and surrender yourself peacefully."

"Bill," Elaine said, "the cops are here. Just give up. Turn yourself in."

"No!" Bill roared with rage. He started to squeeze the trigger. Elaine elbowed him in the solar plexus, and as he doubled over she broke free and ran into the hall.

"Get out of the way!" a voice ordered.

Several dark figures with MP5A3 sub-machine guns, Kevlar body armour, and face shields were stationed at both ends of the hall.

"Get down, now!" A tactical officer of the Toronto Police Service Emergency Task Force sprang from her crouched position.

A shot rang out.

Elaine felt two impacts. The first was the bullet going into her back. The second was the tactical officer, pushing her out of the way a split second too late.

Elaine's body twisted around roughly as she and the cop went down together. From that vantage point, Elaine saw two more black forms spring from their cover positions and converge on the office. She saw Bill trained his gun on one of them.

The other cop fired first. Dark liquid erupted from Bill O'Leary's chest. For a split second, he stood there like a puppet with its strings cut.

Then, as if in slow motion, he collapsed to the floor. Beside his head lay a red baseball cap and an orange-brown toupée. Elaine had no idea Bill was bald.

An officer spoke into her radio. "Medical emergency. We need paramedics up here, *stat*. We have two casualties, repeat two casualties . . ."

The cop who shot Bill went to the body and put two fingers on his carotid artery. She shook her head.

Elaine was still conscious when the paramedics wheeled her out on a stretcher to the waiting ambulance. As she and her rescuers left the McLennan Laboratories building, Elaine noticed a group of reporters and onlookers outside the main entrance. She turned her head and recognized a local crime blogger, an infamous lawyer—and a young woman with long, curly light brown hair.

Maria Alighieri.

Elaine wanted to say something, to thank her for saving her life. Maria must have been the one who had called the police. But her gratitude was tinged with guilt. *The only reason she works so late is because those idiots won't leave her alone during the day.* But Elaine had never done enough to help her. She had *never* done enough.

Once she was aboard the ambulance, the doors slammed shut, the siren sounded, and the vehicle moved. One of the paramedics gave Elaine an injection.

When Elaine woke up, she was momentarily confused by the fact she was not in her apartment. Her hands probed the bed, and she was surprised to feel a metal rail along the side. Slowly, the antiseptic features of the hospital room came into focus.

"Hey, hey. It's all right."

She turned to the speaker. "Derek?"

"Yeah, it's me." Derek Tsai smiled. "Surprised?"

"How . . . why?"

"I had to see you. See if you're okay, and also . . ." he sighed. "And also to say . . . I'm sorry. I have a drinking problem. I know that now. But I'm getting help. I'm seeing a counsellor, going to a therapy group. I'm going to beat this, Elaine. I swear."

"I believe you, Derek."

He nodded gratefully. "The doctors tell me you're going to be fine. They took the bullet out, and the wound is healing. They say you'll be out of here really soon." He handed her a tablet. "Hey, have a look. The story's out already. It's the talk of the town."

Elaine took the device. "Police Shoot Suspect in U. of T. Murder" proclaimed TheGlobeAndMail.com. "Armed Standoff at U. of T. Tied to Military Funded Research" was TheStar.com's lead story. TheVarsity.ca, the University of Toronto's official student newspaper since 1880, had a brief report after a feature article on lap dancing in Tibet.

She groaned. "How much trouble am I in?"

"You don't want to know." He put the tablet away. "So, what are you going to do after you get outta here?"

Elaine frowned and her shoulders tightened. "I'm quitting the Physics Department, and then I'm going to work with Maria Alighieri and Ibrahim Zaher to file formal complaints with the University Ombudsperson. After that, I don't know."

Derek fidgeted. "Do you want to maybe, like . . . do something with me?"

"What did you have in mind?"

"Well, after all the hospital slop they'll be feeding you, I'll bet you could really go for a nice meal. How about dinner?"

"That sounds nice," Elaine said. "Where would you like to go?"

"How about Mövenpick Marché?"

It took an effort for Elaine to hide her disappointment. She sighed heavily, sinking back into the hospital bed. "Sure, that sounds . . . fine."

Derek smiled. "I love you, Elaine."

"I know."

His lips met hers, and then . . .

Author's Notes to My Younger Self: An important life lesson that I would tell my younger self is to have the courage to speak up. If there is something you want, you must ask for it. If you are unhappy, you must not keep it to yourself. If something is wrong, you must say something. And if something is right, you should speak up, too.

THE SABHU MY DESTINATION

Maurice Broaddus

STAGE ONE: Relaxation

Walking down the basement steps, fear filled me since I rarely went down them even when my father wasn't home. Richard Pryor's That Nigga's Crazy *blared from the speakers. Lamont Little, Sr., my father, spun a stack of vinyl records—Gil-Scott Herron, Last Poets, James Brown, Isaac Hayes—the way some people ate chicken and mashed potatoes for comfort. In the corner, he and my mother huddled together, wearing matching dashikis, swathed by shadows; cigarette smoke curled around them. My father surrounded himself with his books, Malcolm X, James Baldwin, Maulana Karenga. Only when he was reading did he seem at anything resembling peace.*

My family was well-practiced in the calculus of colour. My mother held his hand, her skin so fair in comparison. Though Lamont Sr.'s father was white, my father was the darkest in his family. So grandfather would always take my uncle to baseball games because he was light enough to pass. Though my mother was from Canton, Mississippi, she was the lightest in her family. No one ever spoke of her father. I favoured her. Most of the kids in the neighbourhood made fun of me for being too white.

"Who is that?" I pointed to a new poster which hung on the wall. A man clad in a leather jacket ensconced in a wicker throne holding a gun in one hand and a spear in the other.

"If I have to tell you, you don't need to know." My father's tone reeked of resenting my intrusion. Or maybe simply me. My mother shook his hand

in silent chiding. He drew on his cigarette and turned away to study the shadows.

"What is it, baby?" my mother asked.

I handed her the folded paper Cathedral High School sent home. The private school marked the first time in my life I ventured beyond the confines of the neighbourhood to attend school. Only one of a handful of black students there, most of the kids made fun of me for being too black.

"This says there was an incident in class." Her voice rose, implying a question.

"My Algebra teacher hates me." Fearing too much gesturing might make me look like I was spinning a tale, I shoved my empty hands into my pockets.

"How so?" Already unconvinced, she released my father's hand and straightened, crossing her arms.

"He seats the class based on how good your grades are. I get A's on just about every test, which frustrates this one kid who sits two seats down." I skipped the part where since he was quick to talk about "that coon" or "that porch monkey," every time a test was handed back, I rubbed my A all in his face. "He looked at his test, jumped up, ripped it up, and muttered 'this nigger' under his breath."

"So, what'd you do?" She parsed my words with care.

"Nothing. I wasn't going to trip over that. He'd already lost."

A quick smirk crossed my father's lips. The memory of his upturned lips and proud glint in his eye seared itself into my memory. With another drag on his cigarette, he drifted back to his thoughts.

"The teacher pulled me aside after class to ask me what I planned to do after high school. I said go to Purdue University to study engineering. He was concerned that I was . . . overreaching."

My mother's eyes narrowed. "So, what did you do?"

"Nothing." I held my breath. Richard Pryor preached in the background. I should have said, "Fuck you and your concern. Sir." *I could picture my mother throwing her hands in the air and yelling* "Lord have mercy. You just like your father. Always such an extremist." *My father might have slid me some skin on that one. "That was when I was sent to the guidance counsellor. They said I couldn't take the Calculus class I wanted."*

"The hell you can't." My mother's eyes locked onto me like a poised cobra. I never had to explain who "us" were. Just like she understood that "they" wasn't just the counsellor. "I am paying good money out of my pocket for you to go to that fancy school."

"They said I was on the 'business track.' All of us were and there was no room in the advanced track."

"Nah. My money's just as green. You can take any class you want." My mother wadded up the piece of paper. "You should never be made to feel like you have to apologize just for existing."

—•—

"Scientists agree that the first person to live to one thousand was probably already alive."

"Negotiations continue with the Holland Accords, to settle the interfaith wars raging across Europe."

"Ghana launches Outer Spaceways Inc. to explore commercial space travel."

A notice blipped, interrupting Hakeem Buhari's scrolling through the headlines of the day, as a holovid informed him of a meeting with his supervisor. In the eighteen months since he'd been promoted to team lead, he'd honed his squad of six into a tight-knit group who'd walk through fire for each other. Half of them huddled in a corner talking mad trash to each other, their topics ranging from the status of their perspective projects, to current events, to issues bubbling up in their neighbourhood. One had missed a few days due to illness and focussed on getting caught up on her work. The last, like Hakeem, kicked back and studied the news of the day.

"Hakeem, come in. Have a seat." Not rising from his chair, Basic Boss Chad—how Hakeem referred to him—gestured to the empty space across from his desk. A half-eaten sandwich swaddled in the remainder of its wrapper rested next to his holograph array of spreadsheets. A series of bars and projections calculating profit in real time. He interlaced his fingers and rested them on the large swell of his belly while Hakeem settled in. "Your team's doing well."

"The top in the division." Hakeem was not about to let management spin any narrative that diminished him or his team's efforts. Their department had recently rolled out a new citywide administrative AI system. In his spare time, he sketched out the design for the next generation system he called Morpheus.

"Be that as it may, they are developing a bit of a reputation."

"What sort of reputation do *we* have." Hakeem leaned forward, correcting the message from *they*, as if he wasn't part of the team. Another one of management's games was to separate the pack.

"That, for example. That tone as if you're already mad about something. Tip toeing on eggshells makes it so hard to manage you . . ." Basic Boss Chad caught himself, his hand waving, passing through the projection of the cost of productivity impacted by this meeting— somehow magically erasing the mine he was about to step on. "Can I be frank? It's much easier to talk if we can dispense with the PC nonsense."

"Sure. I'm not going to trip over petty nonsense." Hakeem smiled, cold and welcoming, a shark not wanting to startle the prey swimming about him. "I always like to know who I'm dealing with."

"Good. It always offended me to have to refer to you as 'African Americans' much less what's the new word making the rounds? Ugenini? What the hell is that? It's divisive, is what it is."

"Yeah, that's what's divisive." It was "frank" comments like that which earned him the nom-de-guerre Basic Boss Chad. Hakeem grew more exhausted than anything else. Over the course of his long life, he'd sparred with management over the same brand of bullshit. But he was more mad at himself than the company. Compromising his dream of chasing his own hustle, remaining free, because the very real pressure of becoming a father and needing medical benefits led him back into the trap of working for someone else. He was tired and didn't know how much fight he had left. "I'm good with 'black.' I run a *black* department. I run *the* black department."

"I was thinking about bringing in a new manager to oversee your *black* division." Basic Boss Chad emphasized the word "black" like it was a cuss word tripping off his tongue. And by manager, he referred to Basic Boss Becky. She'd been chatting up the superintendent for months, as if the entire floor hadn't noticed her ambitious-at-the-cost-of-anyone-else ass.

"No, we're not doing that," Hakeem said flatly.

"I don't think you get to . . ."

"I get it." Hakeem held his hands up in mock surrender. "Your masters have yanked on your chain to bring us field folks under control. The superintendent probably thinks we're shiftless and don't get enough work done."

"What do you think about that?" Basic Boss Chad's eyes widened with mild surprise.

"According to the reports of any folks like Ba—" —he caught himself before he ended up in HR's office— "based on her whispers in his ear, it's true. Because when there's no work to be done, I'm not going to have my crew fake like they're doing something. That said, our team of six gets more done in a week than your department of thirty does in a month."

"Well, as you said, she has the ear of the superintendent."

"I don't care if she's got God on speed vec." Hakeem glanced through the office window. His team watched him like he was an athlete in a sporting event. Assuming management had promoted him to provide an opportunity for him to fail, he'd assembled his team on his terms. Built on a philosophy of relationships over everything else, when shit hit the fan, they knew the accountability stopped with him and he wouldn't let anything land on them. "My team is my team."

"I'm gathering that neither you nor your team would respond well to new oversight?" Too cheap for implants or genetic sequencing to fix his eyes, Basic Boss Chad lowered his head to study him over his photo-electric lenses.

"An overseer's an overseer when you're on the plantation. I'm simply saying, as long as I'm here and they're under me, we're going to remain free. If you don't mind *my* frankness."

Basic Boss Chad's face flushed a red so deep, Hakeem feared he might need to summon a medic unit.

Finally, Basic Boss Chad scooted toward his desk. "I like to know what I'm dealing with, too." With that, he dismissed Hakeem, turning away like a captain surveying a new series of star charts to make course adjustments.

———•———

STAGE TWO: Reminder

Paint flecked from the siding of our house. The concrete floor of our porch was in desperate need of touch-ups, the steps reduced to a burgeoning scree of pebbles. But none of that mattered. What mattered was that the space was ours. Other kids came to hang out on our stoop mostly because my mother was always quick with a pitcher of Kool Aid for us.

"Look at 'em." His government name was Montaque Harding, but everyone called him Q. Tall and thin, basketball flowed deep in his veins, his every move ending with a practice juke or a layup. He managed to be fifteen and sound like an embittered old man. "Pulling up on a brotha knowing good and got-damn well he ain't do nothing."

As I was the youngest kid on the block, the other kids often felt they had to explain things to me. But this particular sight was all-too-familiar. A cop car squatted in front of a house where Kenny Washington, a famous jazz player, once lived. His family moved away a while ago as the neighbourhood continued to change. Developers bought up properties to use as rentals, leaving scores of neighbours moving about like cicadas in the summer. The police officer remained in his car, surveying the comings and goings of the block.

"Fuck him," I said, testing out my newfound ability to cuss from my front porch. Out of habit, I checked over my shoulder to see if my mother was coming at me, shoe in hand. Still, part of me wondered what the house occupants had done wrong to have police crawl up on them. The thought was pure reflex, and it angered me. Being under constant scrutiny, as if we lived in a zoo exhibit, trained us to feel suspected, embarrassed, and ashamed, just for living in our neighbourhood. The cop's car growled to life and began to ease into the street. It crept by the porch, words locking and loading in the back of my throat. "Get out of here, pig!" I shouted.

The car rolled on for three houses before the brake lights blared. The tail-lights flashed white and the car began to reverse. My friend Michael peeled off the side of the porch, tumbling over the ledge before he was seen by the patrolman. In plain sight, me and Q froze as the vehicle stopped in front of my house.

The cop waited in his vehicle for several heartbeats, taking his time to unbuckle. His short-sleeved shirt revealed a thick mat of light red hair along his burly arms. A trimmed moustache gilded his youthful face, like he'd just graduated from the academy. Slowly removing his sunglasses, he levelled his unflinching gaze at us and unholstered his weapon. "Who called me a pig?" He put his entire weight into making his voice boom with authority.

Not risking even a sideways glance at each other, our attention focussed on the gun looming huge in his hands.

"Come on now, fess up fellas. You were all kinds of bold a minute ago. Who's got something to say now?"

"What's going on . . . officer?" My father said from the doorway. Tall, straight, and proud, his black leather jacket matched his shirt and pants, like he wore the uniform of the community. "What you got the gun out for?"

"The boy called me a pig." The way he emphasized the word "boy," we knew he meant a different word.

"So what?" My father kept marching down the stairs, deliberate but easy. His hands remained in plain sight, not giving the officer an excuse to shoot. "He can call you a cat, dog, rat, pig, any creature on God's green earth . . . it ain't a crime. Especially one worth drawing a gun for."

The pair of them faced off, neither one giving an inch. My father's bold defiance sprang from being used to marching in tandem with others from the neighbourhood. But there were no others today. The officer's lips upturned in a cruel smirk. He holstered his weapon.

"Name and identification." The cop's tone didn't invite debate.

The moment shifted, the way clouds had a way of turning green before a tornado ripped through your life.

"I'm a man on his property not doing anything wrong." My father shifted his weight from one foot to the other as if suddenly unsure of the ground he stood on.

"Refusing to obey a police officer's directions." With that announcement, the officer seized my father. He barely had a chance to grunt a protest before the officer had him on the ground. Knee in his back. The officer rifled through his pockets, turning them out as if my father were no more than a toy he decided to play rough with. "Got anything in here that will stick me?"

"I don't do drugs," my father coughed out, each breath a desperate exhalation. But he refused to give the officer the satisfaction of hearing the sounds of his pain.

"Get off him! He can't breathe!" I wanted to yell, but the words caught in my throat. I wanted to throw myself on him, or even run away, but I couldn't will any part of my body to move.

"You'd be the first on this block not to." The cop ground my father further into the dirt. Like he wasn't a man, wasn't human. He wasn't anything. Something to bend and torture at will as the officer pushed my father's arms, drawing them back, nearly tearing them out of their sockets, until he cried out.

Cuffed, chained, my father's eyes locked onto mine. His face contorted, a miasma of terror and pain and anger. And shame. His gaze grew distant, resigned, like he both needed me to witness him and yet somehow could not watch me see him broken this way.

For something I did.

"What's going on out here?" my mother shouted.

"Ma'am, I'm going to need you to keep back." The officer tugged my father's wallet from his back pocket.

"What's going on? These boys make you fear for your life? Officer." She spat the last word out.

"Lamont Little, Sr." Little more than glancing at the name, he turned my father's license over in his hands. "You know this man, ma'am?"

"He's my husband."

"You managed to get a man to stick around?" He remained on my father's back long enough to drive his point home to each of us.

It wasn't just him. It wasn't just this city. It was an entire system, so completely part of the way we lived it was like air we all breathed. He unshackled my father and tipped his cap to my mother. "You have a nice day. Ma'am."

My father remained on the ground. Only once the police car's door slammed shut did he begin to gather himself and raise up. Avoiding meeting our eyes as much as we did his, allowed him space to hold onto the remaining tatters of his dignity. But he walked as if something had been beaten within him.

A few months later, my father had another one of his shamanistic experiences. Through the years, it was simply not something we talked about. Shamanistic was what I called them, based on what little information I had. I struggled to wrap my tiny head around this figure who moved in and out of my life, gone for long stretches of time. In the story I created, he was a shaman on a retreat, experiencing a mystical way of seeing, which took him to another level.

One day when I returned home from school, the living room looked like someone had broken in and tossed the place, searching for secrets. The family—mom was also gone—said he'd been checked into a hospital in Marion.

———·———

". . . so what did you do?" Dona, Ms. Jywanza as she preferred these days, leaned over the counter of the Weusi Press Bookstore. She gestured toward the seating area. Her college days' vision come to fruition, she called the store—*weusi* being the Swahili word for blackness—her base of operations. Ever since the two of them were kids, growing up in the same neighbourhood, Dona had believed they had to run and control their own institutions, or they could never be free. She built a digital publishing house and coffeeshop that doubled as a staging area for her community work. When they were kids, he had the same dreams.

"After that conversation, management did what management does. They dangled trinkets in front of each member of the team. New projects. Pay raises with new titles to work under Basic Boss Becky. Promotions which shipped them off to different departments, even different cities."

"They completely dismantled your team?"

"Right from under me. Management was willing to hurt themselves. I'm talking complete setbacks on some projects—my Morpheus initiative was a non-starter—just to put me in my place. They left me in the department, a leader without a team. Some of my crew pleaded with me to talk to management."

"So, you . . ." Her voice trailed off, raising it to signal a question but allowing him space to answer in his own time. Ms. Jywanza gestured for a servo unit to bring over another cup of coffee.

". . . did what I had to do. Packed up my shit and turned in my notice."

"How are you holding up?" She rested her hand on his arm in that easy, comfortable way they always shared.

"Good, I think. I have my work." Hakeem patted his wrist. A holovid activated and a file displayed a logo for Morpheus. "I just . . . I guess I need to figure out what's next."

Ms. Jywanza left him to his thoughts, allowing Hakeem to sip his coffee in something approximating his own space. As the young people used to say, he was ride or die for his community, but he needed to figure out what the third act of his life was going to be. The downside to better technology and healthcare was longer life. The laws hadn't caught up to the realities of such longevity. To be unemployed at his age: too old to come in at an entry level position, too young to accept retirement with so many decades ahead of him. All but unhireable. *Unmoored* best described his unsettled spirit. Unattached to any foundation, unable to get traction, not knowing how to start or where to go if he did. Gone were the days of one job, one employer, for the length of a career. Now he had to recreate himself every decade or so. Had to think about who he was, what he offered, and dream of possibilities for himself. The uncertainty was the worst, not knowing what came next. The kind of panic which led to him accepting the job he'd just quit.

A buzzing started. Like a swarm of every negative thought he'd ever had about himself. His heart pounded. His hands sweated. Tears welled in his eyes.

On the television screen, a scene sharpened into view. His brain placed the picture as familiar until the images coalesced into memory and he realized it was his childhood home. Words crawled along the bottom of the screen warning that the vid about to be shown might be disturbing to young or sensitive viewers, which wasn't going to stop them from airing it. Drone footage captured every angle, surveillance so routine people rarely took notice of the machines.

A police car pulled over a vehicle. The officers leapt out and approached the car from each side. The officer on the driver's side dragged a young black man out and slammed him against the hood. The man struggled to his feet, hands raised, protesting his mistreatment. Charged batons were in the officers' hands within moments.

The man's terror mounted, splayed across the screen for the commentators to dissect in slow motion and close-up. The batons landing all along his body. Each blow sent waves of shock through him. Hakeem recognized the successive expressions, anger, to powerlessness, to shame, to resignation. The light fading from the man's eyes, the word "why?" dying on his lips. A reporter speculated about the possibility of the incident being ruled an accidental mishap from the man ducking into an officer's blow.

The roar of engines filled Hakeem's ears. The room smelled of burning wood. He grew light-headed. His breathing became heaving gasps, overwhelming him with fear he was being crushed.

Striding into the shop, a postman—dressed as if from the 1800s, with a blue-grey sack coat, matching pants, and a panama hat—drew a letter from his satchel. He prepared to hand Hakeem the proclamation when it was snatched from his hand by a hooded Klansman who ran out the front door.

Hakeem stood to give chase. When he reached the door, a torrent of water from a firehose blasted him back into his seat.

Before him, a cop pressed a figure to the ground. The image resolved into a series of puzzle pieces with the one meant to cover the figure's face, missing. Yanked up, the figure morphed into his friend Michael, shoved into and struggling in the back of the police officer's car. The report of a gunshot stilled his movements.

On the screen, Hakeem's home bursts into flames.

Rising from his chair, he walked through the flames, emerging unsinged, but dressed as an astronaut. He closed the door behind him.

In the distance, over the sound of his sobs, Ms. Jywanza's voice called for medi-drone.

———•———

STAGE THREE: Remembrance

The first time I got really angry, I had been a newspaper carrier for two years. The newspaper station was a large white bay with stacks of papers bundled next to pylons. When I approached my lot, a folded piece of paper had been tucked into the top bundle instructing, "Please stuff the inserts before delivery." Staring at the message, re-reading it a few times, I glanced over to the stack. My blood pressure rose with each calculation of my time spent and lost with each paper. "Aw hell, nah," I cried out, stopping all work in my vicinity.

"Little. My office," my manager said. Blue corduroy jacket, two days of unshaven grey-speckled stubble. Thin but wiry-strong, missing one of his cigarette-stained teeth. I might as well remember him as Bossman Chad.

I grabbed the offending stack of ads and followed him into his office.

The door barely closed behind me before he went all in. "What's your problem this time?"

"You messing with my money. Again." I had visited his office the previous week complaining about my pay rate. For me to get paid, I had to collect money

from each house along my route for the papers I had delivered to them. No matter how much I collected, the first cut went to the Indianapolis Star to cover the papers I delivered. Only after that nut was paid did I see any money for myself. My customers' slow pay or no pay didn't matter to the company since it came out of my end. It took two years to realize just how bad I was being fucked.

"This is the job," Bossman Chad said.

"I'm not going to make the motherfucker and then deliver it. That's not what I signed up to do."

Bossman Chad was three syllables worth of shitty. His yellow teeth ground back and forth. "You can put the inserts in the paper and deliver them or you can consider this your resignation whining session."

We stared at each other, each waiting for the other to move. Finally, I sucked my teeth and headed to the door. Bossman Chad muttered something, too pleased with himself. I tossed the inserts into the trash can. Not satisfied, I fished in my pockets for my book of matches. Turning to him, I lit one and dropped it into the trash bin. I strode out of the office to a chorus of profanity as he stomped out the flames.

That might have been the first time my mother called me an extremist.

———•———

Life ran in cycles, intricate spirals of self-repeating loops holding the universe together. Whenever I came to a place where it looked as if I were about to travel the same road as my father, I made a course correction.

In junior high school, I qualified to be in the band. My music teacher beamed at the possibility. According to him, I had a natural gift and he wanted me to play the trombone. My dad played trombone, and our household was always filled with jazz music. I remember the first time my father played Miles Davis' Kind of Blue. I was transported. Then he left on one of his shamanistic retreats. I quit the band.

Early in high school I wanted to be an astronaut, fantasizing about one day going into space. I read book after book on anything about space. Then I found out that to qualify to be an astronaut, I had to join the Air Force. Before he took up with the Black Panthers, my father was in the military. I quit my dream of going into space.

———•———

By my sophomore year of college, my schedule filled with classes that carved out and explored a black space like Introduction to African American Studies,

Cinema in Black & White: African American Presence and Absence in American Film, Introduction to Black Literature, *and* Health & Healing in Africa. *The exception was my computer programming class.*

"Let's hear from our friend from Rhodesia." Professor Becky was a tall woman who strode about the class with a poise and elegance that demanded the whole world be her model runway. There was no calling her by her first name, as she reminded everyone of the title she had earned.

"There she go again," I whispered.

"What's up?" Dona asked. Hair drawn back into Afro puffs, she glanced at me over the rims of glasses whose thick black frames echoed those worn by Malcolm X. Other than "our friend from Rhodesia," she and I were the only black students in the thirty-person class.

"Whenever the brotha lands on her radar, she disrespects his name. And his people. Keeps calling his country Rhodesia. The first time she did it, I let it slide. Everyone was due a slip up. It was not like the news covered civil wars in Tanzania and Zimbabwe. Folks over here don't care about that."

"Can barely spell Apartheid. And that shit's still going on," Dona said.

"That's what I'm saying. Following week, Professor Becky makes another run at him. Let's Rhodesia trip off her lips again. Turns to me and winks. I'm like, this motherfucker's purposely disrespecting him. Us."

"You ask 'our friend from Rhodesia' about it? See what he wants to do?"

"He doesn't want to make a big deal of it. With no tests, a lot of the grade in here is subjective." I shrugged. "That's his call. It's just . . . I can't let it be. She can't just disrespect us."

"That's cool, but you need to be strategic." Dona patted me on my shoulder, her way of calming me. "Step to her wrong, and you're surfing a wave of white woman's tears right off campus."

"Is there a problem back there?" Professor Becky interrupted. The sharp edge in her voice caused the rest of the class to stop taking notes and turn toward me.

I glanced at Dona. She shrugged, leaving it my choice. "It's Zimbabwe."

"Excuse me?"

"The people of Zimbabwe fought and won a war liberating them from white oppressive rule." I met the eyes of each and every one of my classmates before turning to Professor Becky. "Their liberation and independence need to be emulated. Their right to choose what to be called needs to be respected. If we don't support freedom everywhere, we can't expect it anywhere."

The students turned back to Professor Becky.

"My apologies." Her tone turned frosty. "Zimbabwe it is."

"You got no chill," Dona said. "I like that. You need to come to the next meeting of the Black Student Union."

"Alright, bet."
I was the only one who did not pass that class.

———•———

Surveillance drones flew overhead like crows scrounging for food. A murder of drones. Hakeem's front porch hadn't changed much since his childhood. Perhaps a little more paint had chipped from the walls. The bricks needed touching up, but the foundation was solid. Hakeem's mother used to say, "you never get rid of land," which was why he inherited the house and was able to buy the one next door. Ms. Jywanza didn't fool him. She had already identified and researched the entire block and then bought the two houses on the other side of him.

Time stood still. The return to his present reality from his shamanistic journey took nearly a year. Rocking back and forth, Hakeem studied the patch of earth where his father had been shoved to the ground. The cold rage stirred again. Torn from his former orientation, he listened to a deeper consciousness, trying to get to a place to understand the shamanistic whispers:

This is America. Here's who you think you are.
This is America. Here's who you really are.
This is Muungano. Here's where you want to be.
This is Muungano. Here's where you will be.

Ms. Jywanza climbed the porch steps carrying two cups of coffee, setting one on the ledge in front of him before settling in next to him. "You finally back with us?"

Taking his cup, he sipped at his coffee. "Glad to see I don't weird you out."

"I've never minded your brand of crazy." She tipped her mug in toast. "If you listen, the universe will take you somewhere. So, here's to embracing the unknown and all that."

Hakeem raised his mug before scrolling through his journal. He'd written several poems, most of them trash, but he was improving. It was important to get the words—his feelings—out, no matter what shape they took. At least, so his healers encouraged. Even as essays. He studied the ground where his father had been shackled and shamed. He jotted down the title, "Lessons on Blackness."

"Did I ever tell you about the time my husband lost his job?" Ms. Jywanza asked.

"I knew he switched careers."

"The most stressful time of our marriage. We almost split up over it. He'd worked in a lab for almost forty years, the only job he'd known since college. One day his boss comes in and lays off a third of the staff. Most folks were devastated, but not him. He saw it as an opportunity to do and become something new. To recreate himself. Do what he always wanted to do, on his terms. He tried freelancing, writing for different sites to push out the message of The Cause. But, you know how it is trying to make a living off your art."

Hakeem made a non-committal sound. He hadn't told her he had been searching for work via commlink. He just didn't know how many more "no's" he could take.

"With no money coming in, I watched what it did to him. Eating at his self-worth. Not being able to provide. Not seeing himself—and fearing that others didn't see him—as a man. All the doubts. All the worry. All the dark thoughts he didn't suspect I knew he had. He just needed a break, some traction under his feet, so he could get his thing up and running."

"At least he knew what he wanted to do." Hakeem's voice reduced to a hoarse whisper.

"Something will emerge. The question is, are you ready to get back out there and try and fail at some things until it does?"

Hakeem recognized that particular glint in her eye. "What you got in mind?"

"Come work at the bookstore. Take some time to do something with your writing."

"I . . ." It was a possibility he hadn't considered.

Ms. Jywanza raised her cup again. "Here's to possibilities."

————•————

STAGE FOUR: Re-Imagine

I rarely visited my father at the Marion Psychiatric Hospital. The place reminded me of a prison and his ward, a cell block. I never wanted to see him in a cage of any kind, even a medicated one. The pills left him so sedated, a drooling version of himself. It wasn't good for him. It only made things easier on the staff and family, not having to fuck with his antics. But I understood: part of me wanted an IV pumping drugs into him non-stop right now.

"Say that shit one more time." His rheumy eyes fixed on me. A slurping sound kept drool from escaping the corner of his mouth.

"My name is Hakeem Buhari now."

"Hakeem." My dad rolled the name around his mouth like it left a bad taste.

"We call it our ritual of name change. Hakeem means 'wise' or 'judicious' and Buhari means. . . ."

"I don't give a good got-damn what it means. It translates into you being ashamed of me. Of your family." My father was on the other side of heated. "Call it what it is: a ritual of rejection."

If only to myself, I admitted that it was.

I spent more and more time with the Purdue University chapter of the Black Student Union. They pushed me into a deeper place. I came to see the world as interconnected. First as a series of systems—capitalism, criminal justice, nationalism, military-technological-industrial complex—linked in service to supremist ideology. Second, as a people—Pan-African, those of the Diaspora and of the mother continent—we were united in struggle.

We needed to reclaim our independence and agency. It began with our own name change. Naming was a way to call something into being. What we wanted to manifest in the world. My brothers and sisters in the black Student Union suggested a name reflective of my talents and I accepted the burden of living up to the name. The ritual of the name change itself was transformational.

Though I still had to break it to my folks.

I expected my mother to call me an extremist. Again. The words started to form on her lips, but she paused, almost in consideration, maybe seeing me for the first time. The final derivative in the calculus of colour. Taking my hand in hers, she whispered, "Jesus renamed his disciples with their new mission to redeem places."

I expected no such consideration from my father.

"Pops, I . . ." Suddenly I was the boy afraid to walk down the basement steps.

"Don't 'Pops' me. I gave you my name. Raised you. Now you spit on me." My father's hand flitted, his fingers pinching in the motions of chasing a cigarette.

"Maybe it's time for your medicine." My father had become a pharmaceutical smorgasbord of disorders: bipolar, schizophrenic, oppositional defiance. Each visit seemed to find a new anti-social diagnosis added to his record.

"Fuck them medications." Storming toward his bed, he bent over to retrieve a bag of pills hidden between the mattress and spring board. "You take these damn pills."

"It hasn't been easy for me," I said. "I'm just trying to sort through things. I'm not . . ." The words trailed off. Broken. Beaten. My father's son. I studied him, not seeing the man he once was, the man he could have been. Only the man who'd had his pride and dreams ground out of him by the system we moved and lived and breathed in.

I'm not him.

I still dreamt. Some part of me still hoped. Some part of me needed the name change for another reason. He knew it, too, and it was like the last string connecting us snapped.

I couldn't meet his eyes.

"I . . . understand." His voice softened. Resigned.

My breathing hitched, something caught deep in my chest.

"Let me put one last thing in your ear."

I managed to look up.

"Wherever you go, tell your story. Your way."

"I've never thought . . ." I rested my hand on his shoulder, still wanting to reassure him, to have his full acceptance.

He pulled away. "You go do you."

My dad killed himself later that year.

———•———

Many of the houses in the neighbourhood had been refurbished. Some torn down entirely, rebuilt with polished regolith, fused lunar material which had become the rage in high end construction. Hakeem had his home restored, not updated. He preferred old things.

"What you no good, Hakeem?" Q sidled up the porch steps. "I mean, I knew you as Li'l Lamont and all, so I figure I got some special dispensation to come up here."

"You're always welcome, Brother Q. Who's this?" Hakeem gestured to the lanky figure uncomfortable in his skin, half-hiding behind him.

"This is my grandson, Keegan Besamon." Q stepped aside, making room for him.

"How are you doing, Keegan?"

"Good, sir." The young man seemed to contort himself into a tesseract fold to disappear.

"Sir. I like that." Hakeem extended his hand and Keegan, though reluctant, shook him up.

"My grandson here's been struggling in school. Can't seem to get out of his own way. The teachers keep coming down harder and harder on him."

"It's like they gunning for me," Keegan piped up, finding his voice.

"I know the feeling. It was that way with my son. I had to pull him from that damn fool school. Teach him at home," Hakeem said.

"Well, that's what I thought," Q said. "I figured you up here with this bookstore, putting out those newsletters and articles. I didn't know if Keegan could . . . I thought he might do and learn better alongside you and your boy. I mean, you up here spouting all of this knowledge and history and economics shit. Figured it might be good for him to see it in practice. You get kids like him. Hell, you *were* kids like him."

"Heh," Hakeem said.

"That a no?" Q asked.

"Nah, it's . . . cool." Hakeem stroked his chin. "Just something I hadn't considered."

"Well, I think it's a great idea." The porch door clattered behind Ms. Jywanza, who carried out a tray of coffee cups. "In fact, I have a nephew I'd been thinking of inviting over here to do the same thing."

"We could do it from right here," Hakeem said. "Our school. Our centre of operations."

"On your porch?" Ms. Jywanza asked.

"A wise woman told me that if you listen, the universe will take you somewhere." Hakeem walked the length of the porch. "There was this group of activists who formed a society named after Thmei, the Egyptian goddess of truth and justice. They called their work, Thmei Research. I always liked that. This will be the space for our school. We can call it the Thmei Academy."

"Let's do this, then." Ms. Jywanza sipped her coffee.

"Just like that?"

"Just like that," she said. "We're not teenagers getting high while laying on the roof of your car. We don't have a lot of time left to play around."

"Well, shit." Hakeem raised his cup to Q and Ms. Jywanza. "To the Thmei Academy."

———•———

STAGE FIVE: Redeployment

"I want to make a real difference." I passed the joint to Dona. I had parked my '98 Oldsmobile near one of the main shelters at Bertha Ross Park. We stretched out along the hood of the car, passing smoke between us. It was our favourite place to think.

"What do you want to change first?" Dona said through pursed breath.

"*Everything. We're trapped into all these human constructs.*" *Getting high always made me more philosophical. I only saw in possibilities.* "*Race. Religion. Money. Nationalism.*"

"*First step, change the construct.*"

"*Just like that?*" *I asked.*

"*Just like that.*"

"*I went to this workshop at the Madame Walker Building. The speaker made the argument that the main issue facing black men was employment. That we needed to fix that in order for us to see ourselves as men.*"

"*I thought the silver bullet was education,*" *she said.*

"*I guess that was last week.*" *I took the offered joint back.* "*Before I went to Purdue, I thought I had it all figured out. Go to school. Study engineering, get a high paying job . . .*"

"*. . . become a perfect cog in the capitalist machine,*" *Dona said.*

"*It's a model built to exploit us. Now I want to do better. Dream bigger. We can't just do things the way they've been done. That'll only bring us right back here. We need to change the paradigm rather than try to fix something out of our control.*"

"*That's the thing about plantations: if you escape, there are always people and systems in place ready to send you back,*" *Dona said.* "*We all have been traumatized. That's what the system does. We need to create a retreat place. Carve out space, allow us freedom of thought. Somewhere we can just recover ourselves.*"

"*An* Uponyaji. *A time of healing.*"

"*Listen to Mr. Fancy-Pan-Africanist's vocabulary. Bet you had to dig deep on that one.*" *She cocked her mouth to the side and released a thin plume of a smoke.* "*Healing time. I like that.*"

Hakeem rode through the heart of the Citadel, the capital of First World, in a hover lift. The small craft was barely large enough for him, Ms. Jywanza, and three of their students. People scurried about in preparation, still about the business of salvaging First World. Hakeem had never been off planet before. Having been invited to Ghana to speak and then to First World, he'd been overcome with speechless awe. He rocked back and forth. Ms. Jywanza patted his arm. He wiped the clamminess of his hands against his pants.

<Preparing to dock,> Morpheus announced. When the figure appeared as a holo-projection, its features remained largely blank. Amorphous.

"He even sounds like you," Ms. Jywanza said.

"Well, it was either me or Keegan. I wasn't convinced Keegan was done with puberty and I didn't want an AI whose voice cracked."

"That's cold, man," Keegan said. "And it's Khamal now."

"My bad, brother Khamal. Everyone's due a slip up. Especially at my age. No disrespect meant."

Khamal nodded, not quite hiding an all-too-pleased-with-himself smile.

"All I know is that it's just like you to design a system where you get to hear your voice bossing people around all day," Ms. Jywanza said.

"Support. Morpheus is a support AI," Hakeem said. "Alright brother Khamal. Show us around."

Hakeem had time to collect himself as Khamal tasked Morpheus to tour them about to see the work in progress. First World, the abandoned lunar colony, was undergoing reclamation. Its inhabitants operated under a special charter from the now-defunct U.N. which was why so many of the young people referred to anything related to Earth as O.E. (Original Earth).

Hakeem envied them. So young, at the beginning of an adventure. He could only sit on the sidelines to observe and advise.

"We've been studying your work," Khamal said. "We want to centre First World's philosophy of operation under an umbrella of African-centred consciousness. We're calling the first phase the 'Ujima Experiment'."

"An African-centred consciousness is more than just performative politics." Hakeem eyed the people watching them drive by. The nods. The smiles. "It's about becoming more intentional and more strategic in how we move through the world. We need to let go of the mindset drilled into us by others' definition of being black on O.E. That can't be our measure."

"But how do you allow for some ideas and mindsets needing to die while looking for new ways of doing things?" Khamal asked.

"That's an excellent question. Someone's been paying attention when I wasn't looking. Y'all will have to forgive me. The Khamal I knew was always looking for any excuse to create a disturbance and shake up the old system, so I have to be careful how I answer this." Hakeem tilted his head in consideration, watching Ms. Jywanza take in everything. "I keep coming back to the ideas of allowing ourselves time to heal. An Uponjaji. A time for healing."

"Giving ourselves space and time to heal all the hidden corners of ourselves," Ms. Jywanza mused. "Figure out what it means to forgive those who hurt us and to move forward on our terms."

"We need to put our energies into a system that's all about how we grow and harvest community," Hakeem said. "We can do healing work here, beginning by valuing each other wherever we are. We learn to speak of our sabhu, the language of the soul." Hakeem slumped in his seat. "Woo, that's all I got for today. Y'all done wore me out."

"You've done good work," Ms. Jywanza whispered. "This is your legacy. Where you belong."

Hakeem wasn't done yet. Maybe he could stick around. Tell the story of their community like an ancient griot. Maybe their calling, their sabhu, was among the stars.

He could wait and see.

Author's Notes to My Younger Self: Always have a growth mindset, a posture of constant learning to continue to challenge yourself. Live from a place of abundance. The people around you are gifts. Begin where you are, use what you have, to do what you can to make the world a better place. Daydreaming is a valuable skillset. Nurture it and always imagine the possibilities in you, your community, and the world.

THE HIDDEN
KNOWLEDGE
SOCIETY

Bogi Takács

Anyunak

No one thought the Soviet occupation of Hungary would ever end.

No one except my grandfather, that is; he looked at me right after I was born, and said, "These kids will see the regime fall."

Some of my family laughed at him, others tried to hush him. "The walls have ears, Jani."

"Even on the maternity ward?" he countered.

He passed away soon after; he didn't see his prophecy come true in just a few years' time.

———•———

"Hidden knowledge is everywhere," I whispered to Tamara, my best friend. I pushed myself into the space between the sofa and the bookshelf, wiggled until I managed to crouch down and reach into the farthest corner. I pulled out a large hardcover Bible and made my way back to her.

We sat on the woollen carpet. It tickled my nose just to look at its thick white tendrils, and it scraped against my bare legs. I tried to pull my bicycle shorts down, but there was just no helping it. Yet I didn't dare sit on the sofa—what if the adults came in and saw us reading the book? They

always said I was "precocious" and "an advanced reader," but I understood the book wasn't meant for me.

"This is amazing, you'll see," I told Tamara, keeping my voice down. "The beginning and the end parts are the best. We can read the beginning . . ."

Tamara wrinkled her nose. "What about the end?"

"That's also really good." I was worried she'd find this boring. I was so desperate to keep her attention. I felt boring. I was a clumsy girl, and all I could do was sit and read. I flipped through the Bible. "The Book of Revelation, by the apostle John. It has all sorts of monsters and the end of the world."

This finally seemed to interest her. She leaned forward, seemingly unbothered by the scrappy carpet, and whispered so loudly I winced. "Does it have aliens? I saw on TV that the Bible had aliens. There was a show about Uri Geller and, and aliens."

"I can read it to you." I was sure she'd complain she could read herself, that we were second-graders already, but she didn't; she nodded eagerly. I could never guess what she was about to say.

We didn't even get a whole page in when we heard the living room door creak. I spun around and saw a dark shape moving behind the translucent, knotty glass—Great-Grandma, always dressed in black.

I shoved the Bible under the sofa and hoped this didn't count as some kind of sacrilege.

———·———

I snuck back later, pulled out the now-dusty Bible and sneezed. I didn't tell Tamara, but I felt skeptical about this book. Grandma told me the Bible was a sacred book copied from generation to generation without a single letter being changed. Yet there was a whole paragraph printed twice on the very first page of Genesis, and some typos too. Maybe this wasn't a very high-quality Bible. I read all the front matter and it had an explanation that this Bible had been verified to be an accurate teaching of the Catholic Church. Published by the Saint Stephen Society.

I knew Saint Stephen as King Stephen from school. He was the first Hungarian king. Our teacher didn't like to say "Saint," and I thought this was similar to how some people said "Saint Nicholas," while other people said "Father Frost." Father Frost and his granddaughter, Little Snowflake. I didn't know the Catholic name for Little Snowflake, and when I asked Mom, she laughed.

I was sure I wouldn't find Little Snowflake in the Bible, but I went on reading. I could read very fast. Last year in first grade, I was asked to correct the other kids when they were reading out loud. Everyone hated me after that. I preferred to read by myself.

Maybe I could find the aliens. There was Moses, who was almost as interesting. And the tablets of commandments he received. Then he threw them down because he was angry, and he had to go back to get another set. This cheered me up for some reason, and I made a drawing of Moses breaking the tablets in the back of the April issue of *Laughter, Children's Humour Anthology*, where there was an empty white page.

I smuggled the Bible to under my bed so it would be easier to read before sleep. But the very next day I got to the part where the Commandments said not to make a graven image. Maybe I did wrong by drawing Moses. My Moses was definitely an image, and I had been so proud of him.

I cautiously showed Moses to my mom over dinner.

"This is a great drawing," she said, poking at her pasta with her fork.

"Isn't it a . . . problem?"

"Why would it be a problem?" She turned back to reading *Hungarian News*—she always read this newspaper, never *People's Freedom*. "This is a free country now. The Russians are gone."

I glommed a large clump of pasta into my mouth, the spaghetti slick from the cheese melted onto it. I didn't care what the Russian army thought of my drawing. I cared about what Moses would have thought. If Mom didn't even understand this much, it would be pointless to ask her about aliens.

"Tomorrow is October 23. There is no school because of the national holiday," our teacher, Mrs. Margit, said. "Does anyone know what we're celebrating?"

I knew! I was so proud of myself. I raised a hand. I wished I could raise both hands.

"Yes, Zsuzsi?"

"We're celebrating the anniversary of the 1956 Revolution!" Mom had explained it was all right to call it a Revolution now, not a Counter-Revolution. The Soviet occupation was over.

"No!" she yelled, her face paling. "We're celebrating the new Constitution of 1989!"

"But Auntie Margit . . ."

"It's *Mrs. Teacher, please.* You're not in kindergarten anymore, to call everyone your *aunties.*" She looked about to give me a black mark in my notebook. I slid down in my desk.

"But, Mrs. Teacher, please? They wrote the new constitution on this day because this is the same day the 1956 Revolution started—to memory, memorialize—" My tongue twisted in a knot.

She glared at me. "I don't want to hear any talk of the Revolution. Revolution, Counter-Revolution, who knows what will happen next year?"

———•———

When I got home, Mom was exhausted from work, her curls hanging in big lumps around her head, and I felt bad about pestering her—but I had to ask. These days I only saw her in the evenings. She was peeling a small orange. "Would you like one?" She offered me a slice.

I shook my head. I hated the way oranges felt in my mouth. The mushy orangey bits and the white tendrils connecting them. Brrr. Instead, I tried to explain what happened in school. This seemed more interesting to her than Moses. She made a face and put down her orange. "You know, this is exactly why they are changing all the street names from names of Communists to names of rivers and streams. Because if the Communists come back after a few years, the street signs won't need to be changed again. No one will be bothered by a street named after the Danube."

I liked that Mom took me seriously. Maybe now it was finally time to raise the question of aliens. "Mom? What do you think about aliens in space?"

"Now where did that come from?" She resumed fussing with her orange. I couldn't fathom how she could eat it, but she also ate plums, which were even more disgusting.

"I was just wondering. Mom."

She was already looking away from me.

"Mom! I was wondering if aliens existed."

"I'm sure they do, somewhere out there," she said. "Space is vast."

"But what about flying saucers?"

"That's so the newspapers have something to write about that's not politics." She finished the orange and wiped her mouth. "The same thing with Uri Geller. Though that's a bit more complicated."

She didn't explain about the complications.

———•———

"Uri Geller is Jewish," Grandmother said. "And he's from Israel, of all places."

"He's Hungarian," I complained. "They said so on TV. They also said he can find oil in the ground while he's flying above in a plane."

"So? They say all sorts of things on TV these days." She yanked at her plastic house robe, adjusting it. It was shaped like a flower-print sack and it never quite seemed to fit her. "Now it's allowed to say that he's Hungarian. For now."

"I decided I'm going to learn Hebrew," I said. "I want to read the Bible in the original."

She almost tore off one of the large pockets sewn onto her home dress. "I hope you haven't told any of your classmates about *that*."

———•———

Tamara and I crouched under the shade of a craggy tree.

"Arise, founders of the Hidden Knowledge Society," I declaimed, and we stood. Tamara looked skeptical. "We don't need to make a blood pact, right? It's allowed to make a pact without the blood?"

I thought Ancient Hungarian blood pacts were kind of cool, and my favourite part of our Reading textbook was the colour paintings of Hungarian history. The seven chieftains, ready to slice their arms open. I shook my head, chasing away the image. "It's allowed to make a pact without the blood," I murmured, then raised my voice again. "We pledge to investigate and uncover hidden knowledge! Like UFOs! The Bible! Telepathy! The ghost of Sándor Petőfi, author of *Arise O Hungarian*! Um . . ."

"The small forest beyond the railroad tracks?" Tamara asked.

I blinked at her. "I don't know about that. That's very far . . ." Tamara lived in a different school district but went to our school because of her parents—I didn't quite understand it.

"My dad can take us," Tamara insisted. "It's at least as interesting as the ghost of Sándor Petőfi. There is someone hiding there."

I nodded. I didn't much care for the ghost of Sándor Petőfi, rumoured to stalk the corridors of our school, and I thought our classmates were into him because he was the only poet they knew. We had to recite

274

Arise O Hungarian on the anniversary of the 1848 Revolution, and I still resented the fact there was no school celebration on the anniversary of the 1956 Revolution. They just gave us the day off. Auntie Margit—Mrs. Teacher—said the school still needed to decide what would be appropriate.

I grimaced. "Fine then. The small forest beyond the railroad tracks. But then we strike off the ghost. It is for small girls."

"Aren't we small girls?" Tamara asked.

"We're not, we're already in second grade! We are *big* girls." I was very firm about this.

———•———

My mom bought me a chalkboard when we went to IKEA. This was the first Western chain store in Hungary, and we had to take the train, and then the subway.

I felt I had to put something very important on this Western chalkboard. Previously, I thought only schools had chalkboards; they belonged to people like Auntie Margit. Having one felt like having power.

I drew Moses, then erased him. I felt that his ghost lingered. Now it was time. THE HIDDEN KNOWLEDGE SOCIETY, I wrote, in block letters. INVESTIGATES—I sneezed. My fingers hurt from the chalk dust.

Then came the bullet points.

- UFOs
- The Bible
- The small forest (the rest didn't fit, but I wanted to put "behind the railroad tracks where Tamara lives")
- NOT the ghost of Sándor Petőfi

How to investigate? The only thing I was good at was reading.

———•———

A stand stood inside the front hall of Children's House, just past the list of after-school classes open for enrolment. With Tamara, we'd already read through the whole list and picked our favourites, but now I was interested in something else. The stand was stacked full of books for sale, both for children and adults, and all manner of glossy magazines. When Grandma wasn't paying attention, I reached into a box and pulled out an issue of *UFO Magazine*.

"If we can get our families to sign us up for an after-school class, we can come here every week," I whispered to Tamara. "I'm sure we can find something interesting."

In the end, we picked Origami for Children. I secretly wanted to sign up for Origami for Adults.

It took a few visits before I managed to sneak two issues of *UFO Magazine* into a stack of children's magazines, then convince Grandma about the purchase.

————·————

We were lying on Tamara's bed, me reading an article from *UFO Magazine* out loud. "Human-Alien Hybrids, and How to Recognize Them," I read.

"This is good." Tamara turned toward me. "I want to recognize them. Then we can arrest them in the name of the Hidden Knowledge Society."

I sighed. "We are not the police."

"Yes, but human-alien hybrids are dangerous," Tamara insisted. "If we find one, we can report it to the police and I'm sure they will do something."

I closed the glossy pages. I wouldn't want to go to the police with anything. My dad told me the police once chased him all the way across the hill, and he only escaped by running into a church. They didn't like his long, dark, curly hair. He said I should always be very cautious and avoid the police. I told him I was blonde, but he pointed out my hair was still curly. He also said they once summoned him for a friendly chat. They told him to sit in a chair, and when he tried to pull the chair closer to the table, it was bolted to the floor. That made him very scared, but the police finally let him go. My mom said they were already feeling the winds of change, and I understood this meant the new regime.

"What's wrong?" Tamara asked. She was sitting crosslegged and staring into my face. When did she sit up? I didn't notice.

"Let's read something else," I said.

"No, no, I want to know about this." She yanked the magazine out of my hands. It flipped in her hands almost of its own accord. "Let's see— here it is—'hu-man, al-ien hyb-rids.' You read." She thrust it at me.

I read.

————·————

Human-Alien Hybrids and How to Recognize Them

Human-alien hybrids have a few discerning characteristics. Most hybrids allowed to live on Earth are not Grey hybrids, but rather Blonde hybrids, also known as Nordics—we know Grey hybrids exist from the testimonies of contactees, but they generally do not interact with Pure-bred humans.

My stomach sank. Pure-bred? Humans were not like dogs, were they? I was sure Moses would have disagreed.

Blonde hybrids have blonde hair, blue eyes, and are generally precocious as children. They learn to read at a young age, often before entering formal education. They seem permanently out of place . . .

"This is you," Tamara said, drawing away from me. "You're a human-alien hybrid!"

"I'm . . . not . . ." But I was hesitant, not sure if I was making a statement or posing a question.

"You're blonde and I've seen both of your parents. They aren't blonde." She pulled closer again. Inspecting me? She tilted her head to the side, her hair falling straight down. "You are so much lighter than your parents."

"I look like both of my parents! I'm sure they are my parents!" I had no idea what to say. I was suddenly scared. What if she was right?

"You are a human-alien hybrid! Nordic hybrid!" She jumped toward me. I raised a hand to fend her off, but I already saw what would happen—she was coming in too fast, I would crack my wrist, then topple backward off the bed, crack my skull—

My hand touched her chest, and I didn't even have time to think about how to push her back when she was suddenly hurled back by a giant invisible force.

How—

She fell off the other side of the bed but scrambled up, her face pale. I stared at her, terrified.

"I said you were an alien!" she screamed. "You, you—threw me across the room with your alien powers!"

"I—I didn't . . ." Or did I? I had no idea what happened. One minute she was charging me, then next—

But I hadn't done anything. Just touched her sternum.

I rounded the bed to help her up. Maybe I had pushed her away, after all. With my *strange alien powers.* The words echoed in my head, round and round and round.

I was sure I would have broken a bone if she crashed into me. I just wanted her to stop—I wanted to stop her—

"Just go away!" she screamed at me.

I blinked. "You don't want to arrest me?"

"Just, just go!" She was crying.

I stumbled from her room, her family home, and not even saying goodbye to her parents.

I ran. Then as my side began to hurt, I slowed to a walk. My sight was blurred, and not even from tears. I walked all the way home from her place, back to the big housing projects, under the giant streetlights shaped like whips.

———·———

Mother was sitting in the kitchen listening to a song on the radio. The singer begged the listener not to allow him to become a traitor to himself. I was a bit confused, but I thought it was about politics. Everything was about politics these days. Except, maybe, UFOs.

"Mom?" I didn't want to nag her, but I also had to ask.

"Mmm hmm?" She turned toward me but didn't turn down the song. She had circles under her eyes. The collective farm had been dismantled after the regime change and she now had two new jobs, and was studying for some certification. I felt bad for nagging her all the time. But Dad was gone.

"Why am I blonde, if you and Dad are . . . aren't?"

She furrowed her brow. "There has been a lot of intermarriage in the family."

"Intermarriage?"

"I wouldn't worry about it if I were you. That's why you turned out so nice. As we used to say in the collective, hybrid vigour is the best!"

She smiled at me. The world swirled.

———·———

Mrs. Margit was talking at the front of the class, going on and on about famous Hungarian writers. I tried to pay attention, but I couldn't. I was so nervous. And when I was nervous, I had to go to the restroom a lot. When I asked to go during class, my classmates snickered. I looked at Tamara, and she looked away. She didn't want to have the Hidden Knowledge Society anymore. She didn't want to see me anymore. Was I really a human-alien hybrid? I couldn't think of anything else.

I grabbed my little bag of paper tissues. The school no longer had money for paper tissues, and I was glad I didn't forget this time. I went to the restroom. I wiped and papered the seat with my tissues, then sat and contemplated.

What if I really pushed Tamara off the bed with my mind? *I did. I really did. Even if I didn't quite dare admit it to myself.* Did that mean I was a human-alien hybrid?

My family had a secret. Was this our secret? Was this why Mom and Grandma were yelling at each other late at night in the kitchen sometimes? Grandma said she didn't want to be on a list anymore. Was the government tracking human-alien hybrids? Had Tamara gone to the police after all? Why would *she* trust the police?

Uri Geller could bend spoons. And he was Jewish—or Hungarian? Could he be both at the same time? And Nina Kulagina, or whatever her name was, she was Russian and she could move objects with her mind. I was glad not all Russians could do that because then they would probably still be occupying us. I wondered if Mrs. Kulagina was a human-alien hybrid. She wasn't blonde, but maybe she coloured her hair. Adults were allowed to do that. I wanted to colour my hair.

I wondered if I could push open the toilet stall door with my mind. Maybe first I could focus on opening the latch. I thought at it, hard. I had no idea how to do this.

Nothing happened.

I tried again.

Still nothing.

I had to get back to class. They would be missing me. Would they? I got up, used more of my tissues—I was running low—and adjusted my clothing, ready to return.

The latch didn't open.

It was jammed. I yanked at it. Swore. Had I broken this thing too? Could I undo it somehow? I yelled at the latch. Rattled the door. Tried to push it out with my shoulder. Kick at it.

The stall door didn't budge. It had looked so flimsy just a moment before. I suddenly felt very strongly that I was not a big girl yet. Surely if I was bigger, I wouldn't get stuck in the toilet.

I looked down. Could I wriggle through the gap? The floor was dirty—the school didn't have a lot of money for cleaners anymore, either. It looked like someone had peed there. Days ago. In any case, the gap looked too small. I might have been a small girl, but not that small.

Maybe above? I closed the toilet lid, gingerly with a piece of tissue—it didn't look clean either. I stepped on the lid. It looked like someone else had stepped on it before me. It held my weight, but the top of the stall seemed quite high, still, and how would I get down on the other side?

I suddenly had a very strong, very vivid feeling I would fall and hit my head. I wondered if this was a human-alien hybrid power. Seeing the future, like my grandfather. Hadn't Moses seen the future? Maybe he was a human-alien hybrid.

And didn't the Bible say the angels had lain down with humans? I knew what adults did when they lay down, they had sex and that was where kids came from. I had a Swedish comic book for kids that explained it in detail. I'd wanted to show it to Tamara before the whole falling off the bed thing, but now I didn't think that was such a good idea anymore.

I hadn't wanted to hurt Tamara. But she jumped me in the first place, and I was just—

"Zsuzsi? Are you in there?" Mrs. Margit sounded furious. "You have to hurry up. I had to leave the class to fetch you." She strode into the restroom.

"Mrs. Teacher, please? I'm stuck in the stall." I stood on tiptoe on the toilet lid, but I still couldn't see past the door. I wobbled and almost fell off. I carefully got back down.

She yanked at the door, but the latch held. "Can't you open it from the inside?"

"It's not coming open."

"It must have rusted shut." It sounded like she bit off a curse. "I'll go get the custodian. He has to have some rust remover, if he hasn't drunk it already."

She strode off. I wasn't sure how the rust remover would help him if he was outside and I was inside. And didn't things take a long time to rust? I'd just gone into the stall and it was open.

The custodian came. He was angry and had a sour smell. He didn't bring rust remover, but he brought a screwdriver, which didn't help either, and a hammer, which eventually did.

The whole class laughed at me when I returned.

———·———

The first snow of the season. The first snowballs hitting my back. I lost my balance and fell.

"Alien, alien," someone yelled. I didn't recognize the voice. One of Tamara's new friends?

I turned around and as soon as they all saw my face, they bolted away. I must have had a terrible expression. I felt terrible. "Come back and fight fair, face to face!" I shouted into the snow.

"No fighting fair with alien *infiltrators*." The kid who'd taunted me turned a corner, racing with the others out of sight.

I stared at the concrete wall where they had gone, at the graffiti that said KRAFTWERK in thin black capitals. I thought it was a band, but I never heard their songs on the radio.

Infiltrators didn't sound like a UFO word. It sounded like a politics word. It sounded like the time in kindergarten when a boy told me, "They would have made soap out of you, the Nazis, you know?" *Nazis* was a politics word, about the War, I knew that now. That had been right before the winter celebration, with Father Frost and Little Snowflake. I didn't tell Mom back then, but now I was beginning to feel maybe I should.

There was no Little Snowflake any more, and Father Frost was called St. Nicholas, even in school. Teachers said Father Frost had been a Soviet import, and that we should get an Advent calendar instead.

I knew I wasn't a small girl anymore, so I didn't say I still missed Little Snowflake. Maybe she would know what to do. I didn't talk to Tamara anymore, but now she was telling everyone else about me. Me, and my strange alien powers.

———·———

I stared out of the bedroom window. The streetlight outside flickered, almost in time with the emotions fluttering in me. I read an article in *UFO Magazine* about how people could not only move things with their minds, but also affect electricity and machines. But it was so hard to tell, when everything was so broken-down and unrepaired, what was me and what was just stuff breaking on its own.

I took a deep breath and thought of Moses marching down the hill.

"Mom." I strode into the kitchen, determined. *With steel in my steps,* as they used to sing in the Communist songs. "I want to talk to you about something very important."

She'd been scrubbing the kitchen sink, but now she turned to me, and she looked like she'd been crying. "I've also been meaning to talk to you about something very important." She nodded. "But you go first. I'm listening."

"Mom, I . . . The kids always want to yell at me, and sometimes even fight. I'm not sure what to do. They say all kinds of things."

"For example?"

"That I'm an alien. Like a . . . UFO alien. From space." I shook my head. "I know it's nonsense, but they won't stop. No one wants to play with me anymore. And today someone told me I was a . . . an infiltrator." I hoped I got the word right.

She sighed. "Well, this certainly simplifies matters. We might need to move to a different town in the spring. But I thought you might like to stay here because you have your friends in school." She looked away and began to fuss with her scrubber sponge—not because she wasn't listening, but because she was nervous, I thought. I hated to touch those scrubbers, but Mom didn't mind.

"Mom, why do we need to move?"

She set the scrubber down on the kitchen table. "I got a good job offer, but it's far away. I wouldn't have to work two jobs anymore, and I could spend more time with you. Learn more about you." She sighed again. "I feel like you're growing up and I don't even know who you are anymore."

Again she treated me like an adult. And that felt good. Even the people who said I was "precocious" generally didn't. But my stomach turned into one big knot. What if she found out about me? About human-alien hybrids and moving things with my mind? About throwing Tamara across the room?

I bit down on my lower lip. "I think that might be nice, actually."

She nodded. "We can discuss it more later. You can think about it in the meanwhile. I'll show you pictures of the town, and we might even be able to visit before we make a decision."

"Will Grandma and Great-Grandma also come? Grandma has a job here."

"Grandma will retire next year, so it's going to be a change either way."

I wasn't sure what that meant, but I nodded. "Mom? Can I ask you something else?" She nodded encouragingly, so I went on. "What do you think about . . . people moving objects with their mind? Do you think it's possible? I read an article about it."

She laughed. My stomach sank like a rock, a knotty rock, but then she hugged me. "It's not a bad question. I'm just laughing because I didn't see that coming."

I relaxed a bit. She let go and put her hands on my shoulder. I fidgeted a bit. I didn't really like being touched, even by Mom.

"I suppose it's possible," she said, completely serious. "There's a lot science doesn't understand yet. *There are more things in heaven and earth, Horatio, than are dreamt of in your philosophy.*"

I had no idea who Horatio was, and she must have guessed this, because she quickly added, "This is in a play written by Shakespeare. He was a famous author. Maybe next year I can start taking you to the theatre with me. If you're mature enough for those UFO Magazines of yours, you are mature enough to see a play for adults."

Grandma sometimes went with her, but Great-Grandma hated the theatre. My mom always told her it was her only indulgence.

"I would be happy to share your indulgence," I said, and Mom laughed again.

"You're eavesdropping on me, I see." She rubbed her eyes.

I almost told her, "And you're reading my magazines," but decided not to say anything.

I needed to think this over.

———

The streetlight burned out before the end of winter. Did I finally ruin it by glaring at it so much? People in municipality uniforms came with a truck and tried to fix it. They gave up after a while, and just left the broken streetlight there. When the snow fell, the moonlight sparkled on it even when the corner was dark.

———

"Are you going to say goodbye to Tamara?" Grandma asked.

I shook my head. "Tamara is not my friend anymore."

"Oh. She looked like such a nice girl."

Mom pulled Grandma away and whispered something; I only heard the word *anti-Semites*. Grandma only responded with another "Oh," but she left me alone after that. I didn't understand, but they wouldn't explain. Anti-Semitism was about Jews and we weren't Jewish. Or were we? We had a Catholic Bible.

I packed my toys into large, boring boxes of brown cardboard. My mom gave me a bag of Hungarocell pieces, but I told her I hated the sound they made when they brushed against each other. So I just put my toys in the boxes and my mom poured the Hungarocell pieces on top.

Outside, the birds were returning. My mom bought me a bird guide for kids. It had drawings of all the birds and where they travelled and when. I liked it a lot, but now it had to go into the box too.

Packing relaxed me and helped me think. No one else flew across the room when they tried to tackle me, though that was also because I learned to fight better, and I wasn't taken by surprise. But there were enough strange things happening around me to keep me wondering.

The news said Uri Geller was a fraud, and there was a big back and forth. I felt bad for him a bit, but I was also angry a bit, because what if he really was a fraud? That would be bad for the people who could really bend spoons and move things with their minds, and maybe even find oil. Now nobody would believe them. Maybe nobody would believe me.

I put my book about Hungarian folk beliefs into the box too. My mom got this for me after I explained the bit about Uri Geller finding oil. She said villagers used to find water underground with a dowsing rod, but not everyone was equally good at it. The book explained how to make a dowsing rod from a willow branch, but I didn't work up my courage yet to try. Besides, would I then dig up the playground? I didn't want to shovel. In any case, I was sure Hungarian villagers back in the day had no human-alien hybrids, and yet some of them could still find water underground, so I decided there was a chance I was human after all. Or maybe a mutant, like in those new American comics I started reading. It was cool to read about people like me, even if they were just in flashy, made-up stories.

Or maybe it was my grandfather who had been the human-alien hybrid. He foretold the future, after all. But it wasn't like I could ask him about it anymore. Or maybe some people were just magic, had always been. Now it was allowed to talk about such things, but after forty years of occupation, no one knew about magic anymore. Instead of strange alien powers, it was strange human powers.

In the new town, maybe I could even learn Hebrew and find out what the Bible *really* said about aliens. Or strange human powers. I grabbed the Bible I'd smuggled into my bedroom permanently during the winter. No one had noticed I had it—that I still had it. I put it on top of the book about Hungarian folk customs, and I hoped that wasn't a sacrilege either way. Could I learn about these, both? I figured I could, and if somebody didn't like it, I could defend myself. With my punches and kicks, if not with my powers.

The chalkboard was the last thing left. It still said THE HIDDEN KNOWLEDGE SOCIETY. Maybe once we moved, I could find some new friends who could join the Society. We could try bending spoons with our minds, though to be honest, I tried bending the spoons in the school dining hall, and they were so weak I could bend them just with my hands.

Maybe this meant I was becoming a big girl, after all.

Of course, then Auntie Margit yelled at me for *destroying school property*, but it was worth it. Even though I had to get extra points in all my math assignments to make up for the black marks because of my *improper behaviour*.

We were moving. Life would get a fresh start.

Outside, I heard a loud rumbling, and I stepped to the windowsill. Next to the streetlight, a repair truck was pulling up, all shiny and new, and people in coveralls jumped out of it, cheerful in the springtime sun.

Author's Notes to My Younger Self: Rabbi Tarfon says in Pirkei Avot (2:16), "It is not upon you to finish the work, but you also aren't free to neglect it". Improving the world is a lengthy process that might appear endless, but every little bit genuinely helps, and contemplating that can help us go on.

THE LIGHT OF STARS

Amanda Sun

Natsumi is sweeping the stone pathway around the main shrine when the elderly couple tumble over the edge of the cliff. She catches the man's eyes for a moment, looking at her with vague recognition, before the two topple with linked arms, their pale blue and dusty rose yukatas billowing behind them. Natsumi's broom clatters to the ground, her body lit with fiery shock as she stumbles toward the vacant clifftop. The path around the shrine buildings is well marked, and far from the edge. And yet they stood there, and now they do not, falling toward the beach far below.

Natsumi leaps over the rope marking the path, her red hakama skirt sticking to her legs in the Okinawa heat, the stones scattering in a spray underneath her. She slows near the edge, her sandals slick against the rock. She drops to her knees, grabs the sharp cliff with desperate fingers, thrusts her head forward to gaze down at the beach and the broken bodies below.

There's no one there. Only a scrap of cornflower blue fabric, swirling with the lapping of the tide, spinning lazy circles in the clear turquoise water.

Has she imagined it? But how can she imagine two entire people, arms linked, with her own eyes wide open? Her heart pounds against her chest, even as relief takes hold. If it was true, there would be bodies. There is only the curl of water and foam on sand. The humidity of a Naha summer has clouded her mind, perhaps.

But she's so certain of what she's seen. She can't forget the man's gaze as the couple willingly dropped forward, his eyes locked with hers, as though he knew her.

After another moment she stands, smoothing her crimson hakama skirt, her long white sleeves. She makes her way back to the rope barrier, steps over the fraying cord. She picks up her broom and sweeps the stones she's scattered back off the pathway.

There are no bodies. And so she must dismiss whatever she is certain she has seen.

She's been at Namanoue for nearly two months now as a miko, a shrine maiden, though she's never seen anyone stray from the path before. It was her grandmother who suggested this as a good part-time job while Natsumi studies at the Naha College of Nursing.

"I'm not sure they will take her on," her mother had said with hesitation. She had run her fingers through Natsumi's hair after, as if in apology, twisting the strands into tiny golden brown curls. "Another job might be more suitable."

"Halfs are so much more common these days," her grandmother had countered. She'd always been as sharp as the prickle of an Adan tree. She didn't believe in making space for feelings. Such things were unnecessary. "No one will bat an eye."

Of course, that hadn't been completely true. One of the priests had raised his eyebrows at Natsumi's brown hair and paler skin, and had turned to whisper to another of the ordained *kannushi*. "Do you think she can read Japanese?"

Natsumi had pretended not to hear, as she had pretended all her life. And in the end they passed her the forms to fill out, all feigning that nothing was different. On hearing her grandmother had once been a miko there, too, they gave her the job. But the weight of their words has not left her shoulders. She has to prove herself as capable as a full-blooded Japanese girl, whatever that might mean.

Which is why she doesn't want them to find her sprawled over the cliff, shouting desperately for an elderly couple that doesn't exist.

When the stones have been cleared away, Natsumi leans the broom against the far side of the shed tucked behind the old maple tree. She walks the slow maze of paths, stopping to politely direct a tourist, then another. She walks around the looming red of the main shrine, bird chirps echoing from high above in the musty, wooden rafters. A woman in a broad-rimmed sun hat grabs hold of the thick rope draped from the ceiling. As she shakes it from side to side, the *suzu* bells rattle and clank above. The lady claps loudly, head bowed. The man next to her is throwing yen into the tithing box, coins clinking against the wooden slats.

Natsumi walks through all of this, feeling at once both invisible and exposed. She is as much a part of this shrine as the bells and boxes and stone Shisa dog-lions that line the pathways. She ducks through the main shrine, under the cloth lightning bolts that drape from the thick prayer rope tied above. There is a small building to the right, and she lets herself in the side door, curving around the boxes stacked on the ground.

"*Otsukare*," she says as she approaches Misato near one of the windows, to let her know she's here to replace her. The other miko smiles, rising to her feet. She's not from Okinawa like Natsumi, but lives with her boyfriend above the steak house near Onoyama Station.

"*Otsukare-sama*," Misato answers, lifting a hand to smooth back her black hair. "We'll need some more of the En-Musubi charms."

Natsumi nods, striding toward the window and the waiting customers. She has barely a moment in between sales to reach for a replacement box, filling the baskets on the table in front of her with *omamori*, the shrine charms.

There are golden pouches with embroidered white flowers, and long crimson ones with stitched gilded kanji. There are floral discs with tassels of crimson and navy blue, and even pairs of bells tied to woven rainbow thread. She nods her head in quick bows as she wraps them for each pilgrim, sliding them with a jingle and crinkle into the tiny white paper bags, sealing them with a Naminoue sticker before she passes the bags through the window with both hands, bowing her head as they're taken. And yet through it all her thoughts fall on the elderly couple, on that moment as they went over the cliff.

A bead of sweat rolls along the curve of her face. It must be the heat.

There were no bodies.

And yet.

"Protection from Evil, please," says the next man in line.

She nods, reaching for the golden pouch with unfurling stitched flowers. She crinkles the bag open, slides the charm inside, traces the red Naminoue sticker with her fingertips to seal the bag.

"Thank you," she says, pressing the bag into his hands. As he turns, she sees the edge of his amused smile, the satisfied glint in his eyes.

Eyes that swirl with stars.

"Success in Exams, please," the girl next in line says, but Natsumi is staring at the man walking away. He wears an old-style kimono, an elaborate golden obi tying the cobalt fabric swirled with embroidered ravens. Half of his hair is swept into a samurai bun, and his wooden sandals clatter against the stone.

The stars in his eyes whirled and churned, the colours in them drifting as though they were lenses into the galaxy. The shock is as cold as space, and as isolating. It is impossible, and fears clings to her as she drifts alone through the chill of something beyond reality.

Bodies falling and vanishing like spirits. Stars orbiting where eyes should be.

She begins to wonder if she's gone mad. And she fears either answer.

———•———

She searches up Naminoue Shrine on her phone as the small four-car train jerks her around the curves of Naha City. She looks for any news articles about an elderly couple plummeting from the cliff, or accidental drownings on the beach. She thinks about looking up eyes made of swirling stars, but even she knows that it's ridiculous. The heat has finally gotten to her, rippling like a mirage. She clings to the explanation the way the heat clings to her skin. She has prayed to the kami at Naminoue countless times; never has she considered the terror of something *answering* her.

She doesn't speak of the cliff or the stars when she arrives home. She knows what she's seen doesn't make sense. Instead, she strips off her hakama and blouse, unties her long brown hair and puts on shorts and a tank. She pores over her stack of textbooks for the pathogens exam she has in the morning. She searches for symptoms of psychosis, of heatstroke, of mental breakdown.

When she turns out her light, she stares up at the spackled white ceiling, and she sees the couple falling, and the kimono man's strange eyes. The edge of his knowing grin.

She rides the train to the Naha College of Nursing, scribbles down her answers on the exam, and attends her lectures. She walks to Naminoue, passing under the towering stone Torii that arches over the entrance to the shrine. She climbs the steps toward the chozuya, dipping a bamboo ladle into the cool basin of water to drip it over her fingers. A ripple extends out from the other side of the chamber, and she looks up.

A little boat made from a walnut shell teeters along the surface of the water, bobbing from side to side as it sails toward her. Someone has put a tiny maple leaf in the centre as a mast and sail. The little shell tips and swirls as it glides between the ladles poised along the edge of the basin.

Natsumi catches the walnut shell in her ladle and lifts it out, cupping the walnut shell in her hand. The chozuya is for purifying visitors before they pray at the shrine. She needs to move this child's creation.

But as she sees its cargo, she drops the shell with a startled cry. Two water bugs dash out as it hits the ground, racing for the safety of the underbrush. They leave a trail of tiny wet footprints that fade quickly in the unforgiving Okinawan sun. The tipped walnut lies at Natsumi's feet. The mast curls against the ground, the maple leaf puckering under the weight of the shell.

She wonders what child had the time and skill to coax two of the horned bugs into the shell, to bring them all the way here to the shrine above the beach. Is such a thing possible?

But it is not old, worn feet pushing away from sheer rock. It is not a dark gaze scattered with swirling light.

She puts down the ladle and carries on to the sales building to get changed.

She walks past the shrine, a child tugging the thick rope back and forth. He's wearing an old-fashioned straw hat like they wear in the ricefields, and overalls that are patched and stained. Is he the one who brought the water bugs? Is he lost? Natsumi looks for his parents, but sees no one else.

The child turns to leave, a tuft of tail swishing behind him.

Natsumi's bag clatters to the ground.

When she looks up again, the child is gone, and a tanuki is scampering toward the stairs. The straw hat lies on the ground, its brim lifting in the breeze.

She hears a laugh, and turns her head.

The man in the cobalt kimono reclines across the tiles of the shrine roof, his eyes swirling with moving stars.

Near her feet two ravens flutter into the sky with a clatter of wings and a squawk as loud as the pound of her heart.

When she looks again, the man is gone.

----·----

"Are you all right, child?"

Natsumi barely makes it over the edge of the foyer before she collapses on the hallway floor. She is studying hallucinations in class, the deterioration of reality. She knows the signs to look for. "Grandmother," she says. "I . . . I'm not well."

"Come and tell me what's happened," her grandmother says. She wraps her short arms around Natsumi, but she's small and old, and lacks the strength to pull her up. Natsumi stumbles to her feet, follows her grandmother into the tatami room of their tiny old house. She pours a glass of cool oolong tea, gives it to Natsumi as she strokes the girl's brown hair.

"Now then," she says. "Tell me everything."

Natsumi doesn't want to speak. She doesn't want to tell her grandmother all the strange things she's seen, how the gold sculpted dragon's eyes moved to look at her, how the Shisa statues wagged their tails and scratched at their stone ears when no one was looking. How a lurking shadow jumped aboard the back of a salaryman who forgot to tie his unlucky fortune paper to the post. She doesn't want to disappoint her grandmother further, the way she must've when she was born with brown hair, when she learned her military father's English faster than her mother's Japanese.

But fear causes her to relent. She has drifted in its isolating grip too long. She sips the cool oolong tea, her fingers like tips of frost on the glass.

"I saw a man and woman fall," she says at last. "An elderly couple, past the rope barrier. They went over the edge, Grandmother."

The woman does not flinch, nor widen her eyes. She waits with lips pressed together, as though she knows that isn't all of it.

Under the pressure of such kindness, Natsumi cracks open, telling her grandmother everything. Of the frogs that cling to the sides of her handbells when she dances kagura, of the fleet of walnut shell boats that clashed in a full-scale battle on the surface of the chozuya yesterday, of the tanukis that fell like dominos up the shrine stairs when one stepped on the tail of another. She tells her grandmother how no one else seems to see them, not even the priests nor the other miko. She speaks lastly of the man in the kimono, the man with the dancing eyes and the ever-present grin.

"I think I should go to the hospital," Natsumi says. "To be assessed."

But her grandmother smiles, smooths out the fabric of her pale pink skirt over worn, tired legs.

"Ah," she says at last. "So you've met the Demon Prince."

And although fear spreads through her at that name, at the admission that what she has seen is real, there is, too, a flickering of warmth that she is believed, that she is not alone.

Through the chill of that isolating space, Grandmother reaches for her hand. Her fingers are rough and wrinkled and warm as they clasp Natsumi's, as the two drift together under the swirl of stars.

———•———

Natsumi steps lightly on the tatami-covered stage, jingling the hand-bells as she arcs to the sound of the flute and the thump of the odaiko drum. Beside her, Misato rings her own handbells, matching Natsumi step for step. Tourists lift their phones to snap photos and videos to bring home from their holidays in Okinawa.

She jingles the *suzu* handbells again, the sole of her socked foot tracing a slow arc across the bamboo floor. She tries hard to ignore the shimmering golden foxes that scurry in figure-eights around her legs, soft fur brushing against her hakama skirt as they dart underneath.

"You're not hallucinating," her grandmother had told her. "I saw them, too, when I worked at Naminoue as a girl. You get used to them."

"Who are they?" Natsumi had asked. "What do they want?"

Relief, then. She wasn't imagining them. But a wave of fear crashed over the ebb of relief.

She wasn't imagining them.

"They're spirits," her grandmother had said. "Memories, perhaps, trapped in the fabric of the shrine's long history. They want what any living thing has wanted—to exist, to be acknowledged."

Natsumi flicks her wrist again, the handbells jingling. A crimson raven flutters down to land on top of Misato's pointed hat, but the miko doesn't seem to notice the added weight. As she turns her head, Natsumi sees the swirling stare of the Demon Prince from the top of the roof beside her, the sun glinting on his ebony horns as he reclines across the curved clay tiles. A pair of ravens peck at the roof near his feet, preening their slick black feathers without the slightest worry about the demon lurking beside them.

He's been changing over the last few weeks, shifting. He's grown larger, with horns that tangle around the bun in his hair. His eyes are brighter, his obi glowing at night like a flickering lantern tied around his waist. His hands are no longer human, but gnarled with knots for knuckles, claws for nails, and his skin holds a pale green sheen. The more Natsumi sees of the spirits under his charge, the more power it seems to give him.

She nearly stumbles as her foot comes down on a sleeping fox. The creature lets out a yelp and dashes off the stage, and she catches herself just before she falls. When she shakes the handbells, she finds them heavier than before—three frogs hang to the golden brim around the handle, their long legs dangling over the back of her hands. The music stops, and the frogs drop to the tatami, scattering at the tourists' applause.

It's magical, she thinks, to see these things, but it's tiring too. Except for her grandmother long ago, no one else can see, nor understand. She must live this world alone, then pack it up with her things, file it away on the train ride to her nursing classes.

Misato takes the handbells from her, smiling, asking if she'd like to go for coffee with her and her boyfriend on Saturday. The crimson raven on her head pecks at the tassel on her hat.

The Demon Prince rises to his feet, his wooden sandals echoing on the clay tiles as he walks to the edge of the rooftop. When he steps into the air, he glides down as though he has wings of his own, as though there is no gravity nor any rules at all.

Natsumi forces a smile at Misato, and the miko leaves. But Natsumi is still, unable to move as the Demon Prince approaches. The Shisa dog-lions wag their stone tails as he walks past them, as he steps onto the raised tatami platform for the kagura dance.

He is terrible and frightening, and Natsumi longs to run away. His very presence seems to pulse with powerful magic, his eyes swirling with red stars and galaxies and the darkness of space.

"Kaori," he says. "You've come back."

At first Natsumi cannot find her voice. She never expected this other world to confront her so directly. She thinks of the demon mask her father would wear at Setsubun, how she would shriek and throw beans at him while she hid behind the couch cushions, how he growled between laughs as the beans pelted against his pale skin.

There is no basket of beans now, no warm and familiar smile behind a paper mask tied with string. But the Demon Prince's voice is as soft as the golden foxes' fur. And after a moment, she finds herself able to answer. "Kaori is my grandmother," Natsumi manages. "I am Natsumi."

His eyes look confused for a moment, then sad. "Ah," he says. "Time is a strange thing to me."

She pities him then, as his power and terror subside to his vulnerability.

"Is it not Showa anymore?" he asks.

Natsumi shakes her head. "Not even Heisei. It is Reiwa now."

"Reiwa?" the demon says. "So it goes." A raven perches on his shoulder, pecks at the cobalt threads coming loose on the neck of his kimono. "Well, Natsumi of Reiwa," the Demon Prince says. "These eyes have seen Tokuji, Bunmei, Genji, Meiji, Showa, and others. And now they have seen Reiwa. Will you walk with me awhile?"

And at his smile her fear melts away, and Natsumi walks with the demon around the shrine, the thick heat of Okinawan summer cut by the flutter of raven wings and the twitch of tanuki tails.

———•———

Natsumi fills with the spirits of Naminoue, her world full of colour and surprise. She bursts to tell anyone who might understand. Only Grandmother listens, but it brings such a sad smile to her face that Natsumi stops telling her everything.

At night, she sneaks out to the shrine, where the Demon Prince waits, and the tanuki in their best straw hats, glasses filled with strawberry juice and plates teetering with purple beniimo tarts. She and the Demon Prince laugh as the water bugs clash their walnut boats against each other in a battle for glory and tart crumbs. Natsumi throws a paper origami ball for the Shisa, and the dog-lions leap from their pedestals with a crunch and a wag of stone tails. The Demon Prince laughs, his eyes lit with bright stars, fireflies catching on the horns that wrap around his head.

At home after, Natsumi lies in the dark silence with a heart full of foxes and tanuki, frogs and ravens. The spirits burst and flutter in her head like cherry petals. She sits up and pulls her laptop from the table beside her bed. It hums to life as she types. She sits up this night, and the next, long past essays and memorization of medications and filled practicum hours. She sends her manuscript to publishers, and waits, and writes another, and waits. Sometimes she writes with the Demon King peering over her shoulder, ravens pecking at her notebooks, tanukis tracking muddy paw prints across her words.

At last her first children's book is published, *Mr. Tanuki's Tea*. She has a signing at a bookstore in Naha, in Okinawa City, and another in Motobu. She laughs politely as children and adults ask about her book, how she came up with a tanuki preparing matcha in a tea ceremony.

She doesn't tell them it's true, that he spun the whisk between his furry paws, that she knelt on the red carpet and waited next to a monarch of ravens and dreams. She doesn't tell them how the lanterns flickered to match the fireflies' glow, or that she's seen the same elderly couple go over the mountain cliff four times now, and that there are never bodies on the beach below.

At her signing in Motobu, the Demon Prince walks in the door. His presence startles Natsumi, but no one else seems able to see him. He stands patiently in line to get his copy of the book signed, while lost fireflies cling to his horns and flash like tiny fireworks. A frog clings to the side of his obi, his back legs pedalling against the fabric, trying to gain his footing.

"Congratulations," the demon says when he reaches her, stars and planets dancing through his eyes.

"I thought you couldn't leave the shrine," Natsumi whispers.

He grins, as always. "I can't, Reiwa Miko. But you are as much a part of the shrine as any of us."

Natsumi watches him leave after, fading into nothing as he touches the sunlight of the street outside. *Will I be trapped in the fabric of the shrine too?* she wonders. Will a brown-haired half-Japanese miko sweep the stone pathways into eternity? Will her soul lap against reality like the waves below the shrine, barely a whisper, but etching the stone away one breath at a time?

She writes more books, after that. Some are published, some stored in desk drawers. It's wonderful, it's painful. It tears her to shreds. But she has no choice. She is overflowing with a magic others can't seem to understand. It is beautiful, and lonely, as she drowns in the light and colour of the demon's galaxy of stars.

———•———

One Saturday, as she goes to the café with Misato and her boyfriend, they have brought a man to meet her. He shyly clutches *Mr. Tanuki's Tea* in his hands, bowing as they're introduced. His leg bumps the table just a little as they sit down. A friend of Misato's boyfriend. He is nothing like the Demon Prince; he is clumsy, unsure of himself. He has short black hair and a wide nose, and he smells of cigarette smoke and the unforgiving muggy heat. His eyes are not full of stars, but they are warm and brown, and they crinkle around the edges when he asks Natsumi what she would like to drink.

The Demon Prince stands a little smaller when she goes back to the shrine that afternoon. His horns have receded from the bun in the back, his sandals more tranquil against the stone. He smiles, still, a raven perched on each shoulder. The water bug navy have struck a truce, and their shell boats lie empty beneath the walnut tree. The chozuya basin ripples only from a gasp of the coming fall wind.

———·———

It is a quiet fall day years later, when Natsumi again steps under the great stone arch of the Naminoue Torii. There are no tanuki tripping up the stairs, no firefly clouds nor walnut shell boats. But the deep red of the shrine is the same as she remembers, the sound of the rattling *suzu* bells as the thick ropes are swung with hope that the gods will hear.

Grandmother stands beside her, the baby girl in her arms. They are tied together with an embroidered crimson kimono, wrapped around them like a blanket. Natsumi chose one stitched with ravens and flowers and Shisa. The girl's eyes are warm and brown, and the edges crinkle when she looks at the towering stone gate. They match her brother's, whose little hand tugs at Natsumi as they bow together under the Torii.

Grandmother starts up the stairs, and Natsumi and the boy follow. She wonders if the Shisa will wag their tails, but then the little girl begins to cry, and Natsumi forgets everything else. She hovers above her daughter's tiny face, cooing gently to her. If the dragon sculpture looks at her, she does not see it. She hears only her daughter's cry, her son's sigh as his patience wavers. She is tired, worn, folded in on herself like a paper crane. She is no longer the paper, but a new shape, creased and bent—the children's mother, one of five mothers here at the shrine for *omiyamairi*, the first visit and blessing. Little children wander around the shrine, their parents pleading for obedience and quiet, bribing patience with sweets and jingling charms to keep the young ones amused.

Natsumi looks to the roof of the shrine, but the Demon Prince isn't there. He faded so slowly before her, his horns shrinking, his obi dulling, his kimono fading from cobalt to a feathery black. The last time she saw him, he opened his mouth, and nothing but the caw of a raven came out.

Her next book is due in five months, but she struggles to write between feedings and laundry and comforting and playing. She isn't sure she'll return to her shift at the hospital after her leave. The world is bursting at the seams again, and she drowns in love and service. She is invisible yet exposed, everything and nothing at once. Longing to exist, to be acknowledged, to unfold just a corner of her origami life.

The tiny rattle tucked into the kimono of her daughter falls onto the stone path with a clatter. It sounds out like handbells, and her grandmother gasps with surprise.

Natsumi apologizes, dusts it off, tucks it back into her daughter's tiny hand. The girl lets out a small yawn on small lips, wraps her tiny fingers around the rattle. Her eyes gleam as her eyelids lower, as sleep overtakes the girl who is too new to know the difference between reality and illusion, the expected world and the spirits.

Natsumi strokes a tired finger along the baby's soft cheek, runs a hand over her son's raven-black hair. There is magic in this, too, she thinks. And Natsumi smiles, even as she drowns in miracles.

As they step forward, she no longer looks for the Demon Prince. As they wave the *tamagushi* and pray over the baby, she no longer peeks at the Shisa or the chozuya or the stone path. Nutshell boats float in her memory, and one day she will tell her children about them, about eyes made of stars and the tails of golden foxes that once swished around her dancing feet.

Her grandmother's eyes widen as she looks at the edge of the cliff across the rope barrier. The elderly couple, Natsumi thinks. But she knows her grandmother will not look down as the two fall under the weight of life, nothing left but a scrap of blue yukata floating on the shore.

She will look up into the sky, where two ravens will fly upward, and always have, their wings stretched over the turquoise water of the sea. They will fly like cranes unfolded, edges creased and ripped, magic from the seasons in their bones. And the sun will glisten on their feathers, swirling on their backs like the light of stars.

※　※　※

Author's Notes to My Younger Self: They are wrong. You are everything you need to be. You do not need to fold into yourself and hide. There will be times when they will not understand, but you do not need their understanding. You will grow and unfold and flourish in the moonlight. And bathed in such bright light, you will not see them anymore.

THE HOLLOW OATH

Brent Nichols

"Afternoon, Doctor."

Marvin Perlman grunted in reply, wondering if the woman was mocking him as he circled around the stepladder blocking the sidewalk.

"You have to see this." She stood on the third step, pressing a palm-sized box against the side of a light pole. She let go, then tapped the box. A giant "25" appeared, projected onto the road. "It's for the anniversary."

Marvin looked at the digits, which sparkled and changed colour. *A quarter century of alien meddling is a travesty*, he thought. *It's not something you celebrate.*

"What do you think?"

"I think it's garish." He stepped off the sidewalk and walked through the numbers, his shoulders twinkling silver, then gold. He headed across the highway that cut through the heart of Fort MacLeod. *Three days until the anniversary. Then all this nonsense will be over. We'll still be in the same handbasket, but at least we can stop pretending we're happy about our trip to hell.*

A young man shuffled along the centre line, face blank, stepping in a rain-filled pothole and stumbling without noticing. Curved strips of metal hugged the sides of the kid's skull. Stepping around him would have been easy enough, but Marvin took a deep breath and marched straight ahead. Their shoulders hit and the kid rocked back. Marvin had time to register an expression of startled hurt before the kid vanished from his peripheral vision.

You've had a moment of awareness there in the fog, he thought. *You should thank me.* He shook his head. *Bloody addicts. Someone should do*

something. "Back in my day," he muttered, then stopped. There had been addicts before the Gliders came. The medical community, to be brutally honest, hadn't done much to help them.

Gwen is right. You're a grump. He couldn't quite help smiling at the thought. She thought he was an old crank, but it didn't seem to bother her. There was always such love in her voice when she called him a curmudgeon that for an instant it would stop being true.

A couple of kids came trotting down the road, dribbling a basketball around the potholes. They swung wide around a woman standing motionless near the sidewalk.

Marvin stopped beside her, compassion replacing his usual annoyance with memory addicts. Ellen was a special case. Her hair, unwashed, hung in tangles that didn't hide the mnemonic capacitors behind her ears. Her face, so gaunt he could trace every bone of her skull, hung slack, just the hint of a smile showing, at odds with the deeply-etched lines of grief.

She was pungent, her clothes grimy and unkempt. They were good clothes, he noted. He couldn't remember the last time he'd met someone with real material needs. Not since the Gliders. No, what she lacked no one could give her.

"Ellen?" he said gently, moving as close as his nose would let him. When she didn't respond, he shook her arm. It took another, harder shake before her smile vanished. She looked around, caught sight of him, and almost focussed on his face before her chin started to wobble. A pair of tears ran down her cheeks, making lines in the grime.

"Ellen, it's me. Marvin. Doctor Perlman."

Her eyes squeezed shut, sending another couple of tears down her face. Her shoulders shook.

"Ellen," he persisted. "How are you doing? Have you been eating?"

"My babies," she said. "My babies . . ." She pressed the heels of her hands into her eyes. She shivered, then slowly relaxed. Her head tilted to one side, and her arms drifted down until they hung by her sides. She'd smeared the wet dirt around her eyes, giving herself a raccoon look. She no longer saw him.

"Leave her alone, for Christ's sake." Marvin didn't turn to see who was speaking. "Let her be with her kids. Jesus. Bloody busybody. You're not a doctor anymore. You never were."

Marvin stood unmoving until he heard footsteps recede behind him. Then, carefully not looking to see which of his neighbours it had been, he turned away from Ellen and continued on his way home.

A figure sat in a shadowy corner of his porch. Gwen, of course. He smiled, then hid the smile with a frown.

The figure stood. It was a man, vaguely familiar. Definitely not Gwen.

The disappointment Marvin felt embarrassed him. No matter how many times he told her to stop pestering him, stop trying to mother a man twice her age, he was honest enough with himself to admit it was nice to have a pretty young woman around. Especially one who, for no good reason Marvin could see, insisted on caring for a grumpy old bachelor.

"Doctor Perlman." The young man (well, young by Marvin's standards, anyhow—he didn't quite look thirty) had a furtive look that put Marvin's hackles up. "I need to talk to you."

"Oh?" Marvin climbed the steps and opened his front door. "Stewart, isn't it? Your mom lives over on Harper Street?"

"Mom moved to the city," the man said. "But yeah. I'm Stewart." He followed Marvin inside, and the two of them took seats in Marvin's front room.

Stewart fidgeted, raking fingers through his greasy dark hair and scratching at a line of red blotches along his jaw. He avoided Marvin's eyes, opening his mouth as if about to speak and then closing it again.

"Looks like you've got a bit of psoriasis there," Marvin observed. "You could swing by the clinic downtown. Glider tech would clear that right up."

That got the other man's attention. He met Marvin's gaze, his eyes hot with accusation. "They're not touching me with their dirty alien technology."

Marvin nodded. "I can respect that." He lived by the same creed, though the creeping indignities of age were undermining his resolve. No one made eyeglasses anymore. If his vision got much worse, he might just get it fixed, and if he was going to have nanobots in his bloodstream anyway, why would he keep the ache in his knees?

For now, though, his principles remained intact.

"I mean, look at us." Stewart flapped an arm toward the street outside. "It's not just the addicts. We're as dependant as children. It's what they want!"

The last part was nonsense—as near as Marvin could tell, the Gliders didn't care one way or the other about humanity—but he found himself nodding in agreement. People as a whole were on the wrong path, and they just kept going, getting farther and farther from where they ought to be.

"You can't tell me it doesn't bother you. I mean, you're a doctor, right?"

Marvin scowled.

"They made a joke of your whole profession! How long were you a doctor before the Gliders came?"

"I wasn't," Marvin muttered. "I was still in medical school when July Nine happened."

"Exactly! All those years of school, and here you are, obsolete."

Marvin did his best to glare a hole in the man. "Did you have some sort of point?"

Stewart kept talking, oblivious. "You're like a symbol for what's happened to us. Everything good and noble, made pointless. Irrelevant."

Marvin looked at the iron poker beside his fireplace and thought about bashing Stewart over the head. Just because he agreed with every word didn't mean he wanted to hear someone spell it out. "Do no harm," he murmured under his breath.

"What was that?" Stewart leaned forward, making his head an excellent target.

Suppressing the thought, Marvin snapped, "I said you're an idi—"

The doorbell rang, and Stewart stiffened. "Are you expecting someone?"

"Yes."

Stewart stood. "Do you mind if I go out your back door?"

"Be my guest. Or rather, stop being my guest." Marvin pointed toward the kitchen.

Stewart was out the back door and gone by the time Marvin got the front door open. A young woman stood on the porch, smiling brightly and holding up a bag of groceries. "Organic vegetables." She moved past him, assuming she was welcome. "I'll put them in the crisper, okay?"

The problem was, Gwen *was* welcome. Hiding his smile was difficult, even with Stewart's visit fresh in his memory. "Organic, schmorganic," he muttered, and followed her into the kitchen.

"Have you been eating, Marvin?"

"Yes."

She was as oblivious to the edge in his voice as Stewart had been. "What have you eaten? I bet it came out of shrink wrap."

Reminding her that she wasn't his mother would just amuse her. He leaned against the kitchen doorway and watched her put the groceries away, a slim, vibrant woman with black hair drawn high over her head in a bun that accentuated the long brown column of her neck. She was beautiful, and so full of life she single-handedly revived his faith in humanity's future.

Not an easy task, that.

"You don't need to take care of me, you know."

She ignored him, of course.

"Shouldn't you be out with your young man? What's his name? Porter?"

Her gaze swung to him, and she scowled. "Peter." She shook her head. "No, Peter and I will be spending time together sometime after he apologizes. Or the freezing over of Hell. Whichever comes first." She turned back to the bags of groceries. "Why are men so irrational, Marvin?"

"It's all women's fault," he explained. "You drive us crazy."

She snorted in reply, but there was amusement in it. "Yeah, that's it."

She chattered as she moved around the kitchen, clanking pans and opening cupboards. "I'm going to make you a kale soup. You'll love it." Her head peeked up from behind the counter, her one visible eye crinkling in amusement. "I know you're annoyed with me, but one bite of this soup and all will be forgiven. Trust me." Her head dropped out of sight. "Ah, here it is."

"I saw Ellen today," he said.

"Ellen." Gwen's voice was muffled. Then she stood up, holding his biggest saucepan. "Someone needs to pry that damned capacitor off her skull."

Marvin blinked. "Come on," he said, even though he'd interrupted Ellen's reveries not an hour before. "She just wants to be with her kids."

"Yeah, well, it's time she learned to let go. It's been, what? Ten years?"

Has it really been that long? And she's still . . . "Being a mother was all she had," he protested weakly. "Her kids were her life."

Gwen set the saucepan on the counter. There was compassion in her face, but there was an uncompromising hardness, too. "Grief is one thing. Ten years in a trance is something else entirely." She shook her head. "Ten years, Marvin!" Gwen planted hands on her rounded hips. "Her kids are gone. Whatever life she might have found for herself is gone too."

He stared at her, wanting to argue. Memory addiction was the biggest sickness facing the human race today. It devoured people. It blighted lives. But Ellen was a special case. How could you begrudge a mother the chance to be with her babies?

"I'm grateful the Gliders found us," Gwen said. "Lord knows. Without them . . ." She shivered. "But I look at Ellen and I almost wish they never came." She shrugged, her voice a bit pointed as she said, "But there's no use dwelling on what might have been."

He stayed silent as Gwen started sharpening one of his knives, her voice a little too casual as she said, "You're a lot like her, you know."

He stiffened. "I've never even owned a capacitor!"

The bun on the top of her head bobbed as she nodded. "True. But you lost something, and it consumes you, and you're completely stuck in the past."

He sputtered. "That's preposterous. I'm the only person around here who's *not* stuck in the past."

"All through High School you did homework every night and studied all weekend while your friends were out having fun," she recited. "You had to make sure your marks were high. Straight A's. That's how you get into the best schools. Then four interminable years getting a degree in molecular biology, and that was before you even started actual medical school." She fixed him with a baleful eye. "Any of this sound familiar?"

He squirmed. "I may have mentioned it once or twice—"

She snorted.

"Well, it's all true!"

"And it's all twenty years in the past!"

Marvin's cheeks went hot. "Well, if I'm so bloody hard to put up with, maybe you should—"

"Oh, no." Her voice was a whipcrack, and he flinched. She waggled the sharpening steel at him. "You're not throwing me out, not after I brought all this food over. We're going to have dinner together, and you're going to like it."

They glared at each other for a long moment, and the absurdity of it was too much for him. He said, "Yes, Ma'am," in his most contrite voice. Gwen maintained her glower for another second, and then both of them dissolved into laughter.

The kale soup tasted better than it smelled. At first, he ate it dutifully, but by the end he was glad when she didn't take the leftovers with her.

The only sour note came as she was stacking their bowls in his dishwasher. "How's Tommy?" she said, her voice gentle.

He didn't answer, just shook his head, and she came over and squeezed his forearm. "I'm sorry. I'll come by in a couple of days, okay? Call me if you need anything. Remember to eat." She gave him a peck on the cheek and headed for the door.

"I'm a grown man, Gwen."

"I know." His grumpiness, as always, rolled off her without making an impression. "Bye."

He watched her go, feeling a couple of decades fall away as if they'd never happened. She was so much healthier than the pinched waif he met twenty years before. Just a kid, but a kid under a sentence of death. It wasn't an official consultation. Her parents were afraid of the aliens, who'd turned the world upside-down just by showing up and saying hello. They wanted a second opinion before they took her to the Glider clinic. They wanted a human opinion.

The diagnosis was pretty straightforward. Cancer. It was all through her body. He wanted to recommend aggressive chemotherapy and radiation. The chances of it saving her were slight, and if it worked, the odds of the cancer coming back were high. But she'd have a chance.

Except you couldn't get chemo and radiation anymore. No one was making the drugs. The machines were in mothballs. Marvin, feeling like a traitor to his beliefs, told her parents to take her to the clinic. A week later, she was playing outside with her friends. Within a month, the shadows under her eyes were gone and she was as healthy as any other kid.

Gwen hadn't been gone for five minutes before Marvin heard a tapping at the front door. It was Stewart again. Marvin let him in.

"Have you been hanging around outside all this time?"

Stewart didn't answer, just stood fidgeting in the front hall. "I've heard you complain about the Gliders," he said. "I know you don't like them." The fidgeting stopped, and he looked Marvin in the eye. "How serious are you about that?"

Marvin gave him a long, careful look. "If there was something I could do, I would do it. But . . ."

"Maybe there is," Stewart said. "Maybe you can help."

He looked deadly serious. The problem was he also looked like a schmuck. A dangerous fool.

But . . . to send the Gliders packing! The dream was irresistible. Impossible, but irresistible. "You have a plan of some sort?" Marvin heard the sarcasm in his own voice and wondered if he should bother suppressing it.

Stewart scowled. "We have a plan. We're organized. We're reclaiming our planet." He looked Marvin up and down, curling a lip. "I'm not sharing the details with an old windbag who's all talk. Call me if you remember where your balls went." He left the house, slamming the door behind him.

The drive to Taber took more than an hour, time Marvin spent trying to distract himself. The coming visit would be ugly. Pointless. Still, he had to make an attempt.

Cathy answered his knock and let him in without a word. Tommy sat in the backyard, a string of drool on his chin. Marvin took a seat opposite him. "Hey, Tommy. It's me. Uncle Marvin."

Tommy didn't reply, of course. He had the gauntness of a long-term coma patient. He ate once or twice a day, but never enough. Sometimes he spoke to Cathy during meals, but he was never entirely there. He always had at least half his attention in the past. Now, without the urgency of hunger to compel him, he gave himself to his memories completely.

"I was thinking about you on the drive up," Marvin said. "I was remembering that time I taught you to throw a football. You remember that day?" *You remember it a damn sight better than I do, if it was good enough to make your playlist. You bloody useless vegetable.* "I don't suppose you want to chuck a football around now?" Marvin's words sounded foolish to his own ears, but he ploughed ahead anyway. "It's a special memory to me, that day. Not so special that I'm going to piss away my life reliving it, mind you. But special. Today could be special too. If you let it."

The boy stared past Marvin's shoulders with unfocussed eyes. Except he wasn't a boy any longer, other than inside his brain. There was grey in his short-cropped hair.

Marvin spent another half an hour talking aimlessly, feeling his blood pressure climb ever so slowly. The urge to shake the boy until he roused from his trance was strong. Marvin had tried that before. It hadn't ended well.

"I might not visit you anymore," Marvin said. "I'm not sure there's a point. Not if you don't even know I'm here. Not if you don't care."

Tommy didn't respond.

"Do you ever think of me while you're zoned out?" Marvin hated the peevish sound of his own voice. "Do you replay that afternoon with the football?" He felt his hands curl into frustrated fists. "Did I ruin your life that day? Was the afternoon just a little too good? So good you can't help going back there, again and again?"

Marvin stood, pacing back and forth with short, agitated steps. "I can't relive that day, you know. One of the best days I ever had. But it hurts too much to think about it now." He planted his hands on his hips and glared down at the oblivious face of his nephew. "I think I'm immune to this stupid memory addiction. No good memories to look back on. Just study and work and homework, and then more study. Nothing I ever need to repeat." He jabbed a finger at Tommy, feeling like a fool but unable to stop himself. "You kids these days, you don't know what it was like—"

He seemed to hear Gwen laughing at him in his head. He lowered his arm, flushing. "Anyway," he said, "you should come back to us. Once in a while, at least. Maybe make some new memories. Don't you get bored, going back to the same days over and over?"

Tommy didn't get bored, he knew. The capacitor experience was so complete, so immersive, that you didn't just get the sights and sounds. You got your feelings from back then, even your thoughts. Every surprise was a surprise all over again. The sweetness of the moment remained just as sweet. What could compete with that?

"Goodbye, Tommy," he said, and headed for his car.

———

When he got home, he called Stewart. "I'm in," he said. "This plague has to stop. Whatever you're doing, I'm in."

———

Marvin made the long walk from his house to the centre of town all alone. It wouldn't do to be seen with his co-conspirators.

He wasn't sure how big the conspiracy was. Stewart sat on the steps of the library building with Nate, a man who looked enough like him to be a brother or a cousin. The two of them fooled with their phones and carefully ignored him. For all Marvin knew, this was the whole cabal.

The air-conditioned interior of the Fort Museum was pleasant after the summer heat outside. Marvin stood in the doorway with goose-bumps pebbling his arms, waiting for his eyes to adjust. It was years since he'd been in the building, and much had changed. A corridor to his right led to the parade ground and museum displays. To his left, though, was a new feature. A high counter, the space above filled by thick plate glass.

"Hello, Doc. Haven't seen you in a while." A security guard stood behind the counter, his voice echoing from hidden speakers. It was a young Chinese man with a cheerful, unsuspicious face, and Marvin's conscience reproached him.

He thought of Tommy and suppressed his remorse. "Keith Lau. Is your mom still at the clinic?"

Keith nodded. "She keeps talking about retiring, but she can't seem to quit. She loves it there."

You're not just deceiving the boy, you're going to get his mother fired, too. He dismissed the thought. If the aliens could be driven away, employment would be better for everyone. Real jobs, doing something that mattered, not just handing out alien potions.

He moved closer to the counter and glanced around. There was no one else on Marvin's side of the glass, and he couldn't see anyone but Keith on the far side. "Do you have the Glider in there?"

Keith grinned and lowered his voice. "Arrived yesterday. The big speech is tomorrow afternoon. I guess they'll come pick him up the day after that."

Gliders were terrible public speakers, never leaving their protective tanks. Still, envoys would speak to communities all over the world in honour of the twenty-fifth anniversary of First Contact.

Marvin edged up to the glass, as if that mattered. This was the moment of decision, and he wanted to hesitate. *There's too much at stake, Marvin. Man up.* "Say, Keith? Do you think I could see him?"

The boy hesitated, looking at Marvin. This was the test, a purely subjective, instinctive evaluation that Stewart, with his sly, furtive air, could never have passed. Marvin, though, was an upstanding member of the community. He was fifty years old. He was conservative. He was a doctor, for God's sake.

"Sure, Doc, come on it." Keith gave Marvin a conspiratorial wink. "But it never happened on my shift, right?"

Marvin winked back. "You know it."

A buzzer sounded, and Marvin stepped toward a door at the end of the counter. *Bullshitting my way past a security guard. This could be the first concrete use I've ever put my medical degree to.* He pushed the door open, then stopped in the doorway.

Behind him, the door to the street flew open. Stewart and Nate darted in, grim-faced and determined, and Keith said, "Doc! Get out of the doorway!"

Marvin held his ground until Stewart's broad hand shoved him through into the room beyond.

After that, things happened quickly. Marvin stumbled to one knee as Stewart and Nate charged Keith. The guard stood frozen, then grabbed the stun baton on his belt. Stewart tackled him and brought him to the floor, and the baton bounced away. Nate moved deeper into the room, unslinging a backpack from his back, while Stewart wrestled with Keith.

Marvin stared, his legs shaking. It seemed suddenly obvious he was making a terrible mistake, but it was too late now. He was committed. His eyes tracked Nate's progress. The room ran fifty paces or so, the walls lined with tables and desks. At the far end of the room, however, all mundane Earthly normalcy ended.

The Glider was at the other end. The creature itself wasn't visible, of course. The tank was a dark, gleaming cylinder the size of a minivan, all strange contours that rippled and flowed.

Nate upended his backpack and spilled a hammer, several chisels, and a pry bar onto the floor. He was going to batter his way into the tank, then take his tools to the alien within. For the first time since the Gliders had arrived, one would die at human hands.

A muffled cry brought Marvin's attention back to the foreground. Keith was on his back with Stewart straddling him. Keith bucked and thrashed, his arms up to block a rain of punches.

Stewart's hand snaked out, closing around Keith's right elbow. In a moment, he had the arm pinned across Keith's throat. Stewart's knee trapped the other arm. Keith couldn't block as Stewart hammered blow after blow into his unprotected face.

Marvin closed his eyes. *It's like chemo,* he told himself. *It's like radiation therapy. Sometimes, you have to do some damage to cure a really serious ailment. Sometimes, good tissue has to be sacrificed to save the patient.*

Keith moaned deep in his throat with every impact. The moan, combined with the meaty impact of fist on bone, made a mockery of Marvin's rationalizations.

Think of Tommy. You're doing this for him. Think of Gwen. Remember how sick she was? She needed chemo and radiation. It would have been bad. Ugly. Hard to face. But it would have saved her. You're a doctor, damn it. You can face hard treatments.

Except Gwen was alive, she was healthy, and there hadn't been any chemo. No radiation. He didn't have to poison her to save her. It wasn't necessary anymore.

Two thoughts crystallized in his mind. First, this attack would achieve nothing. It would take more than one senseless murder to drive the Gliders from Earth. And if the Gliders left, it wasn't as if everyone would simply throw fifty years of technological change aside. Knowledge was a river that only flowed downstream. There was no going back. Memory capacitors existed now. Killing Gliders wouldn't make them go away.

Second, if he could roll back the advancements of half a century, it would be an obscenity. More little girls would develop cancer. Would he really wish chemo on them? For that matter, did he want to wear glasses for the rest of his life, and wince every time he straightened his knees? Could he visit that fate on everyone else?

Marvin opened his eyes. Keith no longer squirmed. There was blood on the floor around him, blood on Stewart's shirt, even a few drops on Marvin's shoes. Stewart had one battered fist raised high, but he lowered it, breathing hard.

"Fucking traitor," Stewart said. "I'll show you." His hand plunged into his pocket and came out with a clasp knife. The blade clicked open. He released Keith's arm to expose his throat, brought the knife up—and Marvin thrust the stun baton under his nose.

"Do no harm," Marvin said.

Stewart, his snarl fading into a look of comical astonishment, twisted his head away from the baton. "What the f—"

"Do no harm," Marvin repeated. "Maybe it really is that simple."

Outrage replaced the bafflement on Stewart's face. "Seriously? We're in a combat situation, and you're thinking about your Hippocratic Oath?"

"No." Marvin twitched the baton, making Stewart flinch. "It's not part of the oath. More of a guiding principle. First, do no harm."

Stewart's eyes narrowed.

"No one ever gave her chemo," Marvin said, "and she's fine."

"What?"

"Gwen." Marvin shook his head. "Pay attention."

In his peripheral vision Nate, frozen like a statue, held a chisel against the tank. *I better get on with it. He won't stand there like an idiot forever.*

"I thought I had to do harm to heal," Marvin said. "But Gwen is fine. I need to get with the times." And he tapped Stewart across the forehead with the baton.

Nothing happened, of course. The weapon would be bio-coded to the security staff. Stewart flinched, then glared at Marvin and heaved himself to his feet.

"Worth a try," said Marvin, and dropped the baton. He raised his hands, palms out. "I can't let you do this, Stewart. It's wrong."

Stewart snarled and swung the knife. Marvin got a hand in the way and stared in disbelief as a triangle of steel appeared, jutting through the back of his left hand.

Then Keith tapped the stun baton against the side of Stewart's leg, and Stewart collapsed.

"Hey!" Nate turned away from his demolition job and came toward them, a hammer in one hand, a heavy chisel in the other. Keith was still trying to rise. He was in no shape to fight a homicidal would-be terrorist, so Marvin stepped past him to the security station. He slapped his hand down on a fat red panic button, and an alarm sounded. A man's crisp voice said, "Emergency services."

"Aw, shit," Nate said. He gave Marvin a murderous glare, then ran past him, pushed the door open, and fled.

"Medical emergency." Marvin fished out a handkerchief, tied it around his hand, and told Keith, "Hang in there. Help's on the way."

———•———

They didn't arrest him. That was a pleasant surprise. An earnest young medic tried to give him first aid, but he declined. It hardly seemed right, under the circumstances, to have Glider tech wash away the consequences of what he'd done. Besides, he had his principles. He stopped bleeding before the handkerchief was soaked through, and when the police were done questioning him, he headed home.

The warm glow of mid-morning sunshine astonished him. It seemed impossible that so little time could have passed. The sight of a memory addict standing dumbfounded on a street corner jarred him further. *The world just changed. Why is everything the same?* He paused in front of the woman, watching watery brown eyes slowly focus on him. *Things change, but human idiocy endures.* When he had at least a portion of her attention, Marvin said, "You're a moron." Then he continued on his way.

His medical bag was deep in the back of a closet and covered in dust. The instruments themselves were pristine, though. After all, most of them had never been used. The antiseptic spray had no expiry date, so he squirted both sides of the cut, pleased to find it had a numbing effect as well.

Stitching his own hand was awkward, but he managed it. He sewed up the hand front and back, then surveyed his work with quiet satisfaction.

Not the best stitching job I've ever seen. But it's the best I've seen in twenty years, and that's something. He would have a scar, but that was all right. A mistake of such magnitude ought to leave a mark.

There was a message from Gwen, and he scanned it quickly. She wanted more kale soup. Unless he told her not to come, she would be there at six. She'd learned long since that he wouldn't actually invite her.

He grinned as he hit the "reply" button. "I got your message. I'd love to have you come over. See you at six." He chuckled as he sent it. She would show up convinced he was dying. What she would say when she saw his hand, he had no idea.

He wouldn't let the conversation be all about him, though. He'd steer it around to this Peter fellow. He might even be able to offer a bit of insight.

It wasn't the role he'd wanted for himself as a young man, he reflected as he put the medical bag away. It wasn't what he'd sacrificed his youth for. But Glider tech couldn't solve every problem. Some things required the human touch. Maybe he could still be of some use.

⁂

Author's Notes to My Younger Self: You are young. You lack experience and the wisdom that comes with it. But your moral compass is perfectly sound. Don't let anyone tell you otherwise. Not even your parents. Especially not your parents. Parenthood doesn't automatically confer rationality, or compassion, or ethics. Only power. Listen only to yourself on matters of right and wrong.

WHEN RESIN BURNS TO TAR

Maria Haskins

---------------------------------*(now)*---------------------------------

It's a sweltering summer's day near haying season, and Kata is carrying wood to the tar-burning pit in the meadow outside the village of Vale, when she sees Mother, standing in the shadows beneath the eaves of the forest. Mother has been dead for a year come this autumn, but there she is, looming as tall and menacing as she ever did in life, wielding her craft and wind-keeper staff at will.

Kata straightens her aching back and gazes across the tall timothy and oatgrass, staring at that darker shade beneath the heavy branches of the spruce trees. It's not that Kata is surprised to see Mother. She just didn't expect she would come so near, so soon.

Kata's calloused hands tighten into fists, and she reaches out with her craft for the reassuring touch of water beneath the ground and in the winding brook beyond the meadow. Weak as her water-sense might be, it has always steadied her in the face of Mother's wrath.

You can't hold me here anymore, Kata thinks, willing herself to believe the words.

She turns away and gets back to work, but Mother's gaze still prickles at her clammy neck and backside beneath the thin wool breeches and linen tunic.

After a life spent caring for Mother and doing farming chores for others, it's Kata's first time working at the tar-pit, hauling sun-dried pine to the men and women stacking the wood for burning. They've been working for

days in the heat with nary a breeze from the far-off Inner Sea. The heady scent of pine and meadow grass mingles with the sharper smell of sweat.

The tar-burning pit is shaped like a wide, gently tapering bowl, dug into the sandy ground of a sloping hillside protected from the wind, its inner surface lined with rocks and dirt. Kata's great uncle Abel, the village pit master, walks the grounds, leaning on his cane, making sure they lay the wood right—fanning out from the centre, a pile stacked in the middle to keep the flow of tar from getting blocked once the burning starts.

With the longships and traders' knarrs coming in down-river at the town of Rivermouth every fall, there is always a good price to be had for tar, and every villager covets a share of that bounty, but it is not easy money. It's taken a year's hard labour to make this pit, as Kata knows only too well, having helped fell and haul logs and stumps here in winter, splitting and cracking them, chopping them into firewood this spring, stacking it all up to dry until summer.

Fifty barrels, that's what they might get from a pit this size, Abel says, if the winds are calm and the fire burns just right, slow and hot, bleeding the thick, golden resin out of all that wood, letting the fire and smoke turn it into tar.

While Mother was alive, the village made do without a wind-keeper at the pit, rightly fearing it might raise Mother's ire, even though she'd never take on such a lowly chore herself. Now, a new wind-keeper walks around the pit with Abel. Her name is Magda, and she's no stranger to the village or Kata. Magda grew up down the road from Mother's house, and when she and Kata were children, Magda was as close to a friend as Kata's ever had. Then, at fourteen, Magda left for the coast and earned her wind-keeper's staff at sea, while Kata stayed with Mother and earned nothing but a lowly water-finder's rod.

Magda is in her early thirties now, same as Kata, and she is much the same as when she left, short and round-faced with tan skin and a raucous laugh, though the years have added a fine net of lines around her brown eyes and a scar on her cheek. Somehow Kata always imagined every wind-keeper would be much like Mother, severe and imposing, but except for carrying a wind-keeper's staff, Magda is nothing like Mother.

Kata works, trying not to dwell on the presence of the shade at the forest's edge. Even so, Mother's voice scratches at the inside of her skull, deriding her dirty hands, her ruddy skin, her thick waist, her tousled mousy hair, her soft voice, her shyness.

A day labourer, that's all you'll ever be, scrounging for scraps at the wayside. Useless, hopeless girl.

She picks a splinter from her hand and thinks of the barrels of tar, thinks of the brightly painted ships setting sail from Rivermouth in autumn, travelling south along the ragged shores of the Inner Sea, through the Narrow Gates, into the Outer Sea where you can sail for days, seeing nowt but water.

What would it feel like, Kata wonders, to be carried by that sea, to touch it, to have it touch you? What would it be like, to travel beneath a wide-open sky, beneath the sails and the wings of birds?

—————————————————————(past)—————————————————————

The dun horses pulling the logging sled snorted and steamed, trudging through the early winter snow. Kata knew how they felt. She had been working since daybreak with Abel and Taryn, daughter of the village blacksmith, felling pines on a rise above the bog, at the farthest reaches where the villagers cut logs and dug up stumps to burn in the tar-pit in summer.

Many of the pines they harvested here had been cut in previous years by Abel with axe or knife, stripping away bark to make them bleed more resin, which would soak into the heartwood and make more tar when the lumber burned.

Below the rise grew the shrubby sweet gale and withered sedge of the bog, and in past years, Kata had often gone there in autumn, braving the marshy ground and the midges to gather cloudberries. She would not do that again, because somewhere in that fen, mother's dead body had been sunk into the boggy depths, wrapped in nowt but a shift and a sheet of rough-spun linen.

When Mother lived, the villagers had stayed out of her way, since she was likely to threaten anyone with storms and worse if her mood darkened, which was most of the time, especially toward the end when the sickness had taken hold in her gut. Once Mother was dead, it was a different story. The people she owed money for food and rent and services through the years might have feared Mother, but they did not fear Kata. Every scrap of value from Mother's time as wind-keeper had been taken—rings, bracelets, necklaces stripped off her body—and Kata had been left with nothing but the run-down cottage and Mother's staff, leaning on the bricks by the hearth, just as she'd left it.

The village even refused to bury Mother in the cemetery, fearing the earth would not hold her. In the end, they'd sunk her in the bog, anchoring the corpse with iron and silver, trusting that metal and water would keep her.

They'd been wrong.

The first time Mother had come to haunt her had been a week after they'd taken the body away. Kata had awoken in the chill dark of night to see Mother in the cottage doorway, silent, smelling of death and rot. After that, she'd burned Mother's clothes, used salt and iron on the threshold to bar the shade from returning, but Mother had haunted her steps ever since, and in the woods, there was no protection from her presence.

Kata cleared away the snow around the pine tree, then stood with Abel, while Taryn wielded the axe. She tried not to, but every now and then, her eyes strayed to the bog.

"She haunts me too," Abel said, his tone not unkindly. "But a shade has no more power than you give it, remember that."

Kata nodded, but all she could think of was Mother's voice, close as breath on skin:

You can't leave.

Mother had spoken those words more times than Kata cared to remember, and every time, Kata had felt something sharp and terrible burn into her, like a nail hot from the blacksmith's anvil, pinning her in place. Of all the abuse Mother had hurled at her through the years, nothing felt more like a curse, and she felt the bite of it, even now.

———————————————————————*(now)*———————————————————————

At noon-day, they all seek shelter beneath the birches near the tar-pit. Mother's shade is gone, and Kata takes her turn scooping cold buttermilk from the wooden pail brought from the village, wolfing down fried herring tucked between soft cakes of buttered barley bread.

"Hey, Kata. How's an old maid like you handling a workload like this?" It's Albert, one of the farm-boys, half her age with scrawny arms and a scrawnier beard. She's too used to the jibes by now to bother answering, glancing at him sideways as she sips from her wooden cup.

"Mind your own work," Magda says, swatting Albert's arm with her staff. "Us old maids are working our share, least as good as you."

Albert gives Magda an exaggerated bow. "No disrespect meant, wind-keeper. Just thinking this one's likely claiming a place meant for someone younger and with more need. Many people have plenty of mouths to feed at home and would like their share of the silver."

Kata has heard that same grumbling at her back all year after Abel took her on, and though she would not give up her spot for anything, it still rankles. "I have a right to earn my keep same as you," Kata says, holding back the sharper words prickling on her tongue.

"And if that troubles you," Magda cuts in, "you can pick that bone with me."

She flourishes her wind-keeper staff in the air with a mock-scowl, and everyone laughs, even Kata. After all these years, it's an unexpected boon to have someone take her side.

"Leastways you won't really curse a storm down on us like Kata's mam," someone mutters, and Kata's face flushes hot.

"Everyone here has earned their place," Abel says, taking his turn at the buttermilk, and the crowd hushes. "Kata has been a trusty labourer and waterfinder for many years. She asked for a place, same as all of you, and she's working for nowt more than two barrels of tar. Anyone else want to take that deal, rather than waiting for your share of the sales at Rivermouth come autumn, you're welcome to it."

"Two barrels?" Albert looks as incredulous as he sounds. "What's an old maid need two barrels of tar for?"

Kata does not answer and when the others go back to work, she lingers in the shade a while.

Magda is helping with the wood and has left her staff in the grass. Like Mother's staff it's carved with wind-runes, its grip worn smooth by handling, but while Mother's staff was studded with bits of obsidian and crystal, Magda's is adorned with beads and shells strung on leather straps and set with bits of turquoise.

Kata thinks of Mother's staff, of the heavy thump it made on the wooden floorboards whenever Mother wanted something—food, drink, or someone to take a lashing. How many times did Kata make herself small and quiet to stay out of the reach of that staff? How often did she take the brunt of Mother's rage, no matter who had raised her ire? Often enough that most people in the village now look at her with scorn or pity, if they look at her at all.

If Mother's shade is clinging to anything, it is that staff.

"It's nowt but wood," Abel told her when they carted Mother off for her wet burial, glancing at the staff beside the hearth. But he would not touch it either.

Nowt but wood.

Kata looks at the wood piled neatly in the pit, breathes in the sticky-sharp smell of sun-warmed pine. Not even Abel knows she tucked

Mother's staff in beneath the first layers of wood in the pit yesterday morning. The staff was cold and heavy in her hands, before she put it down and covered it up with pine. Soon, the pit will be set alight, and every stick of wood will burn, slow and steady, resin and lumber turning into smoke and tar beneath the ground. Then, Kata will be free.

That's why Mother's shade has come, because she knows it too.

———•———

That night, asleep in the workers' hut by the pit, Kata dreams of Mother.

It's not a nightmare, not at first, but a memory. Kata was a small child the one and only time Mother took her to the coast outside Rivermouth. Mother borrowed a sailing skiff and they sailed out beyond the grey granite shores of the inlet.

In all her life before or since, Kata never saw Mother stir such gentle winds, a thin smile curled on her lips as she told Kata how to handle the sail and ropes. Later, Kata sat in the prow, one hand trailing in the water, staring through the silky-blue sheen of that rippled surface, pretending they were never going back, that everything would be different now, that they would keep sailing until the world around them changed, until she and Mother changed as well.

Kata touched the sea, and the sea touched her. It was perhaps the first time she felt the stirring of water-sensing in herself. Closing her eyes, she imagined the entire Inner Sea, its currents and eddies and tides, like a sheer net strung with pearls, rippling beneath her, tugging at her fingers.

Eventually the dream, like the memory, darkens like a bruise.

Mother saw a trading ship, headed for the harbour, crimson sails furled, oars striking the water, its dragon prow gleaming in the light. Mother's face turned hard as she reached for her staff. Kata cowered, gripping the railing while Mother shook her staff and called a wind that ripped apart their small sail and crashed the skiff onto the stony shore, the gusts rocking the ship as it passed.

———•———

When Kata wakes, she stares into the dusky indigo of the summer night, waiting for Mother's shade to come, to hook its wet fingers through her ribs, to pin her in place, to tell her she can't leave, that all her plans and purposes are futile. She waits until dawn breaks, but nothing stirs in the meadow but the moonlight.

———

They light the tar-pit the next day. Abel sets the wood alight, after covering the pit carefully with dirt and peat and white moss, Magda standing by to calm the winds if needed.

"Two to four days for burning all the wood to tar, but it'll need constant watching," Abel tells them, sounding stern. He will watch the smoke, regulating the fire by opening and closing holes in the top, making sure enough air comes in to ensure it burns slow and steady. Too little wind, and the fire will go out before all the wood has burned. Too much and the pit might burn to ashes and coal without giving any tar at all.

The barrels are made ready in the space below the slope where the tar will come pouring out of a hollowed log.

"You've done good work," Abel says, "but it's not done yet."

Kata is sitting by herself in the shade when Magda offers her a swig of lingonberry drink from a jug, and suddenly the years between them don't seem so long. They talk. Mostly, it's Magda talking, about where she's been, about the places she's seen, how she got the scar on her cheek in a bar-brawl with a raider. How she's crisscrossed the Inner Sea more times than she can count.

"I'm not cut out for ship life," Magda muses, looking up through the birch leaves at the sky. "I miss the green, the earth, small winds through the woods. These days, I travel the coast, helping wherever people pay me."

"You ever travel the Outer Sea?"

Magda shakes her head.

"No. I turned back at the Narrow Gates. Too much water. Too much wind." She gives Kata a shrewd look. "You were always talking of the Outer Sea. Is that where you're going? With your two barrels of tar?"

"If I can." Kata gives her a careful look. "No law against an old maid travelling the seas, is there?"

"I should hope not. Plenty of old maids travelling lands and seas."

They sit in silence for a while. Again, Magda speaks first.

"How was it, with your Mother, before the end? Everyone here tries hard not to talk about her."

Kata shrugs. "You know what she was like. She birthed me and raised me and never forgave me for either, and then she got sick and took ten years to die."

"Do you miss her, hard as she was?"

Kata has no answer. If she could find the words, she would tell Magda how she missed Mother more when she was alive, when Kata hoped she still might change, than now when she's dead and sunk into the ground.

Magda plays with the beads and shells on her staff, making them jingle. "Thought you might be married by now. Children. All that."

Kata braids a blade of grass into a ring, slips it on a finger. "Attur asked me, once. But I sent him away and then he left, just like you. No one has been fool enough to ask since."

Kata thinks of Mother's fury when Attur stood on the steps of the cottage, the way she struck the window pane with her staff, shattering the dearly bought glass.

Magda shakes her head. "Attur was always more trouble than he was worth. You're not pining for him still?"

Kata laughs at that. "No, I'm done pining." She takes another swig from the jug. "I saw him at the harbour in Rivermouth the year before Mother died. He captains a ship of his own now. He's done well for himself. Away from the village. Away from me."

She thinks of Attur, thinks more of his ship: its gleaming prow and broad, tarred hull, the sea glinting like grey glass behind it.

"You could have left, too, Kata. Long ago."

"No, I couldn't. Not then."

"Yes, you could." Magda looks down at the grass beneath the birch roots, picks up the ring Kata dropped. "You could have come with me."

Kata wants to say something, but what is there to say after all this time? "I can't undo any of it. Whether I wish it or no. I never had much of a purpose in my life. I've only muddled through, and these last few years even the muddling got harder. But if I don't leave now . . ." I'll rot as surely as Mother rots beneath the bog, she thinks, but does not say.

"Then go. The Outer Sea is still there."

"A place on a ship is not easy to come by for an old penniless maid, at least not one without wind-craft."

"Plenty of people in the world would pay good money for a skilled waterfinder."

"Not at sea. And water-finding is not grand like wind-keeping. No staff to wield. It's good for nothing but chores and well-digging."

It makes Kata wince to hear Mother's words spilling from her own mouth, but Magda only chuckles.

"Things don't have to be grand to be worth doing. Living is grand enough, most days. And the staff, well, it's just a stick of wood. I mean, for your waterfinding, do you use a dowsing rod?"

Kata nods.

"Can you do without it?"

Kata thinks of the feeling of water, the tickle of it at the edge of her senses wherever she goes, the liquid threads of it, aquiver in her mind even now. "Yes. But people expect the rod, so . . ."

"Same with the staff. No one takes a wind-keeper seriously without one." Magda gives her a mischievous look. "You want to feel some wind-craft?"

"That's not how it works. No one can touch both water *and* wind."

"You'd be surprised. I've learned a few things since I've been away." Magda puts her hand on top of Kata's, its warmth heavy and reassuring. "It's like reaching for water, I've heard, but . . . different. Try it."

Kata sighs, but closes her eyes and takes a breath, as if she were dowsing, and there, quivering through Magda's hand, she feels it. Something swirling at the edges of her mind, like breath, like mist and light and gossamer. She gasps and lets go.

Magda smiles.

"Something I learned at sea. That any craft is stronger if two or more work together, no matter what kind of craft they have. Met a man once who told me all craft is one and the same, water, wind, runes . . . it's all connected like weft and warp. That we can all strengthen each other. Granted, he was trying to bed me at the time, but there might be something to it."

Kata leans back in the grass, thinking of Mother, glowering at the world through the cottage window, wrapped up in her loneliness and darkness.

You can't leave. The burning spike of the words are still inside her, the threat of rage and storm behind them. Kata wants to reach for Magda's hand again, but Magda is already on her feet, talking to Abel. He is watching the smoke from the pit, studying the wispy clouds, and Kata tenses when she sees worry marring his face.

"What of the wind?" he asks Magda, voice low and cautious.

"It's stirring," Magda nods. "But the storm's further inland, not headed our way yet."

"Not supposed to be storming at all, this time of year." Abel glances at Kata, and she thinks about Mother's shade, looming in the woods. "Well, you let me know soon as you feel it shift."

"A storm?" Kata asks.

Magda gives her a crooked smile. "Don't worry, you'll get your tar. What *do* you need those barrels for?"

Kata hesitates. She wishes she could explain to Magda how these two barrels of tar have become her purpose these last few years; how working toward this moment has been the only flame lighting her way as the world went dark around her.

"It's for a trade," she says finally. "Two barrels of tar to take an old maid to the Outer Sea."

———————————————————*(past)*———————————————————

"Greetings, Kata. How's your mother?"

Kata looked up at Attur where he sat, astride the railing of his ship, his long black hair pulled back in braids, a beard on his chin that made his face look like a stranger's. She hadn't expected to find him at Rivermouth. All she'd wanted at the harbour was to catch a glimpse of the sea while she waited for Mother to be done at the healer's hut, but there he was, large as life.

Attur had been a friend and more, before he left to go on the ships ten years before. She'd heard he captained his own knarr now, trading along the shores of the Outer Sea, and here it was, its dragon-headed prow glistening gold and green.

How's your mother?

After ten years, that was the first thing he thought to ask her. What he meant was, is she still alive?

"Mother's sick. She's dying."

"She's been dying for a long time."

Kata winced. She thought of Mother at the healer's hut, waiting for whatever tincture he would give her this time. Half a day's ride from Vale, rattling around in a merchant's cart, had done nothing to improve Mother's mood or pain. In years past, Mother had searched out every healer up and down the coast, demanding they rid her of the thing growing in her gut. Lately, Kata suspected, all she wanted was something to numb the pain.

She breathed in the smell of brine and tar and looked across the inlet, listening to the gulls screeching above the ships anchored at the docks or pulled up on the pebbly beaches.

"When do you sail?" she asked, looking back at Attur and at his crew, all of them hard at work, securing cargo, stowing supplies, mending sails, and tarring boards.

"Tomorrow, with the tide if the ship's ready. We're already a week late leaving, for want of tar for the sails and hull. Every year tar's harder to come by, and every year it costs us more. You should tell your uncle Abel to build a bigger pit at Vale."

"Would you take me with you if I asked?"

Kata had not meant to speak the words, but they could not be unsaid. She thought of Mother and shivered at her own guilt.

"I have a full crew," Attur answered, looking away. "And you've got no useful skills with sails or wind."

"I'd work hard," Kata said. "I'd learn whatever trade was needed. I'm a water-finder, I could . . ."

"We need no water-finders at sea." Attur climbed down from the knarr's railing, wiping the tar from his hands with a rag. When he spoke again, his tone was softer. "I wonder that you haven't left before. I wonder why you did not take the chance when it was offered."

"You know why. Mother . . ."

"And that is why you won't go now. What would you bring me, Kata? What storms would Ragna call down on your head and my ship if you came aboard?"

Kata went cold at the way the crew looked at her now, even those who had pretended not to be listening before. "You're afraid of her."

"Aren't you?" Attur asked. "They still talk about her up and down the coast. Ragna Firewind they call her. People at home, in Vale, they never spread the full tale. Maybe they never knew it, but anyone sailing the seas, they know."

"It was a long time ago," Kata says.

"So it was. But people still remember her. Your Mother might have been the most powerful wind-keeper to walk this world in living memory, and she did her bit in the old wars down south, even sunk a fleet, some say." He peers at Kata. "Did she ever tell you the true reason why she never went back to sea?"

"She had a child," Kata answers, barely able to look at him, thinking of Mother hurling that in her face, how Kata had wrecked her life by simply being born. *A sailor rat's daughter.*

"So she did. But she could've left you or brought you on board. Some wind-keepers do. Truth is, one day, Ragna didn't get the pay she thought she was owed from a captain, so she burned his ship. Set it alight and spun a wind to fan the flames. Twenty ships burned to cinder. Afterward, no one could prove it was her, but everyone knew, and no ship would take her. No one dared lay a finger on her, mind you, but they would not have her on board either. She went home to Vale knowing she'd never sail again. So, I ask again, Kata. What would you bring me, except ill winds?"

Kata felt the breeze blow through her, cold and bitter. She imagined every gust at her back to be Mother's doing. *Useless*, Mother's voice whispered in her ear. *Hopeless*.

Kata looked at the sea, then down at the tar staining Attur's hands.

"If I brought you a barrel of tar next year, Attur, would you take me then? Would that be useful enough?"

Attur laughed.

"That would be useful, but you'd have to bring me two at least to earn a place."

He was jesting, Kata knew, but she was not. Two barrels of tar were worth more money than she'd had to herself in her entire life, but here and now she needed a purpose, even one as small as this, to keep her from walking into the sea until she could walk no more.

"You give me your word?" she asked. "If I come here, in another year with two barrels of the best pine-tar out of Vale, will you take me on board?"

"Kata. . . . Whether I give my word or not, whether you bring two barrels or none, do you really think your Mother would let you leave?"

"I'm asking you, not her."

Attur looked at her then, and it seemed he saw her at last, saw her true, saw what she was now, not what she'd been when he left. He nodded, and Kata felt it kindle then, a small hope, flickering beneath her skin.

(now)

That night, when Kata is sitting fireguard, a gust of wind stirs her hair. She hesitates, not sure if she's awake or dreaming, before she gets up and walks closer to the pit. The wind follows, swirling 'round her like the eddies of a stream. There's a sound in that wind, a sound Kata does not want to hear nor heed, and yet it commands her all the same. It is the thump of a heavy staff striking wooden floorboards with all the weight of Mother's rage and pain behind it.

In the ever-dusk of the summer night, the meadow's supple grass bends and sways, rippling like the sea as it parts for her, laying bare a path toward the woods. Kata does not want to tread that path, but she walks it anyway.

A shade has no more power than you give it, she thinks, trying to believe it.

Mother's shade is waiting at the forest's edge, and for the first time it shows Kata its face. It is not the shrivelled scrap of bone and flesh Mother was reduced to in the end, but the face Kata remembers from when she was a child. Tall and dark haired, Mother is wearing the shift she was buried in, the one Kata embroidered with her own hands around the neck and wrists. Mother's skin is pearlescent in the dusky summer night, but her eyes have lost their blue gleam and turned to pebbles.

Kata can smell her too: wet and rot, bog and mud.

Kata.

Mother's voice is a sigh and hiss, summoning all of Kata's memories.

Mother, at the window, cursing the winter storm outside, daring it to take her, the howling snow and air tearing at the house like a beast.

Mother, sitting on the porch beneath the stars, sipping berry-wine and whispering tales of ships and storms and battles, drinking until she falls asleep. Kata curled up by her side, dreaming of the sea.

Mother, waiting for Kata that blighted day when she'd seen Attur in the harbour, a skull's grin carved into her face. "He sent you away, didn't he? Because you're useless. Hopeless. Too old to accomplish anything. If you've not shaken the world by the time you're twenty, you never will."

"I put your staff in the pit," Kata says, holding on to her defiance like a shield, even though her hands are trembling. "It's nowt but a piece of wood. It will burn with the rest."

Useless, Mother whispers. *Hopeless.*

Kata shakes her head but cannot turn away.

You can't leave.

The old curse settles like rocks and iron in Kata's chest, weighing her down until she is sinking, as surely as Mother's body sank into the grasping wet ground. The shade steps close enough to touch, its presence rank with the fetid breath of the bog, and Kata stumbles, falling to her knees, waiting for the shade to take her, to claim her, to pull her down beneath the earth, to end it.

"Kata!"

It's Magda's voice. Clear and sharp. Cutting the bonds laid on her.

Kata struggles to her feet. The shade is gone, but a wind is rising, tearing at her hair, shaking the trees around her until they bend and creak.

No.

Kata runs back through the meadow, the gusts rising to a storm around her.

Magda stands by the pit, feet planted wide, staff raised in the dawn-light, holding back the wind. Abel and the others are there too, doing what they can to cover the pit in case the storm breaks through.

Mother's wind. Sent to burn the tar-pit down.

In a flash, Kata sees how it all must end: in ruins, the tar-pit burned to ashes, everything lost.

She screams, howling at the wind, howling because she is too old, too weak, too useless, too hopeless. Mother will have her way, same as always. Kata screams, until Magda takes her hand.

"Help me," Magda says. "I'm holding off the wind best I can, but this storm is strong."

"I can't! It's Mother. She . . ."

"Just anchor me," Magda says. "Like I told you, every craft strengthens the other."

Gripping Magda's hand, Kata feels the swirl of the storm around them, but it's hazy and muddled, nothing like her grasp of water. Dipping down beneath the ground, she senses the water below the meadow, the creek further off, and she anchors herself in the steady flow of it, hoping Magda feels the strength of it too.

Magda holds off the wind, but it roars around them and around the pit, whipping the grass in the meadow, shaking the trees beyond. Kata feels Mother's presence, and across the meadow as the sun rises, she sees the shade. It's grown vast, high as the tallest pines, a grim and grasping shadow, rearing up toward the sky, feeding off the wind and Kata's own despair.

Magda sees it too. Kata knows it by the way Magda breathes a curse and grips her hand tighter.

In a rush, Mother's fury descends on them, battering at her own and Magda's craft, tearing at the bond between them. A heavy gust knocks the breath from Kata's lungs, and for one fleeting, eternal moment, Kata wields the wind. It's as if Mother's wind-craft has rushed into her, filling her to the brim, and it is glorious and terrible to feel it: the wind, everywhere, like a weft and warp strung throughout air and sky, every thread there to weave, or unravel.

Unleash it, Mother whispers in the air. *It's yours.*

Kata knows she could do it. She could take the power that is offered, unleash it, let it ravage the tar-pit and the village beyond as Mother would have done. It's all there for the taking. She holds on tighter to Magda's hand.

You can't leave.

Mother's voice is inside her head, wailing, scolding. *Where would you go? What would you do? Who would want you? Useless. Hopeless.*

And there, in the roar of the wind, is the last memory of Mother when she lay dying, her rheumy blue eyes burnished bright by rage or drink or pain or fever, breath rattling in her throat, bony fingers closing around Kata's wrist.

You can't leave.

Kata thinks of her life, all those years, hoping for Mother to change, knowing she wouldn't; caring for Mother while no one cared for her, fearing what disasters might befall her and the world around her if she left. All those years of being useful to others, not herself. All that name-less guilt she carried, thinking she was the one who chained Mother to a lesser fate.

And Kata sees it then, sees Mother for what she was: full of power and purpose, once, but hollowed out by anger and disappointment and bitterness until she was brittle and broken in the end.

You can't leave, Mother said, not to curse Kata, but because she was afraid of being left alone, of being nothing to no one.

Kata straightens her back, holding on to Magda who is still holding off the wind. The shade is all around them, whirling in the storm.

It isn't the staff you cling to, Mother, Kata thinks. *It's me.*

Mother's shade is still in her head, cursing and cajoling, tearing at her memories, ripping asunder anything it finds, love and pain, grief and rage. Kata feels it all, and then, she lets Mother go.

Letting Mother go is neither forgiving nor forgetting. It is like taking a breath when you thought you were drowning, like pouring cold water on a blistered burn, and Kata knows that deep in the tar-pit, wood and resin are burning, slow and steady, turning into tar and coal, and Mother's staff is burning too, turning to ash and dust because it is nowt but wood. But inside Kata, in the space Mother occupied for so long, something else is burning too, the heartwood and sap of Kata herself changing into something new. She'll never be as grand and glorious as Mother wanted to be, but neither will she be as small as Mother meant to keep her.

At the forest's edge, Mother's towering shade wavers in the sunlight, and then it's gone. Kata crumples in the grass, and Magda is there with her, holding her.

"Oh, Kata . . . that better have been worth two barrels of tar," Magda snivels, long hair tangled around her head, tears running down her face even though she's laughing. "Was it?"

Kata looks up at Magda, at the other faces gathering above her; she looks up at the sky, at the blue windless, endless, stillness of it.

"Yes," Kata answers, thinking of the Outer Sea, of wide-open waters as blue as this sky, of sailing beneath the wings of birds, of travelling until the world changes, until nothing is the same again.

☽ ☽ ☽

Author's Notes to My Younger Self: While you will have to adapt and adjust as you move through life, never give up what you are, your true self, for what someone else thinks you should be, not even when it seems convenient to do so.

EXCHANGE OF PERSPECTIVE

Alan Dean Foster

Evelyn Olsen was sitting at the desk in her bedroom when the sparklies came. A flickering, scintillating swarm of silvery particles half her size appeared in the air between her white chiffon-covered bed and where she was seated. Turning away from her homework she stared at the hovering, slowly-interweaving cloud of shimmering flakes and specks. After putting her computer in sleep mode, she proceeded to activate her sense of wonder. This being highly developed, she had less difficulty than most accepting an alien presence.

"Are you a pixie?" It struck her as a reasonable question, under the circumstances.

"*I am not a pixie.*" Maqkin applied itself directly to the inside of her head, bypassing her ears and much else, as it considered this a much more efficient means of communication. "*I am Maqkin.*"

She considered this thoughtfully. "I've never heard of you. I've never heard of a Maqkin."

"*My kind is unknown to you. Until a moment ago, your kind was unknown to me.*"

Turning sideways in her chair, the diminutive redhead rested her arms against its back and her chin against her arms. "You're very pretty, for whatever you are."

The Maqkin hesitated as it searched for an appropriate, non-threatening response. "*You're very pretty, too, for what you are.*"

A smile jilted freckles awake. "My name's Evelyn Kay Olsen. The 'Kay' is from my mother's mother. I'm eleven."

"*My name is . . . I am Maqkin. I am thirteen and three-quarter billion years, six months, four days, eight minutes, and twelve seconds old in your time units. I can refine my age further if you request it.*"

She sat up straighter, her chin coming off her bare arms. The curtains on the window behind her desk were closed, but her tenuous visitor pulsed with glimmer nonetheless. "Now you're joking with me. Not even pixies are that old. Not even wizards and sorceresses."

"*I am that old. I come before you in the guise of a probing tendril that is to the rest of me infinitely smaller than the end of one of your hairs is to you.*"

Reaching up, she ran the fingers of her left hand through her shoulder length red-brown hair. "Then you need to be careful. My cousin Robert is fourteen, and he's kind of a probing tendril. Sometimes I have to slap him. I wouldn't want to have to slap you." She studied the migrant cloud of shine. "I'm not sure I'd know how to slap you."

"*I sense dissatisfaction with your relation. If you like, I can seek him out and slap him for you. It will remove him and part of the continent he is on.*"

"Don't do that. Some day I might want to visit the part of the continent he's on, and my mom says he'll probably get more mature as he gets older."

"*That is true. Many things mature as they get older.*" In the warm Nebraska summer air, shards of silver, like fragments of a shattered crown, twinkled and danced. "*Would you like to see some of them?*"

Her eyes widened slightly. "Well, sure! I always want to see new things, even if they're old. My mom says I've always been like that, even when they came to adopt me." She hesitated. "Do you have a mom? Or a dad?"

The cloud fluxed, a rococo emulation. "*I have a birth. Nothing more can I define in relation to your queries.*"

Evelyn Olsen pushed out her lower lip. "Then we're both orphans. We have something in common."

"*Only thought,*" the mass of pirouetting dazzle told her, not unkindly. "*It is necessary that I make you a small environment.*"

An orb materialized before her; vitreous of surface, perfection incarnate in its dimensions. Extending from floor to ceiling, it was an ideal sphere. "*Step within. The substances you require for your constant exchange of gases will be continuously renewed.*"

Rising from her chair, she walked toward the transparent bubble. A gentle feathery sensation tickled her skin as she pushed her way into the containment. "I might get thirsty." As she studied her new surroundings, she sensed that the sparkling was watching her.

"More gases, different consistency. Doable."

Within the sphere a second, much smaller bubble appeared beside her. As big as a pumpkin, it had a surface as reflective as a ball of mercury. She frowned. "I'll need a glass, or a straw, or something."

"You have all that you need," insisted the Maqkin. *"Drink freely when you will."*

Pursing her lips, she placed them tentatively against the curve of the sphere and sucked gently. Drawn from the water globe, a thin stream snaked into her mouth. It was cool and refreshing and tasted just right. When she stopped drinking the flow ceased and the surface of the gleaming sphere, ever so slightly reduced in diameter, was restored.

"I can raise it to boiling, if you prefer," the voice of the Maqkin told her, *"or make it flow almost at absolute zero."*

"It's fine." Turning, she once more directed her attention to the mass of shimmering dust, or stars, or whatever a Maqkin was. "You were going to show me some things?" Leaning to her left enabled her to make out the clock that hung on the wall above her desk. "We have two hours until my mom gets home from work. Will that be enough time?"

"Two hours." There was a faint tickle of amusement in the reply. "It will have to do. We will be doing some travelling, Evelyn eleven. Do not be frightened."

She smiled boldly. "Nothing frightens me."

"That's interesting. Nothing is also all that frightens me. But I am not going to show you that."

Her room vanished. Or rather, it fell behind. So did her house, and the town in which she lived, and the Earth itself.

The Maqkin used the two hours well. There was a blur, and then a wonder, and then another blur, and then another wonder. Evelyn witnessed a supernova in the final act of self-destruction. Looked upon nebulae millions of light-years across that were all the colours of the rainbow (as well as all the colours that were not). Saw pulsars whose pulsing would have shattered her bones from her eardrums to her toes had not the Maqkin's bubble muffled the vibrations. Like a stone thrown across the surface of a pond, the bubble skipped across magnetars and danced with dark matter. She marvelled at the impossibly thin, unimaginably tough creatures that inched their way across the surface of neutron stars; teared up at the beauty of a stellar nursery blazing with the brilliance of ten thousand suns aborning, and was rendered solemn and silent by the darkness at the edge of the universe.

Two colliding galaxies flashed and thundered, though both the sound and light of their interaction were carefully muted so as not to damage her rudimentary senses.

"It's so beautiful!" she could not keep from exclaiming. "All those stars and shapes blending and swirling and merging together!"

"All that you see is being propulsed by two Maqkin," the voice told her. *"They are making love."*

From the stupendous interfacing spread out before her, she looked to her right to eye the glitter. "I know what that is. I mean, I know the idea but not the details. That's something else we have in common."

"It is not quite the same thing." The Maqkin involved itself in her mind and smiled to itself again. *"But there are some similarities of thought."* A pause. *"Two hours of yours. That time is done. Are you certain you do not wish to continue? There is so much more I can show you if you will but allow me another million or so of your years."*

She chewed her lower lip. It was very tempting, but. . . .

"My mom will be mad if she gets home and I'm not there. I don't like to make her mad. She works hard to support us and ever since my dad passed away. . . ." Her voice trailed off into a sniffle with none but the majesty of the Maqkin to hear it. "Do you know what love is? That's why I can't go on with you. But maybe we can do this again another time."

"Do you know that the time I offer you is less than the blink of your eye, and the knowledge greater than all that your civilization has amassed? Still, I will respond only maybe. Even the thoughts of a bacterium are valuable."

"So are yours," she replied.

"Perception is also commendable. I will take you home."

Another smudging of spectra, another handful of intergalactic interstices jumped, and she found herself back in her room. The clock on the wall read six o'clock.

"Goodbye, Evelyn eleven." A silver vivacity danced between her desk and the window, a twinkle of effervescent evanescence.

"I won't see you again, will I, Maqkin?"

"Not in this iteration of existence, I fear. You will be gone and fossilized before I might think of you anew."

"I always liked fossils. Thank you for showing me some things."

"I wanted to show you every things, but there was not enough time."

The front door slammed as the infinitesimally tiny fragment of Maqkin vanished. By the time her mother knocked and entered, Evelyn was back at her desk working at her computer.

"We're having spaghetti for dinner." Terri Olsen could not keep a touch of pride from her voice whenever she saw her little girl hard at work. So studious, so intense. "Spaghetti and garlic bread."

Evelyn looked up from where she was sitting. "I've decided I'm not going to be a boat captain, Mom. I'm going to be an astronomer."

Her mother's brows rose slightly. "Well, that's quite a change from last week. I suppose tomorrow you'll want to be a doctor, or a model, or a guitar-shredder, or whatever it is musicians are these days. You're growing up. Why an astronomer?"

"Because astronomers aren't afraid of nothing."

Her mother smiled tolerantly. "Aren't afraid of 'anything', darling. No matter what you decide to be, you need to use proper grammar."

Evelyn eleven nodded quietly. There was no point in trying to correct her mother.

The grammar might be wrong, but she knew the physics were correct.

Author's Notes to My Younger Self: Nothing you do is as important as you believe it to be: act accordingly toward others. At the same time, always act as if you know what you are doing . . . because most people do not. It will make you stand out in a crowd and help you through life.

THE ASTRONAUT'S FOUR SEASONS

Jane Yolen

1. Spring in New England

The astronaut walks gingerly, like a pilot
on Martian day-leave,
not sure yet if her feet can carry her
through the surprise of birth, of spring.
The grass after snow
seems too soft to sustain her.
She raises her face to the sky,
holding up a hand to a cumulus,
where bits of bright sun strain through.
She uses the word she knows
to call things to her. "Mine!"
There is laughter all around,
the sound of ice in drinks,
birds calling to new mates.
But no one brings her what she wants.
She knows, somehow, even this young,
that she will have to get it herself.
But she does not yet know the word
or concept for time.

2. Summer in the Camper

> She is used to the camper,
> the "cramper" she calls it,
> so different from their farmhouse
> and its sixteen rooms.
> When she first learned math,
> she told everyone that meant
> they got four rooms apiece.
> Her mother told her she was smart.
> Grandpa, who lived with them then,
> added as he often did, "Alec!"
> She chose the attic first, and it became
> her study, her library, the globe room
> and where the family telescope lived.
> But in the cramper they got to explore.
> She is the one who—on serendipity trips,
> finds the best things to put in her diary,
> to save in her camping boxes:
> hidden flowers, leaves like hearts,
> an arrowhead, four Victorian buttons,
> the tracks of animals she identifies
> with her field guide. A fisher cat.
> A flock of turkeys. A bobcat's large stride.
> She is sure of them all.

3. Fall in the NASA Station

> The one season in Florida she can stand,
> the air soft, water not too hot,
> and the excitement attending
> each new flight. It is as if the sun
> decides for two months to compromise
> with humans. She wears a sun amulet
> around her neck. Talks to it
> when no one listens. Tells it
> how she, too, is a kind of sun,
> the navigator circling the pilot.
> Numbers have always spoken to her
> in a private tongue. She speaks math.
> In ten days she will have her first flight.

The space station awaits.
A bit of a cramper, but then
she knows how to live in one.
Just as she knows the numbers
to get there and back,
not needing a map or computer,
though they will both be at her command.

4. The Astronaut in Winter

She is too old now to go back in space,
Her bones brittle, her blood anemic.
But she has written a final trip
in her will. She has made her husband,
made her children promise
that when she dies, her ashes—
all that will be left of her seasons—
will be shot into the sun.
It is not, as her poet husband thinks,
a metaphor for her life.
It is where she already lives.
She will travel past the clouds
she wanted to hold in her hand,
past the cramped space station
(now only a training base).
She will pass the nearer planets
and the moon, now destinations
on every vacation map.
And her earthly ashes will plummet
onto the far side of the sun,
to be burnished, reconnected,
welcomed home at last.

※ ※ ※

Author's Notes to My Younger Self: After 113 rejections on my poetry before selling my first poem, I should have told myself: "You're in this for the long haul, not for the short spurt of adrenaline of publishing. Editors aren't saying you're hopeless or stupid. Just that those particular poems don't resonate with the editor(s). I would have saved myself much anxiety and doubt.

AFTERWORD

Susan Forest

In my late twenties I had the exciting opportunity to leave my work as a teacher and return to university to earn my Masters' Degree. As a rule-bound, obedient child, I'd made most decisions in my life with an eye to my responsibilities, and my M.A. was a good career decision—but it also afforded me the chance to study *drama*! One morning in a black box theatre, the professor dimmed the lights for an exercise: in our own space, we were to visualize ourselves at a younger age, then approach that former self to impart a mote of wisdom. Later, our professor said he wasn't sure why it worked, but it invariably helped actors get in touch with deep emotion.

Although my experience of this exercise was not traumatically significant, the memory of it has remained with me. The *me* I visited was a shy girl of eleven in the spring of Grade 6, who'd chosen one particular recess break to roam a bit of vacant field at the far boundary of the school yard, alone. It was the day I vividly remember deciding what I wanted to do with my life. I would become a teacher, and once I was established and stable, take up my career as a writer.

Funny how things work out.

Identity and memory.

There is a poignant moment in the Star Trek television episode, *Is There in Truth No Beauty?* when Spock allows a Medusan to inhabit his body. The alien, deeply moved by his experience, remarks, "You are so alone. You live out your lives in this shell of flesh. Self-contained, separate. How lonely you are. How . . . *terribly* . . . lonely."

This is a profound human truth.

No person can ever truly *know* another. Each of us seeks intimacy in our closest relationships. We study psychology, philosophy, and literature in an attempt to understand what makes human beings tick. The nature of identity—another's or our own—is a question that can never be answered, though we seek it until the universe goes dark.

One reason may be: because identity is not static. None of us is the same person today that we were yesterday, or will be, tomorrow.

Some elements of identity persist. Like that hyper-responsible child of eleven by herself on the playground, I think I shall be rule-bound until the day I die; and though others may find this surprising, I consider myself an introvert. Other elements of identity progress along maturational arcs. I love the self-confidence I've developed over the years. Other elements are "seasonal": in my twenties, I could not fathom any reason why I might want to stay home one night a week; a seven-day rehearsal schedule was fine with me. Today? Yeah, not so much. And, when I have lived my life and given of my experience, I hope to transcend the flesh's drive to *rage against the dying of the light,* and be content to die.

But the key is this. Every day, every moment, we grow and change. Every day, every moment, we cross borders between who we were, who we are, and who we will be. Being and becoming. The twenty stories and two poems in this volume drill down into the Medusan's intimate wonder at the state of *being,* and the process of continually *becoming.* They explore new discoveries by young people—and old—of evolving and reinterpreted relationships; of new understandings of our world; and of new understandings of ourselves.

Memory.
Identity.
Seasons.

—Susan Forest, Calgary, 2021

ACKNOWLEDGEMENTS

Susan Forest

I would like to thank the members of Calgary's Imaginative Fiction Writers' Association, for their support; to Lucas K. Law for inviting me to participate, and whose knowledge and professionalism continue to teach me so much; and finally, to the remarkable authors, whose creative imaginations gave flesh and spirit to this amazing compilation. Thank you.

Lucas K. Law

Many thanks go to the following:

- Susan Forest, my co-editor, for her never-ending enthusiasm and continuing guidance for this anthology series;
- The Lim family (June, Brian, Christina) for their continuing kindness toward my parents;
- Leslie Carlyle-Ebert, Alice Spencer, Camelia Horvath, and Kristian Christensen for reminding me that there is a second act (or third act) and future adventures could be as fulfilling as the previous ones, maybe even more;
- Awang Armadajaya bin Awang Mahmud, Tim Howlett, and Sim Kui Hian for a friendship that neither time nor distance can take away—a rare gift not to be taken for granted in our busy world;
- Tim Feist, my partner, for his patience, understanding, and encouragement;
- Samantha M. Beiko and Clare C. Marshall for their generous support whenever I need it;
- Jared D. Shapiro for his sharp attention to the details in this anthology's interior layout;
- Veronica Annis for her insightful advice on the cover design;
- Candas Jane Dorsey and the authors for giving their unwavering commitment to this anthology;
- Everyone who buys this book and support social causes (please continue to talk about issues such as mental health/mental illness, caregiving/caregivers, affordable housing for all ages, eldercare, and ageing)

ABOUT THE
CONTRIBUTORS

Maurice Broaddus is a community organizer and teacher. His work has appeared in magazines like *Lightspeed Magazine, Weird Tales, Beneath Ceaseless Skies, Asimov's, Cemetery Dance, Uncanny Magazine*, with some of his stories having been collected in *The Voices of Martyrs* (Rosarium Publishing, 2017) His books include *The Knights of Breton Court* (urban fantasy trilogy, Angry Robot), *Buffalo Soldier* (steampunk novella, Tor. com, 2017), *Pimp My Airship* (steampunk novel, Apex Books, 2019), and *The Usual Suspects* (middle grade detective novel, Katherine Tegen Books, 2019). As an editor, he's worked on *Dark Faith, Dark Faith: Invocations, Streets of Shadows, People of Colo(u)r Destroy Horror*, and *Apex Magazine*. Learn more at MauriceBroaddus.com.

Vanessa Cardui has been writing songs to celebrate Laksa Media's new releases since *Strangers Among Us* in 2016. She is a singer-songwriter, multi-instrumentalist, and storyteller. She has numerous recordings available, including *Filk and Cookies* (2014) and *Patience* (2017), featuring songs both whimsical and tragic. She especially enjoys writing on literary, historical, mythological, and mental health topics. One of her songs was an Aurora Award 2019 finalist for best poem/song.

C.J. Cheung writes science fiction and fantasy stories inspired by his Chinese and Japanese roots but reflecting the diversity of his Canadian upbringing—a unique cross-cultural blend of East and West. A self-proclaimed geek, he managed to wrangle his wife and two sons into board games and Shotokan Karate (not necessarily in that order, and not without injury).

Joyce Chng lives in Singapore. Their fiction has appeared in *Where the Stars Rise: Asian Science Fiction & Fantasy*, *The Apex Book of World SF II*, *We See A Different Frontier*, *Cranky Ladies of History*, and *Accessing The Future*. Joyce also co-edited *The Sea is Ours: Tales of Steampunk Southeast Asia* with Jaymee Goh. Their recent space opera novels deal with wolf clans (*Starfang: Rise of the Clan*) and vineyards (*Water into Wine*) respectively. They also write speculative poetry with recent ones in *Rambutan Literary* and *Uncanny Magazine*. Occasionally, they wrangle article editing at *Strange Horizons* and manages *Umbel & Panicle*, a poetry journal and ezine about and for plants and botany (which they also founded). Alter-ego J. Damask writes about werewolves in Singapore. You can find them at http://awolfstale.wordpress.com and @jolantru on Twitter. (Pronouns: she/her, they/their).

Eric Choi is a Hong Kong born writer, editor, and aerospace engineer currently living in Toronto. The first recipient of the Dell Magazines Award for his story "Dedication", he has also twice won the Aurora Award for his story "Crimson Sky" and for the Chinese themed SF anthology *The Dragon and the Stars* (DAW) co-edited with Derwin Mak. He was also the co-editor (with Ben Bova) of the hard SF collection *Carbide Tipped Pens* (Tor). In 2009, he was one of the Top 40 finalists (out of 5,351 applicants) in the Canadian Space Agency's astronaut recruitment campaign. Please visit his website www.aerospacewriter.ca or follow him on Twitter @AerospaceWriter.

Candas Jane Dorsey is the internationally-known, award-winning author of novels *Black Wine* (originally Tor 1997, 1998, re-released Five Rivers 2013) and *Paradigm of Earth* (2001, 2002, Tor); upcoming mystery series *The Adventures of Isabel*, *What's the Matter with Mary Jane?*, and *He Wasn't There Again Today* (2020-2022 ECW); upcoming YA novel *The Story of My Life, Ongoing, by CJ Cobb*; short story collections *Machine Sex and other stories* (1988), *Dark Earth Dreams* (1994), *Vanilla and other stories* (2000) and *ICE and other stories* (2018); four poetry books; several anthologies edited/co-edited, and numerous published stories, poems, reviews, and critical essays. She was editor/publisher fourteen years of literary press The Books Collective, including River Books and Tesseract Books. She teaches writing to adults and youth, professional communications at MacEwan University, and speaks widely on SF and other topics. She was founding president of SFCanada and has been president of the

Writers Guild of Alberta. She has received a variety of awards and honours for her books and short fiction. In 2005, she was awarded the Province of Alberta Centennial Gold Medal for her artistic achievement and community work, and in 2017, the WGA Golden Pen Award for Lifetime Achievement in the Literary Arts. She was inducted into the City of Edmonton Arts and Cultural Hall of Fame in 2019. Other awards include the Canadian Science Fiction and Fantasy Hall of Fame (2018), YWCA Woman of the Year Arts and Culture 1988, and an Edmonton Arts Achievement Award 1988. She is also a community activist, advocate, and leader who has won two human rights awards and served on many community boards and committees for working for neighbourhoods, heritage, social planning, and human rights advocacy.

S.B. Divya is a lover of science, math, fiction, and the Oxford comma. She is the Hugo and Nebula nominated author of *Runtime* and co-editor of *Escape Pod*, with Mur Lafferty. Her short stories have been published at various magazines including *Analog*, *Uncanny*, and *tor.com*, and her short story collection, *Contingency Plans For the Apocalypse and Other Situations*, is out now from Hachette India. Find her on Twitter @divyastweets or at www.eff-words.com.

Alan Dean Foster has written in a variety of genres, including hard science fiction, fantasy, horror, detective, western, historical, and contemporary fiction. He is the author of several *New York Times* bestsellers and the popular Pip & Flinx novels, as well as novelizations of numerous films, including *Transformers*, *Star Wars*, the first three *Alien* films, and the most recent one, *Alien: Covenant*. Foster and his wife, JoAnn Oxley, live in Prescott, Arizona, in a house built of brick that was salvaged from an early-twentieth-century miners' brothel. He is currently at work on several new novels and media projects.

Bev Geddes is a school-based speech/language pathologist and author. Her short story, *Living in Oz*, appeared in the Aurora Award winning anthology, *Strangers Among Us: Tales of the Underdogs and Outcasts* (2016) and was also short-listed for the award, receiving an Honorable Mention in Gardner Dozois, *The Year's Best Science Fiction: Thirty-Fourth Annual Collection. The Gift* was published in the Aurora Award winning anthology, *The Sum of Us* (2017). *Witch of Glencoe* was included in *Tesseracts 22: Alchemy and Artifacts* anthology

(2019). When not reading, writing, or running away to her cabin on Lake Winnipeg, she enjoys playing the harp, aided and abetted by a menagerie of cats, dogs, children and chums.

Maria Haskins is a Swedish-Canadian writer and translator. She was born and grew up in Sweden and debuted as a writer there. Currently, she lives just outside Vancouver on Canada's west coast with a husband, two kids, and a very large black dog. She writes fantasy, science fiction, and horror, and her short fiction has appeared in *Fireside, Beneath Ceaseless Skies, Shimmer, PseudoPod, Cast of Wonders, Kaleidotrope,* and elsewhere.

Tyler Keevil was born in Edmonton, grew up in Vancouver, and moved to Wales in his mid-twenties. He is the author of several novels and the story collection, *Sealskin* (Locarno, 2018). He has received a number of awards for his writing and is a past recipient of the Writers' Trust/McClelland & Stewart Journey Prize. His speculative fiction has appeared in a wide range of magazines and anthologies, and has been selected for inclusion in *Best British Fantasy* (Salt) and *Best British Science Fiction* (NewCon). He is the director of the MA in Creative Writing at Cardiff University. His most recent novel is *No Good Brother* (HarperCollins, 2018).

Rich Larson was born in Galmi, Niger, has lived in Canada, USA, and Spain, and is now based in Prague, Czech Republic. He is the author of the novels *Annex* (Orbit Books, 2018) and *Cypher* (Orbit Books, 2020), and the collection *Tomorrow Factory* (Talos Press, 2018), which contains some of the best of his +150 published stories. His work has been translated into Polish, Czech, French, Italian, Vietnamese and Chinese. Find free fiction and support his work via patreon.com/richlarson.

Karin Lowachee was born in South America, grew up in Canada, and worked in the Arctic. Her first novel *Warchild* won the 2001 Warner Aspect First Novel Contest. Both *Warchild* (2002) and her third novel *Cagebird* (2005) were finalists for the Philip K. Dick Award. Her books have been translated into French, Hebrew, and Japanese, and her stories have appeared in anthologies edited by Nalo Hopkinson, John Joseph Adams, and Ann VanderMeer.

Brent Nichols is a fantasy and science fiction writer, book cover designer, bon vivant, and man about town. He likes good beer, bad puns, high adventure and low comedy. He's never been seen in the same room as Batman, but that's probably just a coincidence. He has two novels with Bundoran Press, and self-publishes military science fiction under the pen name Jake Elwood.

Heather Osborne is an English instructor at the University of Calgary, where she works on science fiction, fantasy, and digital literatures. She is the associate editor for *Foundation: The International Review of Science Fiction*. She has worked as the Assistant Program Director at the Alexandra Writers' Centre Society, a Calgary arts non-profit, and as assistant editor for *dANDelion*, a literary arts and experimental poetry magazine.

Y.M. Pang spent her childhood pacing around her grandfather's bedroom, telling him stories of magic, swords, and bears. Her fiction has appeared in *The Magazine of Fantasy & Science Fiction*, *Escape Pod*, and *Strange Horizons*, among other venues. She dabbles in photography and often contemplates the merits of hermitism. Despite this, you can find her online at www.ympang.com and on Twitter as @YMPangWriter.

Karina Sumner-Smith is the author of the Towers Trilogy from Talos Press: *Radiant*, *Defiant*, and *Towers Fall*. In addition to novel-length work, Karina has published a range of science fiction, fantasy, and horror short stories that have been nominated for the Nebula Award, reprinted in several Year's Best anthologies, and translated into Spanish and Czech. She lives in Toronto with her husband and a small dog. Visit her at karinasumnersmith.com.

Amanda Sun is a YA and Fantasy writer, and author of The Paper Gods, a series set in Japan about dangerous drawings coming to life. She also wrote *Heir to the Sky*, about floating continents and monster hunters, and has contributed to several award-winning anthologies. Many of her novels and short fiction have been Aurora Award nominees and Junior Library Guild selections, as well as Indigo Top Teen Picks and USA Today features. Her recent story "The Travellers" was long-listed for the Sunburst Award. When not reading or writing, Sun keeps busy as a mother, cosplayer, and geeky stitcher.

Patrick Swenson edited *Talebones* magazine for 14 years, and he still runs Fairwood Press, a book line. He was nominated for a World Fantasy Award for his work with the press. His first novel *The Ultra Thin Man* appeared from Tor, followed by sequel *The Ultra Big Sleep*. His new novel *Rain Music* is now available. He has sold stories to the anthologies *Unfettered III* and *Like Water for Quarks*, and to various magazines. He runs the Rainforest Writers Village retreat every spring at Lake Quinault, Washington. A high school teacher for 35 years, Patrick lives in Bonney Lake, Washington with his son Orion.

Bogi Takács is a Hungarian Jewish agender trans person (e/em/eir/emself or they pronouns) and an immigrant to the United States. E is a winner of the Lambda award for editing *Transcendent 2: The Year's Best Transgender Speculative Fiction*, and a finalist for the Hugo and Locus Awards. Eir debut poetry collection *Algorithmic Shapeshifting* was published by Aqueduct Press, and eir debut short story collection *The Trans Space Octopus Congregation* was published by Lethe, both in 2019. You can find Bogi talking about books at http://www.bogireadstheworld.com, and on various social media as bogiperson. Bogi lives in Kansas with eir spouse (writer R.B. Lemberg), child, and an assembly of books.

Hayden Trenholm is an award-winning editor, playwright, novelist and short story writer. His first novel, *A Circle of Birds*, won the 3-Day Novel Writing competition; it was translated and published in French. His trilogy, The Steele Chronicles, were each nominated for an Aurora Award. *Stealing Home*, the third book, was a finalist for the Sunburst Award. Hayden has won five Aurora Awards—thrice for short fiction and twice for editing. He purchased Bundoran Press in 2012 and is its managing editor. He lives in Ottawa with his wife and fellow writer, Liz Westbrook-Trenholm.

Liz Westbrook-Trenholm has published or aired mainstream and speculative short fiction, most recently in *Shades Within Us* (Laksa Media), *Over the Rainbow* (Exile Press), *Tesseracts 22* (Edge) and *Amazing Stories*. She won the Aurora Award for short fiction for *Gone Flying* in 2018 and was nominated in 2019 for her story *Critical Mass*. She is a long-distance, founding member of Imaginative Fiction Writers Association in Calgary, and of East Block Irregulars writing group in Ottawa, where she now lives with her husband, writer, editor, publisher and inspiration, Hayden Trenholm.

Jane Yolen, often called "the Hans Christian Andersen of America," is the author of over 382 books, including *Owl Moon*, *The Devil's Arithmetic*, and *How Do Dinosaurs Say Goodnight*. The books range from rhymed picture books and baby board books, through middle grade fiction, poetry collections, nonfiction, and up to novels and story collections for young adults and adults. She is a Grandmaster of SFWA, SFPA, and the World Fantasy Association. Six New England colleges and universities have given her honorary doctorates for her body of work. One of her awards set her good coat on fire.

Alvaro Zinos-Amaro is a Hugo and Locus award finalist who has published some forty stories and over one hundred reviews, essays and interviews in venues like *Clarkesworld*, *Asimov's*, *Analog*, *Lightspeed*, *Tor. com*, *Locus*, *Beneath Ceaseless Skies*, *Nature*, *Strange Horizons*, *Galaxy's Edge*, *Lackington's*, *The Los Angeles Review of Books*, and anthologies such as *The Year's Best Science Fiction & Fantasy 2016*, *Cyber World*, *Humanity 2.0*, *This Way to the End Times*, *18 Wheels of Science Fiction*, *Shades Within Us*, *The Unquiet Dreamer*, and *Nox Pareidolia*.

ABOUT THE EDITORS

Susan Forest is an award-winning author and editor of science fiction, fantasy, and horror. Her novel, *Bursts of Fire* was released in 2019, to be followed by *Flights of Marigold* (2020) and *Scents of Slavery* (2021). She has published over 25 short stories, contributes to When Words Collide, and has appeared at many international writing conventions. With Lucas K. Law, she co-edited *Strangers Among Us, The Sum of Us, Shades Within Us*, and *Seasons Between Us*. Susan loves travel and has been known to dictate novels from the back of her husband's motorcycle. Visit her online at www.speculative-fiction.ca. Follow the Addicted to Heaven series online at www.addictedtoheaven.com.

Lucas K. Law is a Malaysian-born award-winning editor and author who divides his time and heart between Calgary and Qualicum Beach. With Susan Forest, he co-edited *Strangers Among Us, The Sum of Us, Shades Within Us*, and *Seasons Between Us*. Lucas is the co-editor of *Where the Stars Rise* with Derwin Mak. When he isn't editing, writing, or reading, he is a corporate and non-profit organization consultant in business planning and development.

COPYRIGHT ACKNOWLEDGEMENTS

LEARN HOW TO MANAGE YOUR STRESS . . .

LEARN DAILY MINDFULNESS.

APPENDIX:

MENTAL HEALTH RESOURCES AND ANTI-DISCRIMINATION RESOURCES

Because of the dynamic nature of the internet, any telephone numbers, web addresses or links provided in this section may have changed since the publication of this book and may no longer be valid.

A listing in the Appendix doesn't mean it is an endorsement from Laksa Media Groups Inc., publisher, editors, authors and/or those involved in this series project. Its listing here is a means to disseminate information to the readers to get additional materials for further investigation or knowledge.

RESPITE IS KEY TO YOUR WELL-BEING.

GIVE YOURSELF A BREAK . . .

How is your Mental Health? Do you think you have experienced one or more of the following recently?

- More Stress than Before
- Grief
- Separation and Divorce
- Feelings of Violence
- Suicidal Thoughts
- Self Injury
- Excessive or Unexplained Anxiety
- Obsession or Compulsion
- Paranoia, Phobias or Panics
- Post-Traumatic Stress
- Depression
- Bi-polar
- Postpartum Depression
- Eating Disorders
- Schizophrenia
- Addictions
- Mood Disorders
- Personality Disorders
- Learning Disabilities

MENTAL HEALTH SCREENING TOOLS

More information:
https://screening.mentalhealthamerica.net/screening-tools

- The Depression Screen is most appropriate for individuals who are feeling overwhelming sadness.
- The Anxiety Screen will help if you feel that worry and fear affect your day to day life.
- The Bipolar Screen is intended to support individuals who have mood swings or unusual shifts in mood and energy.

- The PTSD (Post Traumatic Stress Disorder) Screen is best taken by those who are bothered by a traumatic life event.
- The Alcohol or Substance Use Screen will help determine if your use of alcohol or drugs is an area to address.
- The Youth Screen is for young people (age 11-17) who are concerned that their emotions, attention, or behaviours might be signs of a problem.
- The Parent Screen is for parents of young people to determine if their child's emotions, attention, or behaviours might be signs of a problem.
- The Psychosis Screen is for young people (age 12-35) who feel like their brain is playing tricks on them (seeing, hearing or believing things that don't seem real or quite right).
- Eating Disorder Test is to explore eating-related concerns which may impact your physical health and overall well-being.
- Work Health Survey is for exploring how healthy or unhealthy your work environment is.
- Worried about Your Child—Symptom Checker: **https://childmind.org/symptomchecker/**

10 Ways to Look after Your Mental Health

(source: www.mentalhealthamerica.net/live-your-life-well)

- Connect with Others
- Stay Positive
- Get Physically Active
- Help Others
- Get Enough Sleep
- Create Joy and Satisfaction
- Eat Well
- Take Care of Your Spirit
- Deal Better with Hard Times
- Get Professional Help if You Need It

MENTAL HEALTH RESOURCES & INFORMATION

If you or someone you know is struggling with mental illness, please consult a doctor or a healthcare professional in your community.

Below is not a comprehensive information listing, but it is a good start to get more information on mental health/illness.

Emergency Phone Number

If you or someone is in crisis or may be at risk of harming himself/herself or someone else, please call your national Emergency Phone Number immediately.

Canada	911
United States	911
United Kingdom	999 or 112
Ireland	999 or 112
Europe	112
Australia	000
New Zealand	111

Canada

- To locate your local Canadian Mental Health Association: **www.cmha.ca**
- Specifically for children and young people (aged 5-20), call Kids Help Phone's 24-hour confidential phone line at **1-800-668-6868** English or French. More information online: **kidshelpphone.ca**
- There are a number of resource materials and list of organizations that you can reach out to on the Bell Let's Talk website: **http://letstalk.bell.ca/en/get-help/**
- Mental Health & Addiction Information A-Z (Centre for Addiction and Mental Health): **https://www.camh.ca/en/ health-info/ mental-illness-and-addiction-index**
- Canadian Coalition for Seniors' Mental Health: **http://ccsmh.ca**

- List of local crisis centres (Canadian Centre for Suicide Prevention): **http://suicideprevention.ca/need-help**
- The Alex—Changing Health, Changing Lives: **www.thealex.ca**

United States
- National Suicide Prevention Hotline: **1-800-273-TALK** or **1-800-273-8255** (More resources at: **https://suicidepreventionlifeline.org/**)

- For more mental health information: **www.mentalhealthamerica.net/mental-health-information**

United Kingdom
- The Samaritans (**www.samaritans.org**) offers emotional support 24 hours a day—get in touch with them: **116-123**.
- A to Z of Mental Health: **http://www.mentalhealth.org.uk/a-to-z**
- Free Mental Health Podcasts: **https://www.mentalhealth.org.uk/podcasts-and-videos**

Ireland
- The Samaritans (**www.samaritans.org**) offers emotional support 24 hours a day—get in touch with them: **116-123**.
- Childline Helpline (**https://www.childline.ie**): Confidential for young people (under 18). Phone: **1-800-66-66-66**
- For more mental health information: **www.mentalhealthireland.ie**

Australia
- Helplines, websites and government mental health services for Australia: **mhaustralia.org/need-help**
- Kids Helpline: Confidential and anonymous, telephone and online counselling service specifically for young people aged between 5 and 25. Phone: **1800-55-1800** or visit **www.kidshelpline.com.au**
- Lifeline: 24-hour telephone counselling service. Phone: **13-11-14** or visit **www.lifeline.org.au**

New Zealand
- Helplines, websites and government mental health services for New Zealand: www.mentalhealth.org.nz/get-help/in-crisis/helplines/
- Youthline (for young people under 25): **0800-376-633**. More information online: **http://www.youthline.co.nz**
- Lifeline: **0800-543-354**
- Suicide Crisis Helpline: **0508-828-865** (0508-TAUTOKO)

International
- Mental Health & Psychosocial Support: International Medical Corps (**https://internationalmedicalcorps.org/program mental-health-psychosocial-support/**)
- International Association for Youth Mental Health (**https://www.iaymh.org/need-help/**)
- Crisis Helpline for Various Countries: **https://yourlifecounts.org/find-help/**
- Emergency Number for Various Countries: **http://suicidestop.com/worldwide_emergency_numbers.html**
- Suicide Crisis Helpline for Various Countries: **https://en.wikipedia.org/wiki/List_of_suicide_crisis_lines http://www.suicidestop.com/call_a_hotline.html**

ANTI-DISCRIMINATION RESOURCES

Discrimination is an action or a decision that treats a person or a group negatively for reasons such as:
- national or ethnic origin
- colour
- religion
- age
- sex
- sexual orientation
- marital status
- family status
- disability

What is Discrimination? For more information (Canadian Human Rights Commission): **https://www.chrc-ccdp.gc.ca/eng/content/what-discrimination**

Canada
- Promoting Relationship & Eliminating Violence Network (Prevnet): Information on bullying, resources on bullying and prevention at **http://www.prevnet.ca**
- List of Crisis Centres in Canada: **http://suicideprevention.ca/need-help**
- Free LifeLine App (Apple & Android): **http://thelifelinecanada.ca/lifeline-canada-foundation/lifeline-app**

United States
- Cyberbullying Research Center: Facts, Information, Blogs, and Resources at **http://cyberbullying.org/resources**
- The **Crisis Text Line** is a not-for-profit organization providing free crisis intervention via SMS message. The organization's services are available 24 hours a day every day, throughout the US by texting **741741**.

United Kingdom
- Bullying UK Helpline: confidential and free helpline service (Phone: **0808-800-2222**). Information, advice and resources at **http://www.bullying.co.uk**
- Anti-Bullying Alliances: Resources and advice at **https://www.anti-bullyingalliance.org.uk/tools-information**

Australia
- Bullying. No Way! **https://bullyingnoway.gov.au**

Books

The Bullying Workbook for Teens: Activities to Help You Deal with Social Aggression and Cyberbullying (by Raychelle Cassada Lohmann and Julia V. Taylor) - Instant Help; Workbook edition – ISBN: 978-1608824502

Violence against Queer People: Race, Class, Gender, and the Persistence of Anti-LGBT Discrimination (by Doug Meyer) - Rutgers University Press – ISBN: 978-0813573151

The Mindfulness Workbook for Addiction: A Guide to Coping with the Grief, Stress and Anger that Trigger Addictive Behaviors (by Rebecca E. Williams and Julie S. Kraft) - New Harbinger Publications; Csm Wkb edition – ISBN: 978-1608823406

Books (Ageing)

Dear Life: A Doctor's Story of Love and Loss (by Rachel Clarke) - Little, Brown – ISBN: 978-1408712528

Elderhood: Redefining Aging, Transforming Medicine, Reimaging Life (by Louise Aronson) - Bloomsbury Publishing – ISBN: 978-1620405468

Against Death: 35 Essays of Living (edited by Elee Kraljii Gardiner) - Anvil Press – ISBN: 978-1772141276

Conscious Living, Conscious Aging: Embrace & Savor Your Next Chapter (by Ron Pevny) - Atria Books – ISBN: 978-1582704388

This Chair Rocks: A Manifesto Against Ageism (by Ashton Applewhite) - Celandon Books – ISBN: 978-1250297259

Also Available from Laksa Media Groups Inc.

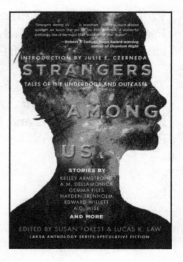

Also Available from
Laksa Media Groups Inc.

THE SUM OF US
Tales of the Bonded and Bound
Edited by Susan Forest and
Lucas K. Law

2018 (Canadian SF&F) Aurora Award winner
2018 Alberta Book Publishing Award finalist

"A strong collection . . . make it worth reading."
—*Publishers Weekly*

"Definitely consider buying a copy, if not for yourself, then for someone who is serving as a caretaker. Hopefully the stories can serve as comfort to them. At the very least, it should make us all appreciate caretakers for all they do." —*Lightspeed Magazine*

"This anthology was one of the better ones, with no 'howlers' and several thought provoking page-turners." —*Tangent*

"These stories take a broad exploration of what care can mean, looking at parental care, long term care homes, social responsibilities for care, foster care, maternal care, elder care, medical care by doctors and nurses, the care relationships of pets, and even the care roles of insectile species' (since care isn't just a human trait) . . . doesn't introduce easy answers about care-giving, but instead invites readers to explore often contrary ideas about care, asking readers to come up with their own critical questions and creative answers to the meaning of care. " —*Speculating Canada (Derek Newman-Stille)*

Original stories by Colleen Anderson, Charlotte Ashley, Brenda Cooper, Ian Creasey, A.M. Dellamonica, Bev Geddes, Claire Humphrey, Sandra Kasturi, Tyler Keevil, Juliet Marillier, Matt Moore, Heather Osborne, Nisi Shawl, Alex Shvartsman, Kate Story, Karina Sumner-Smith, Amanda Sun, Hayden Trenholm, James Van Pelt, Liz Westbrook-Trenholm, Edward Willett, Christie Yant, Caroline M. Yoachim, and Dominik Parisien (Introduction).

READ FOR A CAUSE
WRITE FOR A CAUSE
HELP A CAUSE

laksamedia.com

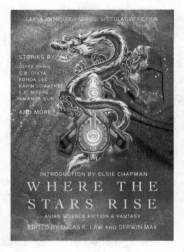

Also Available from Laksa Media Groups Inc.

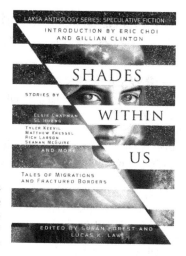

SHADES WITHIN US
Tales of Migrations and Fractured Borders
Edited by Susan Forest and Lucas K. Law

2019 (Canadian SF&F) Aurora Award finalist
2019 Alberta Book Publishing Award winner

"Addresses issues surrounding migration and borders at a very poignant moment in history. Readers are encouraged to understand that our journeys in life do not start and stop when we find new homes but rather are a series of constant, ongoing experiences that have an impact on who we are entirely." —*Booklist*

"An engaging collection of poignant travel through time and space. Highly recommended for its breadth of stories that look at having to leave home—or discover it." —*Library Journal*

"An intriguing addition to short story collections." —*School Library Journal*

"Political and daring, this collection adds to the future imagined by Philip K. Dick, George Orwell, Margaret Atwood, and Aldous Huxley." —*Foreword Reviews*

"A timely collection that invites us to ask whether we still do (or still should) live in a space of national borders and national definitions of identity. It invites us to use our speculative imagination to think through new ways of understanding selfhood in relation to the borders, boxes, and categories that are placed around us." —*Speculating Canada (Derek Newman-Stille)*

Original stories by Vanessa Cardui, Elsie Chapman, Kate Heartfield, S.L. Huang, Tyler Keevil, Matthew Kressel, Rich Larson, Tonya Liburd, Karin Lowachee, Seanan McGuire, Brent Nichols, Julie Nováková, Heather Osborne, Sarah Raughley, Alex Shvartsman, Amanda Sun, Jeremy Szal, Hayden Trenholm, Liz Westbrook-Trenholm, Christie Yant, Alvaro Zinos-Amaro, and Eric Choi & Gillian Clinton (Introduction).

READ FOR A CAUSE
WRITE FOR A CAUSE
HELP A CAUSE

LMG
LAKSA
MEDIA GROUPS
laksamedia.com

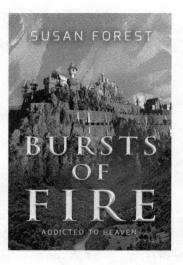

CPSIA information can be obtained
at www.ICGtesting.com
Printed in the USA
LVHW031525040821
694432LV00008B/1166